"*Enduring Justice* is a dynamic and powe   t to the Defenders of Hope series. Amy Wallace has crafted a   gaging, tense story of racial hate, repressed pain, and redeemed lives. *Enduring Justice* is a great read!"
          —MARK MYNHEIR, homicide detective and author of
              The Night Watchman

"In *Enduring Justice*, Amy Wallace has done what few writers can. She's given us a realistic portrayal of life, while finding hope in the despair. Pay attention to this one. She'll be around for a long time to come."
          —BRANDT DODSON, author of *White Soul* and *Daniel's Den*

"Amy Wallace writes spine-tingling prose. Prepare for plenty of adrenaline spikes as *Enduring Justice* races relentlessly from crisis to crisis. Wallace seamlessly blends the characters' personal triumphs and tragedies with a time bomb of a domestic terrorist plot that threatens the core liberties of the nation."
          —JILL ELIZABETH NELSON, author of *Reluctant Burglar* and
              Evidence of Murder

"The third book in Amy Wallace's *Defenders of Hope* series is the crème de la crème! *Enduring Justice* is another multilayered FBI suspense novel that will keep you hanging on to your seat until the last page. While struggling with the fine line between revenge versus justice, Michael Parker learns to rely on God while the storms of life are raging. Amy does such a beautiful job in bringing her characters to life that you feel like part of the family. I look forward to more of Amy Wallace's books!"
          —LORI KASBEER, *Christian Women Online* magazine

"Amy Wallace packs an emotional punch in her new novel, *Enduring Justice*. She deftly confronts the shame and horror of child abuse by opening up the bruised psyches of its victims. Yet she also finds a way to take readers inside the emotional struggles of FBI agents sworn to bring the perpetrators of this most shameful act to justice. Wallace has penned an unforgettable novel that won't soon be forgotten."

—NANCY MEHL, author of *Cozy in Kansas,* Ivy Towers Mystery Series

"If you love breath-stealing suspense, unforgettable characters, and re-markable spiritual depth in your fiction, *Enduring Justice* is a book to savor. Amy Wallace is at her best with this poignant, grace-filled addi-tion to her deeply satisfying Defenders of Hope Series."

—CLAUDIA MAIR BURNEY, author of *Wounded: A Love Story*

ENDURING
JUSTICE

DEFENDERS *of* HOPE, BOOK THREE

ENDURING JUSTICE

A NOVEL

AMY WALLACE

MULTNOMAH
BOOKS

ENDURING JUSTICE
PUBLISHED BY MULTNOMAH BOOKS
12265 Oracle Boulevard, Suite 200
Colorado Springs, Colorado 80921

ISBN: 978-1-60142-014-5

Published in the United States by WaterBrook Multnomah, an imprint of
The Doubleday Publishing Group, a division of Random House Inc., New York.

MULTNOMAH and its mountain colophon are registered trademarks of
Random House Inc.

Library of Congress Cataloging-in-Publication Data

Wallace, Amy, 1970–
    Enduring justice : a novel / Amy Wallace.
        p. cm.—(Defenders of hope ; bk. 3)
    ISBN 978-1-60142-014-5
    I. Title.
    PS3623.A35974E53 2009
    813'.6—dc22
                                        2008045767

Printed in the United States of America

2009—First Edition

10 9 8 7 6 5 4 3 2 1

To my husband.
You knew what this book would require of me and asked me to write it anyway.
Thank you for listening to the Lord and trusting He would carry us through.

To all who have walked dark paths of pain and shame.
You are not alone. And you are loved.

ACKNOWLEDGMENTS

W riting *Enduring Justice* required a terrifying step off the cliff of comfortable. But God was there to catch me. So were a beautiful band of fellow travelers who prayed hard and loved well.

My amazing family wrapped their arms around me and kept the prayers and chocolate coming. They also mastered the artful balance of prodding, pushing, and cheering me along this journey. Not to be forgotten is their platinum-level skill in cooking, cleaning, and encouragement.

Thank you, David, for being the first human hands to catch me before I drowned in the darkness of pain. You heard my heart and saw beauty when I didn't have eyes to see. Michael and Hanna's love exists because I first experienced it with you.

Thanks to my precious princesses too. You are the song in my heart, the laughter that is good medicine, and the sparkling sunshine that welcomes me into each new day. I love being your mommy. And I love you—to infinity and beyond.

Mom, Dad, Josh, Heidi, Zack, and the Wallace clan, thanks for clapping when I bowed, laughing when I attempted a joke, and loving me through tears, tantrums, and growing up. I love you.

Special thanks to the incredible team who continues to pray me through and point out that God is at work in it all: Ane, Anna, Cheryl, Cindy, David, Elizabeth, Heather, Jen, Jennifer, Julie, Kelly, Kristian, Laurie, Meg, Melissa, Michelle, Pam, Patty, Sally, Stephanie, Susan, Tiff, Tricia, and Vicki. Your prayers and encouragement were lights for the path and a safe place to be real and reminded of truth.

Thank you, Chip, for believing in this newbie and making me

laugh when life hurt. Having you in my corner kept me in the writing ring and at least marginally sane.

It's an honor to partner with such an awesome team at WaterBrook Multnomah. Editors extraordinaire: Julee, Diane, and Pam, along with Liz, Allison, Leah, Amy, Lori, and Stuart, you make being an author a dream come true. Thank you for everything!

So many wonderful people added depth to this story with their expertise: Jack Branson (retired federal agent), Corporal Lou Gregoire, Jim Bell (thanks for helping me get this "close enough for government work"), Scott Stewart, Dr. Ronda Wells, photographer Sherri Winstead, the great folks at the Union Station Godiva store (you made research and our last day in DC wonderful) and Gwinnett County District Attorney Danny Porter. Thank you all so much for sharing your time and talent. This story is richer because you were a part of it.

My long-suffering and miracle-working crit partners, Jen Keithley and Meg Moseley, I thank God daily because of you! You're right up there with chocolate and Starbucks on my list of favorites. Mary Griffith and Dee Stewart, thank you for helping me keep it real and being Evelyn to my Hanna. The Writers of Remarkable Design group, amazing ACFW folks, CL Beans and loving journey and laughter buddy, Sharon Hinck, you've made this journey a joy. My words are better and my heart fuller because each of you have walked this path with me. Thank you.

Finally, to my Safe Place and Heart Healer. You have caught and kept me in Your loving arms. Thank You for holding me when I cried, filling me when I was empty, and smiling when I danced. It's all for You, Daddy.

And what does the LORD require of you but to do justice,
to love kindness, and to walk humbly with your God?

—MICAH 6:8

1

The wall she'd built with years of secrecy started to crack.

Hanna Kessler wrapped trembling arms around her waist and stared through the glass door into her parents' backyard. A place she'd avoided her whole stay. Sunlight danced in the still water of her mother's koi pond and highlighted all the landscaping changes Dad had made since Mom's death.

Hanna closed her eyes against warring memories of past and present. As a child, she'd loved feeding the beautiful orange fish and hearing Mom laugh as the koi swarmed to the food. Now the little pond area was the only bit of her mother remaining. Maybe that was why she'd glanced outside and then stood transfixed. She needed her mom now more than ever.

Swallowing hard, she opened her eyes and focused on Mom's teak-wood dolphin statue and the white rocks around the water, glinting in the late afternoon sun. She reached out to touch the warm glass but couldn't force herself to open the door. Goose bumps trailed her arms and she shivered.

She couldn't go outside.

But she had to do something. Had to get away. So she stumbled into the rustic living room, her favorite place in the house. The surrounding family snapshots reminded her of simpler times. Boating on Kentucky Lake. Thunder over Louisville. Playing at Iroquois Park. Times when Mom and Dad and her brother, Steven, had wrapped her in their protection and love.

The front door rattled, then creaked open. "Anyone home?" A

man's deep voice carried through the safe place she'd escaped to months ago. It wasn't safe anymore.

But her frozen feet refused to move. Where could she hide? Footsteps thundered through the front hall, drawing closer. She had to get out.

Choking down the lump of panic in her throat, she ran back to the sliding glass doors and forced her feet to move outside, onto the concrete patio. She could get to her car from there.

The keys! Turning back to the house, she focused on the tall form stepping out of the house and walking toward her.

"Hanna-girl, what's gotten into you?"

Her brain snapped to attention. The man in front of her was no threat.

"Daddy!" She ran into his outstretched arms.

Andrew Kessler kissed the top of her head and chuckled. "You looked like you'd seen a ghost. Didn't you get the message I left this morning?"

Heartbeat still pounding out of her rib cage, she inhaled a few deep breaths before answering. She hadn't checked messages today. And no way could she admit she'd listened to most of the messages her family had left, never intending to return the calls. "I…I must have missed it. Sorry, Daddy."

Try as she might to hide it, calling her father Daddy only happened when she was terrified. Or hiding. And she'd done a lot of hiding.

Dad stepped back and tilted his head, still holding her in his arms. "Well, I'm in Louisville for the weekend and had to see my girl. I miss you. So does everyone back in Alexandria."

Even Michael? She wouldn't ask. She had no right. Not after ignoring all the calls and letters he'd sent. The ones declaring his love even though she'd run away from everyone after her brother's wedding.

She couldn't meet Dad's eyes.

"Hanna, look at me." He tilted her chin up. She fought to not pull away. "Steven asks about you every day. I'm surprised your brother and Clint and the rest of their FBI friends haven't hightailed it up here to drag you home."

"They wouldn't." Especially not Michael. Not after almost two months of her frosty silence.

Dad laughed again. He had no idea the pain his questions, his presence here, caused. "Steven's planned it. So has Michael. But they're waiting for you to come back, on your terms."

As if that would happen.

"Susannah's birthday party is a week from Saturday. Clint and the rest of us are praying you'll come. Take pictures. Let us show you how much we love having you in Alexandria."

A week from Saturday. The twenty-fifth of August. She wouldn't be there. Couldn't face Clint Rollins. Not after her negligence had nearly cost Clint's son his life.

Tears slipped past her clenched eyes.

"Oh, honey." Dad gathered her back into his arms. "No one blames you, Hanna. No one. You need to let the past go. Everyone is safe now. All the Rollins clan. Even Conor."

So Sara's baby was still alive. Just like Steven's and Clint's messages had said. Relief rushed through her, causing her knees to wobble. But other guilt arrows pierced her heart. All the lies she'd told Steven and Michael. Dad too. Clint's son wasn't the only reason she'd fled Alexandria.

"You'll be there for Susannah's party, right?" His hopeful blue eyes begged.

She pulled out of his arms and walked back into the house. Dad followed. "I...I need a Kleenex." Searching through the oak cabinets in the kitchen didn't produce any tissues. So she grabbed a paper towel from the counter. "What brings you in town? During our phone calls last week, you never mentioned coming home."

"If I had, would you have been here?"

Ouch. "Yes, Daddy." Another lie. "So are you here to check on the Mall St. Matthews coffee shop? I've been working there every day, just like you arranged. It's going well." And she was babbling.

"I'm here to meet with some old friends on Friday and talk about upcoming business opportunities."

Old friends. The memories rushing in unbidden surfaced more tears. And more cracks in the wall of secrecy. She needed to get out of the house, out of the neighborhood. Now. Maybe then she could exhibit some self-control.

"Why don't we grab a late lunch at the Cheesecake Factory? After your long drive you're bound to be hungry, right?" She forced a smile.

"Okay, Hanna-girl." He wiped away one of her stray tears. "On one condition."

Please don't ask about the party, Daddy. Please.

He lifted his bushy graying eyebrows. "Promise you'll come back to us and take pictures at Susannah's birthday party next week."

The very thing she couldn't do. How would she get out of this without telling more lies or spilling everything? She had to avoid that. Maybe one last fib would get her though the weekend with Dad.

Then she could find somewhere else to run.

2

Another Friday stuffed in a suit and having to smile for congressional district work.

There were plenty of other places RJ would rather be on a summer morning than his sparsely decorated office. On his computer at home—alone—was high among the choices.

"Congressman Reeley?" His young intern poked her perky red head through his open office door. "It's almost time for the meeting to start."

"Are all the business leaders present?"

"Yes sir. Everyone you invited. And all the talk indicates positive interest in a Kentucky branch office for the National Center for Missing and Exploited Children."

"Good. Very good."

"Any last minute details I can help with?"

"No, Brittney, but thank you. Is my wife already in there?"

"Yes sir. Working the room. She's amazing. Everyone will be begging to help with whatever you propose." Brittney gave him a megawatt smile and left the office.

So Helen had ignored his request to stop by his office first. No matter. She was the perfect political partner. Money, charm, and pure ambition had cemented their wedding vows fifteen years ago. She guaranteed his future in the White House.

He stood and stared out the window at Kentucky's bluegrass and a few old oaks swaying in the breeze. The wind did nothing to abate the blazing temperatures of mid-August. And unlike his fellow representatives on the Hill, he'd take air conditioning over a golf green any day.

Unless he could be outside working in his backyard garden like he'd done so many years ago. When life seemed full of promise. When Gloria was still alive.

A knock on the door startled him out of the idyllic memories of summers past.

"Come in." He straightened his green tie. Better to avoid red or blue so as not to offend the alumni of rival Kentucky colleges. Life was all about keeping up appearances and making everyone happy.

"Hello to the Honorable RJ Reeley, Kentucky's favorite US representative." Andrew Kessler stepped through the door and turned back the clock with his smile.

"Well, hello to you, old friend. Long time."

Andrew shook his hand and clasped him on the back. "I keep thinking I should call and set up another fishing weekend. Especially since we both spend most of our time in DC nowadays. But I talk myself out of it, knowing you're far busier than I'll ever be."

RJ fought with his representative persona, longing to be back on Kentucky Lake with Andrew talking about coffee shops and flower gardens. He leaned back against his desk. A very physical reminder of the present. "Last report you were taking the coffee business by storm and enjoying every spare minute with your beautiful new wife."

"New?" Andrew's graying hair belied the spark of life still bold in his eyes. "Compared to the thirty years Cindy and I had together, I suppose Sue and I are still in the newlywed stage. But we'll have been married six years this October. Six very happy years."

"I'm glad for you, Andrew. But I apologize that so much time has gotten away from me." RJ's guard dropped with every tick of the clock. A dangerous situation. "Cindy was a wonderful woman. I imagine Sue is just as special."

"Yes. She is." Andrew's eyes pierced him. "I remember your wedding to Helen. God has been good to both of us with such incredible second chances."

Second chances? "Yes…well. You're right." This conversation drew too close to memories better left untouched. Yet no way to change the subject entered his rattled mind.

The buzz of a cell phone broke the awkward silence.

Andrew reached for his belt and checked the display. "That's Steven. Mind if I slip into your sitting room and take this?"

Steven Kessler. FBI Agent. Not a man RJ wanted to tangle with or delay. Best to stay off his radar. "Please, be my guest. I'll wait for you."

Andrew stepped to the door and paused. "No need to wait. I'll slip in when I'm done here."

RJ nodded. But wait he would. Who knew what information might be gleaned from phone calls with the FBI?

"Hey, son."

RJ walked to the sitting room door and strained to hear.

"How long has the child been missing?" A stretch of silence. "How old is the little girl?" Andrew's voice dropped when he continued. "She's the same age as Gracie's students?" Another pause, then RJ heard something about the child being Asian.

A missing Asian child? RJ's pulse hammered. Ignoring images from last night, he listened again. He had to know more.

"I'll be praying, Steven." Andrew's voice wavered. "I'm sorry. Sorry any child or parent has to deal with this."

Andrew's footsteps moved closer.

RJ rushed to his desk and shuffled papers.

Andrew entered the office and stopped short. "I thought you were going to the meeting."

"A few notes to go over first." He held up the papers. "I couldn't help hearing you talk about a missing child. Is everything all right?"

Andrew sighed. "Nothing is right when someone abducts a child."

"I couldn't agree more." RJ swallowed the tremor in his voice. "When did she disappear?"

"She went missing yesterday afternoon."

Not the answer he'd hoped to hear. "How old was she?"

Andrew's raised eyebrows drew into a knot. "Why do you ask?"

Why indeed. RJ smoothed damp hands down his slacks. "Well…my interest in our country's missing children is why I'm proposing the branch office for the National Center for Missing and Exploited Children."

Andrew released a deep breath, and the stiffness in his shoulders lessened. "Of course, RJ. That makes perfect sense. It's why we're here, right?"

He could only nod and try to slip back on his congressional mask. Work beckoned. His safe place. "We'd better join the party in the conference room. Elizabethtown's elite will only wait so long."

"Ah, but you have the support of leaders from all over Kentucky. They'll back your proposal for opening an NCMEC branch in our beautiful state. I, for one, hope the groundbreaking takes place in Louisville."

"I'll bet you do. Always the champion of Louisville's development."

"My hometown is in my blood. That's why I accepted the city council's invitation to participate in this grass-roots project. Steven wanted to be here today, but work kept him busy in DC."

"He's still with the FBI?" Not that RJ could forget that monumental fact. He motioned Andrew through the door, then walked with him down the hall.

"Yes. Still working with the Crimes Against Children Unit. He's passionate about protecting children."

Sweat beads trickled down RJ's back. "It's too bad he couldn't join us. He's a perfect fit for fund-raisers. His expertise and hero stature would be a great sell."

"When it comes to keeping our nation's children safe, Steven's the first to step forward." Fatherly pride oozed out of Andrew's grin. "Time allowing, I'm sure he could be persuaded to help."

Parental pride was something RJ had never experienced. Never wanted to either. One of many things that separated him from Andrew Kessler. No surprise they hadn't stayed in touch much after Gloria died.

For that and a multitude of other reasons.

And now he had to remove his old friend and Andrew's FBI son from the mix. Things were safer that way. But for today, he'd keep up appearances and land support for his altruistic efforts to help the National Center for Missing and Exploited Children. Then he'd be well on his way up the ladder.

Obliterating his tainted past with present good.

O nce a Kessler, always a Kessler, right?

Hanna gripped her favorite camera with shaky hands. Sitting in her car outside Sara and Clint Rollins's house, she rehearsed her speech. The one she'd give to Steven and the rest.

She'd promised Dad.

Thus, her long journey back to Alexandria to meet with who knew what.

"Leave the past in the past." Dad's words echoed a hollow rhythm in her brain. But she couldn't let her father down. Couldn't run away again.

Unlocking the door and stepping out, she smoothed her pink sundress and shivered despite Saturday's late August heat.

"'Bout time you showed up, little sis." Steven's strong arms around her softened his words. "You're shaking, Hanna. What's going on?" His concerned eyes, so much like their dad's, seared her conscience.

She'd lied to him once before when he asked that question. She couldn't keep doing it. The wall of secrets surrounding her cracked a little more.

"I'm just nervous about facing everyone. Maybe I shouldn't have come." She stepped back toward her Chevy Equinox. "I can take birthday pictures later. I don't want to ruin Susannah's party by making a scene."

Steven shook his head. "You're family, Hanna. We miss you and don't care how or why you left." An obnoxious smirk spread over his face. "I mean, after all, just because the house is full of FBI agents trained in every form of interrogation known to man, there's no reason to worry. None at all."

"Ha-ha."

"Come on." His arm around her shoulders, Steven moved her toward the front porch. "Michael's been asking about you. He wants to see you, even if you haven't called."

He does? Despite her apprehension, her heartbeat raced and her stomach backflipped. She should chide herself for being so affected by a handsome man, but she couldn't. Michael wanted to see her.

"Is Champ with him?"

"Yep. The old dog's not been his happy-go-lucky self since you took off…" Steven stopped walking and stared at the porch steps. "I'm sorry. I know you had your reasons. It's just hard to understand without any explanation."

She batted her lashes and cocked her head. "So you *do* care why I left. Your investigator self can't handle the mystery."

"And you'll tell me soon, right?"

"Maybe." Teasing Steven kept the guilt down to the middle of her throat. It still mixed with her churning stomach and created havoc from head to toe.

Clint stepped through the front door. "Hanna Kessler, don't you go leavin' like that again, you hear?" He pulled her into his six-foot-five bulk, all muscle now that his chemo had ended and he'd started working out again. "I was worried about you."

Tears pricked at the corners of her eyes. "I'm sorry."

Surrounded by larger-than-life big-brother types with badges and guns wasn't making her return any easier.

Distraction. She needed a distraction. "Did you know I took more photos to put up in Dad's coffee shop? The one in DC."

Clint and Steven shared a look. Steven beat his Texan partner to the draw. "That means you're staying this time? For good?"

Great distraction. *Not.*

"Aunt Hanna! You're home!" James flew through the open front door and attacked her waist with his almost-seven-year-old strength. So much like Steven. "And you'll be here next week for my birthday too, right?"

Scooping the brown-haired, blue-eyed cutie in her arms, she snuggled him close as they walked inside. "You bet. I wouldn't miss it for the world." But she had last year. She'd stayed caught up in her own personal hell, leaving Steven on his own to deal with his ex-wife and her threatened custody battle. James's sixth birthday had hardly rated a mention for anyone in the family.

This year would be different.

Soon the whole Kessler and Rollins clans engulfed her. A very pregnant Sara Rollins encircled her neck and held on tight. Everyone joined the hug and welcomed her home. But Steven's new wife, Gracie, hung back watching, head bowed a little.

Praying.

Gracie had probably been praying hard for her all this time.

Hanna willed away the tightness in her chest.

"Hanna."

One word. Her knees liquefied as everyone smiled and cleared the room, feigning interest in preparations for the soon-to-arrive party guests.

Michael stepped forward, right into her personal space, and kissed her with a force that lit a fire all the way up from her toes.

She blinked and almost pinched herself. Instead, she pulled back to catch her breath, still not willing to meet his probing chocolate-colored eyes.

"I've missed you."

"I'm sorry I didn't call." All the excuses she'd practiced for her speech fell flat before she could voice them. "I had a lot of things to work out."

He tilted her chin up. "I want to understand, Hanna. I need you to trust me and talk to me."

"I will." Just not right now. For this perfect minute, she wanted only to enjoy Michael's passionate presence and attention.

If they could move on from here, like this, maybe the whole truth wouldn't have to be told. The worst could stay buried in the past.

Forever.

❋ ❋ ❋

Michael wrapped Hanna in his arms again. He'd dreamed of holding her like this far too often. Other times, he'd yelled at her until his lungs burned for leaving without so much as a "See you later."

She tugged at her pink sundress, the one he remembered so well. She'd worn it the day she brought Champ to live with him. Hanna would laugh at his cataloging every little detail like that.

But his memory served him well in his job. Not so much at midnight, alone in his bed, wondering where Hanna was and why she ignored his calls and e-mails and letters.

"Can we grab dinner alone tonight, after the party cleanup?"

Hanna didn't answer. Instead, she stepped out of his arms and surveyed the Rollinses' living room, snapping a few candid pre-party photos. The place was filled with balloons and party stuff for a bunch of second graders to pounce on when they arrived. Kids at seven were inquisitive, still trusting, and full of energy. Spunk like that kept them alive.

He'd seen a few of those kids. Prayed Mattie Reynolds would be one of them. The boy he and Steven had rescued in April had been little more than a rag doll when they'd taken him home.

Hanna took more pictures as he waited for her response. Pushing her now wouldn't work. She'd crawl back into her shell. Just like she'd done after he shot and killed the man who'd stolen her joy. The one who'd killed too many little boys too similar to James Kessler and Jonathan Rollins.

He threw that memory away. Use of deadly force still had him talking to the trauma counselor, and he didn't want to think of it outside the shrink's office.

"Hanna?"

She stepped back over to his side. "I'm sorry, Michael. I needed a little space. But...I would like to go out to dinner with you later."

He let out the breath he'd been holding. "Good. How about we grab some Chinese takeout and go back to the apartment? Champ will make sure I stay an honest man."

She forced a smile. He shouldn't joke with her about stuff like that. Physical intimacy had never been a comfortable subject.

"Is your dad coming to visit?"

So she had read his letters. At least they hadn't landed unopened in the circular file. "Doubt it. He's pretty content with his Florida lifestyle and has never been too impressed with my work here."

Turning off her camera, she stared at him, her beautiful blue eyes filled with pity. He hated that. "I'm sorry, Michael."

"It's not a big deal." *Liar.*

But she didn't push the issue and steered the conversation to photography as they headed into the living room. A quick visit with Champ outside, then taking pictures inside, and before long, Hanna's smile, the one he'd known and loved, returned. She came alive behind her camera. Like all was right with the world.

He hoped talking with her tonight would make everything right between them.

The party got underway on time. Just what he'd expect for anything Clint or Steven touched. Little girls squawked, or giggled, as Gracie and Hanna called it, louder and longer than imaginable.

And there was a whole lot of pink everywhere.

Not his thing, but he'd known Hanna would be here when Steven mentioned the party last week. So here he sat, punch in hand, waiting for tonight and willing the clock to tick off the hours faster.

His cell buzzed. Answering it, he noticed Steven and Clint kissing their wives and then walking out of the room, phones to their ears.

"Parker."

"National Center tip is going out to your team and the Baltimore Task Force." Jan Bryant's voice remained calm but clipped with fear. Their best administrative assistant got personally involved with every case concerning the youngest kids. "Katrina Chu's been spotted again. The Baltimore field office is gathering warrants. They know you're coming, but those guys won't wait for you to go in."

"Thanks, Jan. We're on our way." He waved good-bye to Hanna and hurried toward Steven and Clint.

Steven held up a hand. "I want you to sit this one out, Clint. I'll call Lee on the way. The new recruit orientation he was leading should be wrapping up, and you need to stay here with your family."

"I'm close to my pre-cancer shape. Don't baby me anymore." Their deadlock stare wouldn't stop the seconds ticking.

Michael stepped toward the door. "We can't wait much longer."

Clint growled and stormed back into the living room.

Steven and Michael jumped into Steven's Explorer and headed toward Baltimore without a word.

Minutes later, his boss rattled off case facts to Lee Branson. Since the shooting in May, Michael and Lee had spent more time together. Lee could handle the shooting details Steven and Clint wanted to forget.

No telling how Lee was taking today's news. Steven snapped his phone shut and focused straight ahead. "Lee's on his way."

"Good."

Steven's monotone filled the SUV. "Kat's alleged sighting earlier this week near an upscale row house east of downtown Baltimore turned up nothing. None of our leads have panned out, and the Baltimore task force couldn't find the child or the white truck. No one in the neighborhood gave any relevant leads."

Why was Steven repeating details of a case they'd worked all week? Michael clamped his jaws shut and listened to his boss organize things out loud.

"But today, another neighbor claims to have seen Kat leave from the house next door in the truck. She caught its plates." Steven rehashed more details from the phone conversation with Lee.

They'd been handed Kat's case when she disappeared nine days ago, and Steven couldn't keep his distance if he tried. The little girl resembled a child in Gracie's class, and Kat's parents had dug their way under everyone's defenses the past week with their quick help and unshakable belief in the FBI's ability to return their only daughter.

Maybe today they'd end this case well.

"I've worked with the agent heading up the Baltimore task force before. And Baltimore PD's Lieutenant Barnes is a large part of the task force's success. They're good cops." Steven wiped his forehead as the air conditioner spit out little relief. "Let's hope their team stays cool. No telling what state we'll find things in."

Michael's jaw almost snapped. This perp better not have... He refused to focus on the options. It'd take all he had to restrain himself when they arrested the guy. But he would. The guy'd do thirty to life if they found Kat and the search warrant turned up anything at all.

He waited for Steven to add more details. As case leader and FBI super agent, Steven always knew more than he let on.

"What are you not saying?"

Steven raced through the Baltimore-Washington Parkway traffic. The hour it'd take them to get into Baltimore still wouldn't put them too far behind the locals. Warrants took too much time some days.

"If the person sighted is the white truck's owner, he's a registered offender."

Michael's lunch rebelled. Taking down a child sex offender had been one thing he hadn't had to do during his four years in the FBI. Until recently. That first one in his year and a half with the Crimes Against Children Unit was one too many.

He must have gotten a lucky break. That, and more than his fair share of domestic kidnappings.

He wished for the laptop he'd left in the Rollinses' front closet. Working while waiting for Hanna's arrival had helped then. It'd prove an even better mind focus now. Instead, the gray outside whizzed past his window.

"10-4, Lieutenant. Copy your 10-7. ETA five minutes."

Michael sat up straighter. Locals had arrived on scene, and Steven's Explorer was only minutes away. The buzz of adrenaline rushed through his veins.

"The suspect is considered armed and dangerous. Let's make our presence here count." Steven pulled in behind an empty cruiser and an unmarked one, just as Lee exited his Bureau car. Their vehicles lined the street in front of a long stretch of renovated row houses. No white truck in sight.

Lieutenant Barnes motioned them inside where he stood with Lee. Two cops came down the steps. Lee pointed toward the basement, his dark forehead a map of worry. "Main level and upstairs are clean. We arrived just in time to search the storage area downstairs."

All three CACU members unholstered and headed toward the stairs. A young Italian cop nodded and followed.

Into the dark, they took one slow step at a time. Michael pushed the storage room door open and pointed his Glock inside.

A bluish computer light ricocheted off the walls and cast an eerie glow over the office setup filling the large room. This was no storage area.

A young bald man flipped toward them and rolled to the edge of the couch pushed up against the far wall.

"FBI!" Michael's voice echoed.

Nothing moved.

The man must be deaf.

Or ignoring them and waiting for a shot line.

"Baltimore PD. Hands up." The cop's voice shook like a rookie's.

The bald guy didn't move.

"Hey, punk! I said hands up!"

This time the guy snapped awake. "Okay, man. Okay." He lifted his hands and dropped his earphones to the side. "But you've busted the wrong place. The drug parties happen four doors down."

Michael moved right while the rookie went straight toward the couch. Bad choice.

"Look, I told you. You're all in the wrong place." The guy stiffened when Lee stepped near him. "And I want that mud race out of here, now."

Why would this guy single out Lee? Michael waited for Lee's response. Nothing but steel eyes fixed on his target.

The cop glanced around and whipped out his handcuffs, moving forward undaunted by the cocky order.

"I don't want any trouble." The man glared at Lee. "But he has to leave. Now."

Lee repeated the cop's instructions. "Put your hands on your head and turn around."

The suspect didn't move.

The other cop in Michael's peripheral vision hung back by the stairs.

"Hands on your head." Lee stepped closer.

The perp's eyes darted between the rookie and Lee. But before Lee could lay a hand on him, the skinhead lunged and sacked Lee like a football dummy before whaling him.

The rookie's gun clanged to the floor, and he threw himself into the fray. The cop took a few punches before landing a righteous right hook into the perp's face.

Blood splattered the floor.

Lee jumped up and hit the skinhead. Then clamped his cuffs on the dazed idiot.

The stocky cop threw one more adrenaline-laced blow to the perp's abs.

"Let it go, Masino." The other Baltimore cop corralled the rookie. "We got him. Down, man."

Michael and the rest of the law enforcement team holstered their weapons. Then Steven took the thug from Lee. "You all right?"

Lee nodded and wiped blood from his mouth.

The perp smiled.

Michael stepped into the handcuffed man's space. "Where's the little girl seen leaving here earlier today?"

"I've been house-sitting this week. No one's been here but me." His eyes raked over Lee and Officer Masino, then flicked to the computer screen. Interesting. "Get that monkey and his friend out of here."

Michael locked eyes with the skinhead. "Why should I? Afraid they'll mess up more of your teeth?"

Steven shook his head and faced the man in handcuffs. "Let's start with your name and go from there."

"Sean Haines."

"Tell me what you know about William Lasser, last time you saw him."

Haines jerked his hands up. "Undo these and I'll think about it."

Michael smirked.

Ignoring the request, Steven studied Haines. "What were you and Lasser doing here yesterday?"

"I haven't seen him."

Masino called from behind them. "Our friend here's lying through his teeth. Big surprise. He exchanged e-mails with his pal Lasser earlier this week. All about meeting again and what to do with Katrina Chu."

Steven turned around and groaned, but checked himself fast. "Michael, why don't you do the honors and read him his rights before we go any further."

Michael began the memorized speech. "You have the right to remain silent..." As he continued, Steven and Lee stepped over to Masino's side.

The handcuffed idiot lost his smile and stared straight ahead.

Michael shoved him. Hard. "Where is she?"

"Not here."

Steven joined them. "Where's Lasser? This'll all go better if you start talking. Now."

"Lasser's gone." He shrugged. "Haven't seen him lately and don't know anything about that brat he mentioned."

"Your computer says you're lying." Michael itched to punch this punk.

"Last time I checked, e-mail wasn't illegal."

The lieutenant stepped down the stairs, flicking on an overhead light as he came. Michael blinked, and the cuffed fool tried to bury his head in his shoulder.

"What do we have, gentlemen?" The large lieutenant crossed the room to the computer with a stride far faster than his years indicated him capable.

Masino snapped to attention. "Our person of interest, Sean Haines, charged the FBI agent, and I had to use force to subdue him, sir." The rookie stood stiff and unmoving.

"Lieutenant, you might want to come see this." Lee's monotone made Michael's skin crawl. He stepped behind Lee's rigid back.

"Dear God, there's a picture…" The older lieutenant moved back. Michael wanted to join him but couldn't look away from the dark-skinned child. The noose around his neck. Hanging from a tree. The disgusting image burned itself into his brain.

Lee didn't move.

"It's a free country. I can look at what I want. There's no law against that either."

Michael spun to face the handcuffed imbecile and fought the urge to finish what Masino had started. "You'd do well to keep your mouth shut."

Steven jerked the creep toward the steps. "Unless you want to tell us where you're hiding the little girl."

"I don't keep chopsticks around here."

Michael clenched his fist. "Where is she?"

The skinhead only smiled.

Lieutenant Barnes snapped his phone shut. "Let's continue this conversation down at the station. We'll deal with the paperwork and take it from there."

Steven shook his head and handed the thug to Barnes. "We'll follow you over."

Michael tugged on Lee's shoulder. "This fool might lead us to Kat. Let's go nail him on that, and then we'll bust him for the rest of this."

Lee walked out of the row house with dead eyes, saying nothing.

Michael couldn't fathom the emotions hammering his friend's soul, so he left him alone as they rode to the station.

He'd beat the smile off that skinhead during interrogations. Get Kat's whereabouts and then find out what this fool had to do with the pictures they'd just seen. Depending on how much they could pull out of him and if he'd done anything to Kat, Haines could be looking at serious jail time. Add in charges for attacking an FBI agent. At least that knowledge would help Michael sleep tonight.

Maybe.

That and finding Kat before this day dragged into tomorrow.

4

Guess turnabout's fair play.

Hanna hadn't talked to Michael since he'd left the party Saturday. And Steven had been beyond evasive with his few comments about white trucks and the wrong suspect.

She ran a hand through her newly cut and styled blond hair and took a deep breath before raising the front gate of Grounded, her dad's idea of a hip coffee shop with a hometown feel. Dad was wise to use retirement investments and add a fourth small deli-slash-coffee shop in Union Station back in March. All his shops had stayed well afloat, and this one continued to give the mall Starbucks a run for its money.

Maybe Michael would come see her at lunch today. She'd left him five messages over the weekend, and that was more than enough. He'd have to make the next move.

The same staff busied themselves around her as they had before she'd left, but no one asked where she'd been. Even so, her first Monday back to work since June excited her. She loved working in Union Station, and if her plan to stay in Alexandria had any hope of solidifying, she needed to get back to normal fast.

One more glance at the toffee-colored walls drew out a smile. She'd filled them with some of her favorite landscapes and a few gallery samples of friends from Louisville. Her college professors had said she possessed a rare eye to capture both the beauty of nature and people. She was beginning to see it for herself.

Through photography she could at least do one thing that didn't end up a mess.

"So, Hanna, is your FBI boyfriend going to start coming for lunch again?" Becky leaned into the back counter with a giggle, then blushed as red as a strawberry and bit her lip. "I mean, I know it's none of my business and all."

Hanna gave the older teen's arm a small squeeze. "It's okay. He might be back soon. We'll see." Hanna shrugged. "So, how's college going? You're attending George Washington U, right?"

"Yes, but classes don't start till September. I'm looking forward to it though. I'm going for an art history degree." Becky checked the coffeepots and then straightened a few sandwiches in the deli case.

"That sounds like a wonderful major."

"I'd like to teach one day and make my parents proud. Maybe then they'd leave me alone about dieting and exercise. Stop talking about fat farms and all."

Becky's words bruised Hanna's heart. How could parents harp on a normal, curvy teen and make her feel overweight? Some things should never cross a parent's lips. Telling your daughter she was fat headed the list.

"Mommy!"

Hanna scanned the entrance of Grounded. A tiny Asian girl ran past the coffee shop and stopped at the stairs, her black hair swinging as she searched the food court below through the open floor area. "Mommy? Mommy! I wan' my mommy."

Hanna's heartbeat kicked up a notch as she ran past the front tables. But before she could reach the little girl, a dark-skinned young woman knelt in front of the crying child. Curious shoppers stopped and stared.

"Hey, sweetheart. It's okay."

"My mommy's gone. She lefted me an' got on the train." More crying and loud sniffles. "I was looking at all the 'tores an' now I can't find her."

The young woman dried the little girl's tears and spoke in a sing-song voice. "I understand. My little girl likes to go see pretty things too. And she doesn't always notice me standing nearby, watching. Let's go to the Amtrak counter and see if we can find her. What's your name, honey?"

"Jordan." The child's tears lessened and she took the woman's hand.

Hanna caught the young woman's attention and searched her calm, coffee-colored face. "I'll go call mall security."

"Thank you."

A striking woman with flowing ebony hair rushed past the main hall's ornate pillars, looking left and right. "Jordan! Someone please, help! My daughter's disappeared."

"Over here!" Hanna waved.

"Mommy!" Jordan ran into her mother's arms, both of them crying. *Thank You, God.*

The crowd of onlookers dispersed as the mom scooped up Jordan and held her close. A few seconds later, she smiled toward the young woman. "Thank you so much for your kindness."

"Glad to help. My little girl has done the same before." She patted Jordan's back. "Stick close to your mommy, okay, Jordan?"

The little girl nodded as she buried herself in her mother's arms.

Jordan's mother dipped her head. "Thank you again for returning my daughter." She walked away and the pair disappeared into the milling crowd.

Hanna turned to face the well-dressed young woman who was in her early twenties at most. "How about a cup of coffee? My treat. For helping that little girl and her mother."

The woman let out a long sigh and smiled, eyes glistening. "Thank you. But I only did what any mom would do."

"Still, I'd love to show you my thanks. It's not every day I get to watch such an act of kindness." That little happy ending meant more than Hanna could explain.

The slender woman tugged at her cropped white jacket and adjusted the matching pants. "Okay. I'll take anything with a huge kick of caffeine."

"How about a large house blend?" Hanna led the way into Grounded.

"Sounds great. My heart's still hammering out of my chest. But that was a good way to start the day, a needed distraction."

Hanna slipped behind the counter and filled a white mug with steaming coffee. "Rough morning?"

"Yeah. My baby girl started school today."

"First day ever? Did she cry?"

The woman smiled. "Denisha's in third grade. And no, she didn't cry."

Hanna blinked. No way could this young lady have an eight-year-old. Then again, what did she know? Lots of people started their families young. And she was a bad judge of age anyway. "The house blend should wake you right up. How about a wonderful cherry-orange muffin to go along with it?"

"Did you make them or are they frozen?"

Hanna grinned at the direct question. "I wish we had the kitchen to bake everything fresh. We do receive a shipment from a large local bakery every morning."

"Okay, then. I'll take my coffee black and a muffin to go with it."

"Good thing you're not a mischievous moose demanding jam as well."

Chuckling, the woman pulled her wallet out of her denim purse. "My daughter loves *If You Give a Moose a Muffin*. I can read it in my sleep."

"Me too. Only it's my nephew. He'll be seven this week." Hanna wrapped a sheet of wax paper around the muffin and placed it on a white plate.

"Here's the money for the muffin." The woman held out a five dollar bill.

"Nope. On the house."

After putting the money in the tip jar, the young woman slid her tray to the edge of the counter. "Thank you. Hope the rest of your Monday passes calmly."

"Me too. And I hope we'll see you back at Grounded again."

The tray hovered at the edge. Dark brown eyes searched Hanna's face. "You wouldn't happen to have any job openings, would you?"

"If you'd like to fill out an application, we can schedule an interview later this week." Hanna pulled out a form from under the counter. Based on what she'd seen already, this woman would be a wonderful addition to Grounded.

The young woman scooted the tray back a little ways on the counter. "Great. Thank you. I'll fill this out before I leave." She extended her hand. "I'm Evelyn Blaine by the way."

"Hanna Kessler." Shaking the woman's hand, they shared a smile. Maybe Evelyn would become the friend Hanna had hoped to find at work. Someone easy to talk to. Someone in no way connected to the FBI. A real need since things were still uncomfortable around Gracie and Sara.

Evelyn surveyed the empty coffee shop, her expression changing from a wide smile to sadness as she studied the small grouping of family portraits Hanna had done for her friend, Trish—engagement photos at the park, pre-wedding photos, and the ones she'd just taken when she was in Louisville, newborn photos with Trish and her baby girl.

Something in Evelyn's wistful expression touched a lonely place inside Hanna's heart. Fixing a smile back in place, Evelyn settled down at a table near the entrance and started filling out the application form.

"So, what else did you do when you weren't off photographing everything?"

Startled by Becky's voice, Hanna turned around. "I'm sorry?"

"Photographing, you know, taking pictures?" Becky wiped the back counter. "That's what your dad said you'd gone to Louisville to do. Something about going back to God's country for some fresh air and beauty."

Hanna turned to wait on a line of customers who had all arrived at the same time. Becky helped fill the orders without any more conversation. Glad for the diversion and the silence, Hanna worked quickly.

Of course Dad had to tell his employees something about her abrupt disappearance. And she had been snapping a final round of compositions for her coffee-table book project. She still wasn't sure what to tell Becky.

Placing the last to-go cup in an older gentleman's hand, she smiled.

"Thanks and have a wonderful day." Hanna wiped her hands on her red apron and noticed Becky still waiting for an answer to her earlier question. "Yes to the photography. I also worked a little in Dad's Mall St. Matthews shop. But nothing interesting to the question about what else I did."

"If I had free time like that, I'd watch TV. Shows on HGTV and the History Channel. Do you ever watch those?"

Even when she had time, TV had never ranked too high on Hanna's list. She preferred nature hikes to couch surfing any day. "I've seen a little bit of their programming, not much. When I'm home, I watch *America's Most Wanted*."

Becky raised her eyebrows. "You like that stuff?"

"Sometimes." Now she wished she'd kept her mouth shut. Opening up to someone she worked with never paid off in the end. They either couldn't relate because she was enough older at thirty-one, or they acted like she was stuck-up and didn't say much beyond surface pleasantries.

"Guess with an FBI boyfriend you're used to all sorts of cop stuff."

She nodded and watched the bustling foot traffic on Union Station's street level. Would Michael show? Turning her back to the outside activity, she let Becky handle the next few customers while she double-checked the menu for the week, reading over the handwritten entries hanging behind the main counter.

Becky's giggle interrupted the relative quiet.

Hanna stiffened. Was Michael behind her, watching her stand there looking stupid?

"It's not Michael, so you can relax."

Steven. She whirled and faced her brother with a huff. "You're so obnoxious."

"Hey to you too." He crossed his arms over his broad chest. That move probably made Gracie sigh. It made Hanna want to toss a cream pie into her brother's smug expression. Then he turned serious. "Michael's not coming in this afternoon. He's been at NCMEC all weekend and is working there today."

He'd spent the weekend at the National Center for Missing and

Exploited Children? Explained the no returned calls. Sort of. "Why's he there?"

Steven shrugged.

"Never mind. I hate when you pull that silent cop routine. So, do tell. Why'd you decide to torment me today?"

"To invite you over tonight so you can assist Gracie and me with some redecorating."

"There are phones, you know."

"It's much more fun to pester you in person."

Hanna stuck out her tongue. "Will you promise to keep the mushy stuff to yourself? Under no condition will I come if you two are going to make kissy-face all evening."

"Deal. I'm married now. I can—"

"Please stop." She remembered far too well what couples did alone at night. Only she'd never gotten a ring to make it right. Old news. "Are you going to order something, or just stand there bugging me?"

"I'll take a turkey on rye, a banana, and one of your fancy chocolate milks to go."

"You are so not a grownup."

"Am too."

She rolled her eyes and gathered Steven's early lunch into a to-go bag.

"So, will you come tonight? Six for dinner and then we'll put in a few hours of work before James goes to bed."

"And if I'm busy?"

"You aren't." Steven handed her a ten. "Keep the change for the tip jar. Service being so good and all."

She stood as straight as she could. "How do you know I'm not busy?"

"Because Michael will be at my house at five thirty." With that Steven sauntered out of the coffee shop, leaving her to stew all alone.

❈   ❈   ❈

"You understand playing cupid is dangerous business?" Gracie wrapped her arm around Steven's waist and tucked her thumb in his jeans as they surveyed their yet-to-be-remodeled basement. The home gym needed updating, and thanks to Sara's influence, Gracie wanted a scrapbooking room.

Steven grinned. "She's my sister. Besides, you're the one who started the cupid thing. Please don't take away all my fun and say I have to play nice."

"All your fun?" His wife rose on her tiptoes and kissed his neck. "Really?"

"Okay, no. But she did say we can't be mushy like Clint and Sara or she'll puke. My paraphrase, of course."

"Gracie," James shouted down the stairs. "My mom's on the phone and asked to talk to you."

"I'll be right there."

"Better you than me, my dear." He kissed her soundly on the lips. "Just remember you're my wife, and you and I decide what's best for our family."

Watching Gracie sashay up the stairs left him second-guessing his cupid plans for Hanna and Michael. He had better things to do with his evenings now that he was married again. And with Angela spending most of her time back in Louisville, still working through rehab, that left plenty of time for his little three-person family to blend and thrive.

Life was good.

Michael, on the other hand, was not so great. Steven had learned long ago to push the blackness of evil to the back of his mind and lock it up tight so it didn't intrude into his home. Of course, now that Gracie had moved in, she insisted he tell her what he could of his cases and they'd pray over them.

He had to admit, his wife's way trumped his compartmentalizing.

But Michael had no wife to coax him out of the darkness he'd fallen into Saturday. He still wasn't thrilled with Hanna dating Michael, but Steven had seen how much they cared for each other. How much Hanna's return had done for Michael's spirits. So if he could get them back up to speed in their relationship, things would be better for Michael again.

Especially when Steven's gut said their search for Kat might end with less-than-hopeful results.

"You daydreaming, boss?" Michael stood in the basement doorway.

"No."

"Planning to ride my tail for being out of the office so much, then?"

"No again, my fine Watson."

Michael didn't even crack a smile. Tonight stretched long before him. "Hanna should be here soon. Why don't we head upstairs and you can help me set the table?"

"I can't stay."

Steven raised an eyebrow but held his tongue.

"I know you and Clint are concerned about me. I'm fine. And I don't need to be set up on a date right now."

Steven walked to the door and stopped in front of Michael. "I told you before not to play games with my sister. I am worried about you, Michael, yes. But that pales in comparison to what I feel for Hanna."

"I know."

"Then what are your intentions? Your welcome home kiss Saturday says she deserves better than the silent treatment you've given her lately."

Michael hung his head and rubbed the back of his neck. "I know."

"Care to elaborate?"

"I waited for Hanna to break her silence until I thought I'd go crazy. I'm still fighting the trauma counselor about how to handle stress, and I can't escape those pictures from the skinhead's computer. I don't want to drag Hanna into that trash."

"I get that. But at least let her know."

"If I see her, I don't know if I can keep from kissing her again and trying to lose the memories that way." He blanched. "I mean, well, I guess you know what I mean."

Yeah, but they were talking about his baby sister. He didn't want the up-close-and-personal version.

"I'll call her. Okay? I just can't face her yet. Give her my apology?" Michael didn't wait for an answer but showed himself out before Steven could think of a good way to keep the young agent there.

Now what? It was too late to cancel with Hanna, and she'd proba-bly had her hopes up all day of finally getting to talk to Michael. Steven had seen the longing in his sister's deep blue eyes, and it caused an ache in his soul. Based on Michael's reaction, Steven couldn't fix things for Hanna this time or chase all the monsters out from under the bed.

Then again, maybe he could. Maybe Hanna would reach out to Michael. A perfect plan started to come together.

He could persuade Hanna to take her portfolio over to Michael's. All the man needed was a reminder that good still existed. What better way to do that than through his beautiful and compassionate sister and her amazing pictures of kids. Innocence and light captured in a smile.

If anybody could snap Michael Parker out of it, Hanna could. Unless she refused. Then life with Parker would get worse. Fast.

5

Another night alone.

Hanna rifled through her kitchen cabinets for a bowl and the microwave popcorn. At least she'd spent the weekend with family. Not by herself like the two months before.

But she should have been spending tonight with Michael, after dinner at her brother's.

Something in Steven's passed-along apology didn't sit right. Cases hadn't hit Michael as hard when they'd been dating. Guess Michael's workaholism was her fault too.

Her leaving had messed up far more than it fixed.

It certainly hadn't helped her keep the past in its place. Hanna pushed aside memories of her parents' backyard and all the tears she'd shed there, the secrets she'd longed to leave unearthed. She'd avoided that place next to Mom's old koi pond as much as possible when she was in Louisville.

Too bad she hadn't avoided seeing Craig and his new wife. When they'd sauntered into Dad's shop in Mall St. Matthews, Craig acted like a total stranger. Until he came back up to the counter for another cup of espresso and chatted like she was an old pal.

Not the woman who'd warmed his bed.

She shoved those snapshots of shame aside and filled her bowl with popcorn. The buttery smell made her stomach growl. Grabbing a small box of Godiva chocolates she'd bought to share with Michael tonight, she headed into the living room.

"Mmm. Steven and Clint can have their steak. I'll take popcorn and good chocolate any day."

She missed Champ's nudges in response to her talking to the air. But Champ called Michael's place home now, and she didn't have the heart to uproot him after she'd abandoned him months ago.

"So it's me and my photography stuff tonight." She'd grown so used to talking to herself it didn't feel strange. But tonight it did. Maybe because she should have been telling Michael all about her first coffee-table book.

The one she hadn't even mentioned to Dad or Steven yet because she wanted Michael to know first.

"Stupid me. I missed my chance with Michael. Now I'll have to celebrate alone." She plopped down among piles of paperwork and portfolio pieces and put her food aside.

Shuffling through her stacks of favorite Kentucky photographs, she found the pictures that Brad, the Cliff Winds Press general manager, had loved. He'd been the first to call and welcome her into the "family." Cliff Winds claimed to have America's top nature photographers creating high-quality landscape coffee-table books.

She didn't see herself as top notch or a true nature photographer, but Brad loved her work. Even the pictures contrasting people and nature. Something most landscape books didn't contain. Brad's compliments about her publicity photo probably cinched the contract deal. Funny, the one picture she totally hated might have been the one to sell her first book. Yuck. Good thing Brad and the rest of the male staff lived miles away in Colorado. No roving eyes or roaming hands to contend with that way. And she had no plans to fly out there anytime soon.

Now all she had to do was eliminate a few photos, write her text and captions, and send everything to Cliff Winds by February. No problem.

Except that the photos of Appalachian children dwarfed by gorgeous mountains and total poverty seared her mind. Even in their tattered clothes they still smiled and played.

Something she seldom did. Even as a child.

She had given in to a few of the little girls' play requests when she'd visited the Cumberland area and helped out at a local ministry to the children. The staff and parents had been thrilled about her photography and even displayed a few of her photos in their small office.

One day she wanted to thru-hike the Appalachian Trail to raise money for their work. One day…

Hanna's stomach growled again. Her lack of appetite at Steven and Gracie's had caught up with her. Pulling the popcorn bowl with her, she scooted away from the stack of photographs and toward the TV. No way would she risk ruining those pictures. After munching a few handfuls of buttery delight, she picked up the remote control.

"Might as well watch the latest *America's Most Wanted* tape while I eat." That way she could pretend to be part of Michael's world and maybe someday help put a bad guy in jail. That'd sure score points with him. Of course she didn't really want to recognize someone from the show.

Munching popcorn, she listened to John Walsh talk with passion about putting criminals away for life. The Adam Walsh Child Protection and Safety Act would go a long way toward that end.

Good for the Walshes.

If only she could be that brave and put her past to good use like John and Reve Walsh had done.

"There's a special place in hell for people who hurt children.
Especially the type of criminal we have to show you tonight.
This is John Doe number ten."

Hanna studied the carpet. She hated this part. The other cases didn't strike at her heart like these special segments. Good thing *America's Most Wanted* didn't run them all that often.

Wiping her hands, she remembered Michael talking about what a great thing the Endangered Child Alert Program was. And how if the FBI didn't get an identification from their "seeking information" Web site section, they'd show the unidentified subject on AMW.

When she'd asked Steven about the program, he'd said the FBI had identified dozens of victims of child sexual abuse and arrested eight per-petrators. All because the creeps put their disgusting videos and pictures on the Web for bragging rights. But her brother didn't like talking about cases like that.

One more reason to keep her past in the past.

After all, that was why she'd run back to Louisville in the first place. Steven's snooping into her past and her lying to him about how many guys she'd slept with in college had started the avalanche that culminated with Jonathan Rollins's abduction. The nightmare for Sara and Clint that was her fault.

All she'd had to do was keep an eye on Jonathan while Sara took Susannah to the restroom. She couldn't even do that. So she ran away from the well-meaning people who would uncover her secret with their concerned attention and questions about how she was doing.

One good thing had come from her time away. She'd decided once and for all that no one in her family needed to know what happened twenty-four years ago. They'd all moved on, and it was time for her to leave Louisville memories boarded up in her parents' old home.

Her family wanted her in Alexandria with them.

Jonathan was fine now, and Clint's family didn't blame her for what had happened.

Taking a deep breath, she refocused on the TV show. John Walsh talked about how the FBI needed the public's help to put John Doe number ten away. Then they flashed his picture again.

Hanna couldn't breathe.

More than twenty years hadn't erased the identical image burned into her brain. No, she'd never forget the large birthmark on the man's upper right arm. The big, rough hands that she could still feel burning into her skin.

The same hands that had offered her cookies every day after she'd worked in his yard all summer for extra money. And then caressed her hair as he told her how beautiful she was.

Right before he—

She ran into the bathroom and barely made it to the toilet. She heaved until her whole body shook, then finally sat back against the tub. Tears stabbed her eyes.

The tears she'd been too terrified to cry as a little six-almost-seven-year-old girl streamed down her face as she curled up into a ball.

"Oh, God, please. Please make him go away." Sobs strained her throat. Two decades' worth of tears soaked her bathroom rug.

And she was right back in her neighbor's bedroom as if she'd never left. The stuffy smell of sweaty clothes and men's cheap aftershave clung to her skin. She'd snuck in the house to get a few cookies before she finished her yard work. Something Mr. Richard had told her was off limits until all the work was done. Then weird noises in the back room made her think he'd been hurt. So she went to check.

Bad. Stupid. Move.

Mr. Richard said she'd come after him because she wanted him.

Hanna curled into a tighter ball and squeezed her knees into her chest trying to cover all the memories. Push away all the shame.

Everything in her had screamed for her legs to run away from the shirtless neighbor when he'd started talking about how beautiful she was. But she didn't.

He'd said she looked at him like his wife had.

But she hadn't. And she wasn't six anymore. She could run now. She could fight back.

She pushed herself up on shaky legs and walked into the living room. Picking up the remote, she rewound the show back to the picture of his right arm, the only identifiable piece of evidence they had against him.

"John Doe is believed to have been abusing little girls for over twenty years. These captured images have been linked to pictures from the early eighties up until five years ago. He has to be stopped. Any information you have on John Doe number ten could help us lock him away forever. Please call our tip line at 1-800-CRIME-TV. Please, if you can help us, call now."

With shaking hands, she picked up the phone. And hung it up again.

She couldn't call. Couldn't tell anyone.

The phone's shrill ring made her scream and drop the cordless.

This was crazy. She was a thirty-one-year-old woman, safe in her Alexandria apartment, far away from her old neighbor. No way was he the one on the other end of her telephone.

Hands still shaking, she pushed the talk button before the fifth ring. "Hello?"

"Hanna, it's Dad. Are you okay? I just talked to Steven and he said you might be having a rough night."

More tears burned her eyes. "Daddy. I need you."

Thirty minutes later she was wrapped in her dad's safe arms with Sue sitting next to her, holding her hand and passing Kleenex her way every few seconds.

"I...I'm sorry. I shouldn't have made you two come over here like that."

"No matter what you need, honey, we're here for you." Sue's soft voice soothed a jagged place inside that only Hanna's mom could have touched.

She hadn't even told Mom about their next-door neighbor. She'd tried a few times but could never get the story past her terror. Who would believe her anyway? And she couldn't bring herself to tell her dad now either. Their neighbor had said he and Andrew Kessler were friends. And Andrew would believe his friend over some imaginative little girl making up stories.

Her dad had never suspected a thing. Or else he wouldn't have made her keep helping with the young widower's yard work that summer. She'd never gone into their neighbor's house again, and he'd moved not long after school had started.

Dad sat her up straight and searched her face. "Is this all about Michael? Did something happen between you two?"

"No. I haven't talked to Michael."

"Then what is it?" Dad's eyes swam with questions and worry. "Is this because of what happened with Jonathan? That wasn't your fault, Hanna. You have to believe that."

She shook her head.

"I'm trying to understand, honey. Please help me out here. It's not like you to be so emotional over anything."

True. She'd learned to hide her emotions so no one would ever find out what her next-door neighbor had done. Even when her mom had died of cancer, Hanna hadn't cried much. At least not in front of anyone.

But now she had to find a way to stop that awful man from hurting other little girls. She just didn't know how without telling her dad who it was.

"There's a man on *America's Most Wanted* that I can identify."

Dad's confusion increased. "What do you mean?"

"A child molester." Nothing like blurting it all out.

Sue gasped and covered her mouth.

"What?" Her dad's eyes narrowed. Most of the time Dad resembled Steven. But right then he'd aged ten years in wrinkles on his forehead.

That he couldn't handle the truth she had to tell was written all over his face. Maybe she'd made a mistake. Another very bad mistake.

"Maybe not. Maybe I'm wrong."

"Hanna." Dad's voice was little more than a whisper. "Did someone…did someone hurt you like that?"

Fear snaked up her spine. She couldn't tell her father that one of his friends had molested her.

No. Dad would blame himself. Maybe even blame her. Dad still talked about his friend sometimes.

One small lie had protected Steven and stopped his snooping months ago. She could do it again. For Dad's sake.

"Maybe I'm remembering what one of my friends in third grade told me about. I think she might have been hurt by her uncle or something. And the TV show talked about how this guy had been hurting people for a long time. I guess I was just thinking about her and all those little girls."

Sue's soft prayers filled with tears for all those children.

Dad let out a deep breath. "I can understand why you'd cry over that. It's unbearable what evil people do to children." He hung his head a minute before looking back up. "But I'm glad it wasn't you, Hanna. I don't know how I'd live with myself if someone hurt you and I hadn't been there to protect you."

Hanna's stomach knotted.

She'd done the right thing not telling her dad.

But that did nothing to settle her churning insides. Her lie would catch up with her. And an untold number of little girls were still at risk if she didn't come forward.

Then she remembered that none of the photos linked to the image on *America's Most Wanted* had been recent. Maybe the man was dead. Yeah. That was probably the case. No sense stirring up trouble for nothing. Their former neighbor might have died a sick, old, disgusting man forgotten in some nursing home. Or maybe his past had caught up to him and he committed suicide.

She shouldn't entertain such wretched thoughts. But they were safer. Far safer than the alternative. Safer than telling Dad the truth about what had really happened.

Right now she needed to lock the truth away in her mind, shove it back into the dusty places where things of the past belonged.

6

Michael paced the Assistant US Attorney's office Tuesday morning, revving like his black Mustang poised for a street race.

If Michael couldn't make good on his promise to find solid evidence leading to a watertight prosecution, Sean Haines would be released today.

Crystal Hernandez, the NCMEC analyst he'd been working with, caught his arm. "What we found this weekend will be enough, Michael, you'll see. Stop your worry." She flipped her straight, black hair and gave him a flirtatious smile like she'd done all weekend. "Sit. Things will go better if you don't wear a hole in Mr. Marks's carpet."

Steven scowled.

Michael ignored him and sat next to Lee. But not seeing Hanna all weekend and avoiding her last night gnawed at him. There was nothing going on with Crystal. Nothing from his end anyway. Maybe he should ask Maria Grivens, the Secret Service agent he'd met last year on the Kensington case, to talk with Crystal and set her straight. Maria had done that for him when he'd invited her out for dinner. Now she was living with another federal agent. But maybe she could employ her gift of direct words and help him out.

Then again, maybe he'd misread Crystal.

AUSA Kenneth Marks strode into his office and placed his leather briefcase on the ornate mahogany conference table. Steven, Lee, and Crystal all straightened in their chairs. Michael gathered his notes and sat forward.

"Steven, I assume you've consulted with Lieutenant Barnes and other task force leadership?" Marks locked eyes with Kessler and sat down.

"Yes. They and Officer Masino regret not being able to attend the meeting today, but they've faxed over case notes and interrogation transcripts." Steven pushed the copied file forward. "Michael and a top NCMEC analyst, Crystal Hernandez, are here to brief you on their findings."

Marks cleared his throat. "I've conferred with the US Attorney for the District of Maryland as well as other top attorneys here in DC. You need to know that almost regardless of what you've found, Sean Haines will walk today. Coerced confessions, police brutality suits, and 'fruit of the poisonous tree' doctrine will silence anything you have to say."

Michael's jaw muscles quivered, about to snap. A warning alarmed in his conscience, but he ignored it. "There's no way this creep can get off with bogus brutality claims and legal mumbo jumbo. It's not right."

Marks sat back and crossed his arms.

Steven's scathing look seared Michael's forehead.

"Haines's lawyer started proceedings against me yesterday." Lee's haunted eyes focused on the bookshelf behind Marks. "And I'm chained to the desk until the investigation is over."

"What?" Michael glared at the older attorney. "That skinhead attacked Lee, and now he's gonna walk while an FBI agent gets slapped down for nothing?"

"Politics and money, Agent Parker, affect far more than Capitol Hill policy makers. Haines is a wealthy and respected business owner whose lawyer is one of the top defense attorneys in Baltimore. And Haines's lawyer is already earning every pretty penny he's being paid." The AUSA paused and studied the case notes. "This case is not going to Grand Jury unless you have something new to report."

"I do." Michael nodded to Crystal. "Over the weekend Ms. Hernandez and I found pictures we believe are of Katrina Chu and Bill Lasser on a Web site frequented by Lasser, the owner of the white truck seen at the residence where we apprehended Haines."

"Have you questioned Lasser or Shale, the owner of the row house?"

Steven jumped into the conversation before Michael could elaborate. "Not yet. We're still trying to locate them."

"Bill Lasser had been identified as being seen with Katrina Chu before we even talked with Haines." Michael ignored his boss and pushed ahead. "And we can link Lasser to Haines with phone records, e-mail, and Haines's Web-browsing cache."

"Because of the fruit of the poisonous tree doctrine, Haines's interrogation is inadmissible. As is evidence obtained based on the illegal search of his computer."

"An overeager rookie cop's mistake. We were seeking information at first, then Mirandized him before we took him to the station and he started talking. Without coercion."

"Doesn't matter. The rookie's mistake taints everything." Marks shook his head. "And even with the link between Lasser and Haines, there's nothing to implicate Haines in anything illegal concerning Katrina Chu."

Lee ground his teeth before speaking. "Being a violent racist isn't enough?"

"No, Agent Branson, I'm sad to say it isn't. We have nothing to implicate Haines in any illegal activity regarding the disgusting pictures on his computer. The First Amendment protects against censorship and gives all manner of rights to people fit to govern themselves. Regardless of our agreed opinion on what type of person Haines is, he has the right to view despicable photographs on the Internet. And for all we know, those could be computer generated."

"Which is what his attorney will argue if this case ever goes to trial." Crystal took a deep breath. "I've run those photos through the National Center's databases and conferred with other analysts. We've found no matches to missing children in the last decade. And there's enough distortion to the photos that we can't provide expert testimony to offset arguments that it could be computer manipulated."

Michael's rage erupted. "This can't be happening. We have evidence linking Haines to Lasser and, before that, eyewitness testimony stating Katrina Chu was in the home where Haines stayed. I don't give a rip what this skinhead or his lawyer claim. He attacked Lee, and there's no way that piece of trash can say he was coerced into a confession of anything."

His conscience pricked again. *But this is righteous anger. Justifiable fury. Right, God?* This time his inner warning system stayed silent.

Attorney Marks sighed. "He can and he has, Agent Parker. In addition, the eyewitness rescinded her statement, saying she couldn't be sure the girl she noticed coming from her neighbor's was Katrina Chu. No DNA evidence related to the child was found at the row house either. And based on the poisonous tree doctrine, a protection against illegal police activity, none of the information we now have will be admissible in court."

Michael forced himself to remain silent while Marks continued. "Everything regarding Haines and his connection to Lasser will be inadmissible. Nothing, and I repeat, nothing, derived from Haines's e-mails or his interrogation, even though the man was talking about Katrina Chu, is valid to hold him beyond seventy-two hours or to press charges for anything more than attacking a law enforcement officer."

"He's playing the system."

"Then according to the system, he wins." Kenneth Marks sighed again. "I'm sorry. Very sorry. Neither the US Attorney in Baltimore nor in DC will prosecute this one."

Steven leaned forward. "Is there any way we can hold Haines until we find Lasser?"

"Do you have credible witnesses that will testify to seeing Haines and Lasser together with Katrina Chu?"

"No. The neighbor who called in the tip about Lasser said she never saw him with anyone but the missing child."

"Any DNA evidence from the white truck that links Haines to the child's disappearance?"

Steven slumped into his chair. "No sir. We haven't found the truck. And we have nothing apart from Haines's computer and his interrogation to link him to our missing child or those lynching photographs."

Marks stood. "Then, gentlemen and Ms. Hernandez, I suggest you

find Bill Lasser and Howard Shale. They may be our only hope for finding Katrina Chu and securing justice in this case."

※ ※ ※

Steven's urge to beat some sense into Michael grew with every step
toward the Hoover building. He didn't care for the company of Crystal
Hernandez either. Her eager attention toward Michael irritated Steven.

"I don't care what Marks says, those phone records implicate Lasser
in Kat's disappearance and prove Haines was involved. How much
clearer can it be stated? Lasser was a high school buddy of Haines and
called his old pal for help with how to handle Kat." Michael jerked at
his unusually conservative silk tie.

Crystal kept pace as the three men dodged tourists on their way
back to headquarters. "I agree. I'll keep working to find more information on Kat and the kids in Haines's photograph collection. It's unheard
of for a sex offender to have a cache of purely violent, nonsexual photographs though. This guy doesn't fit any of our profiles."

The last thing Steven wanted to hear was shoptalk on sexual preda-
tors. Besides, Lee needed some attention. The man deserved more than
the raw deal he'd received. "You still good for dinner tonight, Lee? Gracie's got all your favorites on the menu."

Lee half smiled. "Wouldn't miss it, boss. She's prayin' too, right?"

"That she is. Along with your parents."

"I can't believe I'm saying it, but I actually miss Mom's lectures
about religion and her earthshaking prayer meetings."

"You should come to services with us sometime and put down some
real roots here in DC."

Lee swallowed hard. "No offense, boss, but Mom's religion is a good
thing for her. And I appreciate your family's prayers. But Rashida and I
aren't planning to uproot from Louisiana. We're still hoping to head
back within a few years."

The personal and professional hit from the ridiculous investigation
of Haines's attack threatened to chase another good agent away from the

Bureau. Steven would do all he could to prevent that. Starting with a fast wrap-up of the bogus claims against Lee by Haines's lawyers.

"What about Howard Shale, the owner of the house Haines was staying in? Do we have anything on his whereabouts, Lee?"

"No. The former white-supremacist leader is keeping a low profile, staying away from any legal problems since he moved from Illinois to Baltimore a couple years ago."

Michael snorted. "And carousing with a lowlife like Sean Haines will help him how?" The small group paused before entering headquarters. "I'll walk you to your car, Crystal. See you two upstairs."

The pair disappeared from view and a migraine started pounding in Steven's head. Michael still hadn't called Hanna, and something was very wrong with his sister again. He sensed it in increasing measure with every phone conversation they'd had since she'd returned to Alexandria. That plus this case equaled an ulcer before it was all over. He trudged into the CACU offices with a thousand-pound weight resting on his shoulders.

"Gonna let me do more than donkeywork in the next century, partner?" Clint's drawl connected as Steven flopped into his desk chair.

"Not today, Clint. I've groveled about Saturday enough. I don't regret my call either. This case is no action and all migraine. You should thank me."

"Nothing doing. My shot's just as good as yours. No more excuses." Clint leaned against the gray partition separating their work spaces, waiting.

"Find Shale or Lasser, and you can personally hogtie and roast them, okay?"

Clint smiled. Every day he was more and more like his old self. "That's what I'm talking about."

Having Clint back in the action was exactly what Steven, Michael, and Lee needed. His partner and best friend didn't shy away from the God-talk Steven still struggled to slip into case discussions. "How's Sara doing?"

"Ready to pop. She's in full nesting mode and driving me crazy. But

I love it. There's not a finer lady or mom anywhere in this world, and Conor's arrival will be a national celebration if Sara Rollins, MD, has anything to do with it."

"You Texans do everything big, don't you?"

"You betcha."

Michael entered and sat at his desk without a glance in Steven's direction.

Clint slid his chair around the partition and sat down. "Want to talk about what's up with Michael and Hanna before you rip into the kid?"

"No. I'm prime for a good rip session. And after his hotheaded performance this morning, Michael deserves it."

"Not to mention all the time he's keeping with a pretty NCMEC analyst."

"Leave it alone, pard."

"Keep it about work during work hours. That's what you always say." Clint slid his bulk back to his cubical without another word.

Maybe he should pray. Gracie would agree. Too bad this wasn't Clint's or Gracie's problem. It was Hanna's. And that made it his.

He stalked over to Michael's desk. "We need to talk."

Michael didn't move from his chair. "Okay."

"In the conference room." Steven turned and walked into the large empty room without glancing back. He shut the door when Michael entered.

They stood and faced each other down for a span of seconds before Michael broke the silence. "Is this going to be a personal or professional tongue lashing?"

"Both."

"You know as well as I do this legal…" Michael clamped his mouth over the colorful words he used to let fly. "It's all wrong and I'm doing my best to right it."

"Yelling at an AUSA is not the way to do it."

"I'll set up an appointment with Marks and apologize."

"Good. And my sister?"

"I'll call Hanna tonight after I'm done at NCMEC."

Steven swallowed and tried to pray. It didn't work. "Will that be before you drown your emotions in an analyst who's begging for it?"

Michael's jaw muscles popped and he turned an ugly shade of angry.

"If you're done with Hanna, at least give her the courtesy of a face-to-face dumping."

Instead of the punch Steven expected, Michael deflated into a leather chair. "Boss, I..." The younger man bowed his head and rubbed his eyes with the palms of his hands. "That's not what I want. And nothing's happened with Crystal. I have no intention of that changing either."

Steven took a deep breath. Good. Michael wasn't slipping back into his old ways. That'd keep their work relationship and friendship intact. "Haines will be released in a few hours no matter what you find tonight. Let it go for right now. Let's watch the skinhead and let him string his own noose. He will sooner or later. They always do."

"What about Kat?"

The child's name made guilt tentacles tighten around his insides. "We're still looking. Unit Chief Maxwell just deployed our newest Child Abduction Rapid Deployment Team. They'll talk with the Chu family and work round the clock to process leads. From all indications, Lasser had every intention of keeping Kat alive. Our Innocent Images Unit is jumping into the mix too because of the photos uncovered."

"We're off the case so the new CARD team can scramble for a notch on their belt?"

"Leave the peacock stance to the other agencies. These are our guys and they're keeping me in the loop. We'll focus on our other investigations while we keep tabs on Haines and dig up Lasser's whereabouts. The more people working this case, the better our chances of finding Kat alive."

"When can I start surveillance?"

"I'll initiate the paper process. Regardless of changed witness statements, Haines knows far more than he let on about Lasser and Kat. Let's plan on Monday to begin surveillance. I'll ask Baltimore PD to keep an eye on Haines until then."

Michael nodded, his eyes and skin returning to normal. "Mind if I take off around four to head over to Union Station?"

Steven half smiled. "Give Hanna my love."

"Will do." Michael headed back to his desk.

Steven leaned against the door frame. God help Sean Haines if they found any shred of physical evidence linking him to Kat's disappearance. And his buddy William Lasser would be better off dead when Steven and his team ousted the pervert from under his rock.

But even that would pale in comparison if Parker had any intentions of playing Hanna or him for a fool. Hell might have a special place for people who hurt children.

But not even hell compared to big brother's revenge.

7

Try as she might to avoid it, Hanna still watched Grounded's front entrance for any sign of Michael. His visit yesterday afternoon, with a too-short apology and a too-long list of excuses about work, left her lonelier than before. He hadn't called later or shown up for lunch today like she'd hoped. But maybe he'd come by before her workday ended. All she had left of Wednesday's to-do list was the interview with Evelyn Blaine. If Evelyn worked half as well as she'd helped that frightened child earlier this week, they'd get along well.

She left the front counter to rearrange the storeroom for the third time today. Keeping her hands busy helped her not resemble a forlorn puppy dog. Even though Champ's sad look was adorable. She missed Champ almost as much as she missed Michael. But Michael hadn't invited her over to his place yet, and after yesterday, no way would she show up unannounced.

A slight sound of metal hitting the floor caused her pulse to race. Eyes wide, she turned toward the door.

No one there.

She took a few deep breaths and then picked up the stray utensil. Just a misplaced spoon that had fallen from one of the shelves she'd disturbed. Nothing to be so jumpy about.

A sharp poke from behind and a man's muffled voice shut off her thinking.

She turned around fast, fist cocked to connect like Steven had taught her. Connect she did. Right with the tall man's nose.

He staggered back, face crumpled into his knees. The man groaned and stayed down. "Did you have to listen to everything I taught you?"

Hanna froze. "Steven?"

"Uh-huh."

Bending over to check on her brother, she tried to process what just happened. "Are you okay? What are you doing here? Are you bleeding?"

Steven straightened, red nose still pinched between his fingers. "I'll be fine. But a bag of something frozen would be good."

She hustled to the back freezer and found an unopened bag of coffee she'd meant to thaw earlier that morning. "Here. This should help."

"Thanks." He leaned back and placed the bag over the bridge of his nose, then sat in Dad's desk chair. "You were a little slow with that right hook. But that'll save me from surgery for a deviated septum."

"What in the world were you trying to do?"

"Pay you back for sneaking up on me all these years." He tried to grin but winced instead.

She put her hands on her hips and huffed, noticing for the first time how much her hand smarted. "Steven Kessler, you got what you deserved then. Wait till I tell Dad. Then you'll get the talking to you also deserve."

"Why don't you get it over with now?"

"Because I have an appointment in thirty minutes and need some time for my heart rate to return to normal." She pulled another chair close to her brother. "Don't ever pull a stunt like that again."

"I don't believe I will. Ever."

She giggled, relieving some of her pent-up stress.

Steven groaned a second time. "Please tell me you won't make me regret this even more by telling Clint."

"Be nice to me and we'll see."

❋   ❋   ❋

Steven left shortly after their altercation, and Evelyn arrived with her little girl at three thirty on the dot. Not on time by her brother's standards, but it worked for Hanna. She pushed any further thought of Steven from her mind.

Evelyn waved and settled an adorably dressed Denisha at the table farthest away from the door. "You do your stuff with homework and I see ice cream in your near future."

Denisha's caramel-colored skin crinkled with a giggle. She took off a cropped and jeweled denim jacket and adjusted the lime and pink slip-dress underneath. "Yes ma'am."

Hanna left the front counter in Becky's capable hands and joined Evelyn at the table next to Denisha's homework station. "I'm sorry the only interview opening I had was right after school."

"Not a problem. I'd have gotten my sister to pick Deni up, but she had classes and couldn't." Evelyn rubbed shaking hands on her tan pants and adjusted her conservative lime green top. "I hope this isn't too unprofessional, me bringing Deni with me."

"Not at all."

"Before we start the interview, can I ask something?"

Hanna nodded and smoothed her blue and white capri outfit back into place, praying the question wouldn't be too personal. She'd kept it together for the last few days by the grace of God alone. Today's scare with Steven hadn't helped. But she couldn't lose it now. Not in front of a potential employee and a beautiful little third grader who made Hanna long for a different past.

Evelyn grinned and adjusted her top again. Deni waved.

If only she had the bright smile and friendliness Evelyn and her little girl exhibited. If only Michael would call and take her mind off everything else. Steven had said she should call Michael, but she couldn't. She needed him to show interest. How else would she know if he cared enough to stick around?

She forced her focus back on Evelyn's question.

"When I turned in my application on Monday, I asked the girl working with you about these photos. She said they're yours. I'm not sure I could afford your fee, but I'd like to see how long it'd take to save up for a family picture of me and Deni. We've never had one done."

Hanna smiled. This line of conversation sent her heart back to a normal rhythm. "If you'll agree to let me use one of the shots for the store display, I'll give you a package deal at my cost for materials."

"You're serious?" Evelyn stared wide eyed. "You'd do that for me?"

"Why not?"

Evelyn swallowed hard. "When I told my sister I was going to ask about your prices, she said white folks don't ever cut African Americans any deals. A lot of the people at Howard University agree with Trina."

Hanna's heart hurt. "My family and I aren't like that. And I'd love to do a photo shoot with you and Deni. Besides…" Hanna touched Evelyn's application, "charging you just for materials is the least I can do for a co-worker."

"You mean it? No kidding? About the pictures and the job?"

"I would like to hear about your future plans for school and make sure you'll be able to put in the hours I need, but if we can work it out, the job is yours." Nothing in Evelyn's application had set off any red flags. And she'd already seen Evelyn's character in action.

Evelyn sat up straighter. "I'm taking a year off from school. After scholarships, my momma is helping pay for Trina and my classes at Howard. I have two semesters left, but I'm missing too much of Deni's growing up trying to go to school full time and work. The job I had in the garment industry burnt me out fast. I need a breather. So I'm looking for employment that will leave time for a little design work on the side and evenings with Deni and Trina."

"You're a fashion-design major, right?"

"Yes. I make all of Deni's clothes and most of mine and Trina's too."

Hanna smiled. "You have talent. No doubt you'll do very well when you're ready to return to the fashion world."

"Thank you. You sound like my momma. Only you're a lot younger."

Bless Evelyn for that ego boost. She'd take a compliment about having a mother's wisdom as long as she didn't look old enough to have a grown daughter.

"Your mother owns a bakery in Virginia, right?" Hanna wanted to ask about Denisha's father, but that would cross over into personal information she didn't need to know.

"Yes. Momma is the best cook in the world. And she's kept the bakery in the black, even with Daddy's passing a few years back."

"I'm sorry to hear about your father."

"Thanks. I still miss him." Evelyn pointed to the application. "I can work Monday through Friday, opening until three o'clock. Will that work?"

"That's thirty hours a week. Not enough for me to offer the full-time employee insurance benefits. But if you're okay with that, you can start next week. That'll help tremendously. I have a few employees going back to school who can't work until late afternoon."

Evelyn stuck out her manicured hand. "It's a deal, then." She practically squealed. "I'm so excited."

"Me too. Welcome to the family, Evelyn. I hope your time at Grounded is a great experience."

Deni jumped up and ran to give her mom a hug. "Thank you, ma'am. My mom's the best worker you ever did hire."

"I'm sure she is." The scent of Michael's woodsy aftershave distracted her.

"There's a huge GQ guy that keeps looking your way. If you don't have anything else for me to do today, I'll get out of your hair so you can have a fun evening."

Hanna didn't want to turn around until she could force her pulse to calm down. "We'll fill out your employment paperwork first thing Tuesday morning. Can you be here a little before nine?"

"Definitely. Thank you, Hanna. I look forward to working with you. And I'll call about setting up a photo shoot. Thanks for that too." Evelyn and Deni gathered up their belongings and scooted out of the coffee shop.

"Hanna."

She stood on wobbly legs and locked on to Michael's dark brown eyes. The intensity missing from him yesterday had returned. In full force.

He smiled. "Can I get that rain check on our Chinese dinner?"

❋   ❋   ❋

Less than a week back in Alexandria, and Hanna was heading over to Michael's apartment. He'd followed her to her brownstone and then insisted on driving them to his apartment. When she was in Louisville she'd dreamed about this. Now here she was.

He picked up their Chinese takeout and for the rest of the drive made small talk about Champ and needing to change out of his monkey suit. "Champ will do backflips when he sees you." Michael slid his Mustang into a front parking place.

She grabbed their food bag and waited for Michael to open her door. If he was anything, the man was a gentleman. Tonight's visit held no cause for alarm.

Even if every cell in her body wanted to escape into Michael's arms.

Shame blanketed her. Would she ever grow past the Pandora's Box she'd opened by sleeping around in college and then trying to keep Craig happy?

"You want me. I can see it in your beautiful eyes."

The memory of her former neighbor's comment roiled her stomach.

They walked up the three flights of stairs in awkward silence. When Michael stuck his keys into the deadbolt, Champ's scratching at the door made her laugh. "Think he'll remember me?"

Slobbery dog kisses and yelps of joy answered her.

"Down, boy. She's not going to visit if you maul her like that." He nudged Champ's backside and the yellow Lab sat obediently, tail beating a staccato rhythm on the floor.

"I missed you too." She hugged the quivering dog and wanted to cry. "I'm sorry. I'm not leaving like that again. Ever."

"That a promise to me too?" Michael's eyes searched her face.

"Sorry. I'll get the food dished up and on the table after I take Champ out for a sec."

He took the food to the kitchen, and then the two males disappeared outside for a few minutes. When Michael returned, he stayed busy in the kitchen with Champ shadowing his every move.

She continued to look around. Nothing had changed, even though it seemed like years since her last visit. The minimal bamboo sculptures and strong earth tones still exuded Michael's very male presence.

Crossing the living room to the entertainment center, she paused and ran a finger over the two silver picture frames there. The one of Michael and Champ taken on their favorite trail at Rock Creek Park brought a smile.

"I still say I'm a great photographer. That picture of you and Champ at the Rollinses' pool is magazine quality." He stepped close. His way of taking charge of every interaction.

"Other than the subject matter, I'd agree you have a knack for the camera."

Something clouded Michael's eyes, but he pointed to the dining room without a word. Once seated, he took her hand. Champ didn't wait for prayers to dig into his dinner.

"Father. Be evident tonight. We need You. Amen."

Michael's prayers had never lacked passion and remained short and to the point. She whispered her own pleas toward heaven and hoped for safe mealtime conversation. Pushing aside thoughts of after dinner, she concentrated on her sweet-and-sour pork.

"How did things go last weekend? I figured you got busy with work." Why did she have to sound so lame and needy? She didn't look up.

"The whole ordeal is a waking nightmare." Michael's bitter words forced her to meet his eyes. "I'm starting to believe justice is a joke and nothing I do will change that."

"Does that mean you're still thinking about leaving the FBI?" His letters last month indicated that possibility, especially when he referenced the shooting in May. Not that he ever gave any emotional details.

"No. My work keeps me here in DC. Near you. For now that's enough. I'll just keep pushing the system to work for me again. Until one of us breaks under the strain anyway."

He inhaled his mandarin beef and fried rice. She picked at her food.

"Are you going to tell me about why you left? I'm not up for dancing around the elephant in the room tonight."

Hanna grabbed her water and washed down the last bite of pork lodged in her throat. She might as well get this over with. Then she'd tell Michael about her photography book and move things off the eggshells they were treading.

"I couldn't shake the guilt of Jonathan's abduction, not with seeing Clint's family every day. That and Clint's struggle to come back after chemo raked like sandpaper on an open wound."

"You could have talked to me about it."

"I'm sorry, Michael. I should have. I just didn't know how to do it then."

"And now?"

If she hadn't known better, she'd have sworn Michael had morphed into a sad little boy begging for someone to say a kind word. No doubt he'd been that little boy growing up. The few stories he'd told of his dad's painful discipline and caustic words left her longing to kiss away the pain etched across Michael's face.

"I spent some time with a counselor friend in Louisville. That helped."

"Female?"

"Yes." Male egos were as fragile as blown glass. "We talked over a lot of the guilt issues. She insisted coming back to Alexandria would help."

"Has it?"

It might if Michael would give her the time of day instead of working twenty-four seven. "Some. It's been good to see the Rollinses are doing fine and to be with my family again. Work is great. This feels more like home than Louisville did."

"What about us, Hanna?"

She pushed her plate away and met his eyes. "If all you have time for is work, 'us' can't survive."

"Do you want it to?"

Did she? More than food and water most days. "Yes. Do you?"

Another strange look flashed though Michael's eyes. Her people-reading skills had grown rusty, and an uneasy silence settled around them.

"I want you to trust me. To talk to me. But you're not there."

"I'm trying."

He stood and moved toward his bedroom, Champ still sticking to his leg like superglue. "I'll be back in a minute. I need to change."

Cleaning the plates and loading the dishwasher provided little distraction. Tension thickened the air. What she wouldn't give to turn back time four months. Twenty-four years for that matter.

Michael's presence filled the kitchen. "When you left…right after Steven's wedding…were you running away from me?"

Deep breath. "No." More lies.

Strong hands gently turned her around. Michael's sleeveless shirt and running shorts didn't give her any good place to focus. "I…I have some good news I've been waiting to tell you. I wanted you to be the first to know."

"I'm all ears."

And muscles. She shook her head and stepped back for some breathing room. "That photography book you were sure I'd publish someday? I did it. Got the call about my first contract a few weeks ago. I have until February to compile everything and send in the completed manuscript and corresponding photographs."

"Congratulations, Hanna. I knew you could do it." He pulled her into a hug and twirled her around. It was so good to see Michael happy again.

Before she could think of something else to say, he lowered his head and claimed her lips. He ran his fingers through her hair and drew her closer.

Pulling back a little, she traced his stubbled chin with her hand.

"You're so beautiful, Hanna." Michael's husky words shattered the moment. He stroked her hair. "Please don't run away again."

"You're too beautiful to keep my hands off." More of her former neighbor's sick words.

She stared at Michael's right bicep. No disgusting birthmark. This was Michael Parker. FBI agent. Her Michael. But his words sounded too much like her old neighbor's that her mind struggled to hold on to reality.

She had to get out of here before the memories came spilling out of her mouth.

Before she ruined one more good thing.

"Michael, I'm not feeling too well."

Concern creased his face. "Is there anything I can do?"

"I'm okay. Just a lot of sleepless nights catching up with me. I need to rest." She was becoming a proficient liar. Her insides twisted tighter.

"You sure you aren't getting sick?"

"I'll be fine after a good night's sleep. I'm positive."

Michael slipped into his running shoes and grabbed his keys and holster before she could locate her purse. Where was the stupid thing? Bile and guilt crawled up her throat as panic seeped into the mix.

"Here's your purse." He held it out to her. "Why don't we plan for a fancy dinner Friday to celebrate your book deal? I'll make reservations and pick you up at seven. As long as you're sure you're okay and all you need is some rest."

She walked out into the muggy August air. "That sounds like a great idea." Something niggled at her memory. She didn't have plans already, did she? Later was time enough for figuring that out. Right now she needed out of Michael's presence and into the safety of her brownstone.

Away from temptation and reminders of past failures. Hadn't she covered all of this already? Why wouldn't the past stay where it belonged?

As Michael drove toward her home, she visualized her evening routine. A shower. An easy stretching routine. A cup of warm tea. Maybe tonight she'd catch up on sleep. Things were fine with Michael. Work was good. She had a date for Friday.

Maybe a good night's sleep really would chase away the scary monsters clawing to escape the confines of her memory.

If not, she was sure they would eat her alive and leave nothing for Michael or anyone else to find.

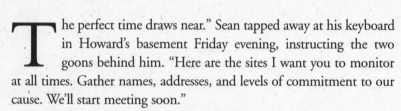

8

T he perfect time draws near." Sean tapped away at his keyboard in Howard's basement Friday evening, instructing the two goons behind him. "Here are the sites I want you to monitor at all times. Gather names, addresses, and levels of commitment to our cause. We'll start meeting soon."

Carl, the larger and wiser of the two brothers, stepped back. "Are these things you set up, what'd you call 'em, social networking sites, safe?"

"Yes. They're configured after the best social sites and programmed to perfection. I've hidden them on one of my father's offshore servers." Leaving Princeton to return home when Dad's health began failing had at first been a bitter life alteration. But working side by side, building a world-class IT business with the indomitable Stewart Haines Sr. had given Sean a greater understanding of his father's brilliant plans.

Memories of Dad's last words charged through him. *I'm trusting you to carry this on.* And further their family legacy Sean would. Not only had his father been a Fortune 500 professional and information technology genius, but also three generations of Haineses had fought the mud-race menace behind the scenes. Quietly. Slowly. Decisively.

Now it was Sean's turn. Total white domination hung in the near future, a carrot no longer so removed from his grasp.

"So when's Howie comin' back?" Don interrupted Sean's pleasant memories. "His pad's a prime party place, but it needs some cleaning."

Don's immaturity threatened to overshadow his usefulness. Now wasn't the time to turn away true followers, though. Sean needed a growing mass of committed men and women, no matter how lacking in social graces they might be.

"Howard will return after the local cops and FBI settle down. Their meddling will end soon."

"That FBI monkey's gonna be a problem."

Carl's words struck truth, and Sean's stomach acids churned with memory. "No. Even if the FBI dismissed their investigation against that wretched excuse for an agent, he's been put in his place. I doubt he's even smart enough to remember my name."

The three laughed.

Don pointed to a recent thread about the growing number of yellow races swarming into the US. It wasn't just the slave minions destroying the purity of America anymore.

"We're well staffed in Florida, Michigan, and New Jersey." Sean scanned the newest post in the discussion about racial cleansing. "Howard has done well in recruiting and establishing the leadership in those regions. We have strong numbers and supplies to carry out our plans for this year." The plans Dad had masterfully outlined before his death. "The mud-race menace will not continue long."

"That kid Lasser brought here is still in the news. Saw her picture last night." Don settled into Howard's couch and Carl took a seat beside him. At least these two were loyal and tried to keep up with the media exposure detailing his exploits. Howard and the rest of Sean's leadership far and away made up for what the Goring brothers lacked in intelligence. Doctors, lawyers, and politicians comprised the top level all across the US. A few law enforcement officers sympathized with their cause as well.

"Yes, well, she's no longer a problem."

"You sent her and Billy-boy into hiding?"

Sean shuddered. He'd done no such thing. William may have been an old high school *friend* and among the first to follow Sean's inaugural white-supremacy group way back then, but his repugnant attachment to mud races was inexcusable.

"Let's focus on the business at hand, shall we?"

Carl shook his head. "You gotta work on that highfalutin talk. I mean, you said you played stupid with the cops and in the slammer, but you go talkin' like that in our meetings and all the non–Ivy Leaguers will bolt."

Carl with his twenty-five-year-old, I-went-to-college pride amused Sean. The young man was still a good old country boy from Tennessee.

"I appreciate your concern, and I will take that into account when we form our first Baltimore chapter." Sean stood and stretched. "But for now, you'll have to pardon my prose and try to keep up."

Don shrugged. He'd failed to make the grade his first college semester. No surprise there.

Sean moved to Howard's well-stocked refrigerator in the basement boardroom and pulled out three Budweisers. "Let's get down to business."

The brothers swooped in and grabbed a brew each. He had to keep them happy in his Baltimore hometown or they'd tuck tail and run back to Tennessee before things were rock solid here. And right now their farm boy good looks would assure a sizable female contingent when they opened up membership.

Howard guaranteed that would happen when he recruited these two from family contacts in the South. It had worked in Florida. Lots of brains at the top, lots of poster boys at the midlevel, and then the masses flocked.

They returned to Sean's state-of-the-art computer system that covered a large portion of Howard's conference room table. An important item the FBI hadn't found on their scavenger hunt. Too bad their warrants hadn't reached into Mother's posh Mayfield residence. Not that Sean would have allowed anyone to torment his aging mother.

Even with her constant criticism on how he ran his father's business, she was still his mother and still in need of his protection.

Back to the present. "Carl, I want you to stir up some talk about targeting the youngest members of the aberrant races."

"You mean kids? That's gonna be a hard sell. Some of these guys still hold to the nonviolent books and stuff put out by other leaders.

They want to win back property and businesses from all the mud races, not kill them."

Problem number one for rich intellectuals. They held too tightly to their pomp and prestige. Win through upper-crust superiority. No matter. They could define the front-face of One Pure Nation. Gain back land and titles. Important legal and political work.

But Sean would control the real backbone of their cause. His accomplishments would far outshine what foolish and weak movement leaders had tried in the past, ignoring his father's exhortations. Followers would now flock to him when he proved smart violence was the best answer.

Violence that avoided prosecution. Stealth. His type of play.

Dad would be proud.

His mother hoped he'd grow up to be a lawyer. But as past white leadership had shown, getting a law license would prove impossible.

He'd contemplated federal law enforcement in college. But they were far too "equality" minded to suit him. Now he'd found his place. And in it, he'd be everything past leaders only dreamt of becoming.

Don swallowed his last drag. "You know, some of them old-time leaders are still talkin' it up in prison."

"Yes. But their power has weakened in the past few years. Our people demand strong, capable leadership. Not ex-cons too full of themselves to organize our ranks."

"Leadership like you, huh, Reverend Sean?" Carl saluted.

"No. I prefer to lay aside those titles. My name will be title soon enough. And when the FBI equality boys crawl back into their government caves, we'll launch Wave One." Sean pierced Carl with a glance. "Provided you lay the groundwork."

"Eliminating the women and children will prevent mud races from populating and polluting our divinely established dominion over our chosen country." Carl quoted his recent tracts well.

"Precisely." Sean drained the last drop from his amber bottle.

The victory well within his grasp would satisfy far more.

❈ ❈ ❈

Hanna's nervous hands twisted the fine linen napkin. The romantic lighting of the exclusive DC hotspot didn't help calm things down. In fact, it created the opposite effect. And her lavender wrap dress might have been a hit with Michael, but it needed three more inches and a winter coat.

Friday night couples buzzed around them with animated laughter and conversation.

Their young waiter, Moe, sauntered toward their secluded table in his crisp white shirt, red and black tie, and razor-creased black pants. His friendly Tex-Mex features and casual compliments had eased her nerves during their arrival. "How were your steaks tonight? Cooked to perfection, yes?"

"Excellent, Moe. Give my regards to your chef." Michael dabbed at his mouth.

Another waiter cleared their plates. "I'll have dessert right out." Moe left with an enormous smile creasing his tanned face.

She leaned toward Michael. "What are you up to? You've been grinning like a Cheshire cat since we arrived."

Enclosing her hand in his larger, warmer one, Michael wiggled his eyebrows up and down. "We're here to celebrate. I called ahead for a few surprises."

Great. She'd been able to keep conversation light and work-focused. Stories of her employee's excitement about starting college next week filled the time in between bites. She'd also groaned a little about her more Barbie-like college employees. Guilt twinged her conscience. She shouldn't classify and judge them like that. Her two beautiful blond co-workers had been faithful and hardworking employees for Dad.

Just not very friendly to her.

"So, are you going to tell me more about your book project? Steven says your newest portfolio additions are amazing."

Her brother's meddling had reached mammoth proportions. No amount of dissuading him this week had worked. To top that, Steven knew she was hiding something.

FBI types were like that.

"Hanna?" Michael brushed a finger down her cheek.

His touch heated her face and chilled her insides. Too intimate. Way too intimate. She'd barely held it together since their last encounter on Wednesday.

"Sorry. I…I was just thinking about how warm it is outside." Sort of. Her foray into truth evasion deepened with every lie. "I'd be happy to show you my collection for the book. I worked on it some more last night and it's coming together well."

"I'd love to see it."

"Maybe tomorrow we could take Champ out for a hike, and then you can help me decide between the two pieces I have left to incorporate. Only one of them will fit in the Kentucky landscapes collection."

"Sounds good. Just like old times." His dark brown eyes redefined flirting.

She squirmed. If she didn't tell him the truth soon, he'd never forgive her for all the lies she'd told to cover up the frightening memories of years ago. "Why don't you tell me about the case you're working on? Steven said you'd stay busy for a good while."

"I start surveillance on Monday. Your brother is convinced our perp will mess up soon and leave clues about the little girl's whereabouts." Michael sat up straighter, his face growing more animated. It always did when he talked about returning kids home. "There was this case we worked while you were gone…"

Swallowing hard, she blinked back tears. Would her leaving ever stop working its way into their conversations?

"We found a ten-year-old boy who'd been missing for a week. And with him, a runaway teen who took off three years ago. What an incredible case, and a great one for raising hope in all the families still watching for their children to come home."

"Are the boys okay?"

"They'll need lots of counseling. Kidnapping is a traumatic experience, compounded by the perversion of their abductor." Michael scanned the small dining area nestled just off of the main seating of the fancy steakhouse. "Crystal says our case is strong. It sure better be. I don't think I can take one more example of justice's failure right now."

"Who is Crystal?"

"A co-worker at the National Center. She works with the Child Victim Identification Program and has been helping with my current case. I don't know how she handles all the database pictures and the damage these perverts cause every day."

Hanna fought to keep her voice in check. "Sounds like you really respect her."

"You sure you and Steven aren't twins?" The edge in Michael's voice caught her off guard.

"No, why?"

"Jealousy doesn't become you any more than your brother's attacking my character."

What? Steven challenged Michael about his involvement with some co-worker and hadn't told her? Little details filtered back through her mind. Maybe this was why Steven insisted she reach out to Michael.

"Do I have a reason to be jealous?"

Moe returned, bright smile beaming as he placed a huge piece of chocolate cake in front of her with the word "CONGRATULATIONS" drizzled over the top of the plate in chocolate. "Along with your proud date, we'd like to say congratulations on your photography book contract. Way to go, ma'am. I can't wait to buy my copy."

All she could do was nod and whisper her thanks.

Moe placed a beautiful serving of warm apple crumb tart in front of Michael and promptly disappeared.

"Congratulations, Hanna." Michael's eyes searched her face. "Please trust me more than Steven does. You're the only one I'm interested in."

Deep breath. "I do trust you. And thank you for this. Thank you for caring about my photography." If she didn't quit, she'd soon be sobbing into her chocolate. No one but her family and a few close friends had ever made such a big deal about her heart's work. She loved photography. The one activity she both lost and found herself in.

They ate dessert without much conversation.

Her cell phone buzzed in her purse. One of the many things Steven had drilled into her—always silence her phone during meals. Otherwise her "Girls Just Want to Have Fun" ring tone would disrupt the few times her brother got to eat in peace.

"It's Steven." She met Michael's questioning eyes and answered the phone. "Why are you interrupting, big brother? I'm with Michael, just where you wanted me to be." She tried to smile into the words.

"Not when you're supposed to be at your nephew's seventh birthday party. The one you promised you'd come to. He asked if you'd left again."

She struggled to breathe. "Oh no. I can't believe I forgot." How could she? "I'm so sorry. Is he upset?"

"So far Angela and her professor are keeping him occupied with too many expensive gifts. But I need you here soon. I can only cover for you so long."

Steven's ex-wife and her husband were there too? How could she have forgotten and failed her brother and nephew again? Because that was who she was. Condemnation slid its slimy fingers across her back.

"I'll be there soon, Steven. I'm so sorry."

Michael signaled for the check, and Moe laid the black book down quickly.

"Why didn't you tell me they'd changed the party to Friday? I don't need another strike against me where your brother is concerned." He slid cash into the folder and nodded to Moe. "Keep the change, my friend. Great service."

"You two enjoy your evening." With a wink, Moe disappeared.

They maneuvered out of the restaurant and waited for the valet without a word. She wanted to light into Michael for blaming Steven's attitude on her. And Steven for pushing her to chase Michael and then getting mad when she forgot the birthday party he changed at the last minute. Men. It wasn't like she'd spent her first week back in Alexandria eating bonbons and watching soaps.

Why couldn't anyone understand? Didn't any of them see her barely hanging on to sanity?

No. All they saw was her running away, hurting them, and evading explanation. Michael hadn't even mentioned how she'd missed his birthday in early August. Or that she hadn't called. But the fact lingered in his sad eyes. Just like Steven's. They didn't understand. And she couldn't make them unless she told the whole truth.

Her brother and Michael were so alike.

And she had no right to be angry at them. Because she was far more at fault for everything than she could bear. The only way out was to tell both of them the truth.

Or run away again and never look back.

9

Michael pushed thoughts of Hanna and the ice-cold reception they'd received at Friday's birthday party from his mind. He had a job to do, even though he preferred Title III to gumshoe stakeouts any day. Wiretaps could be managed in comfortable surroundings.

A far cry from his third day of perching in the back of a cramped utilities truck with a Baltimore field agent monitoring his every move. Wednesday's muggy September weather didn't help anything either.

The FBI might be a band of brothers in some ways, but when headquarters' agents crossed the line into field-office territory, watch out. Stalking lions had nothing on law-enforcement territorialism.

"You really think watching a gentrified row house in Patterson Park will turn up new evidence?" Bart Charles groused and fidgeted on the bench too small for his bulk.

"Yes." Michael kept his binoculars fixed on Sean Haines's form trolling around the main floor kitchen. If not for overpriced lawyers making a mockery of justice, his bald head would be behind prison bars.

Even with Charles's daily garlic-laden lunch, this short-term assignment beat sitting under his boss's fiery diatribes or trying to pull Hanna out from the shell she'd crawled back into Friday night. That she might bolt crossed his mind every nonfocused second.

But all he could do was pray and hope she'd be in Alexandria when he returned. For now he intended to make the most of his two weeks of authorized surveillance and overtime. And he'd stay busy with the work he had planned for his few off hours too.

He'd find Bill Lasser and Kat. Or keel over from lack of sleep trying.

The pair of vendettas to settle with this perp kept him focused. One for the Chu family and one for Lee Branson. His friend had returned to full duty with no impugning marks in his file. The same couldn't be said for the man's mind.

Not only that, but the mess allowed Haines to walk out of jail free and clear.

"We got a house lined up for your use starting tomorrow." Charles unwrapped his sandwich. "Good thing the local PD and your unit chief think you hung the moon."

Michael ignored the unspoken challenge. He'd already made a name for himself cutting through red tape whenever the situation warranted. No apologies for that.

"You'll have a good sightline from across the back commons area. Baltimore PD is overjoyed to throw Haines your way." Charles tore into his food and spoke with his mouth full. "This guy really stays holed up here until night? I'd die from boredom."

"Yeah, the guy goes fishing by day for bottom dwellers of the Caucasian-pride sort, using the computer. At night he's all over the place. I've trailed him for two evenings now, and he's finding devotees in droves." No surprise the creep only slunk around in the shadows after dark. Fitting. What didn't compute were his years at Princeton and his squeaky clean management of his late father's computer-programming business.

Charles finished his sandwich and drank his third Pepsi of the day. "I'll leave you to your data analysis and paperwork, Parker. Another guy will be around to relieve you tonight, and then I'll check back in tomorrow." He buttoned up his utility coverall. "Hope you find what you're looking for, man."

Once alone, Michael virtual desktopped into HQ and skimmed his e-mail. Nothing from Hanna, but lots of short messages from Crystal wishing him well on his assignment. She must have tracked down his whereabouts from one of the Innocent Images guys. Her notes about recent additions to their victim ID program turned his stomach.

Hanna had called his feelings for Crystal respect. Maybe. The lady possessed a cast-iron stomach and the fearlessness of seasoned federal agents. He deleted the e-mails without responding to any of them. Better to avoid rather than court trouble.

His cell buzzed. "Parker."

"How's the first week of party work treating you?" Clint's deep Texas drawl filled Michael's eardrum.

"Slow and boring. Haines is a busy scumbag on the World Wide Web, but so far nothing too exciting or criminal. No doubt that'll change soon."

"Just watch yourself. Keep safe and outta sight. We don't need his lawyers claiming police harassment."

"You got it. Glad to know I'm missed." *Lay the bait and Clint will bite, like always.*

"Both Kesslers are missing you. For different reasons, of course."

Pay dirt. He waited for Clint to fill in the rest.

"Hanna's staying busy at work, and Steven's barreling through white-supremacy reports from the Counterterrorism Division in his spare time. Other than that, we have a few choice assignments from Maxwell. He misses you too." Clint chuckled. "Then there's my favorite part, the low-key ninety percent of our job. Mountains of paperwork."

"Right. Gotta love the donkeywork." He'd gathered most of Clint's info from data transfers. But talking to a friend broke up the monotony of another day. And Hanna remaining in Alexandria ranked the highlight of his week thus far.

Clint cleared his throat. "I'm giving you a heads-up so you can make use of the time to cool your jets before Steven contacts you."

Michael clenched his jaws and started grinding. "Spill it."

"Maxwell is clamoring for budget cuts and looking for anything and everything to trim fat and tighten our spending. You might not get your full allotment of authorized time."

"Figures. One more example of justice's blindfold. There's a kid missing and a sex offender that's dropped off the face of the planet. All roads converge at Sean Haines. But if I can't somehow force this termite to start digging his own grave, I'm outta luck."

"I hear you. Steven does too. This is where we pray and hang on to trust. God has a reason for His timing in everything."

Easy for Clint to say. Okay, maybe not. Fighting cancer and a serial killer stalking him bought Clint Rollins some clout with the God-talk. Michael wished for the thousandth time his newfound faith didn't crumble at the first sign of a quake.

Haines stepped outside in the daylight and shoved computer equipment into his souped-up Viper. Show time. "Gotta run. Haines is breaking his routine. Pray it's not just to handle some stupid problem at Daddy's business."

He needed something soon or he'd be watching Sean Haines walk away a free man for the second time. Which was two times too many.

❊   ❊   ❊

Steven paced the length of his den, phone in hand, and kicked the brown leather recliner for good measure. His Saturday night couldn't have gotten much worse. "You're sure it was my team member at Haines's business posing as a potential client?"

Lieutenant Barnes's voice boomed through the phone. "The boy's got pluck, can't fault him there."

"Officer Masino both saw and spoke with Parker?"

"Station grapevines climb all the way to the top, Kessler. Masino's kept his eye on Haines. Hasn't forgotten the beating he took from our resident skinhead. Or how he messed things up. And after he talked to Parker, he was bragging about the FBI agent with backbone making a move to bring Haines to his knees."

"You spoke to Parker?"

"No. I only contacted the Baltimore SAC to let him know your bionic Parker wasn't sleeping but was going undercover during his downtime. Then I called you. I don't want your guy slipping up from exhaustion and causing a police harassment suit to come down on all of us."

Steven ended the phone call and flopped into his overstuffed chair. Michael had gotten his hopes up with trailing Haines on Wednesday.

Turned out to be nothing more than a sightseeing tour. As if Haines decided to have a little fun at Michael's expense. But that wasn't possible. Michael was good, too good sometimes. Except for this last stunt.

Gracie slipped onto his lap. "Bad news?"

If Hanna wasn't upstairs putting James down, he'd have turned his night around and gone to bed right then and there. As it was, he had business to discuss with Hanna, namely her avoidance techniques ever since James's party. "Yes. Michael's getting antsy and pushing beyond the jurisdiction of his assignment. He's apparently not sleeping and using his few off-duty hours for unauthorized and dangerous escapades. I'm gonna have to pull the plug sooner than I'd hoped."

"The system failed him, and he's fighting to make it right. Reminds me of you." Gracie ran her fingers though his hair.

"What? You see me as dumb enough to endanger my co-workers and throw my career away for some skinhead punk?"

"Maybe not for a skinhead, but for a Hope Ridge vice-principal bent on murder."

His wife's words connected and knocked the air from his lungs.

"But I didn't. I walked away and have been worn out keeping you safe ever since." He pulled Gracie to his chest and kissed her grin away. How she could find humor in one of the most painful memories of his life was beyond him.

She pulled back and looked him square in the face. "Forgiveness, Steven. That's how I can talk now about what happened without crumbling into pieces."

"Now you can read my mind?"

"I know that look. I remember that you almost killed a man in cold blood because he tried to hurt me. I also know that the passion you have for keeping kids safe and loving James and me the way you do can be pushed beyond godly limits unless you're careful. You could teach Michael a great deal if you'd look beyond the man's impulsiveness and stop dogging him about Hanna. And pray."

"She's right, brother of mine." Hanna leaned on the doorpost, sadness cloaking her every move.

Gracie hopped up. "I'll go fix some coffee." *Be kind,* she mouthed as she stepped out of Hanna's view.

"So you're avoiding me because you're mad about how I'm treating Michael?"

"No. But you could have told me about Crystal."

He stood and walked over to Hanna. "Crystal's not an issue."

"Because you threatened Michael or because he cares about me? I can't tell the difference anymore and it's too confusing to sort through."

Nudging Hanna toward the couch, he draped an arm around her shoulders. She stiffened and jerked away. "What's got you spooked? If I didn't know better, I'd think you were still sore about my sneaking up on you last week. Before that, you never acted this skittish with me."

"But I do with everyone else?"

They sat on the leather couch staring at each other. "I've seen it enough to know you have issues with male contact. But you're safe with me."

"I know."

He ran his hand though his hair. "Michael loves you and Crystal wasn't an issue worth mentioning. I didn't threaten Michael. He set me straight on my concerns a week and a half ago. There was no need to worry you."

Hanna sighed. "That's what Michael said."

"So now that's clear, explain why you're avoiding me."

"It's complicated."

Gracie returned with three cups of coffee and placed them on the table. Black for him and two with chocolate and too much milk for her and Hanna. His wife remembered all the little details of hospitality. "I can head downstairs if you'd rather."

Tears started flowing down Hanna's face. Gracie wrapped her in a hug.

All he could do was sit in stunned silence. Nothing made sense.

"I came tonight because you'll find out anyway and it's been killing me. A week alone with nothing to do but work and think and pray convinced me to tell you." Hanna wiped her face with the Kleenex that Gracie had handed her.

He waited, reminding himself that Hanna wasn't an interrogation subject.

"I tried to tell Dad the Monday after Susannah's birthday party. But I couldn't. I couldn't break his heart like that."

More tears.

Gracie stroked Hanna's blond hair and moved her lips in prayer.

Time crawled.

"Hanna, tell me what's wrong. Please." He needed something to fix. Something tangible to do for Hanna to chase away the rawness spilling from her eyes.

"I watched *America's Most Wanted* on tape before I called Dad. When he came over all I could do was cry. I ended up telling him I was upset about seeing a man on TV who might have molested one of my friends in third grade."

His stomach clenched and collapsed into itself. "It was you."

Hanna nodded and balled up into a fetal position against Gracie's chest.

Red-hot rage ripped through his veins. "Who, Hanna?" By the grace of God he hadn't killed the man who'd tried to murder Gracie. But this time? This time he'd do well not to tear the pervert who hurt his baby sister limb from limb.

"Please, Hanna. Tell me his name."

Gracie shook her head.

He started pacing. He had to know. If this man was still alive he'd find him and guarantee he spent the rest of his life rotting in a jail. Until prison justice took care of the problem.

"Hanna, help me find him and put him behind bars."

"Richard Reeley."

He must have misheard his sister's whisper. "Who?"

She blinked twice and stared with the eyes of a wounded child. Haunted eyes like he'd seen in far too many rescue cases. Memories rushed in and puzzle pieces clicked into place with sickening clarity. It all made sense.

Hanna had changed the summer of his twelfth year. She'd always been quiet, but that summer she'd almost stopped talking. She sat in the backyard and dug holes in the dirt, saying she was burying dead things. Hanna had entered second grade a shadow of the girl he'd loved to tease. Why hadn't he done something then?

"He was our next-door neighbor. Dad and Mom made us call him Mr. Richard. But his full name was Richard Reeley. Daddy's old fishing buddy."

No. Impossible. "Hanna, do you know who Richard Reeley is?"

Gracie and Hanna stared at him with frozen expressions.

"No. I'd hoped he was dead. That's why I didn't call the tip line that night."

"Hanna, Richard Reeley is one of Kentucky's representatives. He works on the Hill."

His sister turned three shades whiter. Hospital sheet white. She rocked back and forth in Gracie's arms.

He slumped into his recliner. Richard Reeley had molested his baby sister. The words sliced through his body and left nothing but numbness. He pictured Capitol Hill with crime-scene tape wrapping around its circumference and Reeley's dead body at his feet.

No. That wouldn't fix Hanna's past. Nothing could.

But Reeley had to pay. Except if she had to relive her attack in vivid detail, to strangers, it would tear his sister to shreds. Not to mention what a well-paid defense attorney or the media would do with the information. And the fact that without some serious legal wrangling, they couldn't prosecute. The statute of limitations had run out for Hanna's case.

"You can't tell anyone, Steven. Promise me. It would destroy Dad to know one of his friends did that. And Michael would never forget it either. I can't handle Michael knowing or the media dragging us all through that. I can't. Promise me." Tears still flowed down her pale cheeks as she sat staring at him.

Gracie handed her another Kleenex and let Hanna collapse into her again.

"Reeley was on *America's Most Wanted*?" Steven's brain whirled into gear. "Then there are other cases, other people who might identify him. I'll put a call into NCMEC and find out." He stood to leave.

"No. Don't. All they showed was the birthmark on his right arm."

Images he couldn't shut out crashed into his mind. Not his sister. This couldn't be happening.

"Is he still doing this?" Gracie's soft question made the air stand still.

Hanna locked eyes with him. They had to stop Reeley. That they agreed on. But how?

"I'll call in an anonymous tip." Hanna's bravery swelled his chest.

Yes. That would work. All they needed was a name and probable cause to launch an investigation. No one would have to know Hanna's story unless she wanted to tell it.

But he knew. And it would eat him alive to keep his sister's secret without doing something. Anything to make it better. "Will you let me call in a favor with a trauma counselor I know here? She's one of the best in the nation. Please let me do something to help."

Hanna hesitated, then nodded.

They had a long road ahead. But they'd make it. They had to. They'd see that disgusting pervert in jail. In time, Hanna would heal and they'd be able to tell Dad and Clint. Michael too. In time.

Steven comforted himself by picturing the snake he would crush underfoot if given half the chance. And he would have his chance. Somehow.

10

Hanna's hands shook as she made changes on the menu board to reflect Wednesday's specials. Her whole body quivered with everything she did. Thankfully, Evelyn hadn't noticed as they prepared to open Grounded in companionable silence. Every night since her full confession at Steven's house Saturday, she'd picked up the phone to call the National Center.

But she couldn't. The people working the tip line might be able to trace her number. She wouldn't risk that. Not when it would destroy her father and everything she'd worked to build in DC. Shoving the past back into the past had to work again. Over twenty years of practice had to amount to something.

Working on her photography book and gathering supplies for this afternoon's photo shoot with Evelyn and Denisha had kept her busy all week. And the over-the-counter sleeping pills helped erase the remaining long hours of night.

Evelyn raised the gate for the soon-to-come morning rush, and then hurried to the back room to finish stocking supplies.

"Good morning."

Hanna jumped at the sound of a male voice behind her. Whirling around, she faced a poster child for German nationalism straight out of *The Sound of Music*. Well, not a boy, but a handsome young man.

"Hello. What can I get started for you?" She wished Becky were here or one of the other college ladies. They'd enjoy this customer's wide smile and flirtatious eyes.

"How about two cups of the breakfast blend and a couple of those huge muffins?" The young man pointed to the display case filled with warm pecan muffins. "I'm Carl, by the way."

"It's nice to meet you." She smiled and punched in his order.

His eyes flicked around the shop and then wandered over her red work apron before meeting her gaze. "Who took those photos?"

"I did."

"Do you have a business card? Your talents could come in handy for my work."

She stopped ringing up his order and spoke in a voice loud enough to bring Evelyn out front. "I don't have any business cards right now, but we'll get your order right up." Better to have two people visible with the over-friendly male customers. There was no such thing as too safe.

Evelyn hurried out and smiled at Carl.

"Evelyn, can you bag two pecan specials?" Hanna turned away from Carl and poured the two breakfast blends. Then she set them in a carrier and placed them next to the register.

Evelyn reached for a sheet of waxed paper.

"Uh, hey, never mind about those muffins. Just the coffee." The man's demeanor had iced. Why?

Evelyn stiffened and turned sad eyes to the wall menu lying on the counter. Her dark hands flew over the board to complete Hanna's task.

"Here's a ten." Carl laid the bill on the counter and picked up his drink order. "Keep the change." With that he hurried out into Union Station and disappeared in the crowd.

A steady stream of customers kept them busy until late morning. Evelyn smiled and did her work well, but the sadness in her eyes hadn't left.

Hanna wiped one of the empty tables near the display counter while Evelyn added sandwiches and other lunch items to the case. "What's wrong, Evelyn? Before our first customer, you were excited about the day. What happened?"

"Nothing." Evelyn forced a smile. "I'm looking forward to our photo shoot after school. Deni's going to wear the fancy Easter dress I made for her last April. As fast as that kid grows, it's a wonder the dress still fits."

"I'm glad. It should be fun." Hanna prayed it would be. She didn't understand Evelyn's attitude change earlier or her forced cheerfulness now. But the need for conversation trumped her desire to push.

Girl talk. She needed a casual friend who didn't ask lots of personal questions. Something to crowd out the things she couldn't forget.

"I'm glad you're staying for dinner." Evelyn didn't meet Hanna's eyes. "I'd like you to meet my sister Trina."

"It'll be nice to spend some time with you and your family." She twisted the rag in her hands, glad the shop had cleared out for a few minutes. A perfect opportunity to ask again if Evelyn was okay. No pushing. Just concern. "But I'd like to know what made you so sad this morning. Did it have something to do with our first customer changing his order?"

"Yes." Evelyn sighed and kept moving items around in the case with gloved hands. "I should be used to it by now. Some white people still hate breathing the same air as black folks. I hoped to leave most of that stuff in Virginia with Trey's family."

"How do you know that's what happened? The guy never said anything."

"I've seen it too many times to count. Trey, Deni's father, tried to convince his family skin color didn't matter. But most of the rich people around there preferred to ignore us and stick to their all-white community activities. When Trey took me to events, his people said all sorts of ugly things. Others just threw silent stones my way with a look or left as soon as I arrived."

"I'm sorry, Evelyn. That's just wrong."

"It's reality." Evelyn finished organizing lunch items and then slipped into the back room.

Hanna focused on the incoming lunch rush that would fill their time until she and Evelyn could leave for the day. But in the back of her mind, she committed herself to showing Evelyn and her sister that not all white people cared about skin color.

The Civil War was over, and the last time she'd been in the National Archives, the Declaration still said all people were created equal.

This afternoon, she'd show Evelyn most people weren't like that customer. Starting with a wonderful photo shoot. Then she'd hang Evelyn and Deni's gallery samples front and center at Grounded. Maybe that'd keep people like Carl from stepping foot in her store again.

※　※　※

A semicool breeze swished through the few trees in Evelyn's backyard. Hanna snapped some candid photos as Deni's tall, skinny form twirled around in her beautiful pink and white dress. Summer innocence radiated from her, and Hanna captured it all with her camera.

The owner of the home above Evelyn's basement apartment had agreed to let them take over the backyard. But from her kitchen window, the older woman kept a protective eye on her flower gardens lining the fence.

Hanna smiled. Soft sunlight and perfect subjects warmed her inside and out. "Beautiful, Deni. Can you give Mom a hug and a big smile?"

Evelyn knelt down in her gorgeous, more grown-up version of Deni's dress and opened her arms wide.

The lens of Hanna's digital camera captured a closeup of the smiling pair cheek to cheek. Pure joy coursed through her. Most, if not all, of the shots she'd taken today would be print quality. And she wouldn't charge Evelyn a cent.

This would be her gift to Evelyn and her family, especially Grandma in Richmond. They would get plenty of wallets and some five by sevens. Hanna held back a giggle and clicked a few shots of mother and daughter dancing together.

The crash of a dumpster lid in the alley next to the house caused Hanna to jump and miss a cute shot.

"I'm getting tired, Momma. Can we be done soon?" Deni cocked her head and laid two little hands on her hips.

Hanna clicked a few more pictures and moved to capture the little girl's eye roll and hand-to-hip attitude. Evelyn would get a kick out of that one.

Evelyn picked Deni up and motioned toward the house. "Do you mind if we call it a day? It is pretty hot out here."

Snapping one last shot of Deni snuggling on her mom's shoulder, Hanna grinned. She loved this. Maybe she'd open up a studio sooner rather than later. Photographing kids like Deni all day would be nothing but sunshine and giggles.

"Sure. I think we have a ton of wonderful pictures."

The threesome stepped through the tall gate and went inside by way of the basement side door. Cool air and the smells of spicy Jamaican jerk chicken greeted them.

"Trina must have gotten home early and started that new recipe I was telling you about." Evelyn pointed Deni toward the one small bathroom in the basement apartment. "She's working her kitchen magic hoping to win the notice of this cute Jamaican guy in her biology class."

"I can hear yer blabbing in der, mon." Trina called from the kitchen right off the tiny living room.

Hanna's eyebrows shot up.

Evelyn laughed. "Trina's faking that accent. She speaks perfect English when she's not practicing for that college cutie."

Trina joined them, wiping her hands on a bright orange dishtowel. "I'm not blabbin' yo business all over da place. What's up with dat?" Her slim features were darker than Evelyn's, but the high cheekbones and deep, piercing eyes proved their shared genes.

Extending her hand, Hanna stepped forward. "It's nice to meet you, Trina. Thanks for having me over for dinner."

Glaring at her sister, Trina straightened. "You can thank Eve. I had other plans for the evening." With that she snapped around and returned to the kitchen. Trina stuck her head back out. "An dat fancy crystal vase you brought my sistah? It has a crack in it."

Evelyn's new vase? The one she'd just bought and filled with pink and yellow roses as a thank-you for dinner? It shouldn't surprise her. Except for photography, she messed up everything.

"Sorry about that. Trina's still bitter about what happened between Trey and me. She thinks whites are all like that and the friends she's made at Howard aren't helping that view." Evelyn pointed to the kente-patterned couch with matching throw pillows in bold green and black.

"What happened with you and Trey, if you don't mind me asking?"

They sat, and Evelyn glanced over her shoulder toward the small bathroom. "Deni knows some of the story, but while she's cleaning up I can give you a quick rundown before I go change for supper."

"You don't have to tell me, Evelyn. It's none of my business." What had been a pleasant afternoon continued to dissipate into tension.

"Eve. Please call me Eve. All my friends do." Eve shrugged and grinned. "Besides, it's too much like my momma's scolding to hear 'Evelyn' all day."

"Eve it is, then."

"Back to your question." Eve's smile disappeared. "It's pretty typical. I was one of two black cheerleaders at our high school, and Trey was a rebellious, rich white kid and football star. Everybody loved him. Until he took a liking to me. On graduation night, Trey slipped away from his parents' big party and asked me to meet him at our special place, the park near my house. When I arrived he said we were going to his best friend's house for a real party. I was the only sophomore invited."

"Had you all dated long?"

"That whole year. A few of the kids at school were okay with it. More weren't. But Trey didn't care. He said he loved me and I believed him." Eve's eyes teared up. "I still do. But his family proved too powerful to stand up against. After I got pregnant that night and Trey's family found out, they threatened to cancel his college tuition and all claims to their money."

Trina stepped into the living room. "Yeah, and dat little wimp cared nothin' when your house got trashed or your car or Momma's bakery. He turned a deaf ear an' ran away. Good riddance." She stalked into a bedroom.

Hanna didn't know what to say. Deni bounced into the living room and broke the uncomfortable silence. "Hey, Momma? There's this boy in my class who says I'm pretty."

Eve smiled. "You are, honey. You're beautiful."

"He said that too. An' he wanted to kiss me."

Hanna's stomach acids swirled. An eight-year-old was far too young for kissing.

Touching Deni's chin, Eve chuckled. "So what happened? You said no, right?"

"I tried. But he got real close, and then he kissed me on the cheek."

Not hearing the rest of the conversation, Hanna's mind filled with pictures. The ones Reeley had spread all over his bed flashed to the forefront. Photos she'd tried to erase from her memory.

"They aren't as pretty as you. You're too beautiful to keep my hands off."
And he hadn't.

She tried to force her mind back to the present with deep breaths and focusing on Deni and Eve talking about the rest of the third grader's day. Deni wasn't dealing with a grown man, just a little boy too fresh for his own good.

But what about the little girls Richard Reeley could still be hurting?

Trina returned to the kitchen and within a few minutes dinner was ready. "Come sit. Hope you like collards, Miss Thang."

Trina's barbs and challenges were nothing compared to the images still threatening to break through Hanna's thin hold on the present. Focus. She needed to focus on Eve and Deni and the beautiful photos she'd taken today. That would get her through dinner and the movie Deni had asked her to stay and watch.

Surely those innocent pictures of Deni and her mom would beat back the ones she'd kept hidden in her mind for twenty-four years. This was why she never talked about what happened. Because the minute she opened her mouth the memories would drag her under. She should have kept everything locked away where it belonged.

But maybe if she called in that tip like she'd promised Steven, she could put all this to rest. With one phone call she could do her duty and the police would handle the rest. Then she'd go back into hiding and shove it all into the past where dirty, dead things like her sixth summer belonged.

She'd make that phone call tonight, for little girls like Deni, the minute she stepped foot into her safe apartment. Her fear of them tracing the call was unfounded.

Dinner passed with Deni's adorable stories about her favorite dresses and where she wore them. Not even Trina's continued put-downs spoiled the fun of Deni's sweet smiles and giggles. After Eve tucked her daughter in bed, Hanna said a quick good night and slipped into her Equinox.

Popping in her favorite Chris Tomlin CD, she tried to relax. But knowing what she had to do tonight frayed her insides. The song "The Way I Was Made" reverberated through the car.

She lived the words about feeling all tied up, praying that today was the day she'd be free.

Free to dance like no one watched in the shadows.

Help me remember what I've forgotten, Lord. And find all that You've promised is true in my life. I want to be the way You made me to be. Help me make this call and do it right. Then keep me safe, Lord. Keep me safe.

❋　❋　❋

Sean pointed his yellow Viper toward DC. Let Mr. Super FBI Agent follow him.

Baltimore cop friends had clued him in to Agent Michael Parker's surveillance work, and he'd had fun leading the monkey-loving fed all over Baltimore last Wednesday. But that hadn't deterred Parker like he'd hoped. No, the top cop tried to pull a fast one on Dad's employees to fish out some incriminating information.

He'd settle the score tonight.

Dad had worked hard, compiling the best staff in the IT world. Sean would make sure Parker didn't harass them again. Protecting all that Dad left behind was now Sean's primary responsibility. One he'd do as expertly as his father had.

Even as a young boy, Sean had been entranced by Dad's deft handling of business affairs. And when Dad established his own company, he dismissed every mud race that showed up begging for a job. Too stupid to even sweep the floors, Stewart Haines said. The man had dominated each mud-race encounter, his steel gaze intimidating and putting them all in their place.

Taking Spellman Parkway to the Beltway, Sean smiled as Parker stayed close on his tail. The agent must have figured the game was up and decided to ditch the pretense. Interesting. This didn't fit the profile he'd concocted from his online digging.

Funny thing, Parker had a few enemies at the Bureau. It'd been easy to pry information from one of the movement's newest adherents. A pretty red-headed FBI administrative assistant who'd dated Parker back in his wild days was more than eager to spill all about the party-boy agent.

After that, locating Parker's girlfriend had been child's play.

Sean pulled into Hanna Kessler's upscale community and parked near her brownstone. Parker screeched to a halt next to his Viper and barreled out of a very nice Mustang. No federal cars for Mr. Hotshot.

"What are you doing here, Haines?"

Stepping out of his Viper, Sean straightened his tie and smiled. "Nice to see you again, Agent Parker. Sorry your undercover work at my business proved so unfruitful."

A blue Equinox pulled up and parked near them. "Michael, what's going on?"

Parker barely acknowledged the cute blond standing by her car. "Go inside. I'll explain later."

She didn't move. Hmm. Feisty and about as attractive as Carl had described. She'd be a fine addition to his leadership team. If only she could be freed from her stupid ideas about mud races.

Parker didn't turn around. "Go inside, now."

She climbed back into her car and drove around the building. Must have decided to use her fancy garage. One of the many perks her community advertised.

"I'll ask again. Why are you here?" The large agent towered over him, too close for comfort. But Sean controlled the scene. Parker had already driven far past professional restraint.

"I'm here on a business call. One of my associates told me of Miss Kessler's photography business. Said she was top rate."

"Stay away from her."

Sean tapped a finger on his chin. "It's still a free country. Or is this a police request? Even so, don't officers on duty require a reason to interfere with an innocent citizen's activities?"

"I'm off duty. Thanks to you."

Parker's off-duty status and the likelihood he packed plenty of fire power made this payback lose some of its original luster. He needed to stay off the radar a lot longer. But he still held the upper hand here.

"Think your boss will enjoy my lawyer's phone call in the morning? What time does he arrive at headquarters? Bright and early, I imagine."

Parker clenched and unclenched his fists but didn't budge. "I suggest you get back in your car and stay far away from here. Climb back under your rock in Baltimore."

Sean smirked. "Good evening to you too, Agent Parker. I enjoyed seeing you again. If you'd like another tour of my hometown, please let me know."

He climbed into his Viper and drove home. His plan had gone better than he'd hoped. After his lawyer put in a call to FBI headquarters, Parker's menace would be eliminated. Then he could return to more important matters.

Ones that would put his name all over the World Wide Web and move the faithful into perfect strike position.

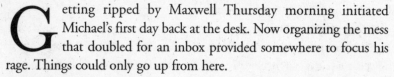

11

Getting ripped by Maxwell Thursday morning initiated Michael's first day back at the desk. Now organizing the mess that doubled for an inbox provided somewhere to focus his rage. Things could only go up from here.

Steven leaned against the partition. "I didn't get my say in that meeting."

Maybe it could get worse after all.

"Haines was in Hanna's brownstone community. In her parking lot. That has to mean something to you."

Steven crossed his arms. "Yes. It does. Hanna called me after you left last night because she was still spooked. So this morning I talked to the property manager that oversees her complex. They're increasing security."

"Good. Haines is dangerous. And Hanna's community could use more police coverage."

"But she wouldn't have been in any danger had you done your job like assigned. You have no excuse to get in Haines's face for paybacks. He didn't get you pulled from surveillance. You did that all on your own with the other stunts."

He stood and squared off with Kessler. "I need to leave for NCMEC. Unless your next move is to collect my badge and side arm."

"Not today. But I suggest you watch yourself and rein it in. Fast." Steven turned and stalked off the floor, the steel set of his shoulders daring anyone to get in his way.

Seconds later, Clint slapped him on the back. "Michael, my friend, you do not want to know what happens when people jerk Steven's chain like you're doing."

"It gets worse?"

"So much worse. And he's still raw over something I can't wrangle out of him. Tread lightly. For all our sakes." Clint pointed to the keys in his hands. "You leavin' us so soon?"

"I'm heading over to NCMEC. Crystal called with some new case information."

Clint shook his head. "Son, you are blinder than a bat in the daytime. Don't let your frustrations with this case lead you where you don't want to go."

"Point well taken."

With that, he sped out to the garage. Revving his Mustang calmed some of the inner chaos. But not much. Hanna hadn't returned his calls last night and all of his previous e-mails had gone unopened. That or she turned off the read receipts he'd requested.

The short trip to Alexandria and some nineties alternative set him in a better mood. Crystal greeted him at check-in.

"Hey there, stranger. Your fingers broken?"

He lifted his hands in front of him. "No. Why?"

She swiped her badge and opened the door leading to her floor of cubicles. "'Cause I'm curious why you never e-mailed back or bothered calling. I'm beginning to think you're just using me for work kudos."

Closing his eyes, he shot up a quick prayer and followed Crystal to her desk. Not even Secret Service Special Agent Maria Grivens could fix this mess he'd gotten into. Based on the smirks he was getting from Crystal's co-workers, everyone, including Crystal, must assume he had something going with the pretty Hispanic analyst.

Maybe he should. Steven couldn't hold Hanna over his head that way. Then again, his boss would make his life a living hell.

Not worth the risk. Not worth losing Hanna either. He loved her, and that wouldn't change. He played for keeps and no one but Hanna Kessler would do.

"I'm sorry. I just didn't want you to get the wrong idea."

She sat down and stuck out her red lips in a playful pout. "No one's wearing your ring. So what's wrong with a little banter and a few drinks between friends?"

The clicking keys around them stilled for a long and silent minute. Crystal's brown eyes clouded and she turned to her computer. "Guess dating the boss's sister off and on is a compelling reason to stay on the straight and narrow. Let's get down to business and then send you back over the river where you belong." Work noise once again buzzed around them.

Michael grabbed a nearby chair and joined Crystal. "I'm not using you for work kudos."

"Play it one way or another, but choose soon. It's not like you're the only FBI hunk to show interest." She pulled up images on her computer that roiled his empty stomach.

He stood up and almost lost it. "Excuse me."

"Bathroom's down the hall to the left."

When he returned, Crystal had cleared the disturbing pictures and was reading an intranet memo. "Sounds like we have a new break in a very long running case. Operation Web Cleaner just got boosted back to primary importance."

"Innocent Images was stagnating on that one a few months back. They couldn't pin down any of the constantly morphing Web domains."

"Or the highly encoded member's list."

Michael was glad to step back into work mode. He and Crystal worked well on this plane. "So what's the break?"

"The CyberTipline logged an anonymous report with a detailed list of information on none other than Congressman Richard Reeley. We were able to use the info to connect an *America's Most Wanted* profile to a huge cache of pictures linked to Operation Web Cleaner's monitored sites."

His stomach burned again. "Can we prove all the pictures and videos link back to Reeley?"

"That's what the Innocent Images task forces here and in Kentucky are working around the clock to do."

If Reeley's alleged connection proved true, it'd be one more example of the appalling failure of a justice system designed to protect the innocent.

Instead of providing protection, a disgusting pedophile made laws on the Hill.

"Yeah, the possibility everything will check out with Reeley has everyone a little cagey today. That's a big media fish to catch in what was a small but growing sting operation."

"I'm glad you all are on this, but I don't see what it has to do with my case."

Crystal pulled up Katrina's missing person picture. "I've mapped Kat's face and compared it to the images we linked to Lasser. They're a positive match. So that piece of the puzzle is a solid linchpin whenever you find Lasser."

If he found Lasser.

"What's disturbing, but profitable for us, is that the same photos are among Reeley's alleged cache too. He could be a link for your case as well."

Michael leaned forward, eyes wide. This could be it. The break he needed to find Kat, Lasser too. And nail Haines. "So this means Reeley could be connected to Kat's abduction?"

"Not sure about that. These perverts trade pictures like baseball cards." Crystal tilted her desk chair back. "All I know for sure is among Reeley's cache there are pictures of Katrina Chu."

"He might know where to find her."

"A possibility. At the very least, he might spill details that haven't been uncovered."

If Crystal were Hanna he'd spin her around and plant a kiss on her lips. He caught himself before fantasy became reality. He only pumped his fist and gave Crystal a high-five. "Yes. So when are the Innocent Images guys bringing Reeley in for questioning?"

"IIU task forces have other scum all across the US caught in their nets. They can't start making arrests until there are solid evidence trails in place. That could take a few more weeks."

Weeks could mean any viable leads to Kat's whereabouts would be long gone. Not to mention the hell the child was living in. Every day mattered.

Crystal continued. "Reeley is a top priority, but as you can guess, we have to make our case foolproof. Better yet politician-proof."

"No chance of this moving any faster?"

"Not likely."

"Can't you contact your tipster and convince them to come forward? A real person with information about Reeley's past could give us grounds to question Reeley right now."

Crystal crossed and uncrossed her legs. "Problem is, it was an anonymous tip. The report was filed with no name or a way to contact her."

"How do you know the person was female?"

"Instinct. I wish I had the info to get in touch with her because I'm ninety-nine percent positive she was a victim. Depending on her age, the statute of limitations might not have run out and he could still be prosecuted. Add to that possession and distribution charges and possibly charging him for production, he could be looking at an enormous amount of jail time."

He nodded. "As it is, unless you can identify Reeley in any of the videos or pictures, he's looking at six years, maybe twelve."

"Don't forget downward departure if he rats on other members or if he manages to evoke sympathetic judicial favors for his good behavior and stellar congressional track record."

His neck knotted and the urge to destroy a punching bag hit him full force.

Crystal checked her watch. "Why don't we go grab an early lunch or walk off some steam? You look like you're ready to blow."

A tempting invitation. He rubbed his neck. "I need to get back to my desk and follow some possible leads on Bill Lasser. The CARD team has slogged through plenty of hopefuls in the last few weeks, but a few about a guy matching Lasser's description might still pan out."

"Sure. I understand." Crystal stared with sad eyes. "Can't blame a girl for trying."

"I appreciate the offer. I do. It's just—"

She held up a hand. "I know. I know. Kessler's sister. You should put a ring on her finger and take yourself off the market so no one else gets their hopes up."

Escorting him out of her work area, Crystal didn't speak. He had no idea what to say, so he waved a good-bye and left the building.

Had he given Crystal an *interested* vibe? Everyone else thought so. What a mess. He needed to see Hanna something bad.

As he pointed his Mustang toward the office, a brilliant idea struck him. He wouldn't call Hanna tonight; he'd just show up on her doorstep with Champ. They could take a walk. She'd open up, and he'd put things back on solid ground. Maybe Crystal's idea about putting a ring on Hanna's finger wasn't a bad idea. Not a bad idea at all.

❋　❋　❋

Sean despised driving clunkers, but Monday's late afternoon plans required low visibility. Something his Viper didn't afford.

"So what are we gonna do with this piece of trash I hot-wired when we're done?" Don air-drummed to the head-banger metal blaring through his iPod.

The kid's adolescent adrenaline wore thin.

Carl shook his head at his brother. "Give it a good bath in the Potomac after we've wiped it clean."

That bit of housekeeping didn't matter to Sean. His prints weren't anywhere on the clunker because he was intelligent enough to use generic driving gloves.

He parked in a well-occupied public lot just beyond the Inner Harbor's crush of tourist traffic. Duffle bags packed to the hilt with a few well-chosen hunters' toys, the three men strolled into the harbor area and marked their trajectories. He'd gained much knowledge over the years from all the hunting and militia types they'd drawn into their group nationwide. Sufficient practical tutoring as well.

"I'm gonna head in and meet Jane. I'll call with the green light to move to the roof." Carl left them milling around outside the shopping mecca. So many mud races passed by, the fire rose in his gut, but he held it in check. For now.

Fifteen minutes later they started inside and met up with Carl and his new romantic entanglement.

The perky brunette droned on as she twirled a strand of hair. Jane smiled and got to the point. "This mall is one my dad's maintenance crews have serviced a few times. They outsource a lot of the work to plenty of different companies. And according to my dad's book, the mall is due for a roof walk to check for damage this week. Your generic uniforms are in a brown bag on the second-floor landing just in case anyone tries to stop you. I'm glad I could help out with this. It's good to be a part of the team."

Sean let her babble on a little longer and tried to keep a smile in place. "Thanks for helping us find a top-secret place to meet. We'll take it from here."

"And if anyone asks, remember you were just here to shop." Carl winked and Jane sashayed away.

"You'd better keep that one happy and quiet." Sean motioned for them to proceed to the stairwell. "I don't need any squealers in our inner circle."

"Jane's from a third generation supremacist family. We're safe."

Twenty minutes later they were out in the growing dusk with no interference. Sean set up his top-of-the-line McMillan with all the necessary adaptations. Foremost, his exquisite suppressor, a key piece to remain undetected.

Since Agent Parker's snooping was over, he'd had a few days to reestablish his marksman skills. And this time, it was show time. All his years of planning and practicing were coming together at this one delicious moment.

"See that Asian group still loitering in the parking lot? The ones I'd mentioned when we were out front?"

Don and Carl nodded as they looked through binoculars. Then their eyes refocused on him in rapt wonder. He loved the power rush of people hanging on his every word, just like they'd hung on Dad's. All Sean had taught these two in the past would prove profitable in the year to come. If they learned well today, the success of their small inner circle would ignite loyal followers across the country.

All they had to do was keep their boasts low key and nameless. Just enough for the masses to know they were on the move. Just enough to incite fear in law enforcement. Or drive them to join their ranks.

"What say we keep it simple and just take out two today?"

"Will I get to take a pull? I've been practicing all this time, just like you said." Carl's eagerness reminded him of a stupid puppy. But a very well-trained puppy should be allowed in on the fun.

Don moved behind them to guard the roof entrance.

As soon as he nodded, Carl set up his rifle and adjusted his bipod. "I'll follow your lead."

Sean regulated his breathing and braced for kickback. His fingers strummed the weapon waiting for just the right moment.

One. Two. Three. And off we go into infamy.

He pulled the trigger. Carl's weapon discharged right after his.

Jumping up and disassembling their gear left no time to survey the damage done. An unfortunate drawback to long-range sniping. They'd be able to gauge some measure of success when they hit ground level.

They took more time going down than they had coming up and chose three different floors from which to exit the stairwell, rendezvousing at the car. No need to look hurried and suspicious. Sean did, however, feign concern as shoppers sped by him to get a look at the commotion's cause.

He reached the brown vehicle first and pulled out a newspaper to scan while he waited. Don arrived next, with Carl bringing up the rear a few long minutes later.

No one spoke until they were in the car and on their way out of the area, headed in the opposite direction of Baltimore's finest rushing to the scene. He breathed a contented sigh of relief as they sped toward one of Howard's residences just outside of Alexandria. One the FBI had no knowledge of. Another night without his mother's gourmet cooking, a small sacrifice.

"I can't hold it in no more. We did it. Man, what a rush. I'm gonna do some more practice so I can play next time." Don left his music off but still jerked around to some strange rhythm.

Carl grinned. "Noise on the street says two yellow women went down and never came up. I'd say that's a success."

"Well done, boys. I say we take in some R and R and enjoy the newscasts for a couple days."

"Gotta stay on the Web sites though. Monitor the jabber explosion."

Don had a point. Good thing Sean had already moved all the necessary equipment and left word with his office manager that he was on his way out of the country to visit a friend in France. Dad's death hadn't changed the loyal employees who took his word for gold and were quick to accommodate his frequent work absences.

He'd even had one of his new recruits from the DC area be his stand-in with all the necessary paperwork. A new passport and tickets in his name. Perfect alibi.

Sometimes, the wonder of his wisdom and forethought astounded him.

"It's genius to have Howard's old hunting buddy's place as our safe-house. Not even the FBI can find us there." Carl nodded his head with nervous energy.

Sean couldn't agree more. *Genius.* He tried the moniker on for size and liked the fit. Soon the rest of his faithful would too. And all the stragglers or holdovers from previous leadership would have to get off the fence and join his new army.

They would. And he'd lead them all into a purified new world too perfect to imagine. But more real than the weapons in the trunk awaiting round two.

12

Hanna wiped her forehead and tried to keep up with Michael and Champ's fast clip around the nearly deserted apartment complex. Catching a quick few minutes with them the evening before her first counseling appointment was a mistake. As Michael sped past buildings and trees, his tirade about Reeley increased in volume. He used no names, but she knew. All too well.

Hanna jangled the car keys in her pocket. She needed to leave now before she spilled everything.

Champ stopped and looked back at her with a tilt to his head. A canine mind reader? She almost laughed. Instead, she bent to rub his warm fur and received a slobbery dog kiss that made her smile. Man's best friend? Woman's too.

"Hanna?"

She startled and jumped up, but tried to play it off with a weak laugh.

Michael nudged their yellow Lab forward and the speed walking continued. "You're awful quiet tonight. Not still spooked about the confrontation last week?"

Yes. "No." Well, her answer wasn't exactly a lie. Other nightmares trumped the creepy run-in with one of Michael's suspects.

"You sure? You're wound pretty tight."

Maybe all his talk about Reeley had something to do with that? Go figure. She could earn an Academy Award for her performance thus far.

"I'm fine. Really."

"Yes, you are." He smiled and leaned in to kiss her.

Her eyes snapped closed, and she forced herself to return the kiss.

Michael had no clue his contact turned her skin inside out and rubbed it with sandpaper.

His smile widened as he stepped back. "I'm glad you're here. Listening. It means a lot."

If only she could reciprocate. Sadness cloaked her like a heavy coat. Before she'd run to Louisville, Michael's kisses were the stuff of happily-ever-after dreams.

Not now. Not when her past could turn their future into a nightmare. One more to add to her collection. She couldn't risk that.

Michael turned and headed back toward his apartment. "You know what riles me the most?"

"No." Not that she wanted to either.

"If this disgusting human being created all the videos and pictures linked to him, he's been hurting little girls for twenty years or more and no one stopped him. And now he's in a powerful position." Michael's disgusted huff rivaled his words for volume. "The system failed in a monstrous way."

"But...but you'll put him behind bars. Right?" *Please, God, let that be right.*

"He deserves worse. Far worse. But the way things have been going, I doubt he'll get it. He'll slip through some legal loophole like Haines did. Makes me sick."

Insides quaking, she fought to hold in the threatening tears. But if she had to hear anything else about Reeley and the other girls he hurt, she'd crumble into pieces.

So she shoved it all down. Like she had for over twenty years. But one thought slipped past her defenses.

It's all my fault.

No counselor could prove otherwise.

Her muscles ached and her head throbbed. Right now she needed to get in her car and go home. Crawl into bed and...and what? Forget? Run?

Oh, God, I can't handle this. Make it go away. Please. Just make it go away.

❋ ❋ ❋

Last night's walk about did Hanna in. And memories haunted the few minutes she'd slept. But the lingering numbness of the sleeping pills took the edge off. Helped her forget. Not enough though. And not at all when Steven's Explorer pulled in front of her brownstone. Of course he'd be here early to pick her up Tuesday morning.

For her first counseling appointment.

She let the curtains fall back in place and took a deep breath. She was ready. *Not.*

Undoing the safety chain, she opened the door. "You really don't have to do this."

Steven ignored her and extended a sweet-smelling venti cup. "Brought you a white chocolate mocha with whip. Let's get moving. Traffic's a bear."

And that was that. No discussion. They left without another word.

Coffee-charged jitters shot through her arms, increasing with Steven's slow, silent driving and infrequent sips of espresso. The strong smell inside and honking traffic outside kept her on edge.

Of course, those concerns masked the real reasons for her nerves and dissipated when Steven parked his Explorer in front of the counselor's office. She stayed rooted to the seat.

"Ready?" He returned some of James's books and toys to the backpack her nephew kept in the car. No wonder Steven refused to drive a Bureau car most of the time.

"Will you always buck FBI protocol? There's no way you'll get that cushy desk job when your unit chief retires, what with you wearing kid-friendly ties and driving your own car to work."

Steven shook his head. Her stalling wasn't lost on him. Not one little bit. "I'm saving taxpayer money and avoiding all the fines I'd otherwise receive thanks to hauling kids and little sisters all over the place."

"Gracie wants you to take that desk job."

Her brother shut his door and circled around to open hers. "Nerves might be making you catty, but I'm not biting. Come on. I don't want you to be late."

Nine minutes early was late for Steven. Some things never changed. As they walked into the brick and glass suite of professional offices, he put his arm around her, letting her lean into his strength. Maybe it was good so much about her brother had stayed the same.

Steven remained the one constant in her ever-crumbling present.

"Do you want me to stay and introduce you to Dr. Nations?" He glanced at his watch.

She stepped into the counselor's office. "I'm a big girl, Steven. I can take a taxi home. It's not that far."

"It's not that I don't want to be here, Hanna, you know that. But the CyberTip you left last week has fast-tracked some big cases. I need to monitor things."

She nodded and straightened her sleeveless sash-tied shirt and tiered skirt in shades of the ocean. Eve had said the classic look worked for her. It looked better on Gracie.

Hanna tried to breathe normally and let the empty rose-scented office with calming periwinkle walls and comfy couches seep into her system. Didn't work. "Will my online tip be enough to put him away for life?"

Steven studied his spit-polished black shoes.

"Tell me."

"I don't know. Maybe. But that's not your burden to bear. It's mine. And I'll have to trust the system to handle this because my way would land me in jail."

"Michael believes the system will fail this time too."

Steven clenched his jaw but said nothing.

Running from the heat in her brother's eyes, she scurried to the sign-in area and added her name to the clipboard. The older receptionist smiled at her. Gentle brown eyes searched her face as the woman moved aside the sliding glass window and placed a number of papers on the counter.

"If you'll fill these out for us, dear, Dr. Nations will be with you shortly."

Hanna took a seat and started scribbling medical facts she struggled to remember.

"Michael isn't your compass, little sister. Don't let his misguided fury keep you from hearing the truth."

She wanted to snap off a curt "Yes sir." But it would hurt Steven. Instead, she met his misty eyes, mirroring the depth of her pain. The heaviness of her hurt lessened a little with his tender smile. "I'm trying, Steven. Thanks for being the best big brother."

"I'm your only brother."

"You're still the best."

After a quick hug, Steven exited before any other words or tears could give away his soft heart. All her courage followed her big brother and best friend. How she'd kept her secret from him all these years still amazed her.

But now he knew. And soon she'd have to tell a complete stranger words she swore would never pass through her lips.

Ten minutes of paperwork kept her sitting in the comfortable waiting room. Soft nature sounds added to the nurturing atmosphere. It still didn't make her want to be here.

"Hanna?" A plump woman, maybe mid-fortyish, stood in the doorway with a welcoming smile. She was striking in her beautiful black and white Greek-border dress and model-perfect red hair.

Hanna stood and followed Dr. Sally Nations into an elegant, simply decorated office. "Betty said your brother had to leave in a hurry. I hope everything is all right."

Sitting on the edge of the tan and emerald sofa, she fought the urge to spill everything and run. "How did you know it was my brother?"

"Steven's an old friend."

Counselor-speak for a former patient. She'd forgotten Steven had set up the appointment and told her over and over what a wonderful counselor Dr. Nations was. He'd probably told Dr. Nations everything about her situation too.

So why did she even need to be here?

The doctor studied her, waiting for her to make the first move. That empowerment awakened her courage. "Steven explained all the confidentiality protections and said I could tell you anything. But I don't know where to start."

"Why don't we talk about what prompted you to come today?"

Steven. Pure and simple. She'd dumped so much on her brother she couldn't live with the guilt of not letting him help in the only way he knew how. "My brother keeps talking about how this will help me deal with some lie or something he's convinced I'm believing."

That came out far cattier sounding than she'd meant it to. What'd gotten into her today? Remnants of her walk with Michael and Champ pushed through her memory. She shoved them back down.

"Let's talk about why you decided to come. You have far more strength than you give yourself credit for, Hanna."

Tell that to her stupid six-year-old terror and all the trouble she'd caused for everyone by not running when she should have. Not telling anyone what happened.

Dr. Nations handed her a Kleenex.

When had she started crying like a baby? Twenty-four years of dry eyes and now blubbering was her typical response to stress.

"Are those hurt tears or angry ones?"

The question stunned her. Steven was the one with a temper. "I'm not angry. I just want this all to go away. Things were far better when I kept the past in the past where it belongs."

"Have you ever experienced anger toward Richard Reeley?"

"No."

Dr. Nations studied her again but said nothing.

An emotion resembling Steven's rage started to rattle free. But she couldn't unleash it. Not in words. Or actions would follow. And if her perfect law-abiding brother wanted to kill Richard Reeley, what was she capable of?

Ice cut a path through her insides.

"How would you describe your feelings toward the man who hurt you when you were seven years old?"

"I was six. It…he…" Oh, why couldn't she get her words to obey? "He molested me a month before my seventh birthday."

Dr. Nations waited.

Hanna's insides churned. "I buried all the feelings in my parents' backyard, by the koi pond. I left them there." Along with all her Ken dolls. She'd told her parents one of her friends had traded for them. "So if there was any anger, it's deep under the Kentucky bluegrass." She sounded like an idiot claiming all her emotions were still buried like she'd prayed they would stay when she was six. Maybe that was the problem. She was still trying to deal with this like a six-year-old kid. Out of sight and out of mind.

It'd worked for twenty-four years.

Or had it?

Dr. Nations talked a little about healing being a choice. About identifying emotions and lies. And how they'd work on these things in the coming weeks. *Oh joy.* The sarcastic slant of her thoughts bothered her. She wasn't acting like her normal self at all.

But what was normal, now that her secret defined her existence?

A lot, according to Steven and Michael and too many news reports. This was one large statistic she didn't want any part of. But here she was. Like it or not.

So much for being free to dance like no one was watching and being who God made her to be.

Now she was forced back in time to face huge monsters whose power had only grown stronger over the years. Not weaker. All because she believed she was smart enough to keep things buried for good.

She couldn't even do that right. And if she kept going to counseling, everyone her life touched would be seared by her runaway emotions. But she couldn't stop, or Steven would feel guilty and keep trying to fix her.

One more choice that wasn't a choice after all.

❊ ❊ ❊

"You ready to go have a little talk with one of the biggest fishes Innocent Images has netted yet?" Lee's words exhibited the first sign of life Michael had seen in his friend in weeks.

He followed Lee downstairs to the interview rooms Friday evening. The cyber guys had given Steven the all-clear to have at Richard Reeley for CACU's open investigation into Katrina Chu's disappearance, but Steven wanted no part of it and passed it off to Michael. His lucky day.

Or whatever phrase Christians were supposed to use instead. One more thing he had yet to figure out. That and why mercy had anything to do with justice. He had no intention of holding back against this pervert, Bible verses shooting around his brain like a pinball or not.

"Crystal joining the fun tonight?"

Not Lee too. "Don't know. I had to cancel my plans with Hanna to deal with this guy tonight. And Saturday's boatload of paperwork follow-up ruins my date with a hiking trail, my dog, and my girl."

Crystal stepped off the elevator just as they approached the interview rooms. Her tight-fitting black dress screamed for attention. He averted his eyes.

"You got your bling on tonight, girl. Please tell me you're not all done up for front-row seats to an interrogation." Lee's happily married self could get away with comments like that.

"Nope. Just stopping by to see justice done before I head out for a late dinner with Mack."

"The IIU superstar can't pick you up at your house?" Michael loosened his Seminoles' tie and forced himself to focus on Crystal's eyes.

"Jealous?" She winked. "It's about time."

Lee cleared his throat and motioned to the observation room. "We'd better get this show on the road. Michael may have cancelled his date, but my baby's home waiting up for me."

Michael groaned.

"Mack asked me to meet him here since he was working late. But the party doesn't start until after ten, and he can drop me off at my car when he comes into work tomorrow. So I'm good. I'll watch this scumbag squirm a little, then show myself out."

She couldn't have come when Mack was doing his interrogation? Guess that wasn't much of a turn-on for the club scene.

They entered the observation area and nodded to the busy technicians. Crystal and her evening wear faded into the background. He and Lee focused on Congressman Reeley pacing the floor while his stiff-suit lawyer tried to calm him down. Good. Michael wouldn't be the only one off his game tonight.

"It's all you, hotshot." Lee slapped him on the back and pointed to the door.

Heading for the interrogation room, he replayed his idea of how things should go. He needed a few pieces of information, not some sordid confession. Innocent Images guys had taken the heat of that responsibility. All he had to do amounted to an easy in and easy out.

But time played against him. Haines had disappeared earlier this week, and Kat was still out there. Somewhere.

Reeley's disgusting cache of pictures shouted his involvement in hurting children like Kat. He'd pay. Just like Haines. But before that Reeley would talk. Because the pervert in custody held a key to finding them both.

❋   ❋   ❋

Richard stiffened in his seat as a young FBI upstart sauntered into the little room. Being treated like a common criminal and subjected to lewd questions rankled him. But what could he do? His past had caught up to him. Legal counsel advised complete cooperation because of the overwhelming evidence against him. No use denying what the FBI already discovered. But if he played his cards right, he could claim a few dirty vices, hand over some tidbits of incriminating evidence, and gain a downward departure recommendation. Then he'd do community service and put this little embarrassment behind him.

As long as the media didn't make him their top story.

According to his aides, he hadn't even rated a passing mention. So far, so good.

The young agent's presence filled the small room. Richard refused to allow the man's chiseled features to ruffle him. The flash of rage in the agent's brown eyes, however, challenged the hold Richard had on calm and collected.

"Congressman Reeley, I'm Special Agent Michael Parker with the Crimes Against Children Unit."

The agent slid a picture of a young Asian girl across the table. A mild head shot. Nothing like the photographs other agents had shoved his way today. But he recognized this one.

Pure terror slithered across his shoulders. He fought a shiver. Had to do a better job of hiding his reactions. What was that about the best defense being a good offense? Worth a try. "Are you hoping for some sort of confession, Agent Parker?"

"Is there one?"

"You have my computer and access to all of my phone records and business receipts too. I made some terrible mistakes and will enter therapy as soon as I'm released on bond. But I've done nothing worthy of the FBI's continued fishing expeditions."

"Child pornography is illegal."

Jaw clenched, he could only nod. And wish for the thousandth time today that he hadn't uploaded any of his old videos. So far the FBI had linked him to some of his photo collection and the one clip shown on *America's Most Wanted,* the most damaging evidence leveled against him. But his defense lawyers would work on the all-digital angle, and no one would ever prove without a doubt the images weren't computerized.

"Being sentenced as a producer carries the penalty of life in prison."

His lawyer stepped in. "Your alleged evidence and empty threats are wearing thin." So much for total cooperation.

"All I want is the online identity you used to download videos containing this little girl." The agent pointed to his picture of the Asian child.

"I've given you all my passwords and user names."

"Lying will not help your case."

His interrogator was a man of few words and barely bridled hostility. Better not to provoke him further. But what were his options? Lie and risk losing all his good-behavior benefits. Or help the FBI with a case that had no real connection to him. Except for a few videos he'd downloaded. And his contact with the man who had made the videos. But the FBI didn't have to know about that. The federal agents had only uncovered a fraction of his collection. He needed to tread carefully so as not to disclose any further incriminating evidence.

Forget total cooperation.

"There was a special edition, encrypted section of the Web site where I found similar pictures and the video in question. I doubt it's the same computer image though."

"This is a real child. One that's been missing thirty-six days."

Sweat slicked his palms. It had to be the same child he'd asked Andrew Kessler about. What a stupid move. And now he had to lie like he'd never lied before. "I know nothing about that. I only saw the pictures and video on the special edition site. I'll give you all the information I have."

As the words left his lips, the FBI agent smirked.

White House aspirations began to crumble around him. But he hadn't kidnapped anyone. Hadn't done anything like the refuse he'd been in contact with over the Internet. If he could prove that, maybe his one dream could still become a reality.

13

Steven hung up the phone and stared at the blinking cursor on his computer. The case report in front of him was supposed to have been the extent of his Saturday work.

Not now.

Gracie would understand. He'd make that call first. "Looks like it'll be a long day after all. I'm sorry." The muffled sounds of unfortunate colleagues clicking computer keys or talking on the phone provided the perfect background for his apology.

"As long as it doesn't change our plans for your birthday tomorrow, I'll manage."

His first birthday as a married man where there'd be no alcohol ruining the night. His first wife had routinely forgotten the day or insisted on partying the night away. But Angela was doing well after rehab and planning to take their son for his first overnight weekend next month.

"You still there?" Gracie's voice snapped him back to better thoughts.

"Just thinking about how glad I am that I get to spend my birthday with you as my wife this year."

"You have no idea what I have planned."

"Doesn't matter. It'll be all good."

She giggled. "Just hurry home. And let thoughts about tomorrow help you forget what you have to see today."

"I sound that bad?"

"Yes. I'll be praying."

That would help. They ended their call with the "I love yous" that kept him smiling. Until he placed the next one.

"You up for meeting with Walters and the Evidence Response Team?"

Clint groaned. "No. But it beats helping Gracie and Sara go birthday shopping. I'll leave them with my order for all things black and over the hill."

"Already forgetting in your old age? That's you next year. I'm still the young and chipper one."

"Ha-ha." Background sounds of vest and holster snaps and clips were sober reminders of the day's upcoming events. "Where we headin'?"

"Baltimore."

"I'll meet you at headquarters in thirty."

Long enough for Steven to get his head into this game and get ready. At least Philip Walters had been assigned to the case. He was top-notch. That'd mean one less stress point.

He contemplated calling Michael but decided against it. Parker didn't need one more reason to run to NCMEC for Crystal's input.

An hour and a half later, he and Clint walked behind a deserted grocery store and tried not to gag at the scent of decaying flesh.

A stocky construction worker faced off with Philip Walters. "Look, I gotta job to do here. How long will this place be swarming with cops?"

"We'll notify your company when our investigation is complete."

"This place has been boarded up for over a year. An' we jus' got this contract for large-scale renovations. New superstore's movin' in. But this delay could ruin everything."

Steven and Clint joined the conversation. "Is there a problem?"

The tanned construction boss wiped a meaty hand over his face. "No. No problem. I'll send my guys to another site for the week." He locked eyes with Philip. "Then can I do my job here?"

The sun reflected off Philip's bald head, but the long-time ERT leader kept his cool. "We'll let you know as soon as we're finished."

The man nodded and walked away yelling colorful instructions to his crew.

"Nice way to start the day." Steven clasped Philip on the shoulder. "What do you have for me?"

The three of them walked toward a huge dumpster that had once been painted a dark green. "Good to see you out here again, Rollins. Wish I had a better ending for this missing person's report."

"Me too." Clint rubbed his full head of dark brown hair. No doubt glad he and Philip no longer shared a similar hairstyle.

"I'll have DNA evidence to you as soon as the lab processes what we collect today. But locals are pretty sure these two near-skeletons match the recent reports on Bill Lasser and Katrina Chu. Judging from the size of the corpses, I'd say that's a strong possibility."

"How long have they been back here?"

"Hard to say. Maybe a month or a little less. They were enclosed in the dumpster, which kept animal predation to a minimum. But the heat and humidity caused decomp rates to accelerate."

Clint stepped away from the dumpster. "If they're near skeletons, why's the stench so strong?"

"Garbage around them, body fluids contained in a small, enclosed space. Take your pick. All together it amounts to one reason I'm thankful for seasonal allergies. I can't smell near as much as you folks are taking in."

"Lucky for you." Steven followed Clint away from the crime-scene markers, making mental notes about each one. "Any idea on the cause of death?"

"Execution-style gunshots to the skulls." Philip shook his head and shrugged. "The dead tell plenty of stories if you're willing to listen."

"Glad you're on this one, Philip."

"All in a day's work."

Steven couldn't relate. Seeing death wasn't part of his usual routine. It happened far too often, but not every day. "I'll keep an eye out for your report. And I think a gift card for another year's worth of Starbucks will be heading your way."

"I'm still working on the last one. Which I appreciate. But no need to repeat. I'll do all I can to help you find the person responsible for these deaths. From what we've tagged at this scene, it appears the perp had no concern for being caught. The killing was sloppy and fast. Plus, he or she picked a good place to hide the bodies until most of the evidence deteriorated."

They said their good-byes to Philip and headed toward Steven's Bureau car. "What's your gut say about this one?"

Clint unzipped his FBI jacket and tossed it on the Bucar floorboard before climbing in. "Michael will swear Sean Haines is behind this. I'm not sure. Close-distance execution shots say the killer knew his or her victims and hated them with a passion. That's all I've got."

"What's Michael told you about his hunt for Haines?"

"He interrogated Reeley and got an online identity Reeley hadn't given to the Innocent Images guys. He was planning to talk to Maxwell today about using it. He wants to set up a meeting with Haines by claiming to have information Lasser shared connecting Haines to Katrina Chu."

Steven white-knuckled the steering wheel and merged with the Baltimore-Washington Parkway traffic. "Michael better back off. The unit chief's beyond fed up with his antics on this case. If he'd come in before we left, I'd have adjusted his plans for the day."

"Aside from his undercover stunt, the kid's just doing his job with passion. It's better than getting cynical."

"A dose of common sense would go a long way."

Clint leaned against the door and crossed his arms. "This have anything to do with Michael's off-duty time at NCMEC and not with Hanna?"

"No."

"You're lying."

"There's more to the story I'm not at liberty to discuss."

"That's hogwash. And it confirms my hunch that something's very wrong with Hanna. She's rejected all our invites to dinner. And she's too busy to babysit. It's like she's terrified of being around Jonathan again."

"It's not that." Steven swallowed down the bile creeping up his throat. Keeping Hanna's secret grew harder every day. Even more with Reeley in custody. Nothing but ethics and Gracie's prayers were keeping Steven away from that sorry excuse for a human being.

Adding Michael's entanglement with Reeley equaled a quagmire of problems. As did Clint's probing. And Steven would have to come clean with Maxwell sooner than he would have liked.

"You gonna tell me what it is or do I have to press Hanna?"

"Leave her alone."

Clint's eyes widened. "This must be big."

"I'm handling it."

"Looks like it's handling you, partner."

They continued on toward the Hoover Building in silence, Steven's thoughts going a million directions at once. He'd talk to Maxwell today. Tell him just enough to pull Steven's team off the Reeley angle of this case. After that, talking to Michael would be a cakewalk.

❊ ❊ ❊

Michael sat at his desk and did his best to process the words coming from Clint's mouth. Kat was most likely dead. It was only a matter of time before forensics backed up that hunch.

Found in a dumpster.

It had to be Haines. Sounded like something right up that sick slimeball's alley. He checked the time on his computer screen.

Clint leaned against the gray partition. "Steven will be done with the big boss soon. But don't go revving your engine and rushing into trouble. For whatever reason, Steven thinks we're better off leaving the Reeley angle to Innocent Images. They'll let us know if they're able to unearth Haines."

"Haines isn't the focus of their investigation. And I need to use

Reeley to get a lead on Haines's whereabouts. My gut says he's behind Kat's and Lasser's murders. And if I can pose as a friend of Lasser's using one of Reeley's identities, I can convince Haines to meet me. I know I can."

"I applaud your confidence. But I'm with Steven. This isn't our forte. Leaving the undercover pedophile stuff to the IIU is a far better idea."

"We'll see." Michael stalked over to Maxwell's office but pulled up short at the raised voices spilling from the partially open door.

"I can't tell you any more than that. Don't you think I've given enough reasons to let my team drop the Reeley angle? We have numerous other cases that deserve our concentration. Kids we might still bring home." Steven's voice boomed off Maxwell's white walls.

"IIU is backlogged too. Why should I give them more work for your case? Parker can handle this."

Michael straightened at that bit of info.

"Ethical reasons demand my team be taken off anything to do with Reeley."

What was Steven's problem? It wasn't like him to back down from any case lead. Not one as promising as this. Finding Kat's killer would be worth the time put into working on Reeley's cooperation. Not to mention using Reeley's identity was one of Michael's more genius ideas.

Maxwell boomed right back at Kessler. "All I have is today's claim that someone you know is connected to turning Reeley in. Unless that person is blood relation, I see no reason to dump this case angle onto someone else."

Long silence. Michael could imagine Steven's clamped jaws and tight fists. Something had his immediate supervisor ticked beyond reason. Why else would he be going toe to toe with Maxwell?

"If it's this important to you, Kessler, I need a name."

Steven slammed the office door, cutting off any further information. Good thing he hadn't seen Michael. Even so, Steven's meeting with Maxwell didn't bode well for getting the okay to use Reeley's identity.

Maybe he should go one more round with Reeley. Make some headway before the official axe came down and cut him off from his one hope of finding Haines.

14

Hanna's hands shook as she opened the door and climbed in her Equinox for the second time Tuesday morning. Earlier, she'd been able to drive to Dr. Nation's office without Steven. Had even gotten there on time. Not early like Steven. That little act of self-assertion strengthened her.

Until they talked about things she'd rather forget.

Her mom's cancer. Jonathan's abduction. More details about the molestation. All the children Reeley hurt. Dr. Nations had pointed out that in all these instances Hanna blamed herself.

It's all my fault.

Yes. She lived with those words banging around her head all the time. But it wasn't a lie like the counselor had said. It was true.

She turned on the Chris Tomlin CD again and just drove. Not until she ended up in a downtown DC parking lot was she willing to admit the counselor's homework was a valid exercise.

"Talk to Michael. Trust him with your story."

If there was any hope of a future with Michael, telling her story would make that clear. Or ruin everything. But after lying to him far more than she'd ever lied to Steven or Dad combined, she had to get the truth out.

And pray that Michael understood.

Walking up to the fortresslike J. Edgar Hoover Building did nothing for her nerves. And she didn't have the courage to walk past the glaring yellow EMPLOYEES ONLY BEYOND THIS POINT sign. That could prove a million times worse than walking into James's high security school. Hope Ridge Academy, where her sister-in-law taught, had the magnetometers and armed security guards. But not the men and women in black who would come after her for entering without an escort.

And unlike Hope Ridge, the Hoover Building had Michael Parker inside.

That thought almost turned her around and back to her car.

But she couldn't keep running from this. She had to talk to Michael. Pulling out her cell with shaky hands, she took a deep breath and punched Michael's number on speed dial.

"Parker."

So not the reception she'd hoped for. "Michael? It's Hanna. I'm outside on Pennsylvania Avenue. Can you come meet me?"

"I'll be down in a sec." Then he hung up.

Her bold move to tell the truth was turning into a horrible idea.

She moved away from the huge beige planters and watched tourists snapping pictures of the imposing building behind her. When Michael stepped outside a few short minutes later, he was stiff and official in his wrinkle-free black suit.

Only his eyes hinted at any measure of concern. This was so not a good idea.

"Are you okay, Hanna? It's not like you to show up at my work unannounced."

People moved closer and listened. Some snapped pictures of them. No way was she going to talk to him in the open like this. "Is there any way we can go someplace more private? There's something I need to tell you before I chicken out again."

After checking his watch, he nodded toward the front doors. "The building is closed to visitors. But if you can hang on a few minutes, I'll take an early lunch and we can walk to a restaurant. Will that work?"

No. Not anywhere close to private enough. But if she waited to talk to him tonight, it'd be too easy to lie again. "What if what I had to tell you involved a current case?"

Michael narrowed his eyes. "Maybe you should talk to Steven."

"He knows."

Stiff as steel and teeth clenched, Michael put his hand on her back and moved toward the brown and glass front doors.

Given Michael's mood, her ploy to get in the building and find a safe place to talk backfired worse each passing second. Bad. Stupid. Idea. She should have known better.

After handing over her driver's license, she waited, shaking more with every tick of the clock. The huge wall of glass in front of her and the small reception area closing in around her didn't help settle her racing heartbeat at all. Minutes later, her ID was returned and Michael ushered her through more security into a labyrinth of halls, finally stopping to enter a small meeting room. The place was one step up from a TV interrogation room. Not the most inviting atmosphere.

Michael sat behind a small metal and fake wood desk, taking out a recording device as he settled in. "Why don't you have a seat while I get this ready?"

She walked over the desk and stood. "I don't want this conversation recorded."

"If this is about a current case, I have to. It's evidence."

Biting the inside of her lip, she started to make up an excuse to get out of this situation with her dignity and Michael's sympathy intact. But it was too late for both.

"Michael, I need you to understand—"

He held up a finger as his cell phone's buzz brought everything to a halt. Concern knit his eyebrows tighter together. "That's my father. He never calls. Do you mind if I take this?"

Before she could answer, he'd flipped his phone open and started talking as he walked out of the room.

What had she gotten herself into? She could have lasted a lifetime without seeing Michael in full FBI mode. All manners were gone and in their place was a cold, hard federal agent intent on solving his cases no matter what.

But she couldn't just run. She'd be a huge security breach walking around the FBI building with no official escort, and she'd get

Michael and Steven into heaps of trouble. Provided she got out without being arrested first.

She took a seat in the metal chair and waited. Praying might be a good idea. Then again, God wouldn't help her bury her head in the hole she'd dug by lying, so there was no real reason to ask His direction. But she couldn't risk telling her story on tape any more than she could risk lying to Michael again. Bad enough that she had to tell him anything.

He reentered the room in an even more sour disposition. "Hanna, does what you have to tell me involve Congressman Richard Reeley?"

Oh, Father. Please help me now.

※   ※   ※

Hanna's sheet-white face told Michael everything.

"H...how did you...find out?" Her eyes filled with tears.

Warning bells screamed for attention. He ignored them. "I overheard Steven talking to our unit chief. Didn't hear his connection to Reeley's case. But after your statement about something to tell me regarding a case, I put two and two together."

"Please hear me out, Michael. I need you to understand."

"And I need you to stop lying to me." He sat behind the desk and fiddled with the recording equipment. If he didn't do something with his hands, he'd take Hanna's quaking form into his arms and forget about his job. Something he couldn't risk right now. Not even for Hanna.

"I won't say anything on record. I can't."

"If you're the person who filed that CyberTip, we need your statement."

"Who's we?" She twisted her shirt with nervous hands. "If your *we* is you and Crystal, I have nothing to say to you. Nothing at all."

"This is work, Hanna."

Standing, she clenched her fists and squinted her eyes. "You have no room to talk about lying. I know from Steven that you've been at

NCMEC far more times than you've told me about. What I had to say was to my boyfriend. Not to some cold-hearted FBI agent who only cares about his job and spending time with some attractive analyst."

"Hanna, listen."

"No, you listen, Michael Parker." She walked around the desk and pointed a trembling finger in his chest. Fury lit her eyes. "All your talk about me needing to trust you is garbage. I've been struggling through more pain than you can even imagine. I came here to tell you what I've wanted to for a long time, but all you can do is treat me like a criminal or some two-bit informant."

"Hanna." He stood and reached for her.

She stepped away. "You've lied to me about Crystal for the last time. I want to leave. Now."

Tears slid down her face despite her best attempts to look tough and mean. His anger melted in the light of Hanna's raw pain. He pulled her into his arms.

She stiffened and tried to pull away. "Let me go."

"No, Hanna. It's me. Not Reeley." He held her there while she beat on his chest and struggled to break his hold.

The heat in her flushed cheeks mixed with the sadness still flowing down her face. The ache in his chest grew.

God forgive me.

Soon she stopped fighting, and anger dissolved into sobs.

He kissed her hair. "I'm sorry, Hanna. I never meant to hurt you. But I couldn't handle you being one of Reeley's victims. Making it about work was safer."

"Not for me." She spoke in a low whisper.

"No. Not for you. I'm sorry." He helped her sit in the chair and knelt in front of her. She grabbed a Kleenex from her purse and waited for him to continue. "I love you, Hanna. And I'm not interested in anyone else but you. Please believe me."

She sniffled and nodded.

"Reeley isn't my case anymore. Steven had our team removed from that part of the investigation. So the Innocent Images Unit is handling everything connected to Reeley. But your statement against Reeley could help so much. Will you please consider talking to them?"

Wringing the tissue in her hands, she studied the floor. "Can we please have a normal conversation before I do that? I don't want to talk to anyone looking like this."

"Sure." He dragged his chair around the desk and sat down, taking her hand and squeezing. "That was my father on the phone earlier. He's coming to visit this weekend and would like to meet you."

"Oh. Why?"

"Because I've told him all about you and how I..." He'd better rein it in, or he'd come close to proposing right here. "I told him that we've been dating."

"Is he still as mean as when you were growing up?" Her blue eyes held so much concern he wanted to kick himself again for the way he'd treated her today.

"I'm so sorry for how I've handled everything since you arrived. Will you forgive me?"

"Yes, Michael. I know your job is important. I should have waited to tell you tonight, when we were both in a safe place and it wasn't about your work."

He wished they were at his apartment right now. Then it wouldn't be a problem to kiss her and find better things to talk about.

"You didn't answer the question about your father."

Smiling, he leaned back in his chair. "Colonel Parker has mellowed some in his old age. Not much, but some. He'll be nothing but a gentleman to you though."

"Why's that?"

Because his mother and father wanted grandchildren and figured Hanna was their greatest chance of ever having any. Not to mention he'd practically told them she walked on water she was so perfect.

"Because you're a beautiful woman who's very important to me."

Hanna's smile disappeared and her eyes watered again. "I...I need to go home, Michael. Can we continue this conversation tonight or tomorrow?"

What had he said to elicit that reaction? And why did her eyes turn haunted so fast? A memory surfaced. His apartment. When she'd told him about her photography book and he'd kissed her.

What had he said? He couldn't quite remember.

Then it hit him. He'd told her how beautiful she was. "Did Reeley tell you how beautiful you were?"

She nodded and more tears rained down her cheeks.

God, what did that man do to Hanna? My Hanna. Please help me see justice done.

It took everything in him not to punch a hole in the wall. Or go find Reeley and put a hole in him. For Hanna's sake, he took a deep breath and released his clenched fists.

"If I walk you out now, will you come back and talk to the Innocent Images people soon?"

"I…I don't know if I can do that, Michael. I'm just not ready."

He stood and pulled her into his arms. "I'll be with you. I promise. If we go today it can be over and done with. And you'll have done a very brave thing to help put a criminal in jail for a very, very long time." He almost added that her actions today would protect untold numbers of other little girls. But that would be like dumping salt into an open wound. No one had protected Hanna.

Taking a deep breath, she closed her eyes. He prayed she'd draw courage from his presence and help put Reeley away for life. They could do this. Together.

"Okay."

They walked out into the hall and waited in front of the elevators. Hanna's face remained ashen, but her eyes flamed. Her courage made him proud.

Steven stepped off the elevators right in front of them. "Just who I was looking for. The front desk called to say my sister was here." One glance at Hanna's face and Steven's grin turned to steel. "No."

"Steven, Dr. Nations said I should talk to Michael. So I did. And I agree that telling the people who are dealing with this case is a good idea."

"No." Steven clenched his jaw and glared. "Parker, I told you we were off this. You have no idea what you're doing in encouraging Hanna to talk to IIU."

Michael didn't back down. "It will help her."

"It'll destroy her." Steven didn't blink. "I will separate you from your badge and side arm if you ever interfere in a case that's no longer yours and push my sister like this again. Do you hear me?"

"Understood."

"I'm right here, by the way. And it's my decision, Steven."

Steven backed up and stared at Hanna. "This is about a case for him. I won't let him talk you into this. Trust me, Hanna. This is not a good idea right now."

Hanna's eyes watered all over again as a sliver of doubt slipped into place. "Michael?"

Nothing he could say would stand up to her brother's accusation. Better not to make a scene at headquarters. He'd try to fix things with Hanna later. Even if things with Kessler were beyond repair.

"I'll call you tonight, Hanna."

She didn't respond. Only walked away, tucked safely under her brother's granite protection. It would take an act of God to find a good way out of the minefield he'd just stumbled into.

15

Richard's hopes for avoiding the media spotlight crumbled as he stared out his second-floor bedroom window. The media still swarmed his Georgetown residence Wednesday morning as they'd done since his return late Saturday evening. All gunning for the inside scoop.

All ready to trample any remaining hopes for the White House.

No one cared that he'd only been charged with possession of some harmless pictures and a few racy videos. No one bothered to mention on the news that he'd voluntarily entered treatment and had fully cooperated with law enforcement.

Unlike other congressmen.

Someone in the know must have leaked to the press. The face of the young FBI agent who'd returned to torment him Saturday came to mind. That man had been angry enough to take matters into his own hands.

At least Andrew Kessler's son and his team had been removed from the case. And Andrew had no way to contact him in DC. No doubt he'd already spoken to Helen back in Kentucky.

Where Helen would stay, threatening divorce until he straightened out this entire mess and cleared his name. Well-paid lawyers and forensic experts would create enough doubt in any jury's mind about the pictures the FBI had linked to him. Videos too. No one could prove his involvement.

He'd had the birthmark on his upper right arm removed years ago by an overseas plastic surgeon. So unless they had a real person giving testimony under oath, this disaster would be put to rest soon and his congressional career salvaged.

Helen claimed he was delusional about working on the Hill again. He'd prove her wrong.

Moving away from the window, he returned to his brooding in the den. No computer to waste his time with, and legal counsel advised against attempting to purchase another one after the FBI confiscated all of his technology at work and home.

All he had were his thoughts. And they tortured him.

Who could have reported him to the National Center for Missing and Exploited Children? The list of possibilities remained short. Not many young ladies had seen his birthmark. Try as he might to ignore the strongest possibility, Hanna Kessler's name and face intruded on his thoughts.

She'd been his first. But he hadn't done much of anything with that beautiful one. Nothing deserving an FBI investigation.

How could he find out if she was the one talking to the FBI? Contacting her right now was beyond risky. Maybe when the media circus died down, he'd find her address and stop by for a chat. Remind her of what really happened. How she'd come on to him in the first place.

A bigger problem existed. The last photos and video he'd downloaded were now connected to a child's murder. And the murder of a man he'd conversed with concerning new video technology. But that conversation would never come to light since the man was dead. Wisdom had kept him secure in this circumstance as he'd had that discussion through an unmonitored chat room the FBI had still not uncovered.

But if he could find the man that young FBI agent had been so eager to locate, maybe he could come out on top of this yet. Become a local hero for turning in the one responsible for heinous crimes like killing a child.

Something he'd never, ever do.

Yes. Finding Haines shouldn't be too hard. FBI Agent Michael

Parker had let a few too many details slip as he pressed for information on Bill Lasser, the producer Richard had once contacted.

Dialing his brother in London would prove a wise time investment.

"Good day, little brother. Can you do any worse on the telly?"

"Thank you for keeping up with the news, George. Any chance you can take a holiday and come home for a visit?" Richard paced the den, knowing his words were being monitored. He needed to remain covert with every statement.

"It's a possibility. What can I do to assist you when I come?"

He'd always said his older brother could read minds. Perfect help that George had learned all manner of new tricks during his semiretirement from an international computer software corporation. And he'd never leave home without at least one computer. "Keep me company. It's a bit quiet since Helen left."

"I'm sure we can find some good board games to while away the time."

"See you soon, George. And thanks." With his brother's help and access to an unmonitored computer, Richard would find the Haines character the FBI had failed to locate.

Things were on the upswing once again.

※　※　※

Michael parked his Bucar across the street from Mrs. Haines's large Mayfield estate, thankful he still had a job. It'd been a tense few days since Tuesday's confrontation with Steven.

"You sure know how to rile Kessler. I warned you to steer clear of Steven's baby sister. Told you it'd be trouble, didn't I?" Lee had been hounding him the entire drive to Baltimore, but Michael hadn't given away anything related to Hanna. It wasn't his story to tell.

"I'm not trying to tick Steven off, believe it or not."

"Then why have I had to babysit you this entire week? Not like I'm sitting at my desk twiddlin' my thumbs. You know the AUSA is still dumping child-support recovery cases on me?"

"You were a superstar with the last one. What'd you think that'd earn you?"

"Too true."

They exited the boring black Bucar and crossed the street. "Be prepared. People like Haines don't come from racially open-minded families."

"As long as the old lady doesn't have her son's lynching pictures hanging on the wall, I'm good." Lee knocked on the door. "Besides, Kessler is gunning for Haines as much as we are. We'll find him soon. You'll see."

An attractive, white-haired woman answered the door and smiled. "May I help you, young man?"

"I'm Michael Parker. We spoke on the phone earlier today." He motioned to Lee, who stepped into view. "This is my partner, Lee Branson."

The woman's smile disappeared. "You're both with the FBI? I'm not feeling too well right now." She eyed Michael. "Maybe *you* can come back tomorrow." No need to guess what her emphasized word meant.

He had to move fast. "Have you spoken to your son recently? He's been out of contact since the seventeenth of September, and we need to get in touch with him."

A strange, pinched look distorted Mrs. Haines's face. "Now I recognize your name. You were the one harassing my son. He's done nothing wrong. You and your *partner,*" she spat the word, "should leave. And don't return unless you have a warrant." She slammed the door in his face.

"That went well." Lee shook his head and started back toward the car. "As long as I live, I'll never understand white folks."

"Just because she and I share a skin color doesn't mean I can relate to her skewed belief system." Michael unlocked the door and climbed in. "You know prejudice is just as real a problem for black people as it is for white."

"No political correctness?" Lee grinned. "I knew I liked you."

"Good to hear."

Michael headed toward the Baltimore field office.

Lee huffed. "You're just looking for a fight today, aren't you?"

"Why do you say that?"

"Let's see, you're still calling Hanna every day even though she's not wanting to see your sorry self yet. You're not avoiding Kessler like someone in your position should be doing. And now you're diving headfirst into a hornet's nest, going to the office where you ticked off all the field agents the last time you were in their fair city."

"Lieutenant Barnes calls it pluck. And the Baltimore PD said my undercover work was genius and gutsy."

"Not at all the words they used, choirboy. But yeah, of course they hailed you a hero. You kept their chicken behinds from getting busted because you went renegade and did what they couldn't do."

"Didn't amount to much."

"The last song's not been sung. You never know what ripple effects your time in Baltimore caused."

Right now he needed a tidal wave of good results. All his cases were in a holding pattern. So much donkeywork for so little return. He shot up a quick prayer. All he needed was to see Hanna soon and catch one small whiff of a trail for Sean Haines. A way to get on Steven's good side again wouldn't hurt either.

Not too much to ask. Was it?

※　※　※

Thursday had already been one of those eternally long and twice-cursed days.

Nonetheless, Michael hustled to the Innocent Images Unit to check the progress of their Haines fishing expedition. Neither Steven nor Clint had been on the floor before he left for Baltimore with Lee this morning, and both were still absent from sight.

Maybe the day wouldn't end so badly after all.

He'd survived a nonproductive ego dance with the Baltimore field agents. And he'd avoided Steven's eagle eyes today. The only negative was Hanna's being too busy to see him since they'd talked on Tuesday. More like she was keeping her distance because of her big brother.

Apologizing to Steven had helped a little. He hoped it would make a difference with Hanna soon too.

Stepping into the Cyber Division brought back some fond and some not-so-happy memories. He'd spent his first two and a half years in the FBI on this floor, thwarting the spread of malicious code and taking a *byte* out of cyber crimes.

"Long time no see, Parker." Special Agent Carrie Medlin flipped her long black hair over her shoulder and smiled.

Great. The first friendly face he'd seen today had to belong to an agent he'd dated years ago.

"Good to see you, Carrie. Any chance Hammack is working with the online profile I netted from Congressman Reeley?"

Carrie's deep brown eyes searched his face. She still had what Lee called bling. The attractive, supersmart computer whiz had been the first to make him feel like he belonged in the FBI. Too bad things hadn't worked out between them.

Except then he wouldn't have met Hanna. Despite the unique obstacles presented by a relationship with his boss's sister, Hanna was worth it.

"Come on back, hotshot. I'm sure your old supervisor would be happy to work with you again." She winked and motioned for him to follow her through the maze of desks back to the computer lab. "We still haven't found a replacement who can match your speed and computer prowess."

"She's still enamored with you, Parker. Don't believe a word she says." Dan Hammack, Michael's first boss and now head of Innocent Images, met them in the hall. Short and built like a Mack truck, only Dan's smiling eyes belied his tough exterior.

"Later, gentlemen. I have work to do. No time to yak about the ones that got away." With that, Carrie disappeared into the jumble of people and high-tech gadgetry.

Dan nodded toward the lab. "Ready to watch a master at work again?"

Michael laughed. "Lead on, oh Great One."

Twenty minutes and some stomach churning conversations later, they stumbled upon a promising hit. "It would appear Reeley doesn't know the extent of our genius. He's using one of the many profiles he thinks we missed." Dan leaned back and stretched his arms in front of him, cracking a few knuckles in the process. Not a pleasant sound.

"That won't help his case in court."

"No one said all our elected officials were playing with a full deck of squeaky clean cards." Dan followed Reeley through a few message board posts. "Looks like our guy made contact with someone who sounds a lot like Haines and his windbag white-pride manifestos."

Michael scanned the disgusting Web site's board. Why would Haines be hanging out here with a bunch of flaming pedophiles? Maybe because Reeley considered this a meeting place away from FBI eyes. Wrong.

"Check this out." Dan pointed to the most recent post in a strange political thread.

The person sounding like Haines left a note for Reeley's online profile. "Our mutual friend's info is intriguing. Post time and date here. I'll contact you in person."

"Sounds like our two characters are trying to plan a meeting. Wonder if they're swapping pictures or top-secret security information." Dan laughed.

Michael didn't. "Sounds like Reeley is trying to bait Haines into a meeting. Maybe he has some intel about Lasser he failed to share with us."

"Could be. Or maybe it's all a bluff. Our congressman hasn't played straight with us from the onset of this investigation. Plus, he has something of a hero complex."

"You think he's trying to find Haines to clear his name?"

Dan shrugged. "Wouldn't put it past him."

"It would clear Reeley of the suspicions racing through the newswires about his involvement with a missing child who was found murdered."

"They already have positive IDs on the bodies?"

"Yes. Philip Walters, an ERT leader, is the best in the Bureau." Kat's parents made a dental match easy and had been notified before anything turned up on the TV. Thank God for small miracles. And this could be the lead he'd prayed for earlier.

A twinge of guilt hit him. He'd blocked Kat's case from his mind ever since Clint had talked to him about the possibility of her death last Saturday. His focus this week had been on finding Haines and forgetting what Reeley might have done to Hanna.

Both situations slammed into his chest with equal force. He needed to pray. For Kat's family. And for Hanna.

"You still here, Parker? Or daydreaming about another of your lovely ladies?"

His reputation would be hard to live down, especially here where he'd sown far too many wild oats and bragged about it to Hammack. "I'm not that guy anymore, Dan."

"That's right. You got religion and Kessler's sister. How's that working for you?" Dan's smirk communicated the rhetorical nature of his question.

"Back to business. Why don't we post Saturday, at noon. See if we can get both to show."

"Sure thing, Sundance Kid. High noon? Very original. But we should be able to pull this off, no problem." Dan laughed as he typed and read out loud. "Saturday, noon. Greenbelt Park. Use this e-mail for details."

Michael stood and stretched his neck. "You'll let me know if we get a hit, right?"

"I'll have to log it in with Kessler first. He'll make the call about whether you get to ride this on to completion." Dan gave him a half smile. "Hope you get to bag and tag these guys, Parker. They're both serious scum."

Leaving the computer lab, Michael breathed a bit easier. Unlike Dan, he didn't want Reeley or Haines meeting a bullet and a body bag. He wanted both in prison. Suffering for the rest of their miserable lives.

The sick churning in his stomach stopped him short of voicing his thoughts. Maybe he was wrong. But he couldn't deny his hope that prison justice finished the job.

Because if it didn't, he would.

16

Michael's father sat in the Mustang's passenger seat like a steel rod. No doubt hating the sports car and preferring a Mercedes escort instead. Michael and the colonel hadn't exchanged a handful of words since meeting at Reagan National thirty minutes ago.

At least the man wasn't in full-dress uniform. And Michael now had a few inches on the elder Parker. He wasn't a cowering kid anymore. Even if breathing the same air made the veil between past and present thinner.

"Are we going to have dinner tonight with your newest interest?"

"Hanna is the only one I've dated in a long time."

"So you tell Mother all the time. It's all you talk about, in fact."

According to his father, he could do nothing right. If he didn't call, he was a terrible disappointment to his mother. If he did call and didn't talk about a girl, his father hinted that he might be gay. And now if he did call and talk about a girl, it was still wrong.

His father's cell phone rang. "Colonel Parker."

The man had been retired for years, but he was still Colonel to everyone.

"Good to hear from you, General Yount. Yes sir. I have a number of meetings in DC during the two weeks I'm visiting my son. Yes, I'd be happy to meet you for eighteen holes next Saturday. An honor, sir."

So family time wasn't the primary reason the colonel was in DC. Shouldn't have been a surprise. It still registered as a low blow hearing it out loud.

The remainder of the trip to his apartment was spent dodging traffic while his father talked on the phone, filling up his two week *vacation* with meeting the top brass at the Pentagon.

Guess golf counted as a vacation activity. Just not with him.

Champ greeted them at the door with his usual yips and excitement. "Hey, buddy. Glad to see you too."

"You have a dog? Why was I not consulted on this?"

Michael kept hold of Champ's collar so the Lab wouldn't soil his father's travel clothes. All pressed razor sharp and worth far more than Michael could afford.

"I'm an adult. I don't need your approval."

"Anyone who needs to assert his maturity has none."

One more quip to add to the others that tormented his mind. "The guest room is the first door on the left. Make yourself at home while I take Champ out for a walk."

The colonel didn't even acknowledge Champ's searching eyes. Twenty years ago Michael mirrored Champ's forlorn look, always watching his father's retreating back. So little had changed between them.

Champ jumped at him and slobbered his hands once they were outside. "Yeah. That's my dog. You're good for the ego, buddy."

They walked in the growing dusk in companionable silence. He should have gotten a dog a long time ago. Champ's enthusiastic welcome made coming home far more palatable.

Champ stopped to listen when a car door slammed nearby.

"Nope. It's not her." He scratched the dog's head. "Maybe she'll come see us tonight. You'd like that, huh?"

Champ nudged his hand.

"Me too, buddy. Me too."

Far too soon, they returned to the apartment. His father already had the cable news blaring. What a way to spend a Friday night.

"Have you called your girlfriend? She doesn't live here too, does she?"

"No and no."

"That's right. You got religion. No more fun for you, huh?"

Not a real question, since his father never took his eyes off the television. "I'll call Hanna as soon as I get Champ some dinner. Would you like anything to drink?"

"Don't suppose you stock any Sam Adams Utopias."

A hundred-dollars-a-bottle beer? Not a chance. "There's tea, sodas, and some Guinness, what you used to drink."

"You moved out a long time ago. Things change."

Not enough.

"I'll take a Guinness."

Michael fought the urge to slip into some of the slang Lee used away from the office. But his age didn't exempt him from his father's fist. And a smart aleck *yessir* would get him a box for sure. Not only that, but the slave lingo he and his high school friends had used as a joke wasn't funny anymore. Not after all he and Lee had been through together. Not when racism thrived.

He handed his father the beer and was dismissed with a flick of the hand. Time to call Hanna and beg her to rescue him from the next two weeks. He went back to his room with Champ on his heels.

"Hi, Michael."

She sounded okay. Not weepy like last time they'd talked. "I know you said before that you weren't ready to see me yet, but I'm willing to beg to have you come to dinner with me and my father."

"Steven is sure you'll try to push me into talking to the Innocent Images people, you know."

So that was why she wouldn't see him this past week. Figured. "This isn't about a case for me, Hanna."

"It's about justice."

"Yes."

"Even if I get hurt in the process?"

Her question damped his flag-laden speech about doing the right thing. He leaned back into his iron headboard. Did he really want Hanna's name in the report, leaving her open to who knew what come court time? No, he didn't want her hurt any further.

He also wanted Reeley behind bars for life. Hanna's statement could help put him there.

"I don't want you hurt, Hanna. You know that."

"I do." Her soft whisper gave him hope she'd agree to see him. He needed that more than he cared to admit.

"If I promise not to bring up the case, will you please join me for dinner?" Champ jumped on the bed and wagged his tail. He wasn't the only male in this home who wanted Hanna here. "I miss you."

"I miss you too." The playful smile had returned to her voice. "But do you want me to come over because your father is driving you crazy, or do you want to see me?"

"Both. But I want to see you more." Need to see her was more like it. Just hearing her laugh would set his world right.

"Do you want me to meet you somewhere?"

"No. I'll pick you up. Twenty minutes?"

"See you then."

He wanted to jump up and whoop. But his father frowned on such displays of emotion. So he just wrestled with Champ. "She's coming, buddy. Maybe we'll survive the next two weeks after all."

※   ※   ※

Sean surveyed the disgusting chat room thread with disinterest. Noon tomorrow. New e-mail address. Was it worth the information?

"Hey, man. When are we going into town for some grub? I'm starving." Don slouched against the cabin wall. "Besides, it's Friday night. Time for a little recruiting action, huh?"

Exhaling slowly, Sean turned to face Don. Too bad this younger brother didn't have half the sense Carl retained. But he'd seen too much already. Better to train him well and let Howard instill the terror of hell reserved for snitches. Howard's infamous training drills were renowned for making the faithful even more committed.

Not to mention Howard's instruction had increased Don's weaponry skill exponentially. A prime piece of the puzzle necessary for their next exploit.

Soon.

Carl joined them and motioned to the computer screen. "What's up on the Net? Not much chatter about our last initiative. Isn't it about time to strike again?"

Sean exited the revolting Web site. The Goring brothers didn't need to know any more about Lasser or the overblown claims some *influential* contact sounded a bit too eager to share.

Lasser had never expressed intent to divulge a shred of blackmail-worthy information. Nothing that mattered. But maybe meeting this man in person would result in another efficacious contact. Something beneficial for the near future. Couldn't have too many friends in high places.

A slight reordering of tomorrow's plans settled the matter. "Yes, Carl, the time is drawing near. Within the next twenty-four hours, in fact."

"So let's slip down to the local pub and do a little celebrating first." Don needed a wife far more than the rest of Sean's chosen leadership. No time for that now.

Carl shook his head. "Sure wish Jane could have accompanied us. Any chance I can take some time off soon?"

Sean had no use for such adolescent entertainment. Not when everything he'd ever wanted rested just beyond his grasp.

He eyed both men with a steel glare. The one he'd learned at his father's knee. "The time for celebrating and for visiting with Jane will come. Don't lose sight of the goal." He stroked his newest acquisition, a present from Howard. The sleek barrel of his McMillan Tactical Rifle heightened his excitement.

"We'll go double-check the preparations for tomorrow." Carl grabbed his brother's arm and tugged.

He smiled. The electric charge of pure fear crackling around him added to his enjoyment. And this time tomorrow would bring an even greater rush.

※ ※ ※

Hanna's smile turned Michael's day around.

"Hey, stranger. It's so good to see you." He stepped into her brownstone and waited for her to make the first physical move. A major exercise in self-control. But she'd mentioned something on the phone this week about her counseling that made him think he'd better work on staying out of her personal space.

When she touched his cheek and dropped her eyes to his mouth, all his plans of slow and sweet flew out the window. Then the fear in her eyes hit him like a blast of frigid water.

He took her hand and placed it in the crook of his arm. "We'd better head back to my place. Champ is probably eating my leather seats waiting to see you."

"He's in the car?" The excitement in her voice made him grin. Good choice to bring their dog along.

"And my father is awaiting our arrival."

Hanna grabbed her purse and pulled the door closed, never moving her arm from his. Good sign.

Champ slobbered all over her when he pulled open the Mustang's door.

She buried her face in his neck and held on tight. "That's my boy. I missed you too."

When they were finished, Michael nudged Champ into the backseat and started the engine. "Do you want to talk about your counseling homework or something light?"

"Light sounds good." She touched his arm. "I'm not shutting you out, Michael. I promise. I just need some space sometimes. I hope you'll be patient with me."

"Whatever you need. I'm in this for the long haul." More like forever. But now wasn't the time to voice his dreams.

"Thank you."

"I should warn you that my father will try to regale you with military stories and his vast knowledge of everything."

"It's going that well?"

"Better." Time for a subject change. "What's happening at Grounded?"

Hanna filled him in on her growing friendship with Eve and her plans for a photo shoot she'd lined up with a new client. Even though she tried to sound upbeat, sorrow clung to her like a security blanket.

"Want to try the Majestic on King Street tonight?"

"Think it's fancy enough to please your father?" Hanna rubbed Champ's head sticking in between them.

"I'm more interested in making you smile. My father will eat wherever we take him."

She shook her head. "A little praying and some real trying on your part could go a long way toward healing the relationship with your dad."

In a perfect world, maybe.

But for Hanna, he'd give it another shot with the colonel. Who knew? Maybe God had big things planned that blew golf games and fancy eats out of the water.

❋ ❋ ❋

Hanna blinked and blinked again when Michael opened his apartment door. "Wow."

Even Champ stood next to her leg staring at the candlelight dinner spread in Michael's dining room. But hadn't Michael said they were going out to eat?

"What in the world happened here? Dinner fairies?" The edge in Michael's voice bothered her.

An older, slightly shorter version of Michael stepped out from the kitchen wearing black slacks and a crisp, red button-up. "I'm Colonel Parker. But I'd be honored if you'd call me Harry." He held out his arm and led them to the table. "I just called in a few favors and had a local caterer deliver us a dinner fit for a woman of your accomplishments."

"Not even you could make this happen in thirty minutes." Michael stiffened but stayed glued to her side.

"No. I made some calls while I was waiting for you at the airport." Harry held out a chair and motioned for her to take a seat.

"You coulda let me know."

Harry shrugged and turned his attention back to her. "Michael's mother tells me you have a photography book coming out next year. I'd love to hear about it. Claire has taken an interest in nature photos and would appreciate any tips you have to offer."

No mention of her looks or her relationship with Michael. Things were off to a good start.

Michael rolled his eyes and sat down next to her.

Even with his glowering across the table at his dad, Michael's nearness charged the room and she longed to escape into his strong arms. But he kept his distance. Just like she'd hinted at earlier this week.

That alone made her want to kiss him senseless. She wouldn't. No use asking for trouble.

Harry cleared his throat. "Why don't you say a blessing, son."

Taking her hand, Michael kept his prayer concise and stopped just short of begging God to make the next two weeks fly by.

Talk of photography and old military stories kept the conversation flowing. Michael even relaxed and laughed with her as she shared about a recent hike they'd taken where Champ tried to chase a squirrel up a tree and got them tangled together in his leash.

"Sounds like you two were made for each other." Harry locked eyes with Michael. "Better walk a straight line and not mess this up."

So the colonel had fangs after all. Hanna squeezed Michael's hand. No matter how much of a charmer Harry was, Michael held her loyalty.

After an unbelievable mint chocolate pie, she helped Michael clear the table while Harry excused himself to go call Claire.

"He does have his good points."

Michael shrugged. "If you steer clear of the minefields."

"I'm proud of you. Even when your dad bared some teeth, you didn't rise to his challenge. Judging from what you've shared before, that's progress."

"Thank you." He moved closer. "I'd really like to kiss you right now."

"I'd like that too."

His eyebrows rose. Then he bent down and touched his lips to hers. She wanted more.

But Michael stepped past her toward the door. "I'm gonna settle Champ in my room. I'll be right back."

She loaded the dishwasher and wiped off the counters. Regardless of what Steven believed, Michael wanted what was best for her. It showed in everything he did. He kept conversation light but let her know he'd listen to whatever she needed to share. Every physical interaction where she would have given more, he pulled back. For her sake.

Harry joined her in the kitchen. "Well, Hanna, it's getting too late for my old bones. It was a pleasure meeting you. And I hope I'll see you again while I'm here."

"That would be wonderful. Thank you for dinner."

Michael stood in the doorway.

"Good night, Hanna." Harry faced his son. "Don't forget you have an early meeting tomorrow. One of your friends left a message."

Michael's eyes narrowed, and he stepped out of his dad's way. The hard line of his shoulders shouted trouble. Which friend had called? Not Crystal. Please not Crystal.

"I'd better get you home." He pointed his chin toward the front door. "My father's right. Tomorrow is a big day. We're hoping to bring our elusive suspect down and catch Reeley in one of his deceptive games."

Reeley again. What she wouldn't give to make him disappear forever.

17

"We have one stop before returning to our perfect strike position." Sean turned to Carl, waiting for the light to change on Saturday morning. "This shouldn't take long."

"Is this about another place for today's fun?"

The light changed, and a series of turns later Sean directed his gray rental into Greenbelt Park, toward the Sweetgum picnic area. A rather unimaginative location for a meeting involving information about his and Bill Lasser's friendship years ago.

"No." Sean parked in a secluded spot near the prearranged meeting area. "This business is of a more personal nature."

And one he'd manipulated so masterfully that his father would smile if he were here.

"That *influential contact* you've been following the past few days?"

Carl proved far smarter and more observant than Sean could have hoped. Leveling his voice, he locked eyes with the younger man. "Yes. I'll remind you how vital it is that you keep this between us."

"Yes sir. Your secrets are safe with me."

No secrets to keep. More like hands-on training for his young protégé. "Focus on the park benches through that clearing of trees." Sean handed Carl an extra pair of high-end binoculars.

"I see a short, older man who looks like he could have been a weightlifter and a black-haired, nice-looking chick sitting at a picnic table. Must be his daughter."

"Anything else?"

"A few guys setting up camp a little ways away from the playground area. Why? Are you supposed to meet any of these people?"

"No." Sean watched the window of a nearby camper for any signs of movement. When he caught a glimpse of blond hair and a very familiar face, he smiled.

"Lesson number one in life, Carl. Things are not always what they seem."

Carl lowered his binoculars and knotted his face into a dumbfounded question. "What do you mean? It's just a bunch of boring people going camping for the weekend."

Movement beyond the cozy little camp scene demanded a closer look. Another car, a step up from his mid-sized rental, parked along the road. Adjusting his binoculars, Sean's smile grew even wider. "So now all the pieces of the puzzle come together."

"What, man? This all seems a little crazy. A waste of time when we have important business today."

Sean grabbed Carl's jacket at the throat and pulled him closer. "Don't ever question me like that again."

The kid's eyes widened as he nodded.

Sean shoved him away and narrowed his eyes. "You have much to learn." He pointed to the tan Cadillac. "That is none other than Congressman Richard Reeley. My initial online contact."

"The pervert in the news? The one they're saying killed that Asian kid and Lasser?"

"The very one."

"He was your influential contact?"

"If my hunch proves correct, his pathetic attempt to locate me will land him right back in jail."

"I'm not following."

No surprise there. It'd taken Sean a while to piece things together. Bits of information from his law enforcement sources sparked ideas that solidified in the early morning hours and were now playing out in front of him. He'd make it easy for Carl. No need to overload the young man's brain this early in the day.

"It's simple. Reeley finds a way to go online without FBI surveillance and tries to find me because some FBI idiot tells him they're looking for me. If he succeeded, he'd be a media and law enforcement hero and clear his name."

"He thinks you killed Billy-boy and that kid? What a joke. You were at the office all morning. Lasser and that nasty kid were long gone by then."

What an alibi. Good thing Carl was more loyal than intelligent. "Yes, well, regardless of Reeley's misinformed beliefs, my hypothesis is that he set up this meeting and planned to alert the police after we began talking."

"How's that gonna land him back in jail?"

"Those boring people you described around the picnic area? Those are FBI agents. They followed Reeley all over the Internet and intercepted our communication." Sean pointed to the camper. "And behind that dark curtain is our favorite FBI agent, Michael Parker."

Carl's open-mouthed stare was amusing.

While he'd rather enjoy watching things play out, he couldn't stay around and risk being spotted. "Learn from this, Carl." He started the engine and retraced his steps back to the main road. They needed to be in DC soon. "Let's do a better job of keeping tabs on our Michael Parker and his pretty girlfriend. They might prove valuable once we change their minds about mud races."

Carl nodded. "You think they'll come over to our side?"

"Who knows? Either way, it will be entertaining to educate them on the power of our movement."

"That Hanna Kessler would be an incredible asset if we could make her see the light."

Sean chuckled. "What about Jane?" Hanna was well beyond Carl's league anyway.

"For you. Not me, Reverend Sean."

Interesting idea. Very interesting.

❉   ❉   ❉

Richard watched the undercover FBI agents for over an hour. Nothing. Sean Haines had stood him up. He rubbed sweaty palms on his trousers and returned home to pick up his brother for another meeting.

The one he had to do before federal agents came knocking yet again.

George met him at the door, his salt and pepper hair all sprayed into perfect place. His brother had become an outrageous metrosexual in recent years, thanks to British culture and too much expendable income.

"No luck for the weary, eh brother?"

"No." Richard motioned for George to follow him. "Join me for this next appointment, will you? I'll need your help to assure all ends well."

"My pleasure."

They set off toward Old Town Alexandria in companionable silence. How good to have family close, especially his dear older brother. Computers had always been George's forte, and his insight cut Richard's search for Haines by immeasurable days.

George's computer had also alleviated the boredom plaguing the long night hours. Good thing he'd learned better how to erase his digital trail across the Web. No downloading. Just looking.

For now it was enough.

Richard pulled into Hanna Kessler's brownstone community and parked near her home.

"Well, are we going in or not?" George reached for the door handle then stopped. "Please don't make all my detective work for naught."

Despite his brother's prodding, Richard waited. Could he face this beautiful one and remain unmoved by their shared history? Could he convince her that her memories were misguided when his mind's eye recalled every detail of their one passionate day together?

Before he lost himself in the past, a black Mustang raced into the parking lot and stopped right outside Hanna's door. Michael Parker emerged and stormed toward Richard's intended destination.

Michael Parker?

He started his Cadillac and retreated faster than ever before. This was no place to be apprehended by that dangerous FBI agent.

So Hanna was the one who'd reported him, just as he had suspected. And she was connected to Parker, the overeager FBI agent with a penchant for destroying his political career. Talking to Hanna could prove more perilous than beneficial.

Unless George went in his stead.

Another time. Yes, they'd return. And George would accomplish what Richard now could not. As long as he avoided law enforcement entanglements, they'd make plans to speak with his beautiful one and convince her of his innocence.

His future depended on it.

❊   ❊   ❊

Sean and Carl set up their custom rifles and perched atop the tall office building owned by one of their newest recruits. Stuffed shirts had their usefulness, and this one's proof of loyalty had far exceeded their main contingent of business contacts.

"Are Don and Howard going to wait for us?"

"No. Howard has trained Don well enough to handle this task without your presence."

Carl's face stretched into a frown. "Too bad I can't see my brother's first kill. I'm sure he'll be stoked and flying high."

He'd do better to stay calm and avoid detection. Their strike in Baltimore and his and Carl's in DC should bring back memories, echoing the sniper-attack panic of years ago. But this time, his race wouldn't fall.

They'd begin a well-organized first wave of decimation. Many members of various mud races would fall today.

The more the better. If only Dad were here to see it.

Carl adjusted his scope and bipod. "Looks like the pickin's are slim."

Yes. Too many of their own pure blood frequented the gas station far below. "Stay alert. We need one mother and child pair here."

"Two if we can, right?"

Sean smiled. Yes. Their totals today might not be extravagant, but the DC attack added to the ones planned for Baltimore, Miami, and Chicago would be enough.

For now.

As he surveyed the scene below, adrenaline coursed through his veins. A large Mexican woman bounced one of her cursed brood on her hip. Another mongrel ran around the station wagon and attached itself to the woman's leg.

What a retching scene.

"On my mark."

Carl's finger curled around the trigger, muscles tight and ready.

Sean regulated his breathing and braced for kickback. His fingers strummed the weapon just like he'd done last time. One lucky rub and he was ready.

"One. Two…"

Three. Their weapons discharged simultaneously. Sean's shoulder absorbed the kickback and taut muscles screamed for more. But within seconds they were up and repacking their gear.

Screams followed along with mass chaos.

A glance through his binoculars congratulated him. They'd both made their mark.

One bullet snuffed out the pathetic mother and child combination. Another ripped into the one clinging to his mother's skirts.

Now they were no longer. And the useless heroes in the gathering crowd could do nothing to change that fact.

"Let's pack up and return to the cabin."

Carl pumped his fists and rocked on his knees. "Man, what a rush." Indeed.

Hours later, the reports streamed in. Carl and Don tapped away on their computers and exchanged far too much blather about the endorphin rush. They were still high on it with no signs of coming down.

Beer and more beer would quiet them in due time.

Sean reveled in the day's results. Three eliminated in Baltimore: a black father and two daughters. Four in Miami. Unfortunately only two in Chicago.

That was twelve less than yesterday.

A good start. An excellent start, in fact.

18

I'm scared, Hanna."

Standing next to Eve on Monday morning, Hanna nodded and stared into the milling crowd outside Grounded. The rainy and cold first day of October did nothing to dissuade tourists and other shoppers from Union Station. Neither did the panic on the television.

"Me too." Hanna gave Eve a sad smile.

"The news says they have no idea who's behind it. Four simultaneous attacks in one weekend. It's crazy."

After Michael's diatribe Saturday about blind justice and one more thwarted attempt to apprehend two suspects he hated with a passion, he'd warned Hanna about being extra careful. Both for Eve's sake and for the possible retaliation black hate groups might stage. Looking again at Eve's beautiful maroon duster and matching corduroy pants, she reconsidered the questions perched on her lips.

"What's on your mind?"

Hanna tried to smile and pray about her answer, but the words flew out anyway. "I...well, I was wondering what Trina and her friends at school are saying about the snipers."

"You mean are her friends gonna go shooting white folks?"

A beak-nosed customer in wire-rimmed glasses stepped up to the counter and eyed them both. Hanna stepped forward. "What can I start for you today, sir?"

"A large Colombian Supreme with organic milk and sugar."

No Starbucks lingo about whip, dry, or with legs? So much the better. "Can I get you anything else? We have cinnamon scones and blueberry muffins today."

"Nothing else."

"I'll have your coffee right up."

The man paid with exact change and stood so close to the counter he might as well sit on it. Hanna handed him the coffee less than a minute later, but he studied his watch and left with a huff. Manners sorely lacking.

Eve handled the next few customers and then helped load the last of the day's pastries into the case.

"I'm sorry about my earlier question, Eve. I didn't mean to imply anything."

"I know you didn't."

"I'm still sorry that I offended you with my question."

Eve wiped her hands on her red apron and leaned against the counter. "Thank you. I know Trina didn't show you any grace last time, but why don't you join us again on Friday? Once Trina gets to know you, she'll soften. And you'll see she's no threat to you or anyone else."

"Really?" She doubted that. Trina despised her for no other reason than her skin color. It didn't make sense.

"Maybe." Eve started wiping the counter. "She's had a lot of reasons to hate white people."

"Did Trey's friends do more than vandalize your home and cars?"

"Yes." The pain in Eve's eyes silenced Hanna's further questions. "You know, with all this sniper stuff targeting minorities, maybe we shouldn't get together again quite yet. It might cause trouble."

Now it was Hanna's turn to take in Grounded's interior with sad eyes. The one work relationship she'd hoped would grow into a deeper friendship was threatened by stupid people with even stupider ideas.

But if Michael was correct, their ideas weren't just stupid. They were downright dangerous.

She grabbed a cloth and swiped at some crumbs on the front table. A small group of suited professionals paused in front of Grounded. One man pointed to the East Street Café upstairs, revealing an FBI badge on his belt. The only female in the little bunch, a beautiful Hispanic woman, stared into the coffee shop. After giving Hanna the once over, the woman flipped her dark hair over one shoulder, smiling at the three men surrounding her. "Let's head down to the food court. I'm not much of a coffee drinker anyway."

The tallest man smirked. "Whatever you say, Crystal."

Crystal? As in Michael's co-worker? The one he'd spent far too much time with?

"Do you know that lady?" Eve nudged her.

"No. Why?"

"Sure looked like she knew you." Eve finished cleaning the front tables.

Things remained far too slow for a normal Monday morning. Not good for business. Not good for her heart. Way too much time to think about Crystal. If the Hispanic lady was the Crystal who worked with Michael, no wonder he hadn't said much about her. That woman was dressed-to-kill gorgeous and a world-class flirt like Hanna hadn't seen since college. She brushed off her simple floral skirt and green sweater set. Wonder where she would have landed in comparison to Crystal today?

Eve added sandwiches to the display case and raised her eyebrows at Hanna. "You sure look like you're stewing on something rotten. What's wrong?"

"Have you ever been jealous?"

"Plenty. But you have no reason to be jealous of anyone."

Hanna straightened her skirt. "Thank you."

She sighed. No way could she talk to Gracie or Sara about this. They'd dismiss her suspicions as ridiculous. Gracie would suggest they pray about things, but she didn't want to pray. She wanted to know if the unease building in her stomach was pent-up emotions gone wild or an internal warning she needed to heed.

"How do you know if your jealousy is warranted?"

"You mean how do I figure out if my guy is scoping someone else?"

Not quite. But yes, that was pretty close to what she wanted to know. Even if Eve was a little young to be doling out advice.

Hanna nodded.

Shrugging, Eve smoothed her tan shirt over her stomach. A move

Sara had been doing more and more these days. Must be a mom thing. "I loved Trey. Wanted to believe he loved me. We couldn't get enough of each other, and he didn't bend to what everyone else said was right." She closed the glass case. "Until I got pregnant. Then he disappeared and trouble took his place."

Hanna wished she'd kept her questions to herself. Better to ignore her feelings. They'd only made life more and more difficult. "I'm sorry. I didn't mean to dredge up bad memories." She had more than enough of her own that she didn't want anyone prying into.

"You should talk to Michael. The way he looks at you, I doubt you have anything to worry about, girlfriend. Not a thing."

Eve hadn't seen Michael enough to know that. But maybe she should broach the subject of Crystal one more time. Not for the next few weeks, though. Between Michael's dad and the anger she'd seen overtake Michael on Saturday, now wasn't the best time. Not when Michael was locked into meting out justice on his elusive suspect and Reeley.

He needed to make his peace with the fact that justice didn't rest in his hands. Until then, she'd keep her fears about Crystal quiet. After all, if he was interested in another woman, Hanna had only herself to blame.

❈   ❈   ❈

Steven hightailed it out of the meeting with the acting chief of the National Joint Terrorism Task Force, Supervisory Special Agent Sonja Foster, and Maxwell. Nothing like time with the bigwigs to remind him what a small wheel he was in the federal machinery of headquarters.

And now he had to tap one of his agents for the Terrorism Task Force in charge of investigating and apprehending the mastermind behind the shootings last weekend.

No small task.

Clint wasn't up for it yet, despite his crowing to the contrary. And it didn't sit right to force Lee into the powder keg of racial issues facing the task force. Not when he still hadn't let go of what happened with Sean Haines in August.

That left Michael.

"Mulling over a sticky admin decision, huh?" Clint met him in the hall outside the Crimes Against Children Unit. "You only make lemon faces like that when you have bad news."

"Walk with me."

"That doesn't sound good."

"How's Sara doing? She looked bad Sunday night, more tired than I've ever seen her."

Clint chuckled. "You're stalling. But I'll be sure to pass along your glowing report of my beautiful wife."

"She'll love that."

"You'd just better watch out." Clint slapped him on the back. "She's begging God for October seventh to arrive today."

"You mean you can't make that happen?" Steven smiled, then let out a long breath. "And you're right. I'm stalling. The Terrorism Task Force wants one of our team on the case that exploded last weekend."

"Because children were involved?"

"Yep. Guess this is a new strategy for domestic terrorism. They think we could add vital information to the huge mix of organizations already onboard."

"You're tapping Michael."

Was Clint clairvoyant? "I'm not sure."

Clint stopped walking and faced him. "You know full well Michael is an excellent choice for this assignment. It'll give him somewhere to focus his pent-up energy."

"That energy coupled with his lack of common sense is what has me worried."

"He's not pushing Hanna."

Steven narrowed his eyes. "What do you know about that situation?"

"Your lack of trust is disappointing." Clint held up a hand. "But it's Hanna, and you've always kept your family close to the vest. So I'm not faulting you."

"Did Michael tell you?" His fists tightened at his sides.

"Hanna did."

"What did she tell you?"

"About Reeley hurting her when she was a kid. Makes me want to lay waste to that guy's face."

"Tell me about it." Steven ran a hand through his hair. "I'm glad she confided in you. Just surprised, that's all. Did she tell you after Gracie and I left Sunday evening?"

"Yep. Give her room, Steven. Michael is. And so will we. She knows we're all on her side and here to help." Motioning back to their offices, Clint started walking again. "Let's go tell Michael about his new case. This time apart from us will do wonders for your friendship. And all of our sanity."

Whatever. Steven hadn't been near as hard on Michael as he'd wanted to be last week. And he'd kept it out of the office.

Mostly.

Not an issue now. Michael would have bigger problems in the near future anyway. Namely one SSA Sonja Foster. Affectionately dubbed the dragon lady by those working under her.

Michael better get prayed up and ready. No telling what was coming his way.

※　※　※

Some kind of wicked headache thrashed Michael's brain as he tried to focus on the paperwork in front of him. Nothing like having to summarize file after file of investigations too far from closure to hand over to another agent. Of course, he'd still have donkeywork for plenty others. And breathing down Innocent Images guys' necks to build a stronger case against Reeley. Soon that scum would do more than make stupid moves on the computer, and they'd toss him back in jail.

But for now, he had to let go of some cases. Thanks to his new assignment.

Domestic terrorism.

What a rotten way to spend the next few weeks or months, however long this investigation dragged on. But if he could track down Haines like this, he'd take it and run.

This might be another facet of the lead he'd asked God to provide.

"Hey, stranger. You look like you need a good dinner and a friend." Crystal stood next to his desk, picnic basket in hand.

"That boy needs something, that's for sure." Lee joined them and gave Crystal a wide smile. "Did you bring enough for an army? There's plenty of us poor unfortunates left with hungry stomachs needin' filling."

She half smiled. "Sorry. I only packed a few things."

Lee smirked and nodded. "I see. He goes and gets a special assignment, and you treat him like royalty. While the rest of us slog on as unsung heroes."

Michael's defenses shot into high gear. "You should be on stage." He shook his head. "Or better yet, take this task force assignment yourself."

Lee's smile disappeared. "No thanks. I've had enough of bigots and murdered black folk to last a hundred lives." He nodded and walked away. "Catch you two later."

Crystal had straightened up some of the mess on his desk and spread out a huge meal before he could tear his thoughts away from the pictures on Haines's computer and Lee's continued avoidance of the subject.

A whiff of jasmine perfume turned his attention toward Crystal's tailored black suit and how it hugged every curve.

Pray.

Yes. That was what he needed to do.

The smell of mandarin beef and fried rice caused his stomach to rumble. His father was out for the night with Pentagon buddies, so he had no plans for the evening. And he did need to eat.

Crystal moved the egg rolls and green tea to make room for fancy plates and cloth napkins. "All your favorites, right?" She smiled and winked, then pulled a desk chair close to his. "Why don't you say a blessing? That is what you do before a meal, or did I get that wrong?"

"No. I do. Pray, I mean. Before meals." When had he lost his ability to form coherent sentences? Probably when Crystal bent forward a little too much and then asked him to talk to God. He was so not getting it clear with her. "Let's pray." His hands stayed tucked into his crossed arms. "Lord, please guide our conversation. Protect Hanna and continue to reveal Your love to her heart."

Crystal served him some fried rice. "So Hanna's not doing well these days?"

"Hanna is fine." He took the plate and dished up the rest of his meal for himself. "But I'm curious. Why all this?"

She took a few bites of beef and swallowed. Then crossed and uncrossed her legs and sighed. "Just doing a friend a favor. I was over this way for meetings and figured you needed some food to keep going with your investigation into Saturday's shootings."

All his favorites too. She'd paid far too much attention during all the working meals they'd shared trying to build a case against Sean Haines. Work that amounted to nothing but lost time.

And hot water for him.

"Crystal, I appreciate your thoughtfulness in bringing dinner, but I made it clear I'm involved with Hanna and only Hanna." He ate fast and kept as far from Crystal as possible. Something he hadn't done well enough when they were working together.

She shrugged and flipped her black hair over her shoulder. Scooting closer, she touched his forearm. "Can't a friend do a friend a favor?"

This was as far from a friend situation as east was to west.

"Besides, you and Hanna are such superspiritual people, I had a few questions."

Who in the world had Crystal been talking to about Hanna? Things were deteriorating fast all around him. No doubt the rumors would be down and dirty tomorrow.

He moved away again. "What kind of questions?"

"I want what you and Hanna have. God. But no one I know is into church or the God you say is your Father."

That answer threw him a curve ball. All he'd been worried about was what Hanna and Steven would think about this dinner. But here was a co-worker seeking God, just like he'd been doing not too long ago.

What if Clint had blown him off like he'd planned to do with Crystal?

Surely God didn't limit Himself to guys talking to guys when someone wanted to hear more about Christianity.

"Well?" Crystal reached out and touched his arm again. "Will you tell me how you became interested in spiritual things?"

Red flags flew all around him. This didn't smack of authenticity like his inquiry about Clint's relationship with God. But what should he do? Maybe God would somehow use this. He'd share his story, thank Crystal for dinner, and then call Hanna on the way home to tell her everything.

No harm there. Right? God didn't live in a box, and he didn't have to accept all the preconceived notions Steven held about right and wrong, what constituted a real opportunity to tell someone about Jesus or not.

He wouldn't fit in a Kessler-sized box anyway. Too stifling.

So he'd pray hard, talk fast, and head home. Nothing to worry about. Nothing at all.

19

Tuesday's beginning started under the shadow of yesterday's mess. The one Michael continued to dig out from under. Crystal had listened to his shortened story of stepping into a relationship with God and then left soon after with no more questions or arm touching. Thank the Lord.

And Hanna handled his recounting of dinner with Crystal far better than Steven had. Of course, Steven's rendition had Crystal pawing all over him and showing more skin than the real version.

Earlier this morning, he'd set Steven, Clint, and Lee straight on what happened. Two of the three acted like they believed him. But even Lee shot him a few smirks.

And now he had to face an SSA with a reputation for fire breathing and then spend most of his day in the Strategic Information and Operations Center. Not the friendliest place on earth.

More like a den of lions roaring at terrorist threats on American soil.

He walked into the large briefing room with stadium seating and tried to focus, to find his fit. Hard to do when huge monitors and flat panel TVs blared news feeds from every corner of the room.

"You'll get used to it." A young, bald police officer in the back row extended a hand. "Brett Hamilton."

Michael hated the bald-headed reminder of Clint's cancer. But that wasn't Hamilton's fault. "Michael Parker." He adjusted his red power tie and took the only empty seat in the room, the one right next to Hamilton.

"Well, now that our last agent is in place, we'll begin." Sonja Foster in the flesh. All six feet of tanned muscles poured into a gray suit with her fire-breathing apparatus covered in red lipstick.

Clint had warned him. No use now hoping the rumors were inflated.

"My task force has kept tabs on various groups of domestic terrorists. The fastest growing faction has been known as One Pure Nation ever since the parent organization dissolved with the arrest and incarceration of their leadership. They're a small and, up until recent months, dormant group. But they're now being credited with many random acts of racial violence."

A skinny uniformed officer took copious notes before raising her hand. "This would include the killing of two Asian females in Baltimore Harbor September seventeenth and the four simultaneous attacks this past Saturday, correct?"

"Yes, Officer Tanner. That is correct." Foster clicked through a Power-Point presentation on the white supremacist groups now considered higher priority domestic terrorists.

"Various pockets of the most active members of One Pure Nation and another religious-sounding group have met in small contingents in three major cities. Chicago, Miami, and Indianapolis. Membership growth has been slow until the last few months. One Pure Nation's newfound fame is drawing interest. But no intel points to any major players in leadership positions."

A tall blond man in a sharp suit raised his hand and stood. "Even with all this information, we still have no hard evidence linking One Pure Nation members to the recent shootings? Ballistics? Eyewitnesses? Web sites? Nothing?"

Foster straightened. "We know McMillan rifles were utilized in two of the recent shootings. But they don't appear to use any specialized ammunition or equipment, so tracing rifle purchases in and around all the major cities hit has yielded few leads thus far." She sneered. "But if you have more to share from your vast cache of information, Agent Matthews, please enlighten us."

Hamilton leaned over and whispered, "Grape vine says Foster and that spook had a fling but neither will step down from the task force. It's usually a good show."

Way too much information. And Hamilton better button his lip before Foster rapped them both over their heads with her pointer. Michael's being the last to arrive hadn't earned him any brownie points.

"What about Howard Shale's activity?" Tanner again. She must be a terrorism junkie. Michael guessed she could quote terrorist information like most men quoted baseball trivia.

"Shale was monitored for years after the disbanding of the largest white supremacist church. But he outlasted tax dollars and slipped under our radar six months ago."

Michael couldn't hold it in any longer. "He owns property in Baltimore being used by a man most likely the leader of this One Pure Nation group."

Foster exited out of the presentation, and her dark brown eyes bore into him. "Yes, Parker, we're aware of your escapades with our Baltimore task force. Unfortunately, you netted your suspect only to throw him back for lack of proper police procedure."

None of which was his team's fault.

A round of snickers and throat clearing increased his ire.

Foster continued. "As stated earlier we have no record of clear leadership and no financial ties between Howard Shale and Sean Haines. Beyond Haines's housesitting for a friend, all we have is the man's wannabe status through Internet chatter. He's not a high priority."

Michael crossed his arms. "He should be."

Stepping away from her podium, Foster locked eyes with him. "Is that so?" She pursed her wide lips. "To encourage your good-faith contribution to today's briefing, we'll issue an updated BOLO for Haines, giving his status as a suspected domestic terrorist. Will that satisfy you, Parker?"

CIA spook Matthews sniffed.

A simple "Be On the Look Out" wasn't enough. But for now, it'd have to do. "Yes. Thank you, ma'am."

Hamilton shook his head and smiled. "Watch your agenda, Parker. We're here to find the perps, not create them."

"Now, if there are no more questions, let's adjourn and move to the SIOC for this morning's National Terrorism Task Force briefing."

Everyone filed out of the room and reconfigured in the Strategic Information and Operations Center along with fifty other multiagency representatives. Computer keys clacked all around the huge room and more enormous screens blared information feeds from all over the globe.

Michael snagged a seat as far away from Foster as possible. One more boring briefing and he'd receive his day's task list, singled out to follow what Foster deemed the "unlikely possibility" of Sean Haines having a leadership role in One Pure Nation. That suited him just fine. With access to so many agency databases, he'd make some headway on his CACU case as well as do his duty with this terrorism task force.

Then, because his father was far too busy to make time for his only son, he'd spend the evening with Hanna and relax. He hoped.

※　※　※

Michael dribbled the basketball and juked around Lee, driving all the way to the hoop and sinking one.

This was the good life. Especially Hanna's cheer from the sidelines.

Lee checked the ball half-court and walked slowly toward the basket.

"Getting tired, old man?" Michael swatted at the ball. "We can call the game if you need a rest."

"Keep your smack to yourself and learn." Lee dribbled the ball through his legs and moved closer. "Kessler and Rollins would agree, huh?"

Lee jumped and Michael smacked the ball into the backyard bushes.

Rashida groaned. "There go my roses. You two need a time-out."

They all laughed. Michael ran after the ball and then joined the group sitting around the Bransons' teakwood table.

"Have some tea, Michael, and give my baby a breather. He sure won't take one on his own."

"Woman, are you on my side or not?" Lee's wide smile earned him a kiss from his wife.

Michael stopped the smack talk about age. Hanna's two-year seniority over him remained a sensitive topic. For her. He could care less.

After five minutes of chitchat, Lee stood and stretched. "Come on. Let's get this game over with."

In the growing dusk, the determined set of Lee's jaw still needed schooling. No way would Lee give one more point if he could help it.

Two lay-ups and a free-throw foul that even the women agreed was the right call gave Michael crowing rights once again.

Lee had just as much to learn as he did.

As they bent over their knees and tried to look less winded than they were, Rashida's quiet voice registered.

"Sugar, you got it bad for that one, don't you?"

Michael hid a smile as Hanna scuffed her Keds against the brick patio. "Guess so. They say the eyes never lie."

"You're right about that. Let's make our men some more tea before they dehydrate or choke on all the testosterone filling the night air."

The back door clicked as it closed. Time for the questions Lee had deflected too long. "Talk to me. No wise-guy cracks either. I want to know what happened in your head the day we busted Haines."

"No you don't."

"Try me."

Lee stared at him a long time before speaking again. "My great uncle was strung up by crazies in white hoods. My dad and uncle were both hospitalized numerous times for going to the white schools in the parish we grew up in. My sisters didn't catch as much physical threats as mental ones."

"And you?"

Lee focused on the brightening stars. "Let's just say I left my mama's faith in a high school locker room where I'd had my fill of turning the other cheek."

"I'm sorry." Michael didn't know what else to say. Growing up military had shielded him from many of the life experiences Lee endured.

"I know not all white folks act like those I grew up around. But no amount of my stories will help you see what it's like to grow up black in a white world."

"At the Bureau?"

"Without quotas, I doubt I'd have been hired." Lee guzzled the last of his tea. "Had a PT instructor at Quantico call me boy and howl about my good-for-nothing pappy who deserved what he got."

"Did you file a complaint?"

"It doesn't always work like that, Michael. Sometimes you got to lay low and hold your head high no matter what gets shoved your way."

"You hold all that in for too long and you're gonna explode."

Lee locked eyes with him. "You want to know what ran through my mind after Haines's pictures? I wanted to scream, 'Dear God in heaven, if You're real You can't let this happen again.' But it's happening."

"Evil men don't mean God isn't real. We live in a fallen world."

Lee studied him for another long stretch. "If that works for you, Michael, that's fine. But it doesn't for me."

What bothered Michael more than anything was the hopelessness infusing his friend's voice. Lee had never been like this in the two years they'd been friends.

Haines had gone too far. Hurt too many. And if people like him weren't stopped, the fabric of America would be shredded, one broken body and soul at a time.

Michael wouldn't let that happen.

And Haines would pay.

20

"News from the FBI terrorism front is not good." The tall blond spook grabbed another beer.

Sean raised a glass of his father's best Riesling toward Agent Matthews. He had little better to do this Friday night than relax in Howard's cabin and continue celebrating their recent triumph. "Do tell, Marcus, what Parker is up to with this new assignment."

Marcus hefted his bulk onto a tall bar chair and leaned against the kitchen island. "I had Foster unhinged with all my questions. Riled her good, like always. But Parker kept returning the issue to you."

"No surprise there."

"He knows too much. You'd better stay off the radar. Postpone your meetings awhile longer." Marcus took a long draw from his amber bottle.

Sean narrowed his eyes. "Still playing house with Sonja when you're off-duty?" One couldn't be too careful with undercover agents. Never could tell whose side retained their true loyalty.

"Whenever I can." Marcus tossed his empty bottle into the metal trash can. "She's back with her husband now, though. So it's a little more difficult to find out all she knows."

"No more pillow talk for you."

Shrugging, the blond hulk donned his suit coat and walked to the door. "I'll keep in touch."

"You do that."

Carl and Don were still out on the town with Jane and some name-less harlot Don met in the two-bit whistle stop where they bought supplies. The one time Sean had been introduced, she was too drunk to even speak his name, let alone remember any details Don would spill to impress.

He'd best not say much. They were far too close to their ultimate conquest to slip now. But he'd allow the Goring brothers some fun. Sean's turn would come in due time.

He meandered into his second-story office. Howard's cabin might look like a hunting lodge, but it had all the conveniences of a military fortress. Nearly invisible electric fencing. High-tech security. Armed guards. He'd need to update his mother's security and the system at Dad's business when he returned to normal life.

Good thing he'd been able to check in via rerouted e-mail correspondence and relate his business dealings in Europe to his office manager. Having a plethora of techies at his disposal in their One Pure Nation ranks served him well.

Pulling up a new favorite Web site, Sean settled back into his ergonomic desk chair. Hanna Kessler's photography was breathtaking. Not that he had much use for such esoteric enjoyment of the arts, but while he researched her he couldn't help noticing the passion she applied to her work.

So much like him.

Sean laughed. Undoubtedly Hanna would disagree. Too bad she didn't know him better.

He clicked onto the section of portraits and scowled. That wretch of a mud race woman Hanna employed smiled back at him. As did her mixed-mutt child. Yet another example of the vile polluting of his pure race.

Disgusting.

He'd have to devise a way to teach them a lesson. Maybe add a little fear into Agent Parker's life too.

Killing two birds with one well-placed distraction elicited a smile.

Carl and Don lumbered into the lodge through the back entrance. He stopped clicking keys and listened. No female voices. Good. No one outside their immediate leadership needed access to their exact whereabouts.

"Hey, Reverend." Don's breath reeked all the way across the office.

"Go sleep it off, you fool."

The kid turned and bumped into the door frame a few times before disappearing down the hall. Seconds later a bedroom door slammed.

"Jane wanted to come stay with us. Said she'd cook and clean and make herself useful." Carl's tall and muscular form filled the doorway. Not intoxicated like his brother.

Sean hated that both younger men towered over him. But he still held the power. In the end, that's all that mattered.

"You told her no."

"Yeah." The downcast tone matched Carl's averted eyes. Was this trouble brewing?

"If you want to leave, do it now." Not that he'd let his protégé walk out. Carl would rest six feet under before Jane had any clue of his desertion.

Wide eyes snapped to attention. "No sir. I'm committed to our cause one hundred percent."

"Keep it that way."

Carl pulled up a chair and changed the subject. "Nice Web site. Little too pink for me, though."

Sean clicked on the photos of Hanna's wretched employee. "It's far too black for me."

Nodding, Carl glared at the screen. "What say I get some of our members itching for a little action and teach her a lesson she'll never forget?"

"Not yet."

"But we will?"

Eliminating Hanna's star employee wouldn't serve his purposes for the time being. Unfortunate. He hated leaving any of her kind alive. Especially the mutt child. That one he'd destroy himself. All in due time.

"Let's discuss some other options for the present."

By early morning they'd outlined the next course of action. Sean smiled. So simple. Yet so potent.

Hanna Kessler would see the error of her ways. Her FBI shadow would run off chasing ghosts in the wind. And that mud-race wretch and her spawn would never forget where they came from.

They might even send that sorry excuse for an FBI agent back to his pit.

Yes. His smile grew. Their idea could eliminate four targets at once. Perfect.

❈ ❈ ❈

Hanna snuggled down into Eve's couch Saturday night with Deni pressed close, her little hands spread around a big bowl of hot, buttery popcorn.

Grabbing a handful of crunchy comfort food, Hanna hugged the child closer. "I'm glad you changed your mind about a movie night."

"Trina said she'd be gone until Sunday night. And I figured letting some bigoted crazies ruin my weekend wasn't smart." Eve smiled. "Now, let's watch this movie that Deni promised would be awesome."

Lots of giggling and a little popcorn throwing later, all three sighed as the two green ogres shared true love's kiss.

"I love that part." Deni beamed at the television. What a hopeless romantic in a petite and way-too-young body.

Eve turned off the movie and a news report blared through the surround-sound speakers. The snapshot of Capitol Hill stole the air from Hanna's lungs. A small female reporter in a gorgeous teal suit stood on the steps, red hair blowing in the wind. "It appears Congressman Reeley has packed up his office for good. The Kentucky representative was filmed earlier today being escorted away by security."

The screen filled with Richard Reeley's angry face.

"Aides claim Reeley slipped into the building last night and left with numerous boxes containing every personal item not removed by federal authorities last month."

The reporter droned on, but Hanna couldn't think past the picture of that man still on the television.

Her stomach clenched into a rock-hard ball. *Oh God, make him go away.*

Eve pulled the DVD from the player. "Press wires are all buzzing about that creep's dirty dealings with little girls."

"What kinda stuff, Momma?" Deni licked her fingers after swallowing the last of the popcorn.

"Hey, baby girl. Why don't you take some dishes into the kitchen?"

"Yes ma'am." She huffed but obeyed.

Hanna's attention returned to the news reporter. "Allegations of Reeley's involvement in the brutal murder of a local Asian child and an online acquaintance of Reeley's forced the congressman to resign yesterday. Reeley issued a statement of innocence to the media but refused further comment."

Jaw muscles nearly cracking her teeth, Hanna slipped shaking hands under her legs. No way could she let Eve see her fall apart.

They both stared at the TV without comment. "Stay tuned for breaking news on the developing story. More details at eleven."

Deni flopped down beside her. "Wanna hear about my new boyfriend?" She smiled a look of innocence that threatened Hanna's hold on her emotions.

Eve turned off the TV and shook her head. "What did I tell you about calling some little kid your boyfriend? You're far too young for that kind of nonsense."

Eyes rolling, Deni shrugged. "He says he wants to marry me. And I let him kiss me yesterday. That means he's my boyfriend."

Hanna closed her eyes and blocked out the ensuing tense conversation between mom and daughter. She had to find a way to excuse herself and call Gracie before the tears started and her mouth spilled far too many details.

Avoiding any deep conversation with Gracie had been such a foolish choice given the mess Hanna was in. She needed her sister-in-law's prayers and guidance more than ever. Especially if her failure to turn Reeley in earlier caused the nightmare she'd just seen on TV.

"Sorry to interrupt, but I'll be back in a minute." She stumbled into the dark hall and locked herself in the tiny half bath. *Please let Gracie answer and not Steven.* Dialing Gracie's number with shaking hands, she sank to the floor.

"Hello, little sister. Not keeping Michael company tonight?" Steven chuckled.

Not funny. Michael's cancelled plans for this weekend still squeezed her insides into a knot of fear. Was he with Crystal again?

"You know I'm not." She wanted to light into him about his rotten sense of humor, but tears started escaping. She needed to get Gracie on the line before Steven figured everything out. "Can I please talk to my far nicer sister-in-law?"

Silence.

"Hanna, I'm sorry. I shouldn't tease you about Michael. I know our work schedule is hard to accept sometimes."

She nodded.

"Hanna?"

Deep breath. "It's okay. I just need to talk to Gracie. Can you get her?"

"After you tell me what's wrong." No laughter in his voice now. She hated the cop perceptiveness Steven, Michael, and Clint all sprang on her. But she couldn't give in this time. She had to talk to Michael before Steven. Or else Michael might start talking to Crystal again.

"Girl stuff." She swallowed the tears in her throat. More lies. Someday they had to stop. But today wasn't that day.

"Ah. I'm no good in that arena. Hang on a sec."

The background noises muffled a minute and then a woman's voice came through the phone line. "Hi, Hanna. Sorry you had to put up with Steven like that. He's incorrigible."

"I...I think it's my fault Reeley killed that little girl." Her throat ached and more tears spilled down her cheek. Her lungs burned.

Gracie gasped, then waited a minute before speaking. "Hanna, that's impossible. What that man did could never be your fault."

If only that were true. It was the same song and dance her counselor kept giving. *"Another person's actions aren't under your control."* Too bad reality didn't back that up.

"If I'd turned him in earlier, he might not have been free to…" She couldn't push more words past her constricted throat.

Gracie remained quiet for another minute. "Maybe you should talk to Steven. I'm sure he knows the exact dates and can put your fears to rest."

No. She had to talk to Michael first. Even Dr. Nations agreed. If Hanna was serious about a relationship with Michael, she needed to confide in him before her brother. Dr. Nations added that her dependence on Steven needed to transfer to God and not Michael, though. But she couldn't quite make that leap yet. Regardless, Michael needed her loyalty.

"I just need your prayers right now. There's a lot of thinking I have to do before I talk to Steven about this."

A long sigh answered her. "I am praying for you, Hanna. Every day. Would you mind if I prayed right now?"

"Please do."

Her sister-in-law sure could pray. Gracie's soft voice filled Hanna's ears with words of hope, peace, and strength. Too bad it all bounced off her heart and thudded around her mind.

"…Amen." Another long pause. "Are you sure you don't want to talk to Steven too?"

Hanna wiped the last of her tears and stood. Glancing in the mirror, she winced. It'd take gallons of ice water and buckets of makeup to get her out of this bathroom looking normal.

"No. Not tonight. And please…don't tell him what I said. I mean, I don't want you to lie or anything. Just tell him I wanted it kept between us. For now." Gracie wouldn't lie if her life depended on it. How far Hanna had fallen. And how much she had to learn from her picture-perfect sister-in-law.

"I'll honor your request, Hanna. I'm praying you'll change your mind, though. Your brother loves you and wants to help."

"I know. Give him my love."

They hung up, and she set to work erasing the shadows and streaks of dried tears distorting her face. She had to see Michael tonight.

It didn't matter that he was home working and it was well past proper visiting hours. If she hurried, she could spill everything to Michael and then get home before midnight, or long before that time if at all possible. Because nothing good happened after midnight. Not to her, anyway.

21

Michael checked the time on his computer screen. Eleven o'clock Saturday night. His father had been absent all day, golfing with General Yount. Probably hit a local pub with Department of Defense brass afterward and stayed well beyond an intelligent amount of brew. But maybe the colonel would exhaust himself and have to stay home tomorrow.

Not that breathing the same air would bring them any closer. No use dreaming about such a nonpossibility. Too bad nine-year-old-little-boy yearnings were hard to dismiss.

Champ flopped his chin onto Michael's knee. "Sorry there's no excitement tonight, buddy." He rubbed the dog's warm fur.

Soon the Lab grunted and made himself comfortable under the desk.

Returning to the computer screen, Michael scoured yet another deplorable white-pride site. These scumbags should all be stuffed behind iron bars. But the first amendment allowed them to spew their disgusting ideas with no legal constraints. Of course, those constraints, once executed, could be used against any section of the population.

The framers of the Constitution were right. So was the estimable former President Reagan when he said, "Without God, democracy will not and cannot long endure." Between the antireligion bias of the press and judiciary, jails filled to busting, and free-speech mongers spouting all manner of evil, democracy took hit after hit.

A loud knock at the door set Champ to barking. His father had a key. Who else would be banging the door down this late? Probably his father, wasted. What a cheery thought. Or it could be a kid playing pranks.

Champ at his side, Michael opened the door with a scowl, ready to wilt any prank player. Or his inebriated father.

"I…I'm sorry to bother you so late."

Hanna. Sniffling back tears. Wet splotches on the shoulders of her pink polo. What now?

Champ yipped a happy greeting and went up on his hind legs, starting to lick Hanna's face. Michael should be as accepting.

"Are you hurt?" Without thinking, he pulled her into his arms and scooted Champ away with his knee.

She stiffened.

Releasing her, he stepped back and closed the door. "Want something to drink?" Lame. But what could he do? Beyond holding her and asking about her counseling for the millionth time, he had no idea how to help. And right now he couldn't handle one more recap of Hanna's counseling.

She shook her head. "It's about Reeley."

Hearing that foul name and remembering the details of her molestation ripped him to shreds every time. He nodded toward the couch.

She clamped her mouth shut and sat down with clenched fists. Anger? It was about time. She'd claimed she wasn't angry at Reeley before. But how could she not be?

"I should have reported Reeley sooner. Now it's my fault he killed that poor little girl." She dissolved into tears.

He pulled her into his arms again and she tensed. But he held her anyway. Soon her shoulders relaxed and the tears subsided.

Reeley killed what little girl? Had he missed a case update tonight? Not likely. Then he remembered. News bulletins ticked across his mind. Reeley resigning. Veiled claims he killed Katrina Chu. Someone was leaking something to the media. Not a shocker. Wonder who?

Hanna stirred and her ragged breathing pricked his conscience. He needed to be more understanding. More patient. Her healing wouldn't happen on his timetable.

She pulled a Kleenex from her jeans pocket and wiped her nose.

"I…I wish I'd listened to you and reported Reeley sooner. Maybe then he wouldn't have killed that Asian child."

Not that Michael wouldn't like to pin a murder on Reeley, but there was no way that man could have killed Kat. The media snitch was more likely gunning for Reeley's congressional seat than leaking truth.

"Hanna, look at me." He tilted her chin up and wiped her tears with his thumbs.

A shiver wracked her body.

He ignored the longing look in Hanna's eyes and the jolt of electricity that zipped through him. "Reeley couldn't have committed that crime."

Nothing like a sicko's name to ice the moment.

"How do you know?" Her question was little more than a whisper.

"He was in Kentucky for summer district work." Trying to raise funding for an NCMEC branch in his home state. What a hypocrite. "We've verified his whereabouts. He couldn't have killed the little girl."

"You're sure?"

He nodded. "Absolutely."

"Oh." She slumped against him again. Willingly. That reality coursed though him.

"What brought all this up tonight?" Not that he minded seeing her, holding her, at all. He hated having to cancel another dinner date and hiking trip this weekend.

"I was at Eve's and saw the news. They think he did it."

"Media isn't known for its aboveboard investigative skills." He chuckled.

Hanna didn't. "I should give a statement. It's important, isn't it?"

He nodded. Steven could kill him later. Hanna needed to know the truth. Needed the empowerment of putting a nail in that pervert's coffin. Reeley didn't have the connections to send people after her for aiding the prosecution. She'd be safe. Michael would make sure of it.

"I promised I wouldn't push. And I won't." He brushed a hand through her soft blond hair. "I still think you need to know that your involvement will make the case against Reeley stronger."

"Steven says you can still send him to prison for a long time without it."

Maybe. More likely not. Reeley's slick lawyers would disprove the media hype about his connection to Kat's case. Then discount all the photos and videos as electronically generated too. A tactic that boiled Michael's blood.

"It's up to you, Hanna. I'm here for you no matter what you decide." He wanted to tell her again that he loved her, but he held his tongue. He'd said those words once before when she'd been crying over the situation with Reeley. No way would he let that happen again.

She reached up and rubbed a gentle hand over his stubble, gorgeous eyes scanning his face. "Thank you, Michael."

That simple gesture nearly broke his resolve. He wanted to kiss her and forget everything. His work. Reeley. Her past. But he wouldn't force himself on her. Not now. Not ever.

She dried her eyes with the back of her hand, then scooted closer. Before he could respond to the strong inclination to flee, Hanna pressed herself into him and kissed him with a passion he hadn't yet seen.

Every fiber of his being responded, deepening the kiss, pulling her closer. She didn't resist.

Running a hand down her back, he lifted her onto his lap.

The point of no return flew past without a sound.

※　※　※

Hanna laid back into the couch, pulling Michael with her, not releasing his lips and holding on to his academy shirt with all her strength. She didn't care where they were headed.

Champ's growl split the night.

Hanna couldn't move. Michael didn't either.

Then a door swung open and hit the wall. "What the devil is going on?"

Still pinned under Michael, she saw nothing. But a loud, slurred voice drew closer, freezing her to the spot. "I asked you a question, son. What harlot are you making out with now?" The words were so full of venom, she couldn't breathe.

Michael jumped off the couch. "How dare you."

Champ lunged forward, but Hanna snapped up and grabbed his collar, holding his growling body in front of her.

Harry stepped into view and shoved Michael. "You're the one sleeping around again."

Michael cocked his fist back and slammed it into his father's face.

Harry hit the floor and stayed down, blood seeping from his mouth.

Michael's curse crackled through the room as he stared at his father. Then he charged into the dark hallway.

She ran to Harry's side while Champ jumped around them. "Harry, are you all right?" Stupid question. Michael had hit him with enough force to break his jaw.

"I'll be fine." Less slurred, but still full of poison. He pulled himself to sitting and searched her face. Recognition widened his dark eyes. "I'm sorry, Hanna." Harry closed his eyes and groaned. "I had…no idea…it was you. You were…out with a friend." He wiped at the blood with his shaky right hand. "I didn't want my son…to return…to his old ways."

The man could barely catch his breath.

"Glad to know you believed in me." Michael stood over them, arms crossed, glaring and colder than ever before.

"He needs some ice. Please."

Michael waited half a beat and then disappeared into the kitchen. A minute later, he extended a bag of peas and a brown kitchen towel. "This is what Mom always gave me when I was in your position."

Harry winced but said nothing as she wrapped the towel around the bag and then touched it to his cheek.

Michael's dad had punched him like that before? Her heart squeezed and her hands shook. She had a hard time holding the frozen peas to Harry's jaw. He tried to help steady it.

"I'm...okay." Harry gasped and fought to inhale. His face drained of color and sweat beaded his forehead.

Then he grabbed his chest and groaned, dropping the towel and bag of peas.

"Harry. Harry are you okay?"

He slumped to the floor. She tried to catch him by the shoulders, but his size prevented her from doing much. Adrenaline surged as she shook him. "Harry! Wake up."

Wide-eyed, Michael joined her on the floor and pressed his fingers into his dad's neck. "Hanna, call 911."

She rushed to the cordless phone by the kitchen and yanked it from the base. *Oh, God, help us.*

"911, what's your emergency?"

She rattled off the symptoms she'd seen and Michael's address, praying they'd hurry. Listening to the operator's guttural instructions, she shouted them to Michael.

But he was already busy performing CPR.

Every time he checked for a breath and returned to pushing on Harry's sternum, her eyes watered more. How could things go this wrong, this fast?

Soon sirens filled the air. She hung up the phone and ran into the stairwell to direct the paramedics to Harry.

Two men, one short, the other tall, ran up the stairs carrying large boxes and a gurney between them. The younger, stocky one took over CPR for Michael. The taller one started an IV.

For a minute, Michael remained frozen on his knees beside the paramedics. She went to him and tugged on his arm, pulling him away so the men had room to work. Then she wrapped her arms around his waist.

"What have I done?" His voice scratched her soul like sandpaper.

"It's not your fault, Michael."

The paramedics lifted an unconscious Harry onto the gurney and raced toward the door. Michael's eyes stayed fixed on his dad, but he didn't budge. She nudged him away and pressed his wallet and cell phone into his hands. "Ride with them. I'll follow and meet you there."

He nodded and rushed out the door after them.

She grabbed Champ's collar again, shutting the apartment door before he could escape. Then she knelt and cried into his fur. "God, please don't let Harry die. Please show Michael the truth." Groans without words filled the rest of her plea. She had no idea the depth of pain both Michael and his dad held inside. But if Harry died...

"Please, God. Please..."

Champ licked her face. "Good boy. Let's get you into the kitchen with some food and water. I have no idea when they'll be home." Babbling while she worked, she filled Champ's bowls and bent down to give him one more hug. "I'll see you tomorrow. Be good."

Shutting the kitchen door, she took a deep breath. Then she grabbed her purse and left Michael's apartment, locking the door behind her.

Only God knew what was ahead. Too bad that brought little comfort.

❈　❈　❈

Hanna entered Alexandria Community Hospital's surgical ICU waiting room and held out a cup of steaming coffee. "Here." She grabbed Michael's arm with her other hand to still his pacing. "It'll help."

"No updates. It's taking way too long back there." He closed his eyes and took her offering. After a few deep breaths, he glanced around the deserted room and spoke again. "I'm sorry, Hanna. For everything. I was out of line. With you. With my father." Looking away, he took a drink that had to scald his insides all the way to his stomach. But he didn't flinch.

Her face reddened with the mention of where they'd almost gone tonight. All Michael's protection and keeping his distance hadn't prevented her from pushing too far. If Harry hadn't come home, she'd have trashed Michael's chivalry in one moment of overwhelming need.

Running to Michael instead of her family wasn't a good idea after all.

"Don't." He stood in front of her and lifted her chin. "It wasn't your fault. I'm responsible for where we go physically, and I failed. Can you forgive me?"

Tears threatened again. But she needed to be strong for Michael right now. "I forgive you. And I'm sorry too. It's just as much my fault. Forgive me?"

Sad eyes stared back at her. He nodded and turned away. "I called my mom. She's taking a red-eye from Tampa. Should be here in a few hours."

"I'll pick her up at the airport." She moved toward a row of chairs. "Why don't you catch some sleep?"

"Not without you getting some rest too." He pointed his stubbled chin toward her purse. "Call Sara and see if you can use her old office."

Glancing at her watch, she fought another yawn. "It's the middle of the night. I won't even call Steven at this hour."

"Then we'll both have to sleep here." He took her hand and led her to a corner of the room. Pulling a few cushioned chairs together, he made a semidecent sleeping place for them. Together.

"Maybe I should sleep over there." She backed toward the middle of the room.

His sad half smile tugged at her heart. "I won't repeat tonight's mistakes. And I promise not to drool on you either."

She wanted to laugh. Wanted to cry. But she did neither. Only collapsed into Michael's outstretched arms. Together they waited for information on his dad. News that could destroy the man she loved with a few words.

Praying herself to sleep, one thought pushed to the forefront. She wasn't the only one who needed healing from past wounds.

22

Michael stood to stretch. He yawned, looking over the still empty waiting room. Hanna had left to pick up his mother over an hour ago.

Pacing, he tried to unknot every muscle in his body.

What a way to introduce his mother to the woman he wanted to marry. In a hospital. Waiting to hear if he'd killed his father or not.

The punch hadn't caused his father's heart attack. But he'd never have leveled a blow if Mom had bothered to mention the colonel's severely blocked arteries before today.

Medical staff had contacted her for permissions regarding the cardiac bypass surgery. They'd shared little with him, and Mom even less. Even though he was flesh and blood.

Just like old times.

And he'd learned long ago that no news wasn't always good news.

Returning to his seat, images from yesterday flooded his mind. Kissing Hanna. Almost…he couldn't let his mind go there. Too heated. Too close. He banged the back of his head against the wall. No way could he let them get anywhere near that again.

Not before he put two rings on her finger. He smiled despite the circumstances. More sure than ever, he started a mental list of plans for popping the question. A long engagement he might survive.

Shifting in his chair caused his right hand to smart again. Why hadn't he used more self-control? That was the million dollar question for everything tonight. He had no answers. Just a ton of memories rushing in unchecked.

Mom holding bags of peas to his eyes and jaw. More often on his rib cage. Too many visible marks and someone might have figured things out. And his father couldn't be reported for child abuse. It would have ruined his career.

Who cared what it did to Michael?

Other snapshots piled over his growing up years. Pictures of kids his team had brought home. And those they'd found too late. Some beaten.

Some…like Mattie Reynolds. At least Michael's father hadn't done any more than hit him. Still, the little-boy groans inside begged for justice, for someone to know all that he'd gone through.

For some way to prevent people from hurting kids like that again.

He stared at his rough hands. Maybe it wasn't just shrinks who went into their field to fix themselves. Clint had been trying to make that point ever since Michael spilled a detail about his father's beatings.

He still longed to hear his father admit he'd been wrong. Apologize for all the pain. Maybe even listen to Michael tell him about God.

Before today, forgiveness hadn't been an issue. He'd forgiven his father. Or so he'd convinced himself. But the surge of justification and the heady taste of revenge after slugging the old man painted a different picture.

His stomach roiled.

No matter what, he wouldn't let the cycle continue. Hanna and their children deserved better than that. So did he.

A young brunette nurse stepped into the room. "Mr. Parker? Michael Parker?"

He stood on exhausted legs and moved forward. "Is my father out of surgery? Is he okay?" His voice sounded prepubescent.

"The surgery is finished, Mr. Parker. He's off pump and his heart is restarted." The nurse's name tag said Heidi Rey. "It shouldn't be too much longer before he's moved to the surgical ICU. Your father is doing well, and you did a great thing getting him such fast medical attention." She attempted a comforting smile. "We'll let you know as soon as possible when you can see him."

She left him alone with his thoughts once more.

Staring into the dark morning sky, he rehearsed what he'd say to his mother. How he'd explain without shaming Hanna. Without letting Mom know just how drunk his father had been.

"Michael Allen Parker."

No time left for practicing. He swallowed hard and turned around. Mom in a maroon warmup suit and no makeup startled him. So did her running toward him, throwing herself into his arms.

"Oh, Michael. Please tell me he's going to be okay."

"He's out of surgery, and the nurse said everything is fine." He held his mother's small, quaking frame in his arms and tried to control his quivering insides. If she'd arrived all self-composed in her normal Sunday dress and warm smile, he'd have held it together with far less trouble.

Hanna gave him a sad smile and hooked her thumb toward the entrance. "See you soon," she mouthed.

"Hanna." Not letting go of Mom, he held up a hand. "Are you going home?" He stopped short of begging her to stay.

Mom swiped at her eyes and stepped to his side. "This dear girl needs some sleep, son. I'm sure she'll return as soon as she can."

Hanna walked into his arms. "Yes. I will."

"Please keep praying." He buried his face into her rose-scented hair and breathed deeply. "I wish you didn't have to go."

With an unsteady inhale, Hanna pulled away and placed her hands on his chest. "I'll be back soon. Promise." She turned to Mom. "It was wonderful meeting you, Mrs. Parker. I wish it was under better circumstances."

"Please, call me Claire." She reached out and patted Hanna's arm. "You're a sweet girl. We'll talk again soon, when Harry and I can get to know you better...together."

"Yes ma'am."

Hanna walked out of the waiting room, waving over her shoulder before she disappeared.

He longed to run after her but, instead, turned to face his mother again. "Did Hanna tell you everything?"

"She said your father had come back to the apartment late, then collapsed from a heart attack." Mom's eyes watered. "That dear girl said you saved your father's life."

God bless Hanna. He'd put a ring on her hand today if possible. When she could have easily spilled everything, she'd protected him and even made him sound like a hero.

Wish that were true.

Mom took a seat and rested her head on the back of the chair. The silence hammered his conscience. He had to tell her what happened.

"Mrs. Parker?" Heidi, the young nurse, returned.

"Yes. Can I see Harry now?" Her voice and eyes begged for a drop of good news.

"He'll be moved to the surgical ICU soon."

Michael's heart thundered against his rib cage. This nightmare was almost over.

"The doctor will answer your questions when he joins you in the private consult area. If you'll follow me." Heidi turned on her heel and walked at a brisk pace.

He reached into his cargo pants expecting to connect with his Glock. But when his hand touched nothing but wallet, he remembered. He hadn't had time to grab it on the way out. And without Hanna, he'd be missing his wallet too.

Still, no gun. Not a pleasant thought.

But better than the one he'd almost unloaded on his mom. She didn't need to know what happened before his father's heart attack. They avoided talk about his father's abuse, so there was no reason to burden her now with more violence. The omission still twinged his conscience, though.

They reached the consult room and waited in silence. Decorators must have hoped the tan and blue décor would inspire calmness and peace. They failed.

His shoulders, back, and calves were nothing more than knots joining liquid bones. Still he paced and waited. Then waited and paced some more. Mom did much of the same.

Too many minutes later, a man of Middle Eastern descent entered the room. "I'm Dr. Fadil, Mr. Parker's cardiac surgeon." He motioned toward the chairs and table in the middle of the room. "Please come. Sit. We will discuss the surgery. Very good surgery, yes." The doctor's heavy accent distorted *v*'s into *w*'s.

"Is Harry going to be okay?"

Dr. Fadil gave a short bow. "I believe he will recover well."

Michael released a long breath while Mom melted against him, forehead still creased with concern.

Again the doctor pointed to the chairs. "Please."

They all took seats around the small table. Dr. Fadil described the last six hours of his father's life. Most of the time Michael could handle technical verbiage, but today he had trouble thinking his own name clearly. Too many late nights on top of everything else yesterday had thrown at him.

He caught words like "coronary artery bypass graft" and "on-pump surgery" as well as details about the severe blockages in three of his father's coronary arteries.

But more than the severity of the doctor's details, his mother's words rocked him to the core. "Yes, doctor. I understand why you did what you had to do. Harry has known about the problem for years but refused to do more than take his medications."

What? Michael leaned forward. Why didn't he know about that? And why hadn't he seen his father taking any medications? "Doctor, did drinking exacerbate my father's condition?"

"Michael, hold your tongue." Her sharp look held more fear than censure.

The doctor glanced between him and his mother for a long minute. "Studies have shown very moderate alcohol consumption is associated with a reduced risk of heart attack. But in your father's case, I do not believe his drinking was beneficial." Talk about an understatement. The doctor paused and studied Mom. "I must tell you that based on Mr. Parker's blood-alcohol levels, it is our medical recommendation that Mr. Parker speak with someone about his drinking habits and—"

Mom sat up board straight, raising a hand to stop the doctor. "We appreciate your concern, but Harry doesn't have a problem with alcohol."

Nodding, Dr. Fadil returned to his previous recommendation. "It remains our wish that you consider rehabilitation."

"We'll do all we can to help Harry recover. But my husband is a social drinker. Nothing more."

His father's blood alcohol count had to have been sky high when they arrived by ambulance. And that wasn't the first time. But his mother's denial shut down any further discussion of his father's alcoholism. A fact Michael had lived with since middle school. Oh, his father hid it well in the social-drinking culture they'd lived in. Never more than a few drinks. At least not in front of friends.

What happened behind closed doors was often a far cry from public impressions.

Mom and Dr. Fadil returned to the discussion of his father's recovery as if Michael weren't there.

"Mr. Parker will remain in the ICU for one, maybe two days. We will watch closely his improvement. Then, he will be moved to a regular room for three to five days."

"Thank you, Doctor. When may I see him?"

Dr. Fadil stood and bowed his head again. "Is not a good idea at this moment. He was fighting the ventilator and required sedation." He blinked at the wall clock. "After we extubate, then we send for you, okay?"

"How long will that be?"

"A few more hours, maybe."

Mom wilted and Michael put his arm around her. "That long?" She took a deep breath. "Well, whatever you say is best, Doctor. Thank you for all you've done. For keeping Harry alive."

"You are welcome. Ma'am. Mr. Parker." With that the doctor disappeared around the corner.

Michael hated being called Mr. Parker. That was his father's name.

"Son, you'd better get some sleep while you can. I imagine you won't be able to take much time off."

More like no time off. Not with his assignment to the task force. He couldn't imagine asking the dragon lady for a break. But he still needed to call Steven and see what kind of hours he could spend at the hospital.

After leaving a message for Steven and Clint, he closed his eyes and tried to rest. When would Hanna get back?

And what would he say when he faced his father once again?

❋   ❋   ❋

Michael ignored the call from Crystal and turned off his phone. News traveled way too fast around the federal water cooler. More like the Internet. It didn't matter. He'd already talked to Hanna and she was on her way back, bringing a change of clothes and some toiletries.

Without her visit on the horizon, he'd have never managed the last four hours. Delays and his mom's nail biting coupled with her constant chatter about weather, her flower garden, and all the home-improvement projects she and his father would do this winter left him on edge.

After a brief visit to his father's bedside, Mom's face was ashen when she returned to the surgical ICU waiting room.

"Is he doing okay?" Stupid question. He was in the ICU, for crying out loud.

"He's still very groggy. The nurses say he's doing fine. But all the wires and beeping things…" She took a seat next to him and sighed like she was a hundred years old. "They scare me."

Half an hour later the morning-shift nurse returned. Karen Kaiser or something like that. Nice lady. Gentle voice. "Mr. Parker, if you'd like to spend a few minutes with your dad, now's the time."

And if he didn't?

His conscience pricked and guilt rushed in. He shook it away and followed her into a room filled with more electronics than his favorite computer store. And none of them made a lick of sense. They beeped and whooshed and hopefully kept his father alive. Maybe even asleep long enough for him to say what he needed to say.

Ten hours in hospital waiting rooms did strange things to a soul. Like bring conviction screaming through his spirit. And rip away another layer of unforgiveness. He didn't want his father to die. What he wanted most was acceptance from the one man he could never please.

"Father. I…" He wanted to call him Dad like Hanna addressed her father and like Steven's and Clint's sons addressed them. But he'd never called Harry Parker by anything other than Colonel or sir. Sometimes Father.

Seconds slipped away. He'd best speak his piece and then find a quiet place to regroup before meeting Hanna.

"I was wrong to hit you last night. Wrong to hate you for so much of my life. I love you." He swallowed the lump of emotions lodged in his throat. "And I hate what you saw in me. I've asked Hanna to forgive me. Now I'm asking your forgiveness. For disrespecting you. I…"

His father stirred and the beeping machines increased in volume, but the man in the bed didn't awaken. And no one came running. Maybe he'd said enough. Yeah. He'd shared all God had put on his heart to say.

He walked away from the bed and out the door without looking behind. Nodding as he walked past the nurse's station, he made his way to the waiting room to speak to Mom before heading downstairs to meet Hanna.

Minutes later, he paced by the hospital's main entrance. Sunlight streamed through the windows. Visitors and hospital employees hurried through the large glass doors and horns honked outside. Life droned on without so much as a pause.

"Michael. There you are. I've been looking for you forever." Crystal. In a tight-fitting jogging suit. Not Hanna. So not good.

"I'm waiting for Hanna."

Crystal stayed a normal distance away and didn't touch his arm. That was new. "I just wanted you to know I'm…" She studied her running shoes for a second. "I'm praying for you. Our talk last week meant a lot to me."

He blinked. It had? She'd listened? Maybe he'd been too quick to jump to conclusions about her intentions.

"Thank you for your prayers. My father's doing okay."

She nodded toward the cafeteria sign. "Why don't we grab a cup of coffee? My treat."

Tempting. The coffee, anyway. But not a good idea.

"You're waiting for Hanna." Crystal's dark eyes told the story he'd failed to confront. She'd fallen for him, and he'd done little in the beginning to protect against that. "She's one lucky lady."

Someone cleared her throat near them.

He turned and met Hanna's questioning eyes, noted the slump of her shoulders.

"Here are your clothes, Michael." Hanna held out a small backpack. "I'll go check on your mom." She darted toward the elevators.

Crystal bit the inside of her lip but said nothing.

He caught up with Hanna in two strides and put a hand on her shoulder. She stopped but wouldn't meet his eyes. "I don't know what you're thinking, but I was waiting for you. Please." He took her hand. "I need you. Stay with me."

She nodded and let him lead her back to where Crystal stood waiting. "Hanna, this is my co-worker Crystal Hernandez. Crystal, this is Hanna." *The woman I'm gonna marry.* He shifted between tired feet.

Hanna stuck out a hand, facial features pinched into a smile. This was such a bad idea. "Nice to meet you, Crystal. Next time you're near Grounded, you should stop in for some coffee. My treat."

So his Hanna had claws after all. He almost chuckled. Almost.

Red tinged Crystal's cheeks. Strange. She wasn't the blushing type.

"I'll do that." Crystal stepped back. "Well, I guess I should go now. Hope your father is released soon, Michael. Good to meet you, Hanna." Crystal turned and walked out the hospital's front doors.

"That was pleasant." Hanna's eyes stayed glued to Crystal's exit.

"I didn't know she was coming."

She turned and searched his face. "I believe you. But I don't want to walk into another scene like that ever again."

"You won't." Right then and there he made a pact with himself. He'd never allow another female close enough to give Hanna any reason to doubt his intentions.

And he'd go ring shopping sooner rather than later.

23

Hanna towel dried her hair early Monday morning. She'd spent all day Sunday with Michael and Claire, leaving her no time to process what happened with Michael Saturday night. Or Harry's heart attack.

Picking up the hair dryer with unsteady hands, she tried to ignore the avalanche of questions fighting for attention. But the noise wouldn't drown out her thoughts. Why didn't God turn down the heat? Or make life move slower and stop thrashing her? She'd been back in Alexandria a little over a month, but she'd already confronted her past, submitted an anonymous tip about Reeley, started counseling, and almost seduced Michael.

What was she thinking?

With a growing headache, she finished drying her hair and stared at the mirror. Deep breathing helped settle her quivering hands. A little.

Truth be told, her behavior with Michael shouted that she wasn't thinking. At least not about how much she loved him. Her desperate desire to forget the past had taken her too close to the mistakes she'd sworn not to repeat. Especially not with Michael.

Applying her makeup didn't lessen the crimson memories scorching her cheeks.

It didn't help that she still wasn't praying enough or transferring her dependence from Steven and Michael to God. Would she ever learn?

A strong urge to pray for Michael washed over her. She checked the bathroom clock. Eight thirty. Michael would be back to work on the terrorism task force, hunting the man she'd caught a glimpse of in her parking lot last month.

No time for him to process his dad's heart attack either.

"Please, God, help Michael heal. Help him catch that awful man. The one killing people just because they aren't white." She shuddered. How could anyone do that? "Keep Eve, Deni, and Lee safe. And Harry. Please heal Harry's heart, physically and emotionally."

She wanted to ask for help in staying pure too, but she couldn't bring herself to say it out loud. So she silently begged God to keep her from tempting Michael. Because regardless of what Michael said, it'd be her fault if anything physical happened between them.

Instead of dwelling on that, she prayed while she got dressed that God would show her ways to stay strong and help Michael in any way she could.

A knock on her front door stopped her prayer time short.

It also kicked her heart into her throat. Who'd be banging on her door before nine in the morning? She fastened the last button on her rose-colored dress with nervous hands. Eve had said this shade was her best color. She wished Eve were here with her now. Or Gracie. Or Sara. She let her mind travel, hoping the person at her door would go away.

Unfortunately, she wouldn't be seeing Sara at her apartment anytime soon. Her friend was due any day and not out and about much. Hanna slipped in a prayer for Conor's safe birth as she clasped her silver watch in place and then picked up the purity ring Dad had given her on her thirteenth birthday.

The one she'd stopped wearing in college.

Before more tormenting memories began, she stepped into the bedroom and planted herself in front of the full-length antique mirror. "I will not return to that behavior. That is not who I am." While practicing her counselor's positive self-talk homework, she forced a smile and shoved the purity ring onto her left hand. There it would stay until Michael offered a fitting substitute.

The knocking at the door started again.

Marching to the door, she was ready to tell whoever it was to go away. She only had a few minutes until she needed to leave for her counseling appointment. Then a full day of work at Grounded and a full night at the hospital with Michael and Claire.

Tiredness dogged her heels.

Through the peephole, she couldn't make out many details of the bothersome visitor. Only that it was a short man with salt and pepper hair. Harmless.

Opening the door but leaving the security chain in place, she cleared her throat. "If you're selling something, I'm not interested."

The older man smiled and lifted his hands in surrender. "Nothing to sell. I just need a few moments of your time to talk about allegations concerning Congressman Reeley."

Fear clamped a hand around her throat. "Are you a reporter?"

"No ma'am."

Who else would know about her tip? Her dad didn't. She'd only cried her eyes out to Steven, Gracie, Clint, Sara, and Michael. Dr. Nations couldn't tell anyone.

Pushing words through her quivery vocal cords proved difficult. "Who…who are you?"

"I have nothing to gain by hurting you." The man glanced back toward the parking lot. "I only want to talk to you about Congressman Reeley."

"There's nothing to discuss." White fingers clamped the door and kept her from fainting. She couldn't do this today. So she tried to push it all away with a closed door.

But the short man stuck his foot in her way. Then a taller, muscular man stepped into view.

Ice replaced the blood draining from her body.

This person was all too familiar. His distinguished features, black hair, and crisp gray suit belied his evil interior. "Please, Hanna. We need to talk."

She wanted to scream. Run. Hide. But she couldn't move.

Not even when Reeley and the stranger shoved the door open, ripping the security chain from the wall.

❈ ❈ ❈

Richard scooted Hanna's shaking form aside and closed the door as soon
as George entered. No need to alert the neighbors.

Thankfully, there had been no movement for over an hour in the
dwellings on either side of Hanna's home. No one to report their little
visit.

Hanna's home. He was standing inside his beautiful one's house,
looking down on her one last time. Too bad she'd outgrown the perfect beauty she'd once possessed. A thrill shot through him at the
memory. Then fear trailed it. One wrong move and everything he'd
worked for would disappear. Forever. That wasn't acceptable. This had
to work.

George entered the living room area and closed the curtains.
Not moving at all, Hanna stayed rooted to the entryway's wooden
floor.

She was scared. More like terrified. Perfect.

All he wanted was to remind her of what had really happened.
Confuse her if necessary. He'd need that edge if his case ever went to
trial. But his mind couldn't focus beyond the shadows of the past. Her
beautiful golden hair in pigtails. Her soft, innocent eyes.

His district office in Kentucky flashed through his mind.

Focus. Convince her to remain silent once again and leave quickly.

"I wish you'd trust me, Hanna. I've never hurt you before."

Her frozen body shivered and her beautiful blue eyes widened.
"How can you say that?"

Nothing more than a whisper. He had her right where he wanted
her. Afraid. Unsure. "I know you've taken childish memories of your
attraction to me and made them more than what they were."

She gasped as if he'd slapped her. Something he'd never do.

He stepped closer again, almost touching her. She was no longer the
beautiful little innocent he'd given his heart to. But she was still attractive. Far more than any other he'd known.

"You understand how important it is to clear up this misunderstanding." He wanted to touch her so badly his arms ached. "All you have to do is admit you came on to me but it amounted to nothing."

"I didn't." The childlike quiver of her voice belied her more grownup words.

The situation continued to improve. The more her fear grew, the more likely she'd forget. Never speak a word. Just like she'd done for over twenty years.

"I know you haven't given your name in connection to the Cyber-Tip." His jaw tightened, and he hoped his bluff proved true. "I know you don't want to destroy the good work I've done for Kentucky as your congressman." Keeping his breathing level, he moved even closer. "We can all forget this little misunderstanding. Can't we, Beautiful One?"

George chuckled and looked out the living room curtains. Hanna still didn't move.

"Leave. Or I'll call the police."

Again, little more than a whisper. But she had more fight than the last time they'd been this close. Then she'd remained frozen. Now she was thawing.

He needed to hurry. "I'll leave as soon as we agree on what happened all those years ago."

"You raped me."

Richard shuddered at the ugly and untrue accusation. "No, Hanna. I kissed you. Touched your beautiful hair." He reached out and stroked her blond tresses.

She slapped his hand away.

"My, my, but you've grown touchy." Grabbing her hand, he exerted some gentle pressure. Enough to remind her who was in control. "You were six, Hanna. Far too young to understand your inner urges. All I did was respond to your advances. And then send you home with some warm cookies. You remember those, don't you? The ones you snuck in my house to steal?"

Hanna's entire body convulsed.

"Isn't that right?"

George stood behind Hanna and moved his head side to side. As usual, his older brother was right. Force wouldn't work in this situation.

Richard released Hanna's hand and stepped back. "My apologies, Beautiful One. No need to be afraid."

She wiped tears away with the backs of her hands.

He swallowed hard. "The media and FBI are trying to pin a murder on me, Hanna. Your accusations add fuel to this fire. A fire you started by wrongly accusing me."

"They know you didn't kill that little girl."

She was back to whispering. And offering him good news.

"I'm relieved they know the truth about that situation. So all you need to do now is what you've done since our last meeting. Forget. Be a good girl. You'll do that, won't you? For me?"

Hanna's growl startled him. Then she lunged in his direction. And connected with a stinging slap on his left cheek.

He caught her wrist again. "Oh, no, Beautiful One. None of that."

George grabbed Hanna's shoulders and shoved her away from the door. "You've no business treating an elected official like that, young lady. You should be ashamed." He pointed to the door. "We'll be leaving now, so you can't attack the congressman again."

Richard allowed George to disappear through the door, pausing before he followed. "Please, Hanna. It's best for everyone if we leave the past in the past. Think of your father. Andrew would be crushed. So be a good girl, Hanna. I know you will."

She made no move, no sound. So he closed the door for her and strolled to the rental car.

Judging from the little girl fear still strong in her pretty blue eyes, she'd do the right thing. Forget. Keep silent. Just like before.

And he'd be back on the Hill in no time.

※   ※   ※

Hanna leaned back from the kitchen sink and wiped the remains of her partially digested breakfast from her mouth.

Oh, God, why this?

How could she ever put her name to the anonymous tip she'd given? She'd never win against a powerful congressman. No one beyond her family would believe her story.

A Bible verse from her reading last week flitted across her mind. One she'd found for Michael. *"Do justice, love kindness, and walk humbly with your God."*

What was justice here? Her hiding? No.

She still didn't know what to do.

Michael's fierce words against Reeley filled her thoughts. The FBI had far more on the man than her tip. But her victim impact statement and identifying him from *America's Most Wanted* would help. Reeley had to know that. Why else would he have shown up at her door trying to intimidate her?

Her skin crawled with the memory of his hands on her wrists. His lies.

Rage rocketed through her limbs.

She'd call Michael and tell him what Reeley had done. Give her statement to the Innocent Images people. Her broken security chain was proof positive of Reeley's guilt. He wouldn't get away this time.

Another verse slipped into her mind before she could carry out her plan. *"Trust in the Lord with all your heart; do not depend on your own understanding."*

Or anger. She didn't want to take up Michael or Steven's rage. Or give full vent to her own.

All the emotions shooting through her confused her more. What was justice? And what did trusting the Lord mean in this situation?

Dad's wise and gentle eyes came to mind. He'd know. Better than Michael. Even better than Steven. Dad would know exactly what to do.

She hoped calling her dad wasn't going against God's command to depend on Him alone.

Because right now she couldn't hear anything over the rush of emotions, memories, and Bible verses flinging around her brain.

Dad would help her sort it all out.

And he'd believe her over Reeley. The image of that man's lying face made her want to spit. Her dad would choose her over that awful man any day. He had to.

She grabbed the phone and punched the number one speed dial. Two rings...

"Hey there, honey. I was just thinking about you." Dad's voice soothed her frazzled nerves. She swallowed back tears.

"I...I need to talk to you." She glanced at her watch. Twenty minutes until her counseling appointment meant she needed to hurry. "Can you meet me at Grounded for lunch?"

"Are you okay, sweetheart? I can be over to your place in fifteen minutes."

Dad had always been her hero, the first one to rush in and hold her when she got hurt. The one who wanted to storm the school when someone bullied her on the playground. Mom had balanced him with her own calmer form of wisdom. Pray first and then act.

What she wouldn't give to have them both here right now.

But Mom was gone. And what Hanna needed was her dad's fast action and sharp thinking skills. Something she sorely lacked at present.

"I need to leave in a minute." How could she tell him about her counseling over the phone? She took a deep breath. "I have a counseling appointment in a little while, and then I'm going straight to work. Please, can you meet me for lunch?"

"Counseling? Hanna, what's going on? Why are you going to counseling?"

The quiver in her dad's voice hurt her heart. She should have told him sooner. Twenty years ago, in fact. If only she'd done that. What mountains of pain she could have avoided.

"I'll explain at lunch. Please pray, Daddy. I need your help." She sniffled back another torrent of tears. "I'm sorry I didn't tell you before, but I will now. At lunch. Please."

Silence.

"Okay, honey. I'm praying. And I'll see you in a few hours."

She hung up the phone and tried to pray. *Please, God...* But she had no idea how to finish that prayer.

24

Hanna's counseling appointment came and went faster than the traffic pouring around her this sunny October day. Dr. Nations had agreed with Hanna's decision to tell Dad everything about Reeley. And to involve law enforcement.

Dr. Nations had even said the anger Hanna exhibited today was healthy. Michael would agree. So would Steven.

She didn't know if God would. Maybe, when it came to what Reeley did. But not to the revenge fantasies she'd begun to harbor.

Pulling into the employee parking area at Union Station, she turned off the engine and took a few minutes to just breathe and compose herself. Touch up her makeup.

Today stretched before her long and taut, like a rubber band ready to snap.

At least Eve would be working with her today. Her friend's cheery voice and bright smile would chase away the ghosts from her past. At least for a little bit. Until she resurrected the whole ugly mess of them with her dad.

She exited her Equinox and pushed the lock button. After a brisk walk in the not-so-fresh DC air, Union Station greeted her with a rush of activity and the warm smells of coffee, cinnamon rolls, and too many perfumes to distinguish.

"Hey, Hanna. You're here early." Eve smiled as she gathered a jean-clad young man's turkey club and large house blend.

"Hi, Eve." She stepped behind the counter and walked toward her office. "Hi, Becky." She waved to the younger girl, busy at the other register. "I'll be in the back for a little while. Call me if you need me."

Becky held up a hand. "Hang on, Hanna. Just wanted to let you know that your dad is in the office. Said he'd be going over paperwork until you arrived."

Hanna tried to swallow the lump of nerves racing up her throat.

A young couple stepped to Becky's cash register and gave their orders. A perfect opportunity to escape. But she wasn't prepared to face Dad yet.

She should have known he and Steven had the same penchant for arriving earlier than expected. A few more deep breaths and she was ready. Sort of. A tremor spread through her arms. Trying to control it, she walked into the storage area and then turned the doorknob to enter her office.

Dad looked up from her desk, shrugging. "Work helps the time pass." He stepped toward the door and enveloped her in a hug.

No knee-jerk response to steel her shoulders and run away. Progress.

After twenty-plus years of hiding, she'd come a long way. Just like Dr. Nations had said today. Michael, Steven, Gracie, Clint, and Sara would echo the doctor's sentiments.

No doubt their prayers and support had a lot to do with her starting to heal from her past.

Now she had to tell her dad.

He pulled back from his hug, keeping his hands resting on her shoulders. "Does your counseling have anything to do with the TV show that upset you back in August?"

The slight gray in his brown hair was more pronounced than before. She sighed and moved to her desk chair. "Why don't we sit down before I get into it?"

They both sat, Dad leaning forward with his knees touching hers. "That man on the show wasn't someone who hurt your friend, was he?"

Swallowing the lump of fear lodged in her throat, she shook her head.

"It was you?" The words were little more than a whispered groan. She nodded.

"Oh, Father, forgive me for not knowing." He started to tear up.

"I'm so sorry, Hanna. My Hanna-girl. I'm so sorry."

She threw her arms around her dad. "It's not your fault, Daddy. I should have told you. You didn't know."

He cleared his throat and guided her back into the desk chair. "You shouldn't be consoling me, honey. You were the one who was hurt. I…I'm here to help you now."

How could she tell him the details without shattering his heart?

Dad gently lifted her chin and forced her to meet his wet, pleading eyes. "Who was it? Who hurt you, Hanna?"

Breathing became difficult. No avoiding the truth any longer. And no way she'd lie now. "It was our next-door neighbor." She rushed on without taking another breath. "I snuck into his house before I finished his yard work. To get a cookie. I didn't mean to and I knew it was wrong. But I did it. Then he sounded hurt in the back of the house. So I went to see what was wrong…"

The tightness in her chest almost suffocated her. Red faced, Dad started to speak.

She held up a hand. "Please. Let me get this out before I lose my nerve." Choking down the bile in her throat, she forced the words out. "He told me I came on to him. That you'd believe him and not me. He threatened to hurt Steven and Mom. So I couldn't tell you. I couldn't tell you that Mr. Reeley…that he…forced himself on me and…"

Dad clutched his stomach. Then he shot up out of his chair so fast it clattered on the floor. "That…that monster. I'll shoot him, Hanna. Or kill him with my bare hands. How dare he hurt my baby? How dare he lie and say I'd blame you or doubt you? How could he… Oh, Hanna. Oh, Lord, how could I let this happen?"

Tears spilled from her eyes and her whole body shook. More raging words about killing Reeley filled the little office as Dad paced. He turned to face her and froze.

"Daddy."

Gathering her into his arms, he rocked back and forth. "I won't kill him, Hanna-girl. I won't. But I want to. God forgive me, I want to."

So unlike her father. But his anger, his wanting to kill the man who'd stolen so much from her, it healed something deep in her heart. Her daddy believed her. It wasn't her fault. It really wasn't.

A knock at the door and Eve's barreling through it startled Hanna and she jumped. Dad steadied her and waited for Eve to speak.

Eve held out a large padded mailer, hands trembling. "I…it…oh, God, help me now."

Hanna rounded the desk and hurried to Eve's side. Her dad did too. "What's wrong?"

"Th…th…this." Eve dropped the envelope and pictures splayed everywhere. "It was addressed to me. Came in today's mail. I didn't think…" The young woman pressed her dark hands to her face and wept.

Dad held her.

Hanna bent to retrieve the pictures. One glance and all the blood drained from her head. She couldn't think. Couldn't speak.

In her shaking hands was a picture that no one should ever have to see.

She coughed and tried to hold back the acid clawing up her throat. "Hanna?"

Dad took the envelope and the pictures she'd gathered. "Dear Jesus in heaven." He scanned the envelope. "No return address. I'm calling Steven right now."

He hustled to the phone. Hanna pulled Eve into her arms. "I'm so sorry, Eve. I wish you'd never had to see that."

She closed her eyes, trying to shut out the awful picture. But it was branded into her memory forever. A large oak tree with three limp bodies hanging from its limbs, distorted faces still discernable.

Eve's. Denisha's. And Lee Branson's.

❆   ❆   ❆

Steven entered Grounded via the delivery doors, Philip Walters close on his heels. The memory of Dad's phone call and photoshopped picture description still churned his stomach.

"Not sure what all I can do here, Steven. But I'm glad to help in any way I can." Philip nodded to the group by Hanna's desk and went right to work.

"Dad. Hanna. Evelyn. I'm sorry you had to see those photographs." He nodded toward Walters. "Philip is an Evidence Response Team leader and also a huge photography buff. He'll take a look around and hand deliver the evidence collected to the FBI lab. We'll find whoever sent these."

"Who would do something like this, son?" Dad held a trembling Hanna and an equally unhinged Evelyn in his arms.

"Don't know. But I have some good guesses." Shaking his head at his father, he pulled out a pen and notepad. "Evelyn, I hate to do this, but I have a few questions for you."

"I'm okay. I'll answer whatever I can." She stepped away from Hanna's desk and walked over to where Philip was cataloging evidence.

"Who delivered the mailer today?"

"Our regular mailman. I'm not sure what his name is."

Dad answered, clicking keys on Hanna's computer. "That'd be Gerald Little. He's worked at Union Station for years. I'll get his contact information for you."

"Thanks." Steven jotted a few notes. "Anything out of the ordinary about the delivery? Different time, more or less volume of mail?"

"No. Just the package addressed to me. I...I didn't even realize there was no return address until Mr. Kessler mentioned it."

"Did anyone besides you three touch it?"

"No." She studied her black boots.

"Have you had any threats like this at home?"

Evelyn snapped her head up. "No sir. Nothing like this. Not since we moved to DC."

Steven raised his eyebrows. "And before that?"

"There was some trouble with my boyfriend's family in Virginia. But that was before Denisha was born. Nine years ago."

"Any violence?" He hated this line of questioning. Hated the answers even more.

"Yes. They…umm…they attacked my sister. Graffiti on my parents' house and bakery. Our car windows busted." Evelyn's eyes clouded over and she steeled her shoulders. "But nothing was ever done about it. No one caught."

He sighed. Too many demented minds and not enough cops or prisons to handle them all. "I'm sorry. Can you give me a list of names? The people you suspect were involved?"

"Yes. But please don't open an investigation about all that. My sister wouldn't press any charges before and she won't now. I…I'm sure Trey's family and friends aren't behind this." She sniffled. "When Agent Branson has come in for lunch with Michael, he's talked about being from Louisiana, anyway. So it can't be Trey's family."

Evelyn's words rang with equal parts fear and truth. No two-bit punks with egos and idiocy bigger than their brains would have the means or the gumption to involve a federal agent in a personal vendetta.

And he'd have no case against them without Evelyn's and her sister's sworn statements. But he did have a strong hunch about who was behind these doctored photos.

He finished his questions with Evelyn and made a few more notes as Dad and Hanna added additional information. Philip gathered his supplies and bagged evidence, then stood by the back door.

Quick good-byes to his family set Steven further on edge. Something besides the photos had Dad and Hanna acting funny. He'd have to deal with that tonight. For now he had a skinhead to find.

He and Philip left Union Station with little conversation. One thing for sure, Lee didn't need to see these photographs. Steven would make that clear to Michael when submitting this evidence to the terrorism task force.

If there was any upside to this mess, it was that Michael's obsession with Haines just received a leg up and some cold, hard facts not tied to some stupid poisonous tree doctrine. That legal roadblock and false claims of coercion wouldn't protect Haines this time.

Not when the fool hadn't bothered to change the background from the photo they'd seen on his computer months ago. The same oak tree and old barn said Haines was sending them yet another message. One that could hang him in the end.

No one ever said criminals were smart. Good thing. It gave him hope they'd cuff and stuff Haines before too long.

❋ ❋ ❋

Michael paced the empty task force briefing room Tuesday morning, TVs still blaring repeated news feeds of last night's shootings. New to the media was old information to him after the all-nighter he'd just pulled.

If not for Hanna's promise to meet him in the lobby two hours from now, he'd have gone ballistic and never come back from her news of Reeley's break-in. Even with the call into work, he wanted to leave his badge at home and beat Reeley all the way to the slammer. Or worse.

Clenched hands and sore jaw said he hadn't let it go.

He stopped pacing and rolled his neck to work out the kinks.

His father remaining in the surgical ICU because of unexplained tachycardia and the CT scan confirming a mild stroke hadn't helped his stress level. Not being able to do anything for his father and Mom's assurances she had everything under control only added to his guilt.

But instead of work action to dissipate the extra adrenaline, he'd had to bottle his rage and spend the night watch with the terrorism task force. At least it'd kept his mind busy.

Not busy enough, though.

Curse words flew through his brain as he pictured strangling Reeley again. How dare that pervert threaten Hanna? But they'd nail him. Hanna's statement to the Innocent Images people today would go a long way in putting that wretch behind bars for good. Even Steven agreed with him now. Remembering the tears from everyone in Hanna's family yesterday evening, he stopped and prayed. Tried to pray anyway. Something that grew harder with each passing day.

Hanna's dad wasn't handling the truth about Reeley any better than Michael or Steven had. They all wanted to do more than send him to prison. But justice would win this time. Prison would take care of Reeley and leave his blood on someone else's hands.

Now they just had to find Haines. Then Katrina Chu's death could be avenged and Lee, Eve, Denisha, and Hanna kept safe. Not to mention the others Haines would keep trying to kill.

Memories of the pictures Haines sent to Eve at Grounded made Michael want to puke all over again.

Without warning, he sensed the dragon lady's presence before Sonja Foster ever opened her mouth.

"So nice of you to arrive early today, Parker." She dropped an armload of papers onto the podium. "But the meeting won't begin for another thirty minutes." Foster's red nails and lipstick highlighted the tight-fitting black suit she wore.

"I wanted to speak with you in private first."

She looked him up and down. "I wonder if this assignment just got too personal for you to be of any good to the terrorism task force."

"You need me on this team."

Eyebrows raised, a slow grin spread across her face. "Do tell." She raised a hand. "But before you state your case, let me warn you. The photographic evidence is not definitive proof that Sean Haines is the man our task force is looking for."

He crossed his arms, his black suit straining at the shoulders. "Combined with all the data I've amassed, it gives a pretty definite trail of guilt."

She scowled. "No one has uncovered rosters or meeting places for any of One Pure Nation's cell groups."

He hid a grin. No way could the dragon lady discount all the evidence he'd compiled this past week. Something her team hadn't even begun to do before he joined them. "The message boards I've decoded give clear proof of Haines's leadership, naming him as the mastermind behind yesterday's string of shootings. And connecting him to the two Asian women killed September seventeenth as well as the killings September twenty-ninth."

"Gunning for an award or a promotion?" Foster crossed her arms, mimicking his stance.

"Neither. Justice. Haines is behind all the recent racial killings, and the Chu murder the CACU is still working. I want to see him behind bars."

"Not dead? I pegged you for a shoot-to-kill-and-ask-questions-later kind of guy."

Not unless necessary. One round with deadly force this year was enough. He'd just completed mandatory visits with the FBI shrink. No way did he want back on that guy's couch anytime soon.

"I'll admit, the evidence you've logged on Haines is convincing. Especially the slipping of names all over the Internet last night after Indianapolis, Michigan, and New Jersey were hit by bigots' bullets."

Fifteen more dead. And hundreds of FBI, homeland security, and CIA agents onboard with terrorism task forces across the US. Not to mention all the other law enforcement agencies getting involved.

"The problem is we don't have direct forensic evidence, nor do we know where Haines, Shale, or the rest are holing up. We haven't even tracked down the actual shooters yet."

"We will." Even with the forensic nightmares a multiple jurisdiction investigation entailed. "Haines isn't finished yet. He'll make a mistake soon."

Foster narrowed her eyes. "Too bad your team didn't bag and tag this guy when you had him before."

Just what he needed today. One more reminder of Lady Justice's blindfolds. It wasn't his fault Haines's top-dollar lawyers and an overeager rookie cop allowed their perp to walk.

"My intel has Haines still in the DC area a little over a week ago." Scoping out a meeting that never happened. Or maybe just playing games.

Once again, Foster smiled her dragon lady smile. She enjoyed pushing his buttons way too much. "It's a shame you weren't on the team before."

"If it wasn't for the CACU's work with the Chu case, your team would still have few leads on your domestic terrorist groups."

That zinger connected and Foster stiffened. "Don't get so full of yourself, Parker. You're not the only agent who logged intel on Haines. But you are the only one holding the distinction of having Haines in custody. Then losing him."

Inside he deflated, but outside his shoulders stayed up and eyes narrowed.

Stupid move, going toe-to-toe with Foster. Time to back down and regroup. This wasn't personal. It was his job. Track and locate the perp. Stop him from killing more kids. Then let justice and the legal system take care of the rest.

He moved to his back-row seat and shuffled through papers as task force members trickled in.

As long as Haines kept his filthy hands off the people Michael loved, he'd see this case to the end. If not, he'd be hard pressed to avoid the use of deadly force.

Justice had better come through this time around.

25

Sean strutted into the living room of Howard's hunting lodge Wednesday afternoon. Ten men snapped to attention. Too bad Dad couldn't see him now. If he'd lived they would have shared this power, conquered the mud races together.

Dad's plan and his under-the-radar generational standing within the white supremacy movement combined with Sean's action—a perfect combination.

"Two very successful campaigns. Let's hear it for our divinely appointed leader." Howard raised a glass and the nine other men followed.

Sean motioned for silence. "Thank you. But the real applause goes to our expert marksmen all over the US."

More toasts and drinks were raised.

"And now, gentlemen, let the plans for Wave Three commence."

They gathered around Sean's blueprints of schools and the time line he spread over the coffee table. "In less than two weeks, we'll have accomplished all of my father's plans for uniting our community and reviving our power, transporting it to higher levels than ever before achieved."

"Then what?" Don stared at the papers in front of him with glazed eyes. It was overwhelmingly clear One Pure Nation needed Sean's vision and organization.

"The next phase will be undercover strategy meetings all over America. A wave of business moves leaving many mud races without homes and jobs. Then we'll start pressing on our political membership for stiffer immigration control and changes in the legal landscape to bend in our favor."

Howard grinned. "Then our country will begin giving the boot to impure foreigners who haven't already run away. They'll flock back to their homelands, leaving our great nation cleansed once again."

Grandiose? Absolutely. Reminiscent of Hitler and other great racial cleansers, but smarter. Attacking from every possible angle. Violence. Business. Legal and political venues. And soon they'd raise a militia, growing in size until it surpassed the disgustingly diverse and weak existing military.

The group brandished ideas like sharpened swords, each growing more precise with every verbal volley.

Sean inhaled the power of the room, his energy burgeoning to new levels.

Hours later, Don, Carl, and Howard remained in the formal dining room. The others had disappeared into the night, back to their home states and hideouts.

"I trust the pictures achieved their intended response." Sean wiped the last of their salmon dinner from the corner of his mouth and tossed his napkin on the table.

Don and Carl nodded with matching Cheshire grins. "Those two monkeys are gonna run anytime now and stay quaking in their holes. Far away from the whites they tried to pollute."

"Let's keep close tabs on them." Sean yawned. "Their genetic weaknesses will do the rest of our job for us. If not, we'll take out the child first."

His table mates grinned. Having tasted first blood, the idea of eliminating women and children had grown on them. He loved it when a plan came together. Dad did too. If only they could have shared this day.

"For now, our challenge is outsmarting Parker and showing Hanna Kessler the truth."

A task he'd happily take on all by himself. The pictures combined with the health of Parker's father should keep that bothersome agent out of Sean's hair for a while.

He loved how far-reaching his network of followers had become. And with plenty of time to think these past few weeks, his mind wandered back to more of his dad's last wishes. After One Pure Nation achieved its rightful standing, Dad desired his legacy to continue for generations. With that in mind, Hanna Kessler's photography and passion for life grew more fascinating. Sure, there were plenty of far more beautiful women joining their ranks every day, but no other woman would prove his dominance like Hanna. Converting her to their cause would destroy Michael Parker, the menace who dared to disturb Sean's mother and employees. And it'd show the world the righteousness of his cause, transforming a mud-race-loving woman into a true believer.

"Matthews checked in." Howard interrupted Sean's daydream and leaned back in the padded dining room chair. "Seems our fame is well established in the domestic terrorism task forces. But they have little evidence to prove anything."

"Make sure Matthews keeps it that way."

Howard nodded. "He will. But Parker is once again a major thorn in our side. He's cracked into too many of our sites, gathering more information than we wanted public knowledge."

"Then we need to see about eliminating him soon."

Howard grinned. "You want that task or shall I?"

"I'll handle that one." Sean smirked.

How to destroy Parker? He'd enjoy counting the ways as he fell asleep tonight.

※　※　※

Michael and Hanna held Mom's hands as hospital staff transported his father out of the ICU and into a private room.

"I'm so glad Harry's taken a turn for the better." Mom smiled at Hanna.

"Me too, Mrs. Parker." She looked at Michael, then smiled back at Mom. "I mean Claire. It'll be good to hear him ordering people around again."

Michael doubted that. But even with mild confusion and obvious memory loss, his father had commandeered his ICU room, calling the shots and making nurses hop to it. All without his characteristic sharp tongue.

At least his father hadn't spilled the beans about the minutes before his heart attack. He'd forgotten. Too much to hope that his father had forgiven him.

Hanna pulled his arm and motioned toward the waiting area before they entered the third-floor private room. "Let's give your mom and dad a little time alone."

He could go for that. Especially when it'd give him some alone time with Hanna too.

She sat in a beige chair and studied the blue carpet. "Is Reeley in jail?"

"Yes."

"And the other man who broke into my apartment?"

Reeley's brother. Money and good lawyers would get him out on the street again far too soon. "Both are in custody."

He hadn't been allowed on that bust. But he'd drunk his fill of reports from Hammack and the team who'd arrested the Reeley brothers and were working hard on the case against them. "They'll never bother you again."

"I know." There was more strength than fear in her words these days. A welcome change. More and more she'd begun to resemble the gorgeous woman who'd walked into his life and stolen his heart eight months ago.

"How's Evelyn doing?"

Hanna shifted in her chair. "Better yesterday. Worse today. I can't imagine what it's like to see a picture like that of Deni. Or herself. If I were Eve, I'd run home and hide for a while."

Not good. He never wanted Hanna to run again. Couldn't handle it now. Not when they were inching toward the altar more every day.

"But I'd rather talk about you."

"Me?" He sat up straighter. "What about me?"

"Your heart is hardening and I'm getting worried." Her eyes glistened. "I know what Reeley did to me affects my family and you. I hate that, I really do. But I can't change the past. Neither can you."

"Am I pushing you, being too physical again?" He didn't think so. He'd tried to be even more careful since last Saturday.

"No. But your phone calls with Lee and the conversations with Steven and Clint are telling. You've let hatred replace the desire for justice, and it's eating you alive, one case detail at a time."

"Justice failed in Katrina Chu's case. Reeley's too. Now more people are dead." Or scarred for life like Hanna. "I won't let that happen again."

What the devil had caused Hanna to jump on this kick? Steven? He'd held his tongue better with Kessler after that boxing match with Foster.

"You're out for blood. And your drive for perfection, pushing harder and harder and working longer and longer, is destroying you." She touched his arm. "How many hours have you slept this week? Or the week before that? Ever since that little girl disappeared, you've been working far too much and sleeping less and less."

"But that's part and parcel of life in the Bureau."

Hanna wouldn't be dissuaded. "Between work and your short visits at the hospital, I don't think you've slept much at all. You can't keep this up. The man you're hunting could stay hidden until after you've worked yourself into an early grave. And none of it will force your dad to change."

What an encouragement.

"Have you forgiven your dad?"

She should talk about forgiving. He clamped his mouth shut. No way would he lash out at Hanna like that. Even if her words cut him to the bone.

"I appreciate that you're worried about me. All I can say is I'm working on the stuff with my father. But my job demands a lot of time. That won't change."

"I understand. It's the hardness in your eyes when you look at your dad that bothers me the most."

She'd noticed. He ran a hand over his buzz cut. Why wouldn't she have picked up on that? She knew hatred. He'd watched her struggle with it since the first time she'd told him about Reeley. Even if it took her a long time to call it what it was.

But was she right? Did he still hate his father? She'd mentioned his issues with Haines before, but never unloading everything and piecing it together as if it was all about his father's approval and nothing else.

He stood up and walked to the large window.

His conscience kicked in and echoed the truth of Hanna's words. Maybe it was all about his father and proving himself.

No. Not Haines and Reeley. That was about justice. About stopping them from hurting anyone else. Nothing more and nothing less.

But even if Hanna was right and justice only a secondary reason for his drive, what could he do to fix it?

Pray?

Catching Haines would help lots of people. Save lives. Make his father take notice.

Hanna joined him at the window and slipped her arm through his.

She'd tell him to pray. So would Clint and Steven and everyone else. At least he'd come up with the idea before anyone mentioned it.

Now he just had to do it.

But like sleep, it'd have to come later. When life slowed down again.

26

Thursday morning Hanna paced the long hall of windows connecting the women's pavilion to the main part of Alexandria Community Hospital. Sara was close to a week late. And despite what Sara's OB said and everyone else's prayers, things could still be wrong with Conor.

That would be all her fault. If only she'd kept a better watch over Jonathan…

She stopped walking and stared out a large ceiling-to-floor window. The clear blue sky and slight October breeze swaying the bright-colored trees did nothing to cheer her mood.

She'd failed Sara and Clint. Jonathan had almost been killed and Conor too when that awful man attacked Sara. But they'd forgiven her. Her family and even Michael believed she'd moved on from the events of last May. And maybe she had. Some. Except she kept failing people. Like Michael last night.

No matter what she'd said, he still wouldn't see that his drive for perfection was all about his father's approval.

A touch on her arm sent her heart thudding into her throat and she jumped.

Gracie's hazel eyes widened. "Sorry to startle you."

"I was just…" Hanna tried to harness her thoughts while she adjusted her rose-colored sweater and wiped sweaty hands on her blue jeans. "I was just thinking about Conor." Not quite a lie. But still not as honest as she should have been.

"Sara's asking for you."

Hanna studied her sister-in-law's face for any sign of trouble, but there were only tired circles under her eyes. Then again, maybe Gracie had learned to hide things like Steven.

"Is everything okay?"

Gracie nodded. "It's been a long morning already, but the doctors say both Sara and Conor are doing fine. He should arrive soon."

Since five o'clock this morning, they'd been on alert. She'd rushed to the Rollinses' house so Clint could bring Sara in when the contractions got serious. And Gracie had called in to work to arrange for her assistant to cover her first-grade class today.

Between the two of them, they'd gotten the kids to the hospital with snacks and coloring books to keep busy. Hanna had even managed to open Grounded and leave it in Eve's and Becky's hands.

Hanna adjusted her watch. Ten thirty. Dad should be at the coffee shop now to keep things running and handle any problems.

Tugging her arm, Gracie grinned. "Come on, I don't think it's wise to leave James and Jonathan in Sara's room for Conor's big entrance."

Susannah didn't need to stick around for that part either. Hanna certainly wouldn't. Prebirth photos and newborns' pictures she could do. The delivery was for the doctor's eyes only. "How's Clint holding up?"

They walked toward the maternity wing with Gracie chattering about Clint's last scan being negative for cancer and how Conor's birth would be such an amazing healing point for everyone.

Hanna paused outside Sara's delivery room and studied Gracie. Everything about her sister-in-law was flawless. Makeup. Chocolate brown, unmussed jogging suit. Glowing smile. Everything but her eyes. "Are you doing okay?" Good thing she'd remembered to ask about Gracie instead of verbalize worries of Conor being brain damaged or having some other complication.

"I'm good." Gracie hesitated. "I'd love to be in Sara's shoes again, but maybe my turn will come soon."

Of course Gracie and Steven wanted a bigger family. They'd mentioned it before. But no pregnancy announcements yet.

Hanna couldn't imagine what was going through Gracie's mind right now. Did being here remind her of her children and first husband? The car accident that killed them years ago? Or was she thinking about James and his first overnight visit with Angela next weekend?

All these thoughts about children and more piled up in Hanna's mind. They were better than images of Conor being stillborn because Hanna hadn't protected Jonathan and Sara well enough.

Gracie smiled. "Let's pray and then focus on Sara and her family."

Good advice. Too bad Hanna wasn't anywhere near Gracie's self-lessness.

Sighing, Hanna followed Gracie into Sara's room.

Three-year-old Jonathan ran over and hugged her legs. "Hey, Nanna! My baby brudder is comin' soon. An dat bad man not hurted him."

So she wasn't the only one thinking about what happened in May.

Gracie squeezed Sara's hand, and Clint scooped Jonathan into his arms, a smile covering the fear that flickered in his eyes. "That's right, big guy. And we'll get to see Conor any minute now."

The faster, the better, judging from Sara's facial contortions with every spiked line on the monitor next to her.

Nurses and Sara's OB entered the room, clean scrubs swishing with every step. "You about ready to meet your new family member, Sara?"

Clint gulped. Even after two kids, the huge tough-guy still wasn't sure about the delivery part.

Hanna almost giggled. But she took Jonathan into her arms instead. "Why don't we go make a picture for Conor while the doctors take care of Mommy and Daddy?"

Jonathan sucked in his lower lip. "I 'tay wiss Daddy."

James and Susannah hurried around Sara's bed. "We'll go with you and help." James smiled.

"And we'll make Conor a name picture and a welcome-home banner for his nursery." Susannah clapped her hands. "Won't that be good, Mama?"

Sara smiled, a few tears slipping down her cheek. "That'll be wonderful."

They needed to leave. Now.

Susannah ran over to Sara's bed. Jonathan wiggled free to do the same. "I lub you, Mama."

"Me too." Susannah kissed Sara and then twirled, her special purple dress spreading out around her. "Bye, Mama. Bye, Daddy."

Gracie herded the three kids out of the room while Hanna retrieved her camera from the bedside chair. One last look at Sara and the swarming medical professionals made Hanna's insides constrict. Without the kids watching, tears and terror filled Sara's face. "Pray, Clint. Pray that Conor really is okay."

Hanna shut the door, her own eyes watering. "Please, God. Please keep Conor safe."

An hour later, Hanna entered Sara's hospital room with Jonathan and Susannah. Her camera in hand settled her nerves. She could do this.

Susannah and Jonathan rushed to the bed, eyes fixed on the baby in Sara's arms. Susannah reached out to touch Conor, and his little hand latched onto his sister's big finger.

Hanna raised her camera and snapped a few shots.

"Oh, Mama, he likes me." Susannah's eyes grew wider.

Jonathan climbed on the bed. "Me too. Me too. Let me see him."

Rescuing Sara from a major pouncing, Clint grabbed his oldest son and chuckled. "Hang on a sec, buddy. Let's give Mama some room and I'll hold you up to see Conor."

Hanna snapped pictures through overflowing eyes. Conor was here. Healthy. God had answered.

Thank You. Thank You. Thank You.

"Can you all look this way?" Clint and Sara beamed as four of them turned Hanna's way. She snapped a gorgeous first family photo while Conor snoozed.

Gracie and James entered the room a minute later and watched Conor with big eyes and bigger smiles. "I called Steven with all the details. Eight pounds, nine ounces, and twenty-two inches long, right?"

Clint puffed up like a peacock. "Yep. He's a strapping Rollins, just like the rest of us menfolk. Right, Jonathan?"

The kids giggled. Susannah shrugged. "At least he's not as big as you yet, Daddy."

The adults nodded and laughed.

"Would you like to hold him?" Sara lifted the little blue bundle toward Gracie. Guess it was moms first.

An old, familiar fear snaked through Hanna. Would she ever experience the emotions written all over Sara's and Gracie's faces? A snapshot of Michael holding a little miniature of himself filled her mind.

She shook that away, not quite ready for the idea. Photography proved a safer venue for her energy, so she returned to snapping pictures. Jonathan kissing Conor. James and Susannah smiling over Conor nestled in Gracie's arms.

Sara beaming.

Clint lifting his face toward heaven, mouthing a prayer with glistening eyes.

"Hanna?" Sara's tone said she'd been talking awhile without Hanna's response.

She moved the camera to her side. "Sorry. Got a little carried away with the picture taking."

"We appreciate you being here." Clint pulled her into a side hug. "Not just for the photos, but because you're part of the family too."

Their little FBI support system. As close as family in many ways.

"Would you like to hold him, Hanna?" Sara's eyes held no reservations. They really had forgiven her. Like nothing else, this one offer filled in some of the broken places in her heart. She hadn't ruined everything for Clint and Sara.

"Yes. I would." She stepped closer to the bed, setting her camera on the nightstand before reaching out to take Conor.

The little bundle wriggled as she positioned him against her chest. Her arms quivered. What if she dropped him?

"He's solid, won't break." Clint put his hands on her shoulders and kneaded. Hanna started to jerk away but didn't. She was safe here.

Looking at Conor's tiny cherub cheeks, she couldn't help but let a few tears spill out. He was so perfect. Ten miniature fingers. An adorable scrunched-up face. She kissed his tuft of brown hair and inhaled a scent beyond description.

Life. Newness and hope all wrapped in baby soft skin and chubbiness.

She couldn't wait for Michael to hold Conor. It'd be so good for him. And if the swelling fullness in her heart was any indication, maybe this would help Michael remember the important things in life too.

Not just justice.

But mercy, hope, life, and healing. Healing, most of all.

�֎   ✖   ✖

Michael couldn't afford this time away from his desk.

But Lee had pestered until he'd given in and agreed to a late lunch on the road and a quick hospital visit. Now his overeager friend stood at Michael's desk, tossing a Nerf football back and forth in his hands. "Come on, man. I told Rashida we'd meet her at the hospital, and I can't let her be there long or she'll be begging to do the baby thing soon."

"Don't you want a little Lee Branson Jr. running you ragged?"

Lee raised his eyebrows. "No sir. Not ready to join my sisters and cousins in being fruitful and multiplying."

Michael laughed and saved the file he'd been updating. It was good to see Lee like this instead of hollow eyed and work focused. "Better watch out." He grabbed a pen and flipped it through his fingers like Iceman in *Top Gun*. "You're starting to sound like Clint with his Bible references for everything under the sun."

Huffing, Lee tossed the Nerf ball on the desk. "Can't work around that man long and not sound like a Baptist preacher." Lee punched him in the arm. "But I'm not there yet, so you and Clint and Steven can put a plug in the God-talk."

Michael tossed the pen back onto his desk. Right. Like Clint would ever do that. Michael would, though. He'd been pushed into religious stuff before and wanted no part of it for a very long time. Until Clint and God broke through his thick walls. But Lee wasn't at that place.

Shrugging on his jacket, he stood and stretched. "You ready to go yet?"

"Whatever, slowpoke. 'Bout time we left."

They navigated out of the federal maze without any last-minute assignments. Thank God. They already had more than enough to keep them busy. Unfortunately, nothing on Haines. And without him, the last piece of Katrina Chu's case couldn't be fit into place.

Lee droned on about his domestic kidnapping case and two others he'd wrapped up just this past week. Nothing like an agent at the top of his game crowing over victories.

At least the scumbag dominating Michael's thoughts hadn't organized another killing spree this week. He had to be stopped before that could happen again.

Headquarters' buzz from the CACU, the lab, and the terrorism task force had Haines bumped up on the watch list and Evelyn Blaine cautioned to stay alert. Lee too. Only he hadn't spoken a word about any of it.

Lee unlocked his Bucar and slipped inside. As soon as Michael snapped on his seat belt, Lee moved the conversation in an uncomfortable direction. "I hear Crystal's going to church now. Looks like you're following in Clint's footsteps after all."

"Wasn't me. Guess she really wanted to know about God."

"Score one for not judging a box by its wrapping."

Interesting analogy. True too. The change in Crystal was evident. At the hospital as well as no more phone calls or flirting or stopping by his office. So why did people keep him informed about Crystal? They'd never been an item. Not even close. Rather than make a stink about it, he let it slide.

Lee, on the other hand, never let anything go. Not until it was dissected and understood inside and out. Very Bureau-minded. Promotion material too. Good for Lee.

One Starbucks stop and several annoying traffic delays later, they reached Alexandria Community Hospital.

"You know what you're getting into, don't you? Gushing women. Lots of kids. You with no ring on your finger." Lee laughed as they rode the elevator up to Sara's floor. "You'll be a boring married man with ten kids and a paunch in no time flat."

Michael failed to see the humor. "How do you know that's not what I want?"

Now Lee cackled. "Hoo, boy. If that don't beat all."

"Shut up." Michael stepped out of the elevator and pointed a finger at Lee. "Don't you go stirring up trouble. Hear?"

Laughter continuing, Lee marched down the hall without answering and knocked on Sara's door. No doubt trouble was exactly what he had planned.

"Come in," a number of female voices chorused.

"Mind yourself now. We don't need any promises of wedding bells or other baby announcements, what with all your *boring* dates." Lee walked in and greeted everyone.

Michael followed and said his hellos. He shouldn't have told Lee anything. Thankfully, Clint hadn't been as much of a problem. And there were no babies on the way from Michael's doing. Might have been, if not for his father's interruption. At least the man had saved him from one thing.

Clint clasped him on the shoulder. "Thanks for coming. Both of you."

"Wouldn't miss it." Michael ignored Lee's smirk and surveyed the sunshine-filled room.

Dr. Marilynn Richards, one of Sara's best friends, and Rashida Branson were cooing over Conor. Sara's tired eyes glowed with pride as she watched every move her baby made.

"Gracie took the kids home for some quiet time, and Hanna went to check on your dad. Says he's doing pretty well now." Clint left the questions unspoken. Had Michael taken Clint's advice and talked to Harry Parker again when the man was awake? Had he forgiven his father and himself for what happened last Saturday?

No and no. But he would. Some day.

"Would you just look at these precious baby booties?" Marilynn held up a tiny boy foot engulfed in blue. "Rashida, your crocheting is amazing."

Lee's wife grinned, showing a perfect set of gleaming teeth. "My momma taught me years ago, and I've been itching to make baby things." She raised an eyebrow at her husband.

Michael smirked. Now he had some ammunition for Lee's next needling.

All the varied skin colors in the room brought Haines to mind. Michael hated how that scum hijacked his thoughts. But wouldn't One Pure Nation's leader despise all this "polluting" going on? Good.

Conor let out a few grunts and pitiful baby cries.

Clint took the baby from Rashida's arms and handed him to Sara, beaming like Michael had never seen him before. "Sounds like it's feeding time for my little guy."

"That means vamoose for the rest of us." Lee ushered Rashida toward the door. "Sara, you're looking beautiful. And Rashida informed me that we'll be stopping by the house soon with some meals for the freezer."

"Thank you. See you then."

Michael turned away and followed Marilynn out. No way did he want to see what came next.

They stood in the hall outside, no one making a move to leave. Rashida spoke first. "That Clint is one fine daddy, and that baby is his spitting image."

Marilynn nodded. "Many prayers and tears went into this pregnancy. It's wonderful to see such good come from it. So many reasons to praise the Lord."

Michael agreed. Lee and Rashida smiled but said nothing. Conversation turned to meals and other ways the ladies could help Sara when she returned home.

One fine daddy.

Rashida's words struck a tender place. Clint was a great dad. Prayed for his family. Worked hard to provide for them. But still made time to just be there.

Nothing like Michael's father.

The one he should go see before heading back to headquarters. But he wouldn't. Not until he could wipe the image of Clint holding Conor from his mind. While everyone else gushed about the cozy scene, all Michael could think of was what kind of dad he'd be.

Not a very good one.

The answer chilled him. But it was right. Clint and Steven both had great examples to learn from. Michael didn't. And no matter how much counselor-speak Hanna spouted about forgiveness and healing and breaking the chains of the past, he knew the truth.

This was just one more thing Michael couldn't fix.

Better to throw himself into work and catch Haines. Then maybe, when all his friends were safe and his father was back in Florida, he could focus on the dad issue.

Only God knew what kind of pain that meant for his future.

27

Sean viewed the revolting scene through a pair of binoculars Sunday afternoon. He'd followed that disgusting Evelyn Blaine and her mixed mongrel from her church to Rock Creek Park.

Now that they'd inhaled their picnic lunch, they were playing Frisbee with Hanna and Parker's huge yellow Lab.

How repulsive.

Too bad the beautiful photoshopped images hadn't deterred any of them nor taught them the intended lesson. No, not even Parker had been kept busy chasing ghosts. On the contrary, the FBI super agent had given the pictures to Matthews's task force and spent his time becoming even more of an albatross, shutting down some of Dad's best social networking sites.

He'd pay for that in due time.

But despite this rejection of his amazing photography work, Sean didn't mind. Not when it meant he'd eliminate these two mud-race menaces from the picture sooner and more permanently.

Less than a week until Wave Three launched. But he couldn't wait until then. He needed a little more excitement beforehand.

"So glad you finally came up to see me." Sherry Crestwell pressed next to him and smiled her sultry red-headed invitation.

He lowered the binoculars and turned to one of his more beautiful recruits. The one Howard had his eyes on. Sherry was too young for Howard's fifty years. But Sean's old friend could have his fill after this Parker business was completed. For now, Sean needed Sherry's FBI admin eyes and ears all to himself.

"Your work thus far has been outstanding. My compliments."

She beamed. "Think you can take a little break for dinner? To celebrate."

Celebrate indeed. He preferred women who didn't throw themselves at his feet. Women who presented a bit of a challenge. Like Hanna Kessler. But for now, he had to keep Sherry happy and devoted.

"I might be persuaded. But tell me first, has anyone figured out where the FBI media leak began?" He led her to a nearby park bench far away from joggers and families out for a nature fix.

"No one has a clue. My sister's been able to deliver information to her cameraman boyfriend without any questions asked." Sherry crossed her long legs. "It's getting him some kudos from the scandal-hungry reporters too. Lots of media coverage on that Reeley character, less news about that dead Asian kid. I was getting sick of watching that coverage anyway."

"Your Innocent Images boss hasn't asked questions of his unit? All the information in the press points back to their current investigations."

She pursed her lips. "Not entirely. Some things could have easily come from Michael Parker's bumbling, thanks to his hotheaded handling of Reeley interviews. At least I tried to make a little of it appear that way."

Sweet revenge. It paid to make the acquaintance of one of Parker's old flames. One of many. Doubtful Parker even remembered her name. But Sherry remembered his. And spouted off about it to her brother, a fine marksman and long-time leader of their cause in the New Jersey area.

Once again Sean marveled at the high level of underground power connections he possessed. And not until he was ready would the media or FBI have more than a small blip of information.

Dad would be proud. His mother was. He'd visited a few times recently, after she returned from her early morning church engagements. With no FBI snoops around, he had a few simple, unencumbered moments with family. *Your father should see you now, Sean. God rest his soul, he'd be so pleased.*

"Where'd you disappear to, Sean?" Sherry tilted her head and held herself more erect. It didn't have the desired effect.

"My apologies. What say I make it up to you over dinner at your house? We'll order in."

"Sounds wonderful." They stood to leave, Sherry slipping her arm around his. "What's my next assignment? You know I'm willing to assist with anything."

He refrained from a lecture about subtlety. "I'm glad you asked. Tomorrow I have plans that will no doubt make local newswires. After that I want you to let the press know Hanna Kessler is the one behind Reeley's recent arrest."

Sherry's smile grew larger. "Definitely. I'm glad that little bit of news I discovered on my own will help you."

One more piece of his personal plan fitting into place. Eliminating Hanna's employee and her offspring next. Then dazing Hanna with media. That'd keep her FBI shadows busy and her unsettled. And as soon as Wave Three thundered to completion, he'd ride in and rescue Hanna from her misguided ideas.

Then he'd have his fun and rest. Yes. His turn had almost arrived.

❋ ❋ ❋

The afternoon sun warmed Hanna's face as much as the physical exertion of keeping pace with Michael and Champ. She wasn't that out of shape. But you could never tell compared to Michael. That man could function on no sleep and still run rings around her.

And look yummy doing it.

She tucked that image away and continued walking. They'd been on the trail ever since Eve had made up some excuse about Deni needing a nap and having homework to do.

Deni had been so cute, rolling her eyes but keeping quiet until after they'd cleaned up from lunch. Then she'd whispered something about true love's kiss to her mom as they left.

"Need a drink?" Michael stopped and handed her a water bottle from his backpack.

She took the offering and smiled, enjoying the reprieve. "Thanks." What an awesome day.

Champ guzzled the water Michael set down for him.

As they returned to walking, images from the photo shoot at Sara's home last night skipped through her mind. She could still feel Conor's chubby cheek pressed against her lips. A deep sigh escaped.

Michael didn't hear.

Probably better. Too much of Deni's romanticized ideas about love and family rubbing off and Hanna would be swooning and asking Michael about a wedding date.

Thankfully, Deni hadn't talked about her little boyfriend today. According to Eve, that episode was over as fast as it had begun. And Hanna hadn't even cringed when the topic came up.

More progress.

Instead of Steven's fears about her statement to the FBI destroying her, it'd made her stronger. Just like Michael had said. She owed him so much. Not only did he listen to her endless reports of counseling, he gave her space and yet let her know his interest.

When he wasn't working.

"I'm glad you have the whole day off."

He jerked his shoulders back and worked his jaw. "Give me some credit, Hanna. I make as much time for you as I can. You know that."

What had she said wrong?

"I know you do. I was just saying it was good to have a whole day together. Church and lunch and now that hike we've had to postpone a couple times."

"I'm sorry about putting it off so long." He remained stiff and aloof.

"Michael, what's wrong? I didn't mean to upset you."

He stopped walking and turned to face her. "There's so much on my mind I can't put into words. Memories of the shooting here in May. Stuff with my father. What Reeley did to you. What that disgusting creep is out there, God knows where, still doing." He took a deep breath. "I'm not Steven or Clint. I don't know how to tell you what's going on without laying too heavy a burden on your shoulders. I won't do that."

"You've listened to me. I can do the same. It helps to talk." She touched his arm and moved closer. If they weren't so sweaty, she'd kiss him.

The light in his eyes returned. "Let's head back to your apartment and get cleaned up. It'd be easier to talk over dinner."

And she was finally at the place to do for Michael what he'd been doing for her ever since they'd started dating.

Listen. Support. Give back.

Maybe even help Michael talk about his dad. Yeah. That'd be a good way to spend the evening. Helping Michael just as he'd helped her.

❊   ❊   ❊

Talking was the last thing on Michael's mind. But with Hanna in the shower and Champ busy with his dinner, he needed something to do.

So he dialed Clint's number and walked out on Hanna's balcony. The cool breeze chilled his still-wet head.

"No-Sleep Hotel, what can I do for you?"

Michael chuckled. He didn't need a baby to fit that bill. "Just checking in. Do you have a minute?"

"You're at Hanna's?"

"She's in the shower."

Clint whistled. "No doubt you need to check in. Hang on a sec. Jonathan and Susannah and I were just watching a VeggieTales. They won't miss me, but I need to make sure Sara and Conor are okay for a few minutes."

Ever the devoted dad. Just the reminder he needed.

"All's well in the Rollins home. For a little while." Clint paused and a door closed. "Please tell me you aren't regularly at Hanna's house when she's showering. That's trouble begging to happen. You need to stay smart."

Nothing like a good dose of down-home accountability, Clint

style. "We were hiking in Rock Creek. This is the only time I've been here like this."

"So what's on your mind?"

Bad question. Except this time it wasn't Hanna. It was the visit to his father's later this evening and all sorts of case details. He'd avoid the May shooting topic. Clint didn't need that reminder. "I feel completely worthless. Too much work time is wearing on Hanna. But I haven't done enough work to nab Haines. He was in my grip and I let him go. Now he's out there killing kids and parents and threatening Lee."

"Hanna's friend Evelyn too."

"Yeah. Hanna's talked about it a lot, but Eve is moving on. Wish I could do that."

"You can."

"It's hard."

"You know the next line, don't you?"

He did. Pray. And he'd tried. But Hanna's speech about everything he did being tied to winning his father's approval wouldn't leave him alone. Neither would the need for justice.

"I'm supposed to check in with my father tonight. Mom's kept busy at the hospital, and they're both okay with all my work hours. But pray, please. I don't know what to say."

"The truth. Be honest with your dad and ask him to forgive you for the punch. Maybe the heart attack has softened him and you'll have a conversation about the past."

"Martians taking over the White House is a more likely scenario."

Clint laughed. "As for Haines, we keep doing our job and praying the Lord lights the path for us to bring the bad guys in."

"Has it always been this easy for you?" Michael regretted the sharpness of the words, but he hoped the answer made things better, not worse.

"Cancer woke me up to a lot of things. The reality of my weakness, for one. Messed-up priorities, for another. Before this year, I hadn't taken family vacations very often or depended on God like I do now. Instead, I pushed and gave my all until I couldn't push anymore. Then God had His say."

"But everyone talks about what a great dad you are, and even those who hate our beliefs respect you."

Another chuckle through the phone line. "What they see is the grace of God. And maybe comparing me to guys who cheat on their wives or leave their kids makes me come off looking great. Reality is we're all messed up and in need of Jesus. Guess I just got an extra dose of that truth this year."

It still sounded too easy. Depend on God. Pray and leave the rest to Him.

"You need to get back to your family. I'm gonna help Hanna get dinner fixed and go see my father. I'll check in with you tomorrow."

"Praying, Michael. You do it too. It makes a difference."

Michael walked back into the living room and hung up Hanna's cordless. She was banging around in the kitchen, and the scents of oregano and sizzling hamburger filled the room. Hanna's homemade spaghetti.

Neither the smell of food nor listening to Clint had altered Michael's mood. Maybe he'd just leave after dinner cleanup and go home to sleep. Talk to his father right before they left for Florida tomorrow.

As good an idea as any. And then, maybe sometime this week Haines would crawl out from under his rock. Even better if Michael was there to cuff him for good this time.

28

Sean detested waiting for anyone. A mud-race mongrel most of all. But this little plan for Monday afternoon would fine-tune his and Carl's stealth and brute force. Something they were both sorely out of practice using.

For now, they sat in yet another mid-class rental Carl's love interest had secured for them. The girl had proven far more valuable than Sean had first guessed.

"Looks like school's letting out." Carl hooked a thumb toward the driver's window. "And I have a great idea about where I'm going to set up for this Friday's fun."

Good. The more prepared they were to get in and out without detection, the better things would go afterward. And the more they evaded law-enforcement problems, the more people would trust and flock to their cause.

"Let's be sure our mark gets on her bus. Then we can beat her home and be ready."

Carl started the car and circled toward the elementary school's bus loading area. So many mud races in one place made his skin crawl. But come Friday, this place would be wrapped in bright yellow tape.

Minutes later, Denisha Blaine skipped her way onto the giant yellow bus. "That's enough of this view. I'm ready to leave."

The short trek to the basement apartment was filled with Carl's raving over Jane's help with plan details. "She sounded so amazing on the phone. Asked for Evelyn Blaine and told the kid at Grounded how she was the best barista ever." Carl made a gagging face. "She didn't even stumble over that lie. And the girl who answered told Jane that mud-race would be off work at three o'clock, no problem. Talk about easy."

"And now we wait for both of them to arrive home." They parked in an alley near the disgusting apartment they'd have to enter. It would be a quick in and out. Nothing too awful.

The ends in this case would most definitely justify the means.

※ ※ ※

Michael helped his mother pack all their hospital items into a small black suitcase. Silence hung heavy in the air as they waited for discharge orders.

"So you're both going to spend the night at my place and fly home tomorrow?" That'd been the plan according to Hanna last night at dinner.

The colonel sat up in bed and raised his eyes at Mom. She smiled.

Michael nearly gagged. For all the backhands he'd taken from the colonel, the man had never, ever raised so much as his voice toward his wife. He didn't have to raise his volume to get a point across. One look, and everyone, Mom included, jumped.

Guess she'd just messed up far less than Michael ever had.

"Claire, why don't you fill Michael in on our decision?" The colonel eyed him. "If you'd come to visit more, we'd have included you in this discussion."

Way to slather the guilt thicker. "What decision?"

Mom patted his arm. Not a good sign. That had always been her way of alerting him to a brewing storm. Her silent communication to keep his eyes open and mouth closed.

Too bad he'd ignored it more than listened.

"The doctor said this morning that because of your father's stroke and continued weakness it'd be a good idea for us to stay close to the hospital for a little while. Not fight our way through the airport bustle and all."

Pure fear knotted his insides. There was far more to his father's condition than they had shared. "Everything was okay. You were walking yesterday and doing fine. That's why they're discharging you." Michael stood at the foot of the bed and leaned into it.

"I am in good condition. Just not ready to travel."

Of course the colonel wouldn't admit to weakness or memory loss. Didn't believe he'd had a stroke. No surprise there.

Fear gave way as the reality of his mother's words seeped in. They'd be staying. At his apartment. Good-bye, home sweet home. "How long?"

"Your father nearly died, Michael. Don't you want to spend some time together? At your house there won't be visiting hours to fuss with or distracting medical personnel."

Like that had been why he'd stayed away. "That…well, that's fine. You're right, Mom. Extra time together would be good."

"See, Claire. Not a problem at all." The colonel shrugged his shoulders. "Michael just has to solve this big terrorism case, and then we'll use our time here as that vacation you've been wanting to take together."

At the rate his work was going, they'd have to stay months for Michael to accomplish his father's goals. *Please, God, not that. Please.* He was close to begging and taking any bargain God dished out. All he needed was for his parents to go back to Florida. Soon. Then he'd do whatever God asked. Anything.

His cell phone buzzed. ID said the dragon lady. Life was looking up. *Not.* "I'll be right back."

Stepping into the hallway, Michael flipped open his phone. "Parker."

"Good news. Ballistics and good old-fashioned cop work netted us a hit. We have recent major ammunition purchases matching the known weapons used by One Pure Nation. Looks like they're gearing up for a big showdown."

"Where?"

"DC, Baltimore, and Miami. That's all we know thus far. I need you back here for a briefing in an hour, ready to present all your profile work on Sean Haines."

"I'll be there."

He hung up the phone and called Lee. "Hey, man. Do I have some good news for you. We're closing in on Haines."

Lee's silence startled him.

"Lee?"

"Yeah, Michael. If your hunch is right about the Chu case and this supremacist, I'm glad you're closer to wrapping it up. But I don't want in on the details, okay? I've seen enough of his hate."

"Just figured you'd want to know we're fighting back."

"You want me to cheer because I'm black? Look, Michael, this case isn't about you saving the day for minorities. It's about justice, doing the right thing regardless of someone's skin color."

"Right."

"So why not call Kessler or Rollins and tell them?"

"You came to mind first. Why aren't you happy about the leads?"

Lee sighed. "Forget it, okay. Sorry to rain on your good news. Let me know how the task force meeting goes. Buzz here says it'll be big."

Michael hung up and leaned his head back against the tan wall. Nothing like a day with the colonel and then a messy confrontation with Lee. About what, he still wasn't sure.

"You look like you could use a good cup of coffee."

Michael opened his eyes and smiled at Hanna standing before him, gorgeous in a pale green dress. "You're right about that. But looking at you is even better." No comments about her being beautiful. He couldn't risk setting her off today too. He'd already struck out twice in the last few minutes.

"Tough day?"

"Yeah. Strange conversation with Lee, and I just found out my father and mother are staying at my home indefinitely. Plus, I have to be back at the office in forty-five minutes to give a huge presentation." He took a deep breath and tried to smile. "We're close to nailing our guy. Finally. Maybe even this week."

She stepped into his arms. Man, did that do something good to his soul.

"Good for you, Michael. I'll help your parents get settled before I go to my counseling appointment, so you can head out. Then maybe we can get some ice cream later tonight."

"Sounds great. You know I love you, right?" He hadn't meant to say it quite like that.

She quirked a grin, then studied her shoes a minute. "Yes. And I feel the same way."

His day was looking up now. "Pray for the task force, okay? I need your prayers more than anything. God has to help us put a stop to this guy's violence soon."

"I will." She paused and stared straight into his eyes. "Just remember that what you believe about God and yourself—not what you're supposed to believe—is what determines your actions."

"Dr. Nations?"

"Yes. I'm working on wrapping my mind around that truth."

"It's a good one." Not that he understood it, but Steven and Clint both spouted some variations of the idea. He kissed her on the forehead. "Will you tell my parents I had to run and I'll see them tonight?"

"You could say a quick good-bye."

"Not this time. I need to go."

She stepped back and nodded. "I'm praying, Michael."

"Thanks. See you tonight." He strode toward the elevators as fast as he could without running. No way did he want to face his father again or his repeated failure to have one real conversation with the man. Besides, he had work to do. Work that could end the string of violence stretching across the US.

Today, if things kept their upward turn.

❋   ❋   ❋

Sean and Carl flanked the inside of Evelyn Blaine's front door. As soon as the first one walked in, they'd complete their business and leave before anyone noticed.

Outside, laughter caught his attention. He listened closer. Yes. They were near the door. Almost time.

"Hey, baby girl, I beat you home today. How 'bout that?"

"Can we make some cookies, then?"

"Sounds like a great idea."

Keys jangled in the lock.

Sean's pulse thundered.

"Why don't you get changed and—"

Carl grabbed the mud-race wretch by her hair and the child by her denim jacket, pulling them inside quickly.

Sean closed the door behind them.

The two females remained frozen in terror in Carl's large hands, their black eyes wide and stupid.

Before that FBI monkey, it'd been a long time since he'd been this close to a mud race. Not since a gang of them tried to jump his father in their business parking lot one evening. But they were stupid, barely armed punks. He and Dad tore through the first two fools and left them broken on the ground. Other late-working employees joined the fray and finished it off.

He was about to enjoy the same rush now.

"Take care of the imp while I get my point across to her mother."

Carl pushed the woman away, but she stumbled and straightened up, fists swinging.

"Deni, run!" she screamed.

The little mongrel bit Carl and tore off toward the back of the house, slamming the door.

"After her. Do it quick." Sean grabbed the woman by her hair and flung her to the floor, as Carl left to take care of the other one.

The woman got up, swinging again. "You will not hurt my baby. I'll kill you first."

Sean dodged her limp-wrist slaps. Then backhanded her to the floor.

Two swift kicks took her across the room and left her in a mangled heap.

Turning toward the back hall, he ignored her moan and walked toward Carl. "Get that little demon in here, now. She'd better not have called the police."

Carl flung his weight into the door, and the splintering wood gave way. The little coward had shoved herself into the closet and tried to close the door. Stupid. And no phone to have alerted anyone. Good.

A gun's safety clicked.

The mud woman limped into the room. "Get out before I shoot both of you."

So she was stronger and smarter than most of her kind. Sean glanced at Carl and nodded his head toward the door. Better to leave before shots were fired than stay longer and risk arrest.

She backed up and let them pass, gun trained on his head.

He glared at her with barely controlled rage. "Tell Hanna not to slum with the likes of you, and this won't have to happen again."

"Get out!"

Turning away, he followed Carl out the front door. At least part of the mission had been accomplished.

He'd finish the rest on Friday.

29

Evie never shoulda called the likes of you."

Hanna ignored Trina's biting remark and handed Eve another ice pack. Eve sniffed, clamping her teeth together as she placed the ice on her side.

"Do you need anything else?" Eve shook her head, so Hanna settled next to her friend on the couch. "We should call the police, Eve. I'll stay and help with everything."

Eve shook her head. "I...I can't."

Trina stalked around the living room, her black jeans and red silk shirt a blur of anger. "Won't matter if she did call." Trina shoved her trembling hands into her jeans. "We've seen what cops do for black folk. They write their notes an' throw them away when they leave."

Was that what had happened when their mother's bakery had been vandalized?

"An' that—" Curse words in a number of languages spilled from Trina's mouth. "He's some kinda bold to come up in here. He would have killed 'em both if Eve hadn't used my gun."

Hanna locked eyes with Eve. "I know you're still in shock. But we need to call the police, then take you to the ER."

Eve closed her eyes. "Trina." She shifted and winced, clutching her sides. "Will you go check on Deni and make sure she's taking a nap?"

Trina huffed but left the room.

"I'm so glad Deni is okay." Eve's eyes watered. "I don't know what I'd have done if those awful men had hurt her."

Hanna knew what she'd have liked to do.

"I called you because..." Eve took a breath and shut her eyes against the pain. "The man who beat up on me…he…he used your name."

Hanna blinked fast and stared at her friend. "What?"

"He said to tell you not to slum with the likes of us."

Eve's whispered words sliced into Hanna's heart. "I don't know any-one who would do this to you. How could he know my name?"

"The big man who grabbed us when we came home?" Eve's eyes darted to the front door. "I've seen him before."

"Where?"

"At Grounded. The man who changed his order because of me."

Oh. No. Hanna's mind flashed back to one of Eve's first days. The German poster-boy who Eve said didn't want black people touching his food. What was his name?

Carl. Yes, that was his name. Even if the incident hadn't lodged in her memory for Eve's sake, she'd have remembered the cocky young man who'd introduce himself and flirted with her.

She'd call Michael and tell him everything. Maybe Carl was some-how connected to the monster Michael was tracking. Michael would catch them both and put them in jail for good.

Movement in the kitchen doorway caught her eye. Then Trina's dagger-sharp gaze pierced Hanna to the couch. "So this be all your fault. You're no better than that wimp Trey." Her volume rose and she stomped into the living room. "You pretend to care about my sistah, then your people beat us up for polluting the likes of you."

"Trina, stop. This isn't Hanna's fault." Eve tried to stand but couldn't.

Trina stalked closer.

Hanna searched for something, anything to provide a physical bar-rier between her and Trina's fury. No pillows on the couch. She eyed the cracked crystal vase sitting on the coffee table. The vase she'd given Eve on her first visit.

Trina jabbed a finger in her face. "This is your fault. You brought this into my sistah's life. Now you get outta here and don't come back. You hear me?"

Hanna swallowed hard. She was here to help her friend. But had she been the cause of Eve's attack? Was Trina right?

Eve stood and stumbled against Trina, grabbing her arm. "You stop this." The strength in Eve's words didn't mask the pain contorting her face. "Your bigotry isn't any better than those men who broke into our home."

Trina rocked back. "How can you say that?"

"Hate is hate. Which skin color you blame for your trouble doesn't matter." Eve's jaw quivered, but her words continued, strong and full of fire. "Hanna is my friend. No white bigot will take that away. Neither will a black one."

Hanna held her breath.

Trina's eyes narrowed and her fists clenched, but she didn't move. Then she whirled around and stomped out the front door.

Eve collapsed on the couch again, tears trailing down her cheeks.

Guilt took over where Trina had left off.

"Will you call Michael?" Eve's voice had returned to a whisper. "I'll talk to him. He'll help us. Right, Hanna?"

She nodded.

Yes, Michael would find Carl and whoever was with him. But what about Trina? Even if Hanna hadn't caused those evil men to hurt Eve, her presence in Eve's life had separated two devoted sisters.

Eve's tears screamed that fact.

Hanna sniffed back her own maelstrom of emotions and reached for her cell phone. Michael would help. But could she?

Not judging from today's events. And there was no telling how much more trouble she'd cause before this was all over.

❈　❈　❈

Sean hung up the telephone and flicked on the TV Tuesday afternoon. Sherry's call had started his day off better than expected. Watching Hanna on the news would continue the festivities.

Too bad Hanna hadn't been smart enough to get rid of that mud-race employee long before.

A job he'd enjoy completing on Friday.

Hanna's blond hair and watery blue eyes filled the enormous flat-screen television. Soon, he'd take away the sadness from her beautiful eyes. But for now she had to learn her lesson.

A skinny reporter thrust a microphone into her face as a crowd gathered around Grounded. "Miss Kessler, is it true your involvement will clinch the case against former Congressman Richard Reeley?"

Hanna's eyes widened. "I have no comment."

"But our sources say you're deeply involved in the accusations against the former congressman."

Michael Parker and that FBI monkey stood by Hanna's side. No surprise about Parker, the pathetic knight in rusty armor. Sean would show him up in no time.

But the mud menace staring into the TV screen caused Sean's flesh to crawl. Disgusting. Carl and Don should get rid of him. A job they'd enjoy. And one that needed doing before Friday's big day.

According to Sherry, some Innocent Images agents—Parker's old friends—now agreed with Parker about Lasser and that yellow kid's disappearance.

Memories of that day rushed to the surface.

The bright sun and sweltering temperatures. Lasser's foolish yet trusting agreement to meet at the old strip mall Sean had frequented in its heyday. The feel of his Smith and Wesson doing what it was designed to do.

It'd been his first kill in ages. Bill should have listened to the truth years ago. But he had to get tangled up in perversion and let it destroy him.

The bullet in Lasser's head saved Bill from himself.

The one in that mongrel's spared the world from more of her kind.

Sean focused back on the television. The tough FBI agents couldn't make the media disappear. His respect for the plucky stalk of a reporter grew.

"One more question, Miss Kessler, please. Wasn't your father friends with Congressman Reeley?"

Oh, infotainment at its best. Where had Sherry come up with that bit of scandal?

The barb struck fire into Hanna's eyes. What a sight.

"Why don't you go do some real reporting? Put your snooping to work for law enforcement and find out who's behind the racial killings and attacks. Those monsters need to be stopped."

Monsters? What a pejorative comment. Here he was, making the world a better place for people like Hanna, and she showed no respect. It might take a considerable amount of educating to change Hanna's mind.

But he'd enjoy the process.

Carl skulked into the living room. Sean ignored him, preferring the three-ring circus filling Grounded. Hanna's diatribe ended, and she slipped past her boyfriend and into the back office. The FBI wall thwarted any further entertainment.

"We have a problem."

Sean clicked off the TV. "What, pray tell, could it be? No one knows where we are or what we're planning."

Slumping into the brown leather couch, Carl scuffed his shoe over the white area rug. "Matthews said they have my name and are linking us together. That stupid witch must've remembered me from the coffee shop and told the Kessler chick. Then they talked to the feds. Matthews warned me to stay hidden and reconsider taking part in Friday's plans."

Sean stood and clenched his fist. "Matthews is not in control here. I am. We will proceed as planned."

Wide-eyed, Carl only nodded.

Their inside contact had begun to overextend his usefulness. Wonder what the CIA did to moles in their midst?

Turning toward the window, Sean squinted through the misting rain to find one of the sentries on duty. A huge man in camo slipped past a tree and faded into the forest. Always good to see everything running smoothly.

"Call Matthews. Tell him to destroy any evidence they try to mount against you. Or exchange any photographs they acquire with falsified ones. Anything to throw them off your trail." Sean crossed his arms, keeping his focus outside. "Your rifle is needed Friday. And nothing will stand in the way of our biggest show yet."

"I'm on it."

"Call Albert too. Have him gather a few of his best men and keep watch over Parker's parents in Alexandria. They should have taken over their son's apartment by now."

Carl cleared his throat, but Sean didn't turn. "Why?" Then he stopped. Doubtless remembering the last time he'd disrespected his betters. "I mean, yes sir. I'm just curious to hear your reasoning."

"Parker's loyalty is obvious. We may need some bargaining chips should his hero complex get in our way again."

"Good idea. I'll go make those calls."

Sean smiled. The FBI couldn't thwart Wave Three, regardless of what foolish attempt they made.

Right, Dad? Sean sensed his father's pride-filled eyes staring down on him. Nothing would stand in the way of completing his father's dreams. Nothing.

30

Steven gripped the coffee mug in his hands, hard. Crushing it might prove a good outlet for the emotions churning his gut. But he'd wait to go a couple rounds with his punching bag when he made it home tonight.

Another glance around the perimeter of Grounded settled his ire. No newshounds waiting to pounce at the coffee store's entrance.

Good thing the reporters' interest in Hanna had dissipated. News clips regarding his sister hadn't filled Wednesday's top stories. No doubt the FBI bodyguards had helped.

"I'm heading back to the office, boss." Lee pulled out a chair and sat down. Looking over at Hanna working the counter, he lowered his voice. "You staying until Baby Sister heads home?"

"No one hanging around out back or in the garage?"

"All clear."

Finishing off his third espresso, Steven set down his mug and met Lee's concerned eyes. "Michael should be here to take Hanna home soon."

"You don't think this Secret Service detail stuff is a little overkill?"

"After what those skinheads did to Eve and what Haines said about Hanna? What that punk reporter tried to pull yesterday? No. It's not too much. I won't let Hanna or Eve be harassed like that again."

"Who's watching Evelyn?"

"Locals are circling her neighborhood regularly. Hanna is there as much as possible, and she's programmed my and Michael's direct numbers into Eve's cell."

Lee chuckled. "That's one tough kid. Too bad she didn't pull the trigger and make our job easier."

Those were the first angry words from Lee's mouth since Haines's legal witch hunt. Good for Lee. Just like Hanna. 'Bout time those two got past the shock and denial and got honest about the anger.

His conscience jabbed at him. Nothing wrong with righteous anger. Then again, righteousness didn't wish someone dead, did it?

"You and Rashida doing okay?"

Lee nodded. "She's a little spooked about what happened to Evelyn. But talking to Hanna helped. Your sister's really stepping up to protect her friend."

"What can I say? Hanna's a good egg."

Chuckling, Lee stood up. "Yeah, well, I think that parental pride belongs to your parents. Don't go back to smothering our Hanna-girl again."

"Point well taken."

"Clint thinks a wedding is on the horizon."

A fact Steven had begun to accept. He'd come to terms with Michael dating Hanna after the mess with Crystal straightened out. And according to Hanna, Michael had been nothing but a perfect gentleman, going over and above his sister's expectations once he learned the truth about Reeley.

As long as that continued, Steven would give his blessing. Not that Michael had asked for it.

Lee cleared his throat. "Still not sure about my buddy? He's the real deal. And he loves that sister of yours."

"I know. And I'm done with the big brother threats."

"That'll be the day." Lee shook his head. "But that's how I am with my sisters, so I get it. My time-off request for November go through yet?"

"We'll be hard pressed to survive without you."

"Ha. See you at the grindstone tomorrow."

Lee slipped past the customers filling Grounded and disappeared into Union Station. Hanna smiled as she worked the front counter.

All normal on the coffee-shop front. Except for Dad's constant presence. Knowing only a small part of Dad's guilt about Reeley, Steven prayed for Dad and Hanna both. Times like this he missed Mom more than ever.

Hanna did too.

He glanced at his watch, remembering the piles of paperwork on his desk.

Setting down a strong-smelling coffee to-go, Hanna smirked. "You don't have to babysit me."

He stood and squeezed Hanna's hand. "But it's so much fun."

"Whatever."

"Dad okay?"

Her averted eyes and sigh said it all. "He's going to see Dr. Nations with me next week. I hope that'll help him as much as it has me."

Hanna's gaze slipped past Grounded's front tables, and her posture straightened. Her entire countenance brightened. Not surprised to see Michael stepping off the escalator and walking toward them, Steven shook his head. Then he picked up his hot coffee. "Time for the changing of the guard."

Hanna smiled. "Glad to see you realize that."

He hadn't meant it quite so literally.

Michael nodded a greeting and stopped right before entering Hanna's personal space. But she closed the gap and kissed him.

Steven shook his head again. His baby sister was growing up indeed.

He caught Michael's eye. "Take good care of her."

"Will do, boss."

He bent down to peck Hanna on the cheek. "See you at Dad's tonight for dinner?"

She scuffed her heel against the floor. "Maybe. I'm going over to Eve's when I leave here."

The slump of her shoulders spelled trouble. But Michael would watch out for her. Keep her safe. And Haines wasn't stupid enough to do anything else this soon. Steven tried to convince himself of that all the way to his Bucar. Sliding into the seat, he started the car and pulled out of his parking space.

Maybe his unease was nothing more than the reality of having to let

Hanna go a little more. Something Gracie had said was a long time in coming. Yeah, that was it.

Still, a nagging thought hounded him. What else did Haines have planned?

✷ ✷ ✷

Michael revved his Mustang and pulled into DC traffic, still trying to figure out what was up with Hanna. The kiss in front of Steven had been a nice surprise. But ever since then, she'd slipped back into sad and silent.

"Tough day at the shop?"

"No. Not really."

Strike one. He hated these types of conversations. Shooting up a quick prayer, he tried another approach. "Any details we need to work out for your dad and Sue's anniversary celebration? With a little over a week, there's time to change things up, and I could handle some of the legwork." Clint would call this event a major shindig and chuckle over Michael's involvement.

"Steven wants to combine it with a surprise birthday party for Dad."

He nodded. "We could do that."

"And have it at Steven's house."

What? "But I already reserved the clubhouse at my apartment complex. And we'll have fun hosting it. Champ will help."

She sighed like speaking was too difficult a task. "I don't know, Michael. We'll see."

Strike two.

Maybe a direct question would earn him a base hit. Or traffic would disappear and this short trip would grow shorter. "I know there's a lot going on…" Talk about an understatement. "But you were okay at Grounded and now you're preoccupied. What's wrong?"

"Nothing."

According to Clint and Steven, *nothing* from a woman never meant nothing.

Tall businesses gave way to more residential areas before he tried again. "It sure looks like something."

She turned in her seat, tears filling her eyes. "I don't want to keep talking about it. It hurts…" Another sigh. "It was awful looking at mug shots, or whatever you all call them, with Eve. Identifying that Haines person. He's evil. And I'm worried about Eve. It's my fault she was attacked, and I need to make sure she's safe."

"What?" His mind fumbled for a response. "There's no way Haines and his henchman attacking Eve is your fault. And the cops have stepped up their patrols in her neighborhood. She's protected."

"It's not enough."

"How about we schedule an alarm company's eval of Eve's apartment? I'll check into who's the best and pay for the installation."

"Trina wouldn't accept our pity."

He turned left off North Capitol Street onto U Street. "It's not pity. Just help."

"She won't see it that way. And I'm getting tired of fighting her sarcasm and hate."

"So don't spend so much time over there."

Hanna's eyes flashed. "Why not? You're busy with work. Or your parents." She crossed her arms. "I can't turn my back on Eve. I have to help her."

How in the dickens had he walked right into this mess? Talk about some serious foul balls. He needed help. "I don't want you to turn your back on Eve at all. I just offered to help her out."

Silence.

"And it's not like I'm a workaholic or hosting tea parties for my mother and father."

She scowled. This conversation was so not going the way he'd planned.

"Have I done something wrong? 'Cause I'm totally lost as to why we're snapping at each other right now."

"Life isn't all about you, Michael."

Ouch. "I didn't deserve that."

"And I didn't deserve what Reeley did to me, what your freak white supremacist did to my friend, or what the media blitz did in ripping my dad's heart out with their awful spin on his past." Tears slid down her cheek. "I can't handle this. And it's all my fault it's happening anyway."

"How can you say that?" He pulled into Eve's driveway and cut off the engine. "No one blames you for anything. Reeley is a pervert who attacked you. Haines is…" He swallowed the colorful euphuisms begging for release. "It's not your fault Haines is killing people or that he attacked Eve. He's the problem. Not you!"

"Stop yelling at me."

Michael checked his volume. How could Hanna believe any of the recent events were her fault? And how had he missed that Eve's attack and the stupid reporter had set Hanna so far back in her counseling progress? He should have paid better attention.

She reached for the door handle. "I'm going to help Eve pack tonight. Then I'm driving her back to Virginia. We both need some time away from DC."

Her words froze him to the leather seat. She couldn't run away again. Not now. "Please don't, Hanna. Don't run." He reached for her hand. "We can protect you here."

Jerking away, she shoved the door open and took off for Eve's apartment.

Everything in him wanted to run after her and force her to use common sense. But a very physical force compelled him to stay put. God would have to rescue Hanna. Michael wouldn't force her to stay.

Third strike, and he was out in a big way.

But God was up to bat now. He'd have to bring it all home. Somehow.

❈   ❈   ❈

Hanna sat on Eve's kente-patterned couch trying to catch her breath and quiet the voices in her head. The engine noise of Michael's Mustang faded into the distance.

She never should have talked to him like that. Never should have run from him. From her past. From her responsibilities here.

Maybe she hadn't changed at all since her cowardly escape after Steven's wedding.

But this time it wasn't about her. It was about protecting Eve.

"Hanna? Are you listening?" Eve tilted her head and reached out to nudge Hanna's knee. "You have no reason to push Michael away. Call him up and ask him to come back and take you home."

"No. He's got too much on his plate already. We both need a break." Her chest squeezed tighter. "Besides, there's something happening with his work on the task force. He's been at the office almost every waking moment since last Tuesday."

"When he's not been babysitting or escorting you home."

"I appreciate his protection. Steven and Lee have done a lot too. But I think the man Michael's hunting is ramping up something. And I want you out of this city so you aren't caught in the crossfire. Let's pack some suitcases and go to Virginia for a while."

Trina walked out of Deni's bedroom, far less hostile than she'd been even yesterday. "Deni's still doing her homework. But I couldn't miss what Hanna asked you to do."

Hanna braced for the sarcastic slap-down sure to come.

But Trina stood watching them, eyes filling with tears. "She's right, Evie. You and Deni need to go to Momma's and be safe."

Did Trina just agree with her on something? Hanna gulped and blinked. And before she could catch her thoughts, her mouth kicked in. "Why don't you come too, Trina? You're in just as much danger."

Trina's face froze, eyes wide open.

"No." Eve stood. Still slower than usual, but refusing to do more than take the doctor's prescriptions and advice to rest her bruised rib cage. It was a wonder she didn't have any broken bones. "I will not turn tail or live in fear. I will not let misguided bigots and their scare tactics dictate my life."

"But Eve, they're killing people." Hanna jumped to Eve's side and took her friend's hand. "I can't handle the three of you becoming his victims."

"Then we'll pray Michael and the task force find him before he can do anything else."

Prayer. She understood Michael's frustration with everyone telling him to pray and still not being able to make himself do it.

"Praying didn't keep those other women and children alive." Trina studied the brown carpet. "Evie, Hanna's trying to help. Let her."

Whoa. Had someone switched bodies with Trina?

"Don't look at me that way, Miss Thang. I'm not saying I like you. I just want my sistah safe."

Eve smiled. "And you don't want to be a black bigot either, right?"

Trina rolled her eyes. "I want you safe. The rest we'll talk about later."

The powerful love of a sibling bridged all kinds of opinion gulfs. Hanna's defenses began to melt toward Trina.

"I love you, Trinie." Eve squeezed Hanna's hand. "And you've become one of my closest friends, Hanna. But I can't run. I ran from the memories of Trey and his friends. I won't continue along that path of fear."

Hanna nodded. Could she stand strong like Eve?

Trina threw up her hands. "I'm going back to help Deni. She has more sense than her mother."

She left the room without slamming the door. Wonders never ceased.

"I'm sorry Trina's been so hard on you. We're working on that." Eve took a deep breath and sat down again. Hanna did the same. "But you need to work on your impulse to run. It won't solve things."

"How can you stay here? Those men might come back."

"So I'll shoot them." Eve let out a nervous laugh. Then winced. "I don't think I could do that. Unless they tried to hurt Deni again. Regardless, I refuse to live in fear."

Hanna shook her head. "How do you deal with what they did to you? What Trey and his friends did?"

"Simple answer? It took me years to forgive Trey and his friends. I was raised on my momma's Bible and didn't believe it. Until fear stole my life. I hid, working at Momma's bakery for a few years after high school. But when I started college, I barely survived my freshman classes. I didn't want to look at any white person, thinking they might do to me what they did to Trina."

"So you just up and forgave them?"

Eve raised an eyebrow. "You know full well it's not that easy. Not like..." She snapped her fingers in a Z formation.

They both giggled.

"I'm still working on what happened Monday, still wrestling with God about it. But I know what I need to do. What you need to do too. You gotta face those demons in your past. Stare them down with the power of God's forgiveness. Then they don't seem so scary."

"Did I tell you about burying all my Ken dolls in my parents' backyard?"

Eve tilted her head again, eyes sad, looking far older than her twenty-four years. "You told me a lot about Reeley last week. But not so many specifics about how you handled it. I'm really sorry, Hanna."

"Thank you."

"Forgiving him isn't about what he did. It's not about unearthing those dolls, either, and what they represent. It's about you being free. Forgiveness frees you."

Hanna nodded, throat too full of emotions to speak. She'd have to mull over Eve's wise words. They were right. Straight out of the Scriptures. She just didn't know how to apply them to her situation.

But the thought of sending the specters of her past packing caused her heart to pump harder. And her backbone to straighten. Maybe it was time to stop running. To take back control, and give those monster memories the boot.

31

Sean held the cell phone away from his ear as he drove up MD-295 in Jane's truck. He'd made a few vehicle switches between Howard's hunting lodge and his home town.

"Don't say I didn't warn you, Haines. The task force caught wind of your Thursday meeting, and they'll be on top of it before you know what hit you." Matthews added some choice verbiage that would have made a drill sergeant blush.

"They couldn't possibly know where it will be held."

"Wrong. Parker is a computer menace, hacking past your encoding and sniffing you out better than a bloodhound's nose. They know you're meeting tonight."

"Keep them thinking it will be tonight. I've already called all the important players and moved the time and location. It's impossible for that task force to get the better of me."

Matthews ended the call saying he had to return to work. He'd better keep his mouth closed as well.

Sean pulled into an innocuous family restaurant well beyond the Inner Harbor's tourist traffic. The sign out front said CLOSED FOR REPAIRS. He drove around back and parked in the small driveway separating the building from a patch of woods, waiting a few minutes before entering.

He hadn't been trailed.

Two raps brought the gray-headed owner, Glen Daniels, one of Dad's old hunting buddies, to the back door.

"Come in. Come in, Sean." Glen slapped his back as he walked past. "You're the spitting image of your father. He'd be so proud."

Sean grinned. He'd been away from home far too long. Unfortunately, after tonight and tomorrow's festivities, he'd be underground and overseas for a few months. Maybe longer.

"How's Stewart's business doing these days? Your mother says everything's in the black, just like Stew would have run it."

"Going well, Mr. Daniels. Very well." Stepping into the large banquet room all set for their lunchtime meeting, Sean nodded in satisfaction. Everything from finger food to the school schematics he'd sent ahead were in perfect order.

Mr. Daniels continued to reminisce about Dad and the company he'd founded. The one Sean now headed. Yes, the business continued to run itself with the employees he and Dad had hired. He sometimes missed the daily meetings and putting out fires with all their IT clients. But his far more important work now required everything.

"Sean Stewart Haines, Junior. As I live and breathe." Mrs. Daniels walked out of the kitchen, wiping meaty hands on her white apron. "You're looking mighty handsome. When are we gonna hear about a Mrs. Haines on your arm?"

Hanna's Web site photograph came to mind. He smiled. "It could be awhile. We shall see." Wouldn't Parker love that?

More loyal leadership trickled into the restaurant, many having met at various places and ridden in together. Sherry and her brother stood talking with Don. Carl had wisely agreed to monitor and mislead their FBI trackers online from Howard's lodge.

When every seat in the large room had filled, Sean stood at the front. Sherry began a clapping spree. Everyone joined in. He gave her an indulgent smile, but raised his hand for quiet. "Thank you all for adjusting plans as our situation warranted."

Pulling out the two local school blueprints, he continued. "Carl Goring will lead the assault on the DC schools." He passed out time lines to the two other marksmen on Carl's team. "My two groups will be in place a short distance from here, a little further northwest of downtown Baltimore. We'll set up on top of row houses owned by some of our loyal members."

"Excellent shotlines to the targets." Mr. Daniels and others nodded agreement.

"Our counterparts in Florida are armed and ready as well. Everything tomorrow commences at three fifteen in the afternoon. Marksmen, be alert and in place. Escape teams, be at your places by three o'clock, no earlier."

An increase in the traffic volume outside moved Sean to the window, gathering his paperwork as he went. One unmarked car pulled into the front of the restaurant. More were coming.

The feds had found them.

A string of curses flew through his mind. Then he focused. Time to disappear.

Mr. Daniels read Sean's movements and gathered all remaining papers for fast disposal, then began ushering the women toward the kitchen, Mrs. Daniels passing out aprons.

Sean motioned to his marksmen to take the west exit.

He slipped out the back door he'd entered less than an hour ago, the driveway now blocked by loyal members' cars. The feds wouldn't get back here in time to find him. Dashing into the wooded area behind the restaurant, more curses filled his mind as his well-orchestrated meeting morphed into chaos.

How could the FBI have located his people this quickly?

At least some of his followers had escaped before the wretched FBI task force swarmed the building.

Shouts of "FBI! No one move!" and the squeal of tires carried on the wind as Sean made his way to the residences on the other side of the wooded area. They wouldn't find him. They hadn't prepared their infestation well enough.

Besides, he had an important lynching to attend.

※　※　※

Michael and Brett Hamilton holstered their Glocks and surveyed the streams of people being led out of the restaurant's front doors in handcuffs.

Baltimore PD had arrived in droves. Good thing too. Some of the cuffed men fought the uniformed officers. Most cursed the pigs violating their free rights.

A few of the women wept. Especially…Michael blanched as he locked eyes with a crying Sherry Crestwell. The red-headed Innocent Images admin glared at him as she was tucked into the back of a patrol car. Haines had people inside the Bureau working for him?

Michael's mind whirled. Acid burned his throat.

No wonder One Pure Nation had evaded the FBI radar so long. A twinge of guilt hit him at the possibility of Sherry going to prison. They'd only dated a few times, a long time ago. But they'd shared more than a few drinks.

He hated the reminder of his past. But he shoved it away and motioned to Hamilton. "Who cleared the woods out back?"

"Tanner and Matthews. They found nothing."

Foster joined them looking almost human in her jeans and FBI jacket. "Haines isn't among those we've identified. One smart mouth said he left as soon as we pulled in, but I find that hard to believe."

"I don't." Michael snapped his mouth closed.

Dragon-lady fire ignited the air, scorching Foster's cheeks. "Let's cull the group and take the top brass back to headquarters. We're bound to get some good intel from a few of these guys."

"Or gals." Hamilton jabbed his thumb over his shoulder. "Parker says one of your own was among the arrested."

Foster glared. "Who?"

"Sherry Crestwell. She's an admin for the IIU."

The head of the task force cursed under her breath. "I figured there was a mole somewhere, given all the information streaming through the media."

Michael should have figured that out. He'd have pegged Matthews, though. But he couldn't worry about it now. At this moment, their biggest concern was tracking Haines before One Pure Nation's mysterious Friday plans commenced.

Please, God, let us find Haines before he can kill anyone else.

❋   ❋   ❋

Sean drove into Alexandria in the truck Mr. Daniels had left parked in front of his row house a short walk from the restaurant. Keys under the floorboard. Dad's old trick.

Wish Dad were here now. He wouldn't have allowed Parker and his FBI team to interfere. But Sean would show them. Today. And tomorrow.

He checked his directions one more time. A few minutes later he pulled into the Bransons' subdivision and parked at the community pool. Several expensive cars passed the small parking lot and whizzed through the community. Visions of his beautiful Viper, covered and stored at his mother's house, leapt to mind. He missed that car.

As he stepped out of the truck, a black Corvette rounded the curve a little too fast and screeched its tires. A CEO late to work after a quick stop at his mistress's house.

Sean had canvassed the area a few times before. The large homes were seldom occupied this time of day. But Rashida Branson would be home on her day off, not at the bank polluting good people's money.

Walking a few houses away from the pool, he stopped in front of their gaudy ranch, the front porch littered with country décor, then slipped around the back of the house. There he watched through the glass patio doors. The disgusting woman was in the kitchen, listening to some Negro spiritual and screeching at the top of her lungs.

When she disappeared into the back rooms, he tried the patio door. Unlocked. *Stupid is as stupid does.* His lucky day.

Entering with practiced stealth, he waited at the corner of the living room wall and the back hallway. Footsteps headed his way.

The big woman stepped past him and stopped, shivering. "Don't be silly, girl. Getting spooked right before Lee comes home for lunch is asking for a messed up day."

What a fool.

Taking the switchblade from his pocket, he clicked it open.

She spun on him and screamed.

"Oh, no. You will not spoil my day like that." He drove the blade into her ample abdomen, and jerked it out, cutting to the right.

She staggered back, wide-eyed with shock.

He kicked the wretch down on her knees as blood dotted the white carpet.

Then the front door swished open. "Hey, baby. I'm sorry I'm a little late for our lunch rendezvous."

Sean cursed and dropped the knife. Reaching into his jacket pocket, he stepped away from the crying, bleeding woman.

"Rashida, what the…"

Sean waited until Lee Branson stepped fully into the living room. Then he fired. One shot and the fool went down.

Now he had to disappear until tomorrow afternoon. He surveyed his handiwork one last time. It wasn't the lynching he'd wanted. But it would do.

32

Michael stomped downstairs to the interview rooms. Foster had assigned him boring observation duty as she interrogated Don Goring. Their one monumental catch of the day. Brother to the creep that had attacked Eve and one of Sean Haines's top men. What Michael wouldn't give for a crack at this kid's skull.

At least he didn't have to listen to Sherry Crestwell's dressing down. When he'd seen Hammack in passing, his old boss resembled a volcano minutes before explosion. He did not envy Dan's job today.

Entering the darkened observation room, Michael nodded to the technician busy with recording details. "Can you turn up the sound?"

The skinny kid straightened his black tie. "Sure thing, sir. If there's anything else I can do for you, please let me know."

Must be new. Veterans at every level mellowed in a short flip of calendar pages.

Foster sat at the metal table, arms crossed and red fingernails tapping on her biceps. "We have evidence against you on multiple counts of assault with a deadly weapon. And eyewitness accounts of your visit to Evelyn Blaine's apartment."

No, they didn't. Michael disliked Foster's tactics more with each clock tick.

"I didn't touch that—" Goring rattled off a dictionary of vile racial slurs. Poor Foster. Words like that might leave a chink in her dragon scales.

"So tell me what you were doing earlier this week, then."

Goring smirked. Then raked his eyes over Sonja. That'd score him big points. Michael chuckled.

Clint's tall frame filled the observation room doorway. "How goes it?"

"Not bad. Not great." Clint's expression caused the hairs on Michael's neck to stand at attention. "Tell me Haines didn't push his plans ahead and strike early."

Tugging at his Looney Tunes tie, Clint cleared his throat. "I have no firsthand knowledge of Haines's plans. Only what you've said in passing, and I don't think they've changed."

"Then why do you look like you've been sucking on lemons?"

"Lee and Rashida are in the hospital. Steven's en route."

Michael stood up straighter, a load of bricks hitting his stomach. "Why?"

"Rashida was knifed in the abdomen. Lee shot in the leg and left to bleed out. Both are in critical condition at Alexandria Community Hospital."

"Haines?"

Clint nodded. "An ERT is scouring the place now. It'll be a while before we know for sure."

"I need to see Lee." Michael tried to step past, but Clint's hand clamped around Michael's bicep.

"Nothing doing." Clint's grip didn't leave room for argument. "They're in surgery, and Steven and Hanna will meet you there later. For now, you need to find out what you can on Haines."

"I'm gonna put a bullet in his brain if it's the last thing I do." Heat ripped through Michael's chest as he yanked his arm free. He needed something to punch. Now.

"That's not our job, Michael. Life and death are not for us to decide."

Michael narrowed his eyes. "Sometimes we do decide. Because that is our job. If I hadn't taken the shot in May, your son would be dead."

Clint leaned back into the gray wall. "Deadly force is what we train for, not revenge. Justice is not yours to mete out."

"Haines didn't execute Lee and Rashida like he did Lasser and Kat. He left our friends to die slowly. In excruciating pain."

"I'm not gonna argue this with you." Clint pointed his chin toward the interrogation room. "But if Foster catches a whiff of your blind fury, she'll officially set you on ice."

"Haines deserves to die."

A deep breath escaped Clint's lips. "Believe the truth, Michael. Not what you feel. Unchecked emotions will get you or the people around you killed."

True. He needed to get his head back into the game. Do like Steven requested. Find Haines.

Michael turned to the technician. "Can you let Foster know I want in there?"

The young techie nodded. "I'll alert her."

"Pray, Michael. You're gonna need it." Shaking his head, Clint pushed off from the wall. "Don't confuse justice and revenge. And don't let your temper overrule your brain."

One more area of life shouting his worthlessness.

"A final piece of advice." Clint stared Michael down. "Call Hanna when you get done here. She's worried about you."

Like he needed a mirror lecture from Hanna. He'd been too busy with the task force to talk with her more than a minute last night. And today would continue the madhouse. Because once again, Haines had slipped through his fingers. Wouldn't his father get a kick out of that?

Foster exited the interview room and narrowed her eyes at Michael and Clint. "Rollins. Good to see you back to speed."

"Thank you." Clint took a step past Foster. "Remember what I said, Michael. I'm praying."

Foster remained silent until Clint stepped onto the elevator. "So he is a religious nut like everyone says. Didn't think you were too." She held up a hand. "Not interested, either way. What I want to know is why you jerked me from my interview. It'd better be good."

He forced a smile. "Maybe a changing of the guard will shake things up a little."

"Think you can do a better job?" Foster crossed her arms, daring him to respond.

Michael stayed silent.

"Be my guest, Parker." She gestured toward the interview room door. "Let's see what a CACU superstar can do."

He wiped the dripping sarcasm from his suit coat and entered the small room.

"The pretty lady need a bathroom break?" Goring laughed at his adolescent humor.

Michael turned the empty metal chair around and sat down. "Where's Haines hiding out while you take the fall for him?"

"You'll never know."

"You do realize he's halfway around the world by now, letting you fry for his crimes."

"The reverend has done nothing wrong."

Now if that wasn't a psycho line, he didn't know what was. "Killing kids. His friend William Lasser…"

Goring whitened. "Sean wouldn't have done that."

"Oh, we're positive he did. Got tired of his old friend. Or maybe Haines's use for Lasser ran out. Wonder what he'll do with you when he's finished with his *waves of terror.*" Mocking the party line of One Pure Nation charged him. He'd pray later. For now, he'd get answers.

Goring said nothing.

"I think maybe your reverend—" Michael choked getting that word out. "Maybe Haines decided to tuck tail and run after we busted up your little meeting."

Laughing, Goring leaned back in his chair. "You know nothing. And your baiting won't work. No matter what you do those"—racial slurs filled the small room again—"stupid friends of yours are being dressed for a funeral about now, aren't they?"

Michael stood up, eyes narrow. Fists clenched.

"Oh yeah. The coffee shop wretch and her mongrel are next. But it don't matter. You'll never find Sean until the last kill is done and he's escaped your grip once again."

Black shoes touching Goring's chair, Michael swallowed back the choice words he'd like to blister this punk with and put him in his place.

"Then purity will be within our grasp. Your pretty girlfriend too."

Michael grabbed Goring's shirt collar and clamped his hand around the fool's thick neck.

Foster threw the door open. "Out. Now."

Releasing the skinhead with a shove, Michael didn't meet Foster's eyes. Only brushed past her and out the door.

Less than a minute later, Foster stormed into the observation room. "I will have your badge if you pull a stunt like that again."

He nodded.

"I want you out of this building until further notice." The dragon lady's breath scorched the room. "You will not destroy my case with your prepubescent temper tantrum."

"I have work to do."

"Do it from home. That's a direct order."

"Yes ma'am."

Refusing to look anyone in the eye, he stalked up the stairs and out to the garage.

Not until he turned the key in his Mustang and revved the engine did he give serious consideration to how close he'd come to throwing away the case against Haines.

And what was that skinhead thinking, talking about Hanna? Haines had better not...

Music from an old Casting Crowns CD blared through the car as he pulled out of the parking garage.

The song "Praise You in This Storm" captured his emotions. He'd prayed, but God still let the rain come and batter the people Michael loved. No saving-the-day rescue on the horizon.

If Lee or Rashida died. If Haines hurt Hanna…Michael slammed his palm into the steering wheel.

No. Lee and Rashida would be out of surgery soon. And Haines couldn't touch Hanna today. Not with Steven standing guard.

Finding Haines shot up to first priority.

Words from the CD about mercy falling and praising the God who gives and takes away registered like a slap-down. Lift his eyes to the hills and see where his help came from? Not today. Today he had other plans.

An hour later, he sat at his kitchen table with his laptop, checking to see what intel had been uploaded so far. His mother and father hovered. Mom had fixed a serious Dagwood sandwich and a cup of hot tea. But he couldn't eat. Didn't want to talk.

"Claire, would you mind leaving us alone for a few minutes?"

Michael's heart kicked into his throat.

Mom stood and forced a smile. "I'll be in the bedroom reading, if you need me."

The colonel waited until the bedroom door clicked. "You look like one of my men staggering back to camp from an ambush."

"I'm not one of your soldiers."

"No. You're my son. I know this, Michael. But I haven't treated you that way."

Against his wishes, his eyes grew wide and his mouth opened and closed without pushing any intelligent words through it.

"You act as if I've never said a kind word to you."

"I don't remember any."

His father's face pinched together, his mouth pulling down at the edges. "Look, son. I know something happened between us the night of my heart attack. But I can't remember any details. The only thing I vaguely recall is your asking my forgiveness."

So his father had heard him. Now what? Spill the sordid facts?

"I don't want to know what happened. But I've had a lot of time to think. And what my mind won't let go of is how little I've been a real father to you."

Michael stood. The apology he'd longed for perched on the colonel's lips. But not even that could right his spinning world. He needed out of here. Needed to check in at the hospital and find out what was going on with Lee.

After everything else, God couldn't let his friend die.

"Can we go over this later? Lee's in the hospital."

The colonel rose from his chair, movements slow, face still sad. "Sure, Michael. I'll be here when you're ready to talk."

Now if that didn't beat all.

Grabbing his jacket on the way out, he studied his father. The large man was more bent, more frail than usual. Maybe he would talk to him later tonight. Much later. "Tell Mom not to fix me anything for dinner. No telling when I'll make it back."

He was out the door before the colonel could reply.

Thirty minutes later, he slogged into the ER waiting room of Alexandria Community. Hanna and Steven stood and walked toward him. The grim lines of their faces shouted news he couldn't handle.

"Tell me they're okay."

"They're in surgery. So far, so good. The hospital notified their families, and I'm waiting on flight information." Steven narrowed his eyes. "We'll talk about work later. For now, I'm heading back to the office and to the airport as soon as Mrs. Branson calls."

"You talked to Foster."

"More like listened to her rant."

Michael hung his head. "I'm sorry, boss. I blew it today."

"You're still in the game. Just get your head where it needs to be." Steven turned toward Hanna and kissed the top of her head. He left without another word.

Hanna didn't fill the empty space with chatter. She only wrapped her arms around his waist and buried her face in his chest.

He led them back to the plastic chairs, Hanna's soft hand enclosed in his. No words needed. Studying the white floor, he let the silence and Hanna's peaceful presence wash over him.

So many images fought for position in his mind. His father's sad face. Lee's haunted eyes. Katrina Chu's picture. He rejected them all. He'd deal with them later. Right now he just needed to be here and be quiet.

Maybe then he'd hear the truth and figure out Haines's next step. Before it was too late.

33

Michael's Thursday blurred into Friday morning, a confusing mix of being recalled to work and arriving at the hospital early this morning to see Lee. Before all hell broke loose somewhere today.

And he had to be there.

The waiting room silence and today's unknowns pressed in on him. Shoulders knotted, he paced. Lee's and Rashida's parents were in their rooms, not getting any more rest than the task force. He didn't look forward to talking with them again today.

Someone entered the small, waiting area with soft steps and joined him by the windows. "Have you slept any?" Hanna touched his arm, her eyes rimmed in red.

"I could ask you the same thing."

She nudged him toward a chair. "Visiting hours aren't for another half hour."

"I need to make some calls before then."

She studied his face but stayed silent. He didn't unclip his phone. Only took her hand and rubbed a circle with his thumb. "You should be at work."

"Dad's taking care of Grounded so I can be where I need to be."

"Where you need to be is far away from DC." Along with Eve, Deni, and anyone else Haines had set his mind on destroying. He was still out there somewhere and planning God only knew what. None of the arrested One Pure Nation fools had leaked a clue regarding today's Wave Three plans.

"I don't want to go back over last night's conversation. I'm not leaving." She released his hand and smoothed her brown warm-up suit. "Eve's right. We won't let these bigots scare us away. You'll catch them."

The fire in her words stoked his pride. She believed in him. Too bad that wouldn't protect her from Haines. Regardless of what his sick mind had conjured about Hanna, Haines would kill her and Eve without blinking.

That couldn't happen.

"You're an amazing woman." He ran a finger down her cheek. "But like I said last night, being safe isn't the same as running away. Will you drive over to Eve's and take all of them to Virginia? Just for the weekend."

"No."

"Please, Hanna. I need to know you're safe."

She blinked back tears and buried her head into his shoulder.

Adrenaline and no sleep ramped up his emotions. Gently taking her face in his hands, he kissed her with everything words couldn't say.

"Michael." Kessler's voice broke Michael's focus.

Hanna jumped back.

Michael only moved his eyes to meet Steven's stony face.

"Lee's asking for you." The hard line of Steven's mouth mellowed. "He'd like to see both of you."

It figured that Steven had beaten him to the punch and already talked to Lee. But Kessler was the boss. And he hadn't made an issue about what he'd walked in on. Good thing. Michael had no intention of apologizing. "Are his parents still there?"

"No. They went down to the cafeteria."

Michael stood and reached out for Hanna's hand. She took it and joined him. "Michael thinks I should take Eve and her family to Virginia for the weekend."

"I agree." Steven met Michael's gaze and gave a slight nod. "You should listen to him." With that, Steven turned and headed down the hospital corridor.

Michael could only stare at the retreating form as a strange emotion surged through him. Someone besides Hanna believed in him too.

✳ ✳ ✳

Hanna tugged on Michael's arm. "Between you and Steven, I guess I have no choice but to go over to Eve's."

"You have a choice, Hanna."

Looking into Michael's dark brown eyes, she wanted to cry. Wanted to kiss him again and stay in that safe place. But nothing around them was safe. And Michael had a job to do.

She'd do her part and follow his request. Because even when he was right and could have pushed, he didn't.

"I'll head over to Eve's so you can talk to Lee alone."

Michael's shoulders relaxed and his eyes smiled. "Let's go see Lee first and then get you some food before you head out of town." He squeezed her hand. "Thank you."

She nodded, and they walked to Lee's room in charged silence. No more running and hiding. They'd work together and see this through to the end.

With a slight knock at the door, Michael entered. Hanna followed.

Lee shifted in his hospital bed. IV lines and leg bandages stayed mostly hidden by the white sheets. But the room filled with plants and bright balloons provided a sharp contrast to Lee's stormy expression. "Thanks for being here. I'm glad I could talk to both of you at the same time."

Her stomach churned.

"I wanted to tell you in person that I'm going back to Louisiana as soon as things are squared away here."

Michael gripped the foot of Lee's bed. "No. You can't let Haines win."

"It's not about winning. It's about keeping my family alive." Lee narrowed his eyes. "He cut Rashida and shot me, not to kill us fast, but to let us suffer before we died. He'd have stayed to watch it too."

"I'll find him and make him pay."

The hardness in Michael's eyes and voice slammed against Hanna's chest. All the tenderness and hope had fled from his face. In its place landed a cold cop hardness that nothing would sway. She had to do something to change the course of this conversation.

"We'll pray, Lee. You and Rashida will get better and Michael will find Haines so he can't hurt you again."

"God didn't do a whole lot of protecting any of us." Lee shook his head. "Thank you for praying, Hanna, and for your friendship. You're both important to me and Rashida. But I need to do what I need to do."

"So do I." Michael straightened. "If I take him out today, will you stay?"

Lee shrugged. "Can't say."

"Then I'll do what I need to do, and we can revisit this issue later." Michael crossed his arms as the two men stared each other down.

Hanna moved in between them. "Michael, don't. You need to pray first. Anger will cloud your better judgment."

"You pray, Hanna." He stepped toward the door. "I have work to do."

She grabbed his arm and held on tight. "If you believe God failed, you'll charge out of here in your strength and…"

"Get myself killed?" Rage lit his eyes.

She dropped her hands. "Please, Michael. I need to know you're safe too."

He didn't move. But his hard expression didn't waver either.

It'd take more than prayer to repair the hurt she'd caused Michael with her fear. And far more than prayer to fix everything Haines had shattered. What, she had no idea.

All she could do was hope they'd both be ready when it came.

※　※　※

Too many minutes inched past before Michael had escaped Lee's attitude of weak surrender and Hanna's doubt. Two more things he couldn't fix.

He'd said a fast good-bye to Lee and now sat across from Hanna at a table in the busy cafeteria. They hadn't spoken more than ten words since leaving Lee's room.

She prayed and nibbled at her omelet.

The smell of pancakes, bacon, and strong coffee assaulted his nose. He couldn't eat. Couldn't think past Hanna's words about charging out in his strength and getting himself killed.

His stomach clenched.

But what could he do? He'd prayed. And like the song running through his mind said, it was still raining. God hadn't stepped in and saved the day. No, everything got worse.

The buzz of his phone jerked him away from his darkening thoughts. Foster's number. "Parker."

"The new site you cracked at dawn is exploding with details about today's plans. And we just received a call from a nervous administrator. Suspicious early-morning visitors at an elementary school on Third Street, near Howard University."

His heart slammed into his throat. Denisha Blaine's school. This was it.

"And another notification from the Baltimore task force about unusual activity around two elementary schools southeast of downtown."

Not schools. *Please, God, not that.*

"All schools in the DC and Baltimore area are on high alert."

"I'll meet you at the school on Third." Michael stood, Hanna's wide eyes locked on to his.

"Only if you can keep a cool head."

"Will do." He closed the phone. "It's going down soon. Pray, Hanna. I'll call when I can."

Less than a minute later, he revved the Mustang's engine and tore off for DC. Traffic on George Washington Parkway nearly did him in. Too much time wasting. Too much time to think.

All the unfinished business with his father buzzed around his brain. Hanna's doubt-filled face. Lee's defeated eyes and the pain not masked by a morphine pump and exhaustion.

Haines would pay.

Michael would rip off justice's blindfold and right the system's wrongs where Haines was concerned. Put an end to his hate speech and the rash of shootings he'd unleashed around the country.

Today. Before another child died at Haines's hands.

Thirty long minutes and less traffic than expected, Michael pulled behind Foster's Bucar and parked.

She met him at his door. "Nothing. Locals swept the school and we've secured the perimeter. If there was anyone here, they're long gone."

Michael doubted that. Given the minuscule percentage of white children and Denisha Blaine's attendance here, there was no way this school would avoid Haines's attention. Unless it only served as a decoy.

But Haines wasn't that smart. Was he?

Matthews and his blond bulk lumbered toward them. He stood way too close to Foster. Didn't look like she minded, either. "Internet chatter says we're at the wrong school." Matthews smirked. "And two men in camo were spotted near Brent Elementary. Locals are moving in and our team's awaiting your word to head that way."

"Let's do it."

Michael shook his head. "I'm staying here. This school is a far more probable hit for Haines and his goons."

Matthews glared. "You haven't been online in the last few hours, have you?"

"No."

"Then I suggest you trust your team and get moving."

Crossing his arms, Michael copied the spook's scowl and stared him down. "Based on a lot more than some blip on the Web, I have a hunch this school's worth monitoring."

Foster shrugged. "Suit yourself. Stay here and keep watch. Maybe some chill-out time for you will benefit everyone."

As Foster and Matthews drove away, a thousand thoughts hammered Michael's brain. Two stood out.

Matthews shouldn't be trusted.

This was the right place.

Maybe Haines had decided to wait until school let out and the early morning menace was nothing more than One Pure Nation idiots almost dropping the ball. Too bad the task force hadn't nabbed them earlier.

He scanned the faded orange-brick school and white pavement surrounding the flagpole, praying his hunch was wrong. If not, it was all up to him to stop Haines.

Or more children would die today.

34

Sean checked his watch and nodded at the two marksmen setting up their rifles next to him. Three o'clock. Perfect, partly cloudy conditions. No glaring sun or too little light. He couldn't have ordered a better day.

Almost show time. At last word, Howard and all their best players were in place. They wouldn't talk again until completion. Three schools in Miami. Three in Chicago. Two in DC. And two in Baltimore.

Even though earlier this morning the FBI hounds had sniffed out their plan to descend on a number of schools, interestingly enough, the two hits in his hometown weren't even on the FBI's radar. Funny how perfectly executed Web chatter worked in his favor. Eutaw and Furman had been mentioned thanks to Jane and her family's help. But hadn't been searched like the two dozen other schools which had been discussed to varying degrees.

Nothing online mentioned Miami or Chicago.

Unfortunate that Sherry couldn't provide his inside information any longer. It would have been interesting to see what scrambling the feds were doing about now. Sherry would be fine, though useless, in the future. He'd provide funding to her family for legal entanglements, but the FBI wouldn't allow her to step foot on federal land again.

Sean scanned the baseball field behind their target location. Soon it would fill, and they'd take their pick of shots before disappearing again.

Too bad they didn't have enough teams to put more schools in their sights.

Today's plans were not as large as he'd hoped Wave Three would become, but it would do. Law enforcement wouldn't know what hit them from all different sides of each city. News crews would swarm. And mass hysteria would erupt. At least in a few places. More would follow suit soon enough.

The FBI hadn't found the most important followers, and the loyal ones they did arrest wouldn't breathe a word of the plans. Only Don knew enough details to be a problem.

Matthews had succeeded in throwing off the task force bloodhounds and diverting them to other locations in DC. Too bad his deadly aim wouldn't be utilized for this project.

Sean readjusted his bipod.

The two marksmen on either side of him stretched out in place and waited for his call.

"On my mark." Soon the school bells would toll and their fun would begin.

Sean's finger curled around the trigger, muscles tight and ready. His other hand strummed the weapon just like he'd done every time. One extra lucky rub and he was ready.

"One. Two…"

But no swarms descended on the field. He checked his watch again. Three seventeen.

Grabbing binoculars, he surveyed the school building. By all accounts everything appeared normal. Except that no children could be seen anywhere.

His abdomen clenched.

Something was wrong.

* * *

Michael wished Foster had agreed to hold off school dismissal longer for the DC system, like the Baltimore officials had planned.

He exited the back of the blue-roofed school and walked the perimeter. SWAT teams had assembled at the two DC schools suspected of being One Pure Nation's primary targets.

But there'd been no movement all day. No one in or out of the buildings. Nothing inside the schools. No additional sightings of anything unusual on school grounds either.

Maybe Haines and his lackeys had decided to postpone their no-longer-mysterious Friday plans.

Schools.

Four, if the task force at headquarters had dug deep enough past the party line.

"I'm impressed you stuck to your guns." Matching Michael's step, Brett Hamilton drew alongside and rubbed his bald head. His jeans and sweatshirt an abrupt shift from his usual uniform.

"Figured you'd be back at your desk after the big no-show this morning."

Brett chuckled. "What, miss all the fun?"

Both men stayed close to the building and kept eyes alert for any movement. There were enough rooftops in shooting distance to make even a hardened veteran squirm.

"You used to be SWAT, right?"

"Yes."

Michael glanced at his task force partner. "Injury or bad scores sideline you?"

"Neither." Brett flashed his left hand. "One too many teary-eyed requests."

Enough said. At least Hanna understood what she was getting into with him. She'd be like Gracie and Sara who never begged their husbands to turn in their guns.

"You really think Haines is going forward with his plans today?"

"I have no doubt. He's drunk with his own superiority, and his pride won't let him back down. Not after we busted things up at the restaurant yesterday."

Brett whistled. "How long till they dismiss school?"

"Fifteen minutes."

"Ever feel like a sitting duck in a carnival show?"

Michael stepped inside the school's front doors and nodded to one of the security guards he'd spoken with earlier today. Stopping Brett from walking toward the office, he nodded toward the back of the school. "Right before you joined me, I noticed a quick glint on the roof of the apartment building across V Street. I had no backup to call, so I kept watching the same spot for a minute. Nothing."

"Coulda just been the sun."

"Or our shooter."

Brett checked his watch. "How long ago?"

"Five minutes."

"How 'bout I keep the back doors blocked and pace outside? If our guy is watching that exit, he should zero in on me fast."

"Let's hope there's only one." Michael picked up his pace through the school halls, slowing to veer right and lift a hand to Brett when they separated. Running the rest of the way, Michael exited the east side of the school and followed the tree line to the street.

A fast dash across V street and he was at the apartment building directly across from the elementary school's back door. Shooting up a quick prayer, he hoped he'd made the right choice. No time to hustle up more than one fire exit before school let out.

Honking cars on the busy street below concealed the minimal noise as he conquered the last escape ladder and crouched down to view the rooftop.

Muscles tightened and his pulse skyrocketed.

Lying prone, face plastered to a sniper rifle, was a black-clothed shooter. Michael had found his mark.

He slipped onto the roof and unhooked his holster. The other man must have been in his zone where nothing registered.

Feet planted, Michael aimed his Glock, trigger finger itching to pull and ask questions later.

"FBI!"

The tall form swiveled onto his back and yanked something from his coveralls.

Michael pulled the trigger.

The man's body convulsed and metal clanked against concrete. Then his chest movements ceased and the tall form lay motionless. Blood pooled around him.

Pulling out his cell, Michael phoned Steven. "One down in DC, boss."

"Haines?"

Michael stepped closer, gun still trained on the shooter's skull-capped head.

The stench of death hit him full force. So did the endorphin crash. Arm muscles quivered and his stomach roiled.

When a young, chiseled jaw line came into focus, Michael wanted to unload another clip. "Not Haines," was all he could force out.

※ ※ ※

Sean scanned the streets around the Baltimore school once more. Normal traffic patterns. No police cars. Could the FBI have every Baltimore school on alert?

There had been no indication of trouble earlier this afternoon, and he couldn't risk calling Howard or Carl and interrupting their assignments.

The young men on either side of him squirmed and re-sighted on the school building.

Sirens sounded in the distance.

"This is not worth getting arrested." The taller of the two men spoke. "Let's break down and try again another day."

"I give the orders here."

The two men exchanged glances. "Yes sir."

Sean threw down his binoculars. "Sight on the middle of a window. You two take different ends of the building. I'll take the middle. Fire on my mark."

Taking shallow breaths, he braced himself and curled his finger around the trigger once more. No time for a lucky rub now.

"One. Two…"

Three. Their weapons discharged simultaneously. Sean's shoulder absorbed the kickback, but taut muscles wanted more.

Screams followed and sirens drew closer.

But within seconds they were up and erasing any hint of their presence.

Less than a minute later they parted ways.

Sean joined his escape team and their beige pickup blended into the cars streaming away from the shot-battered school.

Tight muscles still screaming for action, he remained silent in the backseat, daring anyone in the car to speak. The married couple he'd chosen for his escape team kept their eyes focused forward and made no attempt to ask questions.

"Once we return to DC, I'll be leaving soon for another appointment." His heart rate picked up just visualizing his next move. "Keep my luggage and the boarding passes at your house. I'll return before nightfall."

"Word is DC and Baltimore transit systems are all on red alert. No one is leaving the cities by bus, plane, or train today." Barry didn't turn around or look in the rearview mirror.

"When you arrive home, place a call to my airline and see about changing the flight to tomorrow, leaving from another city if necessary. Tammy, use hysterics as required."

She nodded. "Will you stay at our house tonight?"

"I haven't decided. It all depends on how well my next stop goes."

Sean double-checked his Smith and Wesson. Shortly, he'd settle his last score. That would make up for the multiple hits he'd been denied at the school.

Then one thing would play out just as planned.

35

Hanna picked up another one of Eve's running outfits, this one bright pink, and folded it for the third time. They'd already packed a suitcase for Deni.

"I need to call the school. They should have let out already." Eve bit her lip and tried to shake the quiver out of her hands.

"The last time I talked to Michael he said everything was secured at the school and he'd be on watch all day. Dismissal was delayed thirty minutes, but there was nothing on the news last time we checked." Hanna grabbed Eve's shoulders and held her still. Her friend still winced with any sudden move. "Sorry."

Eve tried to smile.

"Instead of fretting, let's keep praying Deni stays safe."

Trina ran into Eve's bedroom, eyes wide and hands waving everywhere. "All the news stations have gone crazy. There was a shooting in Baltimore and two men arrested before firing on another school. Minutes ago. And kids were shot at three schools in Miami too. What are we gonna do?"

They left the clothes and stood in front of the living room television.

A red-headed local reporter shouted over ambulance sirens and full-scale chaos behind her. "One gunman down and no others found at—"

"Oh, Lord! That's Deni's school. Please Jesus, let her be okay."

Trina and Hanna both hugged Eve gently and kept her standing.

The reporter droned on. "The widespread chaos in DC and neighboring Baltimore schools amounted to little more than federal overreaction. One school, out of the twenty federal sources claimed would be hit, was fired on today."

Hanna wanted to spit. That reporter had no clue how many federal agents and local officers put their lives on the line and probably stopped all the other instances from occurring. Talk about ingratitude.

"Local parents can expect severe delays in bus drop-off schedules and are advised not to flood the school buildings in search of students. Once again, no DC school children were harmed today, and the lone sniper threat at this location has been neutralized."

"Oh, thank the good Lord."

Hanna released the breath she'd been holding and clicked the TV remote's Off button. "Let's pack some dinner while we wait for Deni to come home."

Grabbing the remote from Hanna's hand, Trina stuck out her chin. "Hey, Miss Thang, you might be welcome here, but you are not in control. Jus' you keep that in mind."

Eve rolled her eyes.

Trina turned the TV back on and flipped to a cable news station.

"I'll fix you some PB and J, Trina." Hanna tried to smile and lighten the fear-drenched room.

Trina glowered.

"Come on. I think there's some turkey and cheese left." Eve flipped her hands toward the kitchen. "Don't you go stirring up anything, now."

They set about packing sandwiches, chips, and fruit in silence.

Eve slipped the food into a large, black cooler and broke the quiet. "How were Lee and Rashida this morning?"

Was it only this morning that she and Michael had visited Lee and then choked down breakfast? Well, she had anyway. And then spent the day waiting for Deni to be released from school, everyone's nerves coiled tight.

Dad had manned the coffee shop all week, leaving her free with no questions asked. Sue had even pitched in to man the front counter. And last time they'd talked, all was well.

Not so with the Bransons.

"Lee is dead set on moving back to Louisiana as soon as he's able to hire a moving company and get transferred."

"Rashida?"

Hanna leaned back against the white kitchen counter. "She's struggling to comprehend what Haines did. And not even thinking past today."

"She's going to be okay, right?"

"Yes. Well...physically anyway." Hanna stuck her hands in the jacket pockets of her warm-up suit. "The knife wound tore into her abdomen. And her uterus. The doctors don't know if she'll be able to carry a baby now."

"Mercy." Eve's eyes watered.

"But Rashida's mom and mother-in-law told her over and over the doctor said it was too soon to be sure. They're praying for healing and trying to help Rashida hang on to hope."

Trina entered the kitchen. "You think this kinda stuff is anything new?"

"Trinie, don't."

Hanna's brain hurt from the reality check she'd received this week. "Yes, all this violence is new to me." She placed a hand on Eve's shoulder and met Trina's frightened eyes. "But I know it's not to many people. I wish that weren't the case."

"Me too."

Trina's quiet words washed over Hanna. Once again she and Trina were on the same side. Maybe even sharing a mutual sadness over all the injustice.

"Since dinner is packed, let's load up the car. I can't watch any more stuff on TV." Trina nodded to the small kitchen clock. "Deni should be home soon."

Hanna longed to call Michael and make sure he was okay. The first TV report hadn't mentioned any details about police injuries, but like Trina, she couldn't handle anymore news right now. Steven would call if anything were wrong.

That didn't loosen the jumble of nerves still tightening around her middle. She couldn't let the TV images or unanswered questions go. Something wasn't right. Besides the obvious, there was a nagging unease demanding her attention.

If she'd learned anything the last few months, it was to not ignore the building urge to pray. She bowed her head while Trina and Eve carried suitcases out to the Equinox.

Fear still churned her stomach. Lies about herself piggybacked on the growing anxiousness. So she prayed harder. And hoped Michael would call sooner rather than later.

❋   ❋   ❋

Sean flung his backup computer against Barry's den wall. How could his plans have gone so ghastly wrong?

"Dad, if you were here…" No use continuing out loud and giving Barry and Tammy any reason to believe his mental abilities were slipping.

He should have been celebrating as he watched television with millions across the nation. All hearing about his triumph.

But that hadn't happened.

He turned off the TV and stalked over to the back window, staring into a normal suburbia afternoon. Children running home for afternoon snacks and homework. Tired parents dragging in from their high-powered jobs.

At least Barry's neighbors were all white. He'd claw the walls if he had to look at another mud race right now.

He punched in Howard's number yet again. No word from Carl. And no one had names of their members who had been shot or arrested.

Howard answered on the second ring.

Sean loosened his white-knuckled fist. "Why haven't you picked up when I called?"

"We've been busy down here in Florida."

"Local media isn't saying enough. And what's been reported is depressing." Rage built just thinking about the five loyal followers in jail and the three school failures. Not to mention an unidentified, deceased sniper. "Brighten my day with your success."

Howard's mirthless laugh filled the phone line. "Everything proceeded like clockwork in Miami. I'm still waiting for our teams in

Chicago to check in." Long pause. "Things should be commencing shortly up north."

At least someone had succeeded today.

"Did you hear what Parker accomplished?"

Sean balled his fist again. "Why are you getting reports when Carl has yet to check in with me?" When he arrived at the meeting place, Sean would dress him down so harshly Carl would never forget it.

"Matthews called with an update. Didn't want to disturb you in case you were still busy in Baltimore."

Translation: the fool didn't want to incur Sean's wrath for the pathetic cover job on their school-shooting plans. How the FBI had discovered so much too soon still infuriated Sean.

"Seems your Mr. Parker ended Carl Goring's future today."

"What?" Sean gripped the phone tighter.

"Carl is dead. Thanks to Parker."

That was the final straw. "I'm calling Albert. He can do the honors for Parker and his parents while I'm making my last stop of the day."

"Enjoy that, my friend. You deserve to end this evening better than it started."

He did. His only regret was not being the last one Michael Parker saw before dying.

※　※　※

The Strategic Information and Operations Center roared with controlled chaos as Michael listened to four news reports at once. Three of a suspected five snipers in Baltimore had been apprehended. Carl Goring dead.

Another two arrested, one wounded, in a skirmish at Minor Elementary in DC.

Brett Hamilton stepped next to him. "Great work today."

"Thanks."

"No casualties besides Goring in DC or Baltimore. Makes for a good day's work, don't you think?"

Michael nodded. "Haines shot up a school, though. Not sure how he failed to kill anyone."

"What, the choir boy isn't shouting hallelujah and saying God saved the day?" Matthews leaned back in a nearby office chair.

Brett narrowed his eyes. "Shut up, you idiot. We're on the same side. In case you forgot."

"Oh, that was scary." Matthews chuckled. "I'll be taking my leave before you break out a 'shucks' or 'golly gee.'"

"Good riddance."

So Michael wasn't the only one wishing Matthews would crawl back under his CIA rock and not resurface. After Matthews sauntered out of the SIOC, Michael turned back to Brett. "Any details on those injured in Baltimore?"

Foster pulled herself away from a computer screen. "Ten are being treated at local hospitals. Two teachers, three boys, and five girls. Only two people shot. The rest were injured running from the three class-rooms that were hit. Could have been far worse."

"Unlike Miami." Tanner shook her blond head and frowned. "In three schools over fifty were injured and at least nine dead."

No intel had prepared them for the assault on Miami.

The videoconference screen blared to life with the Chicago Assistant Special Agent in Charge glowering long distance. The room quieted. Foster stood at attention with Acting Chief Lowell of the National Joint Terrorism Task Force while the Chicago ASAC bellowed. "Three Chicago schools were just hit by sniper attacks resembling earlier assaults in Baltimore, Washington DC, and Miami."

"Casualities?" Lowell straightened his shoulders and waited. News from around the world buzzed in the background while dozens of other agents continued working.

"It's too soon to call. I need all the updated information on these One Pure Nation terrorists ASAP."

Foster ducked behind her computer. "I'm on it, sir."

Michael lowered his head. What was next?

His cell phone buzzed and he glanced at the screen. His father. Why would the colonel be calling him at work?

Probably nothing more than Mom watching the news with everyone else in the US and wanting to be sure he was okay. He slipped out of the SIOC to answer the call.

"Hello?"

"Michael, it's your mother." Her voice sounded like she'd run a marathon.

"Mom, what's wrong?"

"Oh…well…I was just checking in to be sure you're okay." Just what he'd figured. But muffled noises in the background sounded like trouble. The hairs on his neck prickled.

"Is the colonel okay, Mom? Or is he just pitching a fit again?"

"Michael, hold your tongue. Your father would never—"

More muffled sounds. Like his father stalking around the room or throwing things. "Mom?"

"Son, I'm sorry. It is your father. I…I think he's having another heart attack, but he won't let me take him to the doctor. He's sure his double bypass surgery fixed everything."

Double bypass? His father had just had triple bypass surgery.

"Don't waylay…I mean…pounce on your brother with the news. Just let him know, okay? And please come home quickly. Drive safely though, Michael."

The phone line disconnected.

Double bypass. Waylay. Brother. What in the dickens was his mom talking about? And was it enough to justify leaving the chaos beyond the SIOC doors?

Brett pushed open the glass doors. "Your presence is required inside." He stopped and cocked his head. "Something wrong, Parker?"

Michael shrugged. "Maybe. My mom just called to see if I was okay. But then she started jabbering about my father's double bypass surgery and him not doing well. Then she said to tell my brother."

"If your dad just had surgery and something's wrong, it makes sense she would ask you to call your brother."

"I don't have a brother."

Brett swallowed. "Does Haines know you don't have a brother?"

Michael's blood froze.

"Not to be all cloak and dagger, but Haines is still unaccounted for, Michael."

"Tell Foster I'm going home." Michael took off down the hall.

Brett ran behind him and jerked him to a stop. "Don't you know the most important law enforcement rule?"

Michael nodded. "Never go it alone."

"Then what are we waiting for? Let's go."

Michael led Brett to the Mustang and called Steven on the way out of the garage. "Something's going down at my apartment. Tell Clint. And Foster." He swallowed hard. "And pray. Please. I don't have a clue what I'm walking into here. But it can't be good."

36

Michael stopped at the management office two buildings away from his apartment.

Brett exited the passenger seat and slipped around the Mustang to the driver's window. "You think going in there alone will work?"

"Better than both of us getting shot."

"I'll give you that. But I'm not sure your confrontation will stall the massacre these guys have planned."

"Stay here. And let me do what I have to do." Muscles tightened to the breaking point, Michael narrowed his eyes. His boss's warning beat a steady rhythm in his brain. "Do not move in. Do not...do not..." Steven's words added an exclamation point to Brett's concerns.

But images of what Haines was doing to Mom and the colonel while Michael sat helpless tore through his mind. What was he thinking, waiting on someone else to do his job?

His buzzing cell snapped him back to the present.

"An HRT is in route. You and Hamilton steer clear of your apartment." Steven's sharp tone heated the phone line. "That's a direct order, Parker."

"Yes sir."

Snapping the phone closed, Michael leaned back into the leather seat. He never should have involved Steven. With Brett's help, Michael could have taken Haines. Might still.

Brett whistled. "I take it we've been instructed to stand down."

Straightening, Michael gripped the steering wheel harder and stared into the cloudy sky. "An HRT is on the way. But I need a visual to know my parents are still alive."

Brett leaned into the Mustang's door. "Haines is laying a trap for you, Parker. And I agree with your boss, it's not wise for you to even be here. Let's wait on your Hostage Rescue Team in the management office."

Deep breath. Brett was right. But it didn't chill the fire building in Michael's gut. Instead of parking the Mustang, he dialed his home phone.

The answering machine kicked on.

He hung up and dialed again.

"Michael, come on, man. Be smart."

Ignoring Brett, he hung up on the monotone message and dialed again.

"Michael…" Mom's voice. "Where…why aren't you here yet? Oh, traffic is that bad…I see."

No doubt someone was there with a gun to her head. But they weren't on the phone extension. Or maybe they were but his mother had no idea. She'd get them all killed if Michael didn't do something fast.

"Mom, calm down. I know you go on when you're nervous, but the colonel will be okay." His mother seldom if ever babbled. But he had to cover her somehow. "I'll call an ambulance if you think things are that serious."

"No! Oh…" Her voice caught and the sound of muffled movement increased. "I mean…well…your father would be furious. He's…he's resting right now and I think he'll be okay. I just need you to come home. I'm…I'm out of frozen peas. You know how your father is about his peas. If you get here to watch him soon, I can run out before he wakes."

Frozen peas? His father hated peas. Another coded message? Then realization hit. Whoever was there had knocked his father out. Mom was something else.

"Michael. I really need you. Here. Now. Please?"

Dread stamped across his knotted shoulders. The HRT wouldn't arrive for another thirty minutes. Too long. Way too long.

"I'm just around the corner, Mom. I'll be there soon." He hung up and re-clipped the phone to his belt.

Brett slapped his fist against the car door. "You can't do this."

"Call a cab, Hamilton. Go back to the SIOC. I'll handle things here."

Cussing a blue streak, Brett spun away from the car. Then doubled back. "No, Parker. I'm here to stay."

"It could cost us both our badges."

"You're sure this can't wait for the HRT?"

"Best I can tell, my father is unconscious. And whoever is there with Haines is getting antsy. Mom isn't going to hold it together much longer."

A quick nod and Brett stepped back. "I'll talk to the apartment management. Give me a few shakes to secure a unit and set up a sight line into your place." Hamilton stepped away from the car. "We'll nail Haines before he can hurt your parents."

"Take my McMillan. Being SWAT, you should be up to speed."

"Affirmative." Brett opened the trunk and shouldered the rifle case. "Wait for my call. I'll settle as fast as possible."

After parking his Mustang a short distance from the management office, Michael weaved his way on foot through the apartment complex. Multicolored leaves still clung to enough trees, allowing him good cover to draw close to his building.

Minutes crawled.

He glared at his cell, daring it to stay silent. *Please, God. Help me do this. Keep my parents alive.*

Now he could tell Hanna he'd prayed. No charging in on his own strength.

The rest of her speech about anger had to wait.

"Come on, Hamilton. Call."

Inching closer to his apartment, he focused on his balcony. Too bad no one stepped outside.

His buzzing cell demanded attention.

"I'm ready when you are, Parker." Brett's voice had hardened to steel. "Two men. One former football player and a short, older man. The old guy is shadowing your mother. I'm locked onto the one standing over your dad. He's on the couch. No movement. "

"I owe you."

"Big time."

Michael stepped up to his apartment building's door. "Give me a few minutes to get my Mom in a safe place."

"Will do. When they demand your weapon, hold it up high. I'll unload as soon as you duck."

Closing his phone, Michael shot up a fervent prayer for God's direction and cycled through possible scenarios. Moving into the building and up the stairwell, he unclipped his holster and tucked his backup into his jeans before he knocked.

"Who…who's there?"

"It's me. I rushed out of the office and forgot my keys. Sorry."

The lock clicked and his front door inched open. Resisting the urge to draw and shoot, he stepped inside.

Mom lunged forward, but was jerked back.

A white-haired man slammed the door shut and grinned. "So good of you to join us, Parker. What an honor to meet a real live FBI hero."

"Let my parents walk out now."

The man pointed his Kel-Tec at Mom's head and held up her rope-bound wrists. "I think they'll stay and enjoy the show."

Michael glared at the mountain of a man guarding his father in the living room. "Where's Haines?"

Half expecting him to slither out from the back hall, Michael glanced that way.

"Attending to other matters." White Hair's smile set Michael's jaw on edge.

Back toward the kitchen, Michael stepped out of alignment with Football Player. Maybe if he got these two talking, he'd unearth Haines's whereabouts. "The Blaines are gone. Or didn't your reverend know that already?"

Football Player guffawed. "You feds are stupid. Keeping schools locked up tight meant our hallowed reverend didn't have to rush to finish up things before disappearing."

Ice shards stabbed into Michael's back. *Please, God, no.*

He couldn't be two places at once. But he was here now. Neutralize this problem, then he could rush to find Hanna.

His hands itched for a weapon.

"Might as well hand over your gun, loser." White Hair's eyes flicked to Michael's holster. "We've already won this round."

He raised his Glock high into the air with slow precision.

"Mom, down now!"

Michael ducked and glass shattered.

Mom's blue-dressed form collapsed the same second Football Player went down.

Crouching, Michael aimed at White Hair and pulled the trigger.

The explosion rang in his ears and he ran to his mother's side. Kicking White Hair's Kel-Tec away, Michael eyed the perp. Pooling blood said he wasn't getting back up.

"Mom?" He shook her shoulder with one hand. "Mom, wake up. It's over."

She shuddered and blinked fast. "Michael? Oh, thank God."

"Stay put." Trigger finger taut, he inched over to the couch. His father lay face down, unmoving. No blood though.

Unlike Football Player.

The stench of bodily fluids and death hit Michael full force for the second time today.

Holding his breath, Michael holstered his Glock and then checked his father's pulse. Slow but steady. White Hair must have drugged the colonel. No other way the two goons would have tied up his mother.

He grabbed the cordless from the end table and dialed 911. While the operator rattled off questions, Michael cut the rope binding his father's hands.

Then he loosed his mother's wrists. She rushed over to the colonel and gasped. "Oh, dear Lord in heaven." Burying her face in his shoulder, she started sobbing. "Michael did it, Harry." She hiccuped as more tears fell. "Just like you said he would."

His father had said that?

The adrenaline crash slammed through his biceps and thighs, stealing his strength.

But he couldn't stop now. Haines was still on the loose.

Brett charged into the apartment. "Cops are on their way." He stepped back and grimaced. "I'll call a cleaner too. Ugh."

Michael pulled his mother into a fierce hug. A minute later, he turned away from his parents and walked to the door, tossing the cordless into Brett's hands. "Finish this for me. And stay with my mom and...dad."

Brow knotted, Brett stared. "Where you going?"

"To meet Haines."

37

Hanna paced Eve's living room for the hundredth time. Trina smoothed her flaming red sweater and grabbed her keys. "While Eve is at the bus stop, I'm gonna run to the store real fast, before Deni gets here."

Heart rate doubling, Hanna shook her head. "But we need to leave as soon as Deni's bus drops her off." They'd be sitting ducks waiting here for Trina.

Unless Michael had already arrested Haines. In that case, they had nothing to worry about, nothing at all.

Her heart didn't buy what her brain was trying to sell.

"I'm goin crazy watching you pace, Miss Thang. I'll be back in a few minutes." She closed the front door behind her.

Good thing there was no slamming involved.

Hanna stepped outside and watched Eve trudge up and down the street, eyes alternating between the reddish sidewalk and the increased traffic. News vans, police cruisers, and far more cars than usual whizzed past the row houses.

"Eve." She waved to her friend. "Come back inside." No use being a target for news reporters angling for a human interest story. School shootings in four cities had rocked the eastern part of the US.

Five minutes of watching TV had soured Hanna's stomach so badly she couldn't bear anymore teary-eyed parents and grief-filled panic.

She reentered Eve's basement apartment and pulled out her cell. Maybe Michael would answer this time. She'd only tried once before and it'd gone to voice-mail.

"Hanna, thank God."

Her heart constricted and she shivered like someone had walked over her grave. Stupid old wives' tale. Swallowing hard, she found her voice. "I'm so glad you answered. I've been worried about you all day."

"Same here."

"Why? You arrested all the shooters, didn't you?" She started pacing again.

"Haines is still out there."

Oh. No. They needed to leave now. Maybe when Eve came in, she could convince her to drive by the school or trace the bus route to find Deni. Something. Anything to keep them moving. Less of a target that way. "We'll leave now."

"I'm en route. If Deni's not home in ten minutes, you and Eve head over to the school and wait for me there. It's still crawling with cops."

"It's too late to leave without Deni. She could be here any minute."

"I'll be there within twenty."

Tears pricked at her eyes. "I won't leave Deni unprotected. What if Haines showed up right after we left?"

Michael's growl and honking horns blared through the phone line. "I'll be faster. Please, Hanna. I need to know you're safe."

"As soon as Deni arrives, we'll go."

A loud sigh. Then silence.

"I can't leave Deni, Michael. You have to understand." Hanna stepped into the tiny hall bathroom and grabbed a Kleenex.

"I do."

"I need to talk to Eve." She wiped her cheeks. "I'll call when we're on our way out of town."

"I love you, Hanna."

Deep shaky breath. "I love you too. Be safe, Michael." The words left her mouth and blazed her cheeks. But she'd said them. She'd voiced the truth buried deep inside. Truth she'd wanted to say a long time ago but couldn't. Not until fear loosed her tongue.

She hung up the phone and tried to shove away the niggling doubt that she'd have a chance to say them again.

"Hanna?" The front door closed and Eve marched closer. "Deni's bus isn't anywhere in sight. What are we gonna do?"

Hanna left the bathroom and met her friend by the couch, pulling Eve into a shaky hug.

Wide-eyed and tear-streaked, Eve shook her head. "We should have left for Virginia Monday night. I wish I'd listened to you."

"No." Hanna stepped back and squeezed Eve's shoulders. "You were brave and refused to run. You taught me a lot about not letting fear control you."

Eve nodded and wiped her eyes.

"Deni will be home soon. And Michael's on his way."

A rattling at the front door halted the conversation. Hanna let a long sigh release. "There's Deni now. Let's go."

As Deni stepped into the room, her saucer-like eyes registered first. Then the gun.

"And so we finally meet face to face, Hanna. Without Parker around." Sean Haines held a gun to Deni's back and shoved her into the room, closing the door with his foot. "I suggest no one move."

Hanna couldn't breathe, much less think. Eve's visible shaking said she fared far worse.

Shorter than Michael with brown hair and brown eyes, Haines's disheveled appearance only served to make the scene before her a thousand times worse.

"Momma!" Deni lunged away from him.

But Haines shoved her to the ground and placed a foot on her back, gun pointed at Eve's head. "I will only say it once more. Do not move."

Shrugging off a backpack, he tossed it at Eve's feet. "Hanna, would you be so kind as to remove the rope from my pack?"

She couldn't make her feet move.

"I can start shooting now." He pointed the gun at Deni. "Or you can do as I say."

Slow as molasses, she knelt down and took the rope from the gray pack.

"Tie up that wretched mud-race woman you stupidly called a friend.

Surely you've learned by now, Hanna, that their kind aren't worth your time." He pressed his foot harder into Deni's back, and she groaned through her sniffles.

Hanna stood, the rope biting into her palms.

"Do it, Hanna. Fast." Eve's whisper spurred Hanna on. Michael would be here soon. Better to get Eve and Deni on the floor and out of sight.

Tying Eve's hands loosely, she hurried. "There." Jaw clenched, she stared at Haines.

"Face down on the floor." He pointed the gun at Eve. Then he kicked Deni forward.

Eve gasped. But lowered herself flat against the living room carpet.

"Don't even think about any heroics." Haines pointed his chin at Deni's coiled form. "Tie her up too, Hanna."

Praying faster than her mind could comprehend, she knelt and wrapped the rope around Deni's shaking hands. "I'm so sorry, little one."

"No talking, if you please, Hanna."

She wanted to spit. And slap Haines like she'd slapped Reeley. Only harder.

"Please step over this way now." His gun stayed pointed at Eve's head. "What's left is you coming with me, Hanna. No struggles. Can you promise me that?"

Teeth about to break, she tried to speak. But nothing came out.

"I need your word, Hanna. Or I start shooting."

Shaking legs barely allowing her to straighten, she swallowed hard. "I...I'd rather die."

Haines tilted his head. "I'd prefer not shooting someone as pure and beautiful as you, Hanna."

The acids in her stomach shot into her throat.

"One more chance, Hanna. I don't have all day."

She said nothing.

Haines pointed the gun at Eve and pulled the trigger.

The explosion didn't cover Eve's scream. Or Deni's wail.

Hanna ran to her friend and fell to the floor. Blood gushed from Eve's knee. *Oh, God, do something.* Hot steel and acrid blood stung her nostrils. More screams split the air surrounding her.

"Shut up!" Haines narrowed his eyes at Eve. "Or I'll shoot the other one next."

Deni gulped in air and silenced. Eve's eyes rolled back into her head, and she made no further sounds. Barely breathed.

Hanna stood. "I...I'll come. Please don't shoot again." She stepped toward the couch. Touching the black and green barrier sent an idea surging through her. Maybe if she stalled, when Michael arrived, all she'd have to do is duck.

"Good choice, my dear." Haines chuckled. "Now, shall we?" He motioned toward the door.

One more look at the blood surrounding Eve stole Hanna's courage. She couldn't move.

"She'll bleed out soon. Come, Hanna." Haines moved toward her. "Promise me you'll join me, and something like this will never have to happen again."

Haines stepped closer.

It's all your fault. The old lie pummeled her heart. But she pushed it away. This was all Haines's fault. And he'd pay.

For now, she needed to do something to stall. Her eyes flicked around the living room, landing on the cracked crystal vase. Within reach.

"Your Web site photos don't do you justice." He touched her cheek, lowering his gun. "You're much more beautiful in person."

Her hand shot up automatically.

Haines grabbed her wrist, clamping hard. "No, Hanna. No more stalling either. We have a plane to catch."

He started to release her, but then pulled her into his chest. "I've been waiting for this day too long."

When he moved to kiss her, she reacted like Steven had taught her long ago. She brought her knee straight up. Hard. And connected.

Haines stumbled back, cursing, and dropped the gun.

Grabbing the vase on the coffee table, she flung herself forward and crashed the flawed crystal against his head.

It shattered on impact, and Haines crumpled to the floor.

❊ ❊ ❊

Hanna screamed, and Michael exploded into Eve's living room.

The image of blood, glass, and four motionless bodies slammed into his brain. "Hanna!" He rushed to her side, his Glock still warm in his right hand.

She groaned and rolled away from Haines's unmoving body.

He checked Haines for a pulse. Weak at best. Kicking the perp's gun away, Michael holstered his weapon. Then he knelt next to Hanna, grabbing her shoulders.

Blood covered her brown warm-up suit and stained her hands. "Hanna, are you shot?"

"N…no. No." Her blue eyes focused. "Michael! Oh, Michael." Sobs cut off her words, and she clung to him.

He held her shaking form for a second. "Hanna, I need to take care of Eve and Deni too." They stood together, Michael almost carrying Hanna as they crossed the living room.

Punching 911 yet again, he stooped down to check Eve's pulse. Stronger than Haines, but still weak. Cutting off Eve's ropes, Michael pointed to the silent child. "Go untie Deni."

Hanna rushed to the little girl and unfastened the knots. "She's unconscious. He kicked her hard, but didn't shoot." She cradled the little girl in her arms, rocking back and forth.

The 911 operator droned on and he answered questions as best he could. "One GSW, right knee. Unconscious." He applied direct pressure to stem the bleeding.

More details poured out of his mouth, but he locked eyes on Hanna.

Alive.

They were all still alive. Not only that, but she'd stopped Haines dead in his tracks. Almost literally.

Sirens drew nearer.

Trina crashed through the doors, panting. "Evie, where's Eve? Deni?"

"Here, Trina." Hanna pointed across the room. "They're alive. Eve's shot."

Trina fell to her knees, tears streaming down her face. "It was only supposed to take a few minutes. I'm so sorry." She leaned her face down to her sister's. "I should have been here, Evie. I'm so sorry."

Michael ended the 911 call and placed a hand on Trina's back. "The paramedics are on their way. It'll be okay, Trina."

"Will it?" Trina sniffled and rocked on her knees, face in her hands.

Soon paramedics and cops flooded Eve's small basement apartment. Eve and Deni were taken to an ambulance first. Next Haines was lifted onto a gurney and disappeared out the door, cops flanking him.

Hanna pressed close, her bandaged hands still trembling. "Is it over, Michael? Please tell me it's over."

He nodded. "Yes. It's over. You did it, Hanna. I'm so proud of you."

"Miss Kessler, we'd still advise a visit to the ER." A young female paramedic stopped in front of them.

"I'll drive her over."

With a nod, the woman walked away.

"You'll stay with me?" Her beautiful eyes begged for comfort.

Wrapping his arms around her, he nodded. "Yes. I'll be with you, Hanna." Forever.

38

Hanna carried in one last tray of coffeecake and set it on the large, linen-covered serving table. Sweets of all shapes and sizes covered every inch of white. Chocolate-chip pound cake, marzipan, pies, brownies, and Dad's favorite cherry-topped cheesecake.

To offset the sugar high a body could get just breathing the air, she started the coffee. Not quite the espresso Steven preferred, but Dad's favorite Colombian blend. And for Sue, she'd followed strict instructions to produce her sugar-shock sweet tea.

Silver and white balloons and streamers decorated the rest of Michael's clubhouse. Over the dessert table, an elegant banner hung. Happy Sixth Anniversary, Andrew and Sue. Its elegant calligraphy in bold blue, the color of her dad and stepmom's wedding.

Once again, tears caused the view before her to swim. There had been a lot of crying in the past week. But today her tears weren't sad.

"None of that, Hanna-girl. Saturdays are officially no-sob days." Steven pulled her into a hug. "Besides, you're a tough chick now."

"Whatever." She brushed away the escaping wetness. "When will Dad and Sue be here?"

"Michael's bringing them over by seven. So you'll only be without him another thirty minutes or so." Her brother grinned as he adjusted his black silk tie and suit coat. "I wish I hadn't let Michael talk me into wearing a monkey suit today. Even if we are celebrating lots of special occasions tonight."

Raising an eyebrow, she tilted her head. "What special occasions?"

"I promised not to say a word." Steven wiped the smile off of his stubbled face. "And you promised not to ask questions."

She had agreed to that when she'd walked in on Michael and Steven talking earlier. The words *babies* and *important question* piqued her curiosity, and she asked what they were discussing. After a round of *"nothing,"* Steven asked her to stop playing twenty questions and just trust him.

"You have something mischievous up your sleeve, but I'll keep my promise and refrain from pestering the truth out of you."

Steven laughed. "Not like you could. But thank you. Especially since I'm honoring your and Michael's request to dress the part and make this evening special for Dad and Sue."

Not only had Michael won the debate on where to have the party, he'd also managed to convince all involved parties to dress up for the combined anniversary and Dad's surprise birthday. But she refrained from ribbing Steven. "Thank you for letting us host. It means a lot."

Steven winked. "Anything for you, sis."

James hurried into the room, dragging Gracie with him. "Come on, Mom. You gotta go faster. I need to set up Grandpa's gift."

Eyes twinkling, her brother's smile widened. "Be gentle, little man."

"Yes, Dad." He waved, but continued to tug Gracie toward the gift table. "Hi, Aunt Hanna. I gotta set up Grandpa's new spaceship. Mom and I finished painting it last night. He's gonna be so surprised."

His little boy excitement charged the room. But it didn't mask his calling Gracie *Mom*. Twice. That was new. Keeping her voice down, Hanna nudged Steven. "Angela's okay with Gracie's new name?"

More of her brother's grinning.

"Enough with the puppy-slobber looks."

Steven turned to face her. "Gracie and I talked with Angela last Sunday when we picked him up from the first overnight."

She tensed. With everything happening to Eve and Deni, Hanna had forgotten to ask about her nephew's first weekend with his biological mother. Angela had never given Hanna the time of day, so she returned the favor and didn't think of Angela much.

"It went okay?"

"Yes." A flash of sadness darkened his eyes. "Angela's turning out to be a better mother than any of us could have hoped. But Gracie is James's mom too. And we told Angela that she and Gracie would be sharing that title."

"James's idea or yours?"

"You know my son." Steven beamed. "He's wanted to call Gracie Mom since the wedding, but decided to wait and see if it was okay with Angela first."

"Sounds like James, all right."

Guests started arriving and silenced further discussion. The Rollins clan joined Gracie and James at the gift table, and more employees from Grounded and the Bureau streamed in. The gift table filled with brightly colored presents.

Kids giggled and ran around the wicker chairs and couch in the sitting area.

A few of the guys started a game of pool. And Steven flipped on the fifties CDs.

Dad would love his party. Not because of the food and piles of gifts, but because so many had turned out to celebrate with him. Her dad was well loved.

Hanna put on her hostess smile and tried to stop checking the french doors for Michael's return. She stepped behind Steven and Gracie's little huddled group, looking out into the patio strung with lights.

"He's gonna do the deal out there?" Clint's Texan drawl mixed with laughter. "Tell me his plan and your big mysterious news will come after we eat. I'm starving."

They all laughed. Hanna cleared her throat. "Who's doing what out where?"

Clint and Steven went stony-faced while Gracie and Sara covered their mouths, eyes still shining with hushed giggles.

Hanna hated being left out.

"You have to stop sneaking up on me." Steven stepped back to make room for her in the little circle. "But there's nothing you need to know right now." He pulled her into a stiff hug. "Isn't Michael due to arrive soon?" He checked his watch.

"This is one major shindig you pulled together, Hanna-girl. I'm impressed." Clint's hug was less stiff than Steven's, but they couldn't bluff their way out of this one.

"Only because I promised, will I refrain from grilling you two." She forced a smile.

Everyone's shoulders relaxed. Sara and Gracie started cooing over little Conor.

Old feelings of being on the outside of a glass house, looking in, crept back. But she wouldn't give in to them. Instead she excused herself and went to greet the people just arriving.

Trina stepped into the clubhouse and waved, her turquoise wrap dress swishing as she moved. "Hey, Hanna."

"I'm so glad you decided to come." Hanna eyed the door. "Where are Eve and Deni?"

Trina studied the floor. "They're waiting in the car. Evie asked me to see...she doesn't want to deal with questions."

Sadness squeezed Hanna's chest. Eve had come a long way just this week. And her friend's willingness to even show up at a party this soon after being shot touched Hanna's heart.

"I'll let my brother know to pass the word around."

Trina left to help Eve.

Hanna rejoined her brother's little group. "Steven, can you let everyone know not to make a big deal about Eve's cast or ask how she's doing?"

He nodded, eyes filled with sympathy. "I'm proud of Eve for coming. Lee and Rashida aren't doing as well." He hooked his thumb behind his back. "I'll let the others know."

Hanna swallowed a flood of threatening tears. Dad would be here soon, and she refused to allow Haines and his evil to spoil this special night. "Thank you."

Minutes later, Eve hobbled in on crutches, Deni and Trina providing a physical barricade to protect her.

"I'm so glad you came." Hanna smoothed Deni's curly black hair. "It means a lot to me."

James ran up with a multicultural mix of kids and spoke to Deni first. "I'm Hanna's nephew, James. Would you like to come play Apples to Apples Kids?"

Deni looked up at Eve. Eve nodded. But Deni didn't meet James's eyes. "I don't know how to play."

Three-year-old Jonathan took Deni's hand. "I'll help you. They teached me and I can teach you."

Hanna's eyes watered.

"We'll all help." Susannah smiled. "Come on. Come play."

As they walked toward the sitting area rug, Susannah's voice continued. "I love your dress. Hanna says your mom makes lots of cool clothes."

"Kids are color blind." Trina's soft words bounced around Hanna's heart.

Hanna smiled. "Grownups can be too."

Eve and Trina nodded. "Well, Miss Thang, when's your dad coming to get this party started?"

Eve tugged an envelope from her cropped denim jacket. The lime green dress underneath swirled around her calves. "I didn't get to the store in time. But I wrote your father a thank-you letter for all he's done for us. And I put some of the pictures you took of me and Deni in there too. Figured these would help erase the other pictures of us he's seen."

Hanna blocked Haines's disgusting photos of Eve and Deni before they fully formed in her mind. A trick Dr. Nations had taught her this past week. Thought patrol or some such name. Handcuff the images or thoughts and shove them in a mental jail, allowing the Lord to destroy them with His truth.

So far, it'd worked well.

She still had a long way to go. Just like Eve and Trina. But she was finally sleeping better, without the help of medication. Thanks again to Dr. Nations.

Steven commanded everyone's attention by turning off the music and turning on a handheld microphone. "Hey, everyone. So glad you all could join us for this special evening." He straightened his tie again. "Dad, Sue, and Michael are pulling into the parking lot now, so if you'll gather around the front double doors, we'll give them a big welcome in just a few minutes."

As directed, kids and adults all congregated in the middle of the clubhouse.

She stood to the side with Eve and Trina. A nudge against her shoulder startled her, and she jerked around.

Steven held up a hand. "Sorry. Didn't mean to spook you."

"I'm fine."

He held up her favorite camera. "You're also the best photographer around, host or not. Will you do the honors?"

Taking the camera from Steven, she smiled. Nothing else fit her hand quite so well.

The french doors swung open, and Dad and Sue stepped inside.

The room swelled with shouts of "Happy Birthday, Andrew" and "Happy Anniversary," so much so that her ears rang. But she captured the teary-eyed smiles of Dad and Sue with her camera and stepped back to snap a few pictures of the cheerful crowd.

Michael stood at her side a few minutes later. "You're amazing, you know."

"Oh?" Smiling despite all the emotions running through her system, Hanna lowered her camera. "How so? Gracie and Sara did most of the cooking. All of us helped decorate."

"You light up the room with your smile."

She groaned at the cheesy compliment.

Michael laughed. "Come on, Steven has a special presentation to make before we eat." He nudged through the group of people and stopped front and center. Dad in his dark blue suit and Sue in a gorgeous cream dress stood beaming. Everyone crowded around them.

Once again, Steven took the mike and the room quieted. "Dad has just requested we get the traditional song over with first."

The crowd of people chuckled.

"So I'm turning the mike over to my beautiful wife."

"Smart move, pard. We all appreciate that," Clint bellowed. FBI agents guffawed.

A rousing chorus of "Happy Birthday to You" filled the clubhouse with every note imaginable. The kids added, "And many moooorre" to cap off the song.

Steven reclaimed the mike. "One more thing before we eat." He nodded to Gracie and James, who stepped forward holding two gleaming space shuttles.

James was a space nut, but Hanna didn't understand why he and Gracie were extending two models. She snapped a few pictures.

"Dad and Sue—"

James hopped up and down. "Grandma and Grandpa, you're gonna be grandparents all over again. Next summer!"

Steven and Gracie beamed as Dad and Sue engulfed them in hugs. More cheers and congratulations rose around them.

Hanna's eyes started to leak once again. "Gracie's pregnant?"

Michael nodded. "Yep. I only found out before I went to get Andrew and Sue. Steven woulda had my head if I said anything."

Hanna took a few more photos, tears flowing. God was surely smiling with them.

"Go join your family, Hanna." Michael nudged her forward. "I'll hold the camera."

She hesitated.

"Steven didn't tell me about the baby. It slipped. They wanted it to be a big surprise for everyone. Something more to celebrate. Especially with things being a little crazy the last few weeks."

Talk about an understatement.

"They're waiting for you, Hanna."

Glass-house pieces crashed to the ground as Dad and Steven hugged her at the same time. "Congratulations, big brother. I'm so happy for you and Gracie."

More hugs and happy tears swirled together. Finally, Steven took the mike again. "Let's pray and dig in, folks. My amazing wife, sister, and good friend fixed us a feast of sugar to enjoy." He held the mike out to Dad. "Will you do the honors?"

Dad cleared his throat and took the mike, bowing his head before he began. "Heavenly Father, You are so good to us. Thank You for six incredible years with my bride. For another grandbaby on the way. And for my wonderful children." He paused. "We also ask that Your healing touch be on us. We need You. Thank You for helping us look deeper into the truth. Beyond skin color, beyond our frail understanding of life. Into hope that endures and perfect justice. Found only in You, dear Lord."

A few quiet amens shot around the room.

"Thank You for tonight, for family and friends. And good food. Amen."

Hanna allowed the crowd and Michael's strong hand on her back to sweep her into the food line. Conversations and laughter filled the air while coffee and chocolate filled her senses. But Dad's quiet prayer shouted above the din.

Above the lies of the past and the evil they'd encountered. Beyond color issues and things she'd never understand. Her heart swelled with a memory she'd almost forgotten this past year.

Choose wisely. Words uttered a million times by her mom and dad came back with tender clarity. She twirled the cool, silver promise ring on her left hand.

She'd listen to their advice this time. She'd choose truth instead of lies. Healing instead of fear and hate.

Eve pressed close. "Thank you for inviting us, Hanna. It was good to be here." She shifted on her crutches. "Your family is wonderful." Looking up at Michael, she smiled. "Yours too, Michael. I've enjoyed getting to know your mom and dad tonight."

Hanna glanced at Michael. "When did your parents arrive? I should have greeted them."

"They came in during the baby announcement." Eve grinned. "Trina and I kept them company in the back, comparing notes on all our hospital adventures."

Hanna bit her lip.

"It's okay." Eve shrugged. "The three of us found some common ground. Besides that, we have you two to thank for us being here tonight."

Words failed, so Hanna settled for a gentle hug.

Eve hobbled back and steadied herself. "I'd like to stay, but I need to get Deni to bed and catch some sleep myself."

"See you tomorrow?"

Eve smiled. "Definitely. Enjoy tonight. You two deserve it."

Watching Eve walk away, Hanna smiled, her heart full.

Michael slipped his arm around her waist and pulled her close. "Let's get some food. And then maybe a dance?"

One of her favorite songs came to mind. "The Way I Was Made." Tonight she'd dance like no one was watching. Because the little girl inside was starting to be free. Really free.

❋   ❋   ❋

Michael adjusted his collar and swallowed hard. Three weeks of in-between-crises planning and eight months of dreaming came down to this one moment.

He drew Hanna close and swayed on the dance floor, waiting for the soft crooning of one of Steven's James Taylor CDs to stop.

"Have you talked to your dad tonight?"

Kissing her rose-scented hair, he smiled. "A little. And more this past week, but you knew that."

"You haven't said how you're doing with it."

He pulled back a little and locked on to the most beautiful pair of blue eyes he'd ever seen. "Better than the first time my father tried to apologize. But it's weird. And it'll take awhile to adjust my thinking. A lifetime of hurt can't be fixed with one 'I'm sorry.'"

"No, but it can open the door for healing to start."

"And it is."

Hanna gasped and stopped dancing.

He glanced over his shoulders to see the reason. "Well, I'll be."

Lee and Rashida made their way across the room. Slowly. Some of the Bureau guys started clapping. Michael and Hanna joined in.

Lee held up a hand. "Thank you. Really."

The noise around them settled back to a medium din. "I'm glad you could make it. The party wouldn't have been complete without you two."

Rashida hugged Hanna and held on an extra beat. "Thank you for all the calls and e-mails."

"And the food." Lee grinned and readjusted his crutches.

They all chuckled.

Continuing, Lee beamed. "We couldn't miss congratulating you both in person."

Michael shook his head.

Hanna's brows knit. "For what? Am I missing something?"

Lee gulped. "For…for pulling off the best and most dramatic bust ever."

Wincing at the bad cover job, Michael tried to avert the conversation. "Yeah. Hanna's pretty handy with crystal."

Oh. Bad. Way bad.

Even so, Rashida and Lee didn't take the hint. Rashida touched her abdomen, mouth stretching into a frown. "I'm just glad he's behind bars and will rot there."

Ouch. Things were deteriorating fast. Michael pointed to the remaining desserts. "Why don't you two grab some food? There's still plenty of chocolate and coffee to spare."

Lee hobbled forward, Rashida close by his side. "We'll do that." Stepping behind Hanna, he mouthed an apology and said to get busy.

That Michael could do.

After the next song.

"You okay?"

"Yes." He pulled her close once again. "Sorry about that with Lee. I'd hoped to avoid any of those topics tonight."

"They'll come up. And I don't want to run from them. No more running for me."

Despite what had almost happened, he smiled. "Glad to hear that."

"Now about Lee's congratulations…what's up with that?" Hanna's blank expression gave nothing away. Except for the mischief in her eyes.

He took her hand and led her out to the back patio.

Rubbing her hands over her pink, long-sleeved dress, she tried not to smile. "Michael?"

The box in his pocket poked him. So he pulled it out and knelt down on one knee. A quick gulp and he pushed through the inner shaking. "Hanna Kessler, I love you and want to spend the rest of my life with you. Will you marry me?"

Not as eloquent as practiced, but he'd gotten it out.

Hanna blinked back tears, a huge grin spreading across her beautiful face. She nodded. But before she could speak, a round of cheers and loud clapping exploded behind him.

Michael stood and Hanna tucked herself into his side.

With her parents and his watching, not to mention his boss, forever the big brother, Michael slipped off Hanna's silver promise ring and placed the marquise solitaire on her left ring finger.

More cheers.

He stuffed the urge to wave them away. But he'd rather be kissing Hanna right now.

Then his father—his dad—shooed them all inside with a grin the size of Texas. "Let's give the new couple some breathing room folks."

Hanna pulled him close. "I love you, Michael."

He tilted her chin up and kissed her like he'd been dreaming about all evening.

Pulling apart, she smiled through the escaping tears. "It won't be all sunshine and flowers. We both have some tough stuff to walk though."

"And demanding jobs."

She nodded. "But with you and God, I'm safe, Michael. For the first time since I was a little girl, I believe that."

"And it's what we believe—not what we're supposed to believe—that determines the course of our lives." He grinned. "I finally understand what Dr. Nations has been telling you. God's been opening my eyes."

"Even in the painful places?"

Thoughts of safety and justice, mercy and forgiveness, held back the darker realities of life. God in His mysterious wisdom wouldn't stop the storms, or shield them from all pain. But He'd walk with them through it.

Hanna's blue eyes locked with his. "Ready to go back inside and dance, as an almost married couple?"

He liked the sound of that. And no matter what, they would dance. Together. Even in the storms.

Dear Reader,

Thank you for journeying with me through the challenges and victories of Michael and Hanna's story. If it's true that every book has bits and pieces of the author somewhere between the pages, then *Enduring Justice* contains the shards of my once-broken heart.

Fifteen years ago, God placed me in a safe place and used my future husband's hands to hold me together while my heart shattered. David was the first person to hear my whispered words about being date raped when I was a teen. For five years I'd denied what happened or hid and blamed myself. When my walls of secrecy started to crumble, I felt alone, exposed, and more terrified than I could handle. But God met me there. He covered my shame with His grace and carried me down the painful path of healing.

He also placed some amazing people in my life who've made this road doable because they've consistently prayed and reminded me it's God who is my Safety, Strength, Hope, and Healer. Many of those folks have shared my skin color and heritage. And many have not. Our differences on the surface and down deep have forced me to confront the boundaries and boxes I grew up assigning not only to God, but also to anyone who appeared different. Many of the challenges Eve and Hanna faced grew from seeds of my experiences. I'm forever grateful for my friends who don't look or think like me because they stretch me and make me grow.

I've been told my stories aren't comfortable to read. In some ways, that makes me smile. Because it's when I've been nudged out of my comfort zone that my understanding of God is deepened. It's my heart and prayer not to cause pain or be edgy for edgy's sake but to shine a light into the darkness so those who are stumbling there might find hope and healing. And to remind those who are no longer there to reach out a hand and bring others to where you are.

My prayer for you is twofold. One, that Hanna and Michael's story challenges you to look deeper into what you believe about God, yourself, and others. Because in the end, it's what we believe—not what we're supposed to believe—that determines the course of our lives.

And second, that you would experience God's amazing, unfailing, and perfect love for you. He's the One who puts shattered lives, hearts, and people back together again. Grab His hand, trust His heart, and take the leap into whatever holds you back. He's there. And He loves you. Forever.

Because of His grace,
Amy

**Please stop by and stay awhile at my Heart Chocolate
(www.amywallace.com) home on the Web.
As always, I'd love to hear from you!**

DISCUSSION QUESTIONS

1. What does it mean to dance like no one is watching? When have you done that?

2. How can we dance in the storms of life? What does Psalm 42:4–6, 8 have to say about our response when our souls are downcast?

3. What was Hanna's biggest obstacle to overcome—the abuse at age six or the walls of secrecy she hid behind?

4. Why did Hanna keep her childhood secret? What do Psalm 56:3–4; Isaiah 41:10; and 1 John 4:18–19 say about one of the biggest reasons we hide and what is a better choice?

5. Hanna believed the lie that the abuse was all her fault, and everything that happened to her seemed to confirm that. Who was behind that, the one the Bible calls the father of lies? God's Word also talks about things hidden in the dark, but what happens when we bring those lies and what happened in the dark to light? What does Isaiah 42:3 have to say about how God tenderly treats us when we bring our brokenness to Him?

6. Dr. Nations talks to Hanna about how it's what we believe—not what we're supposed to believe—that determines the course of our lives. What does this mean to you?

7. Michael realizes he's spent most of his life pursuing justice for others in an effort to heal the wounds of his past. Was this effective? Why or why not?

8. Michael struggles to pray when God doesn't seem to be answering. Have you ever been there, done that? What scriptures do you turn to in those times?

9. Micah 6:8 says, "And what does the LORD require of you but to do justice, to love kindness, and to walk humbly with your God?" What does it mean to "do justice" in circumstances like Hanna's? Like Michael's? When people hurt you?

10. Healing from wounds like Hanna and Michael experienced takes time. Sometimes a very long time. Michael's and Hanna's friends and family all reacted differently to their abuse. If someone in your life has experienced similar pain, how can you be a safe place for them? What do Psalm 91:1–2; Proverbs 18:10; and 2 Corinthians 1:3–4 encourage us to do when we need a safe place?

11. When people talk about putting God in a box, what does that mean? Michael found he couldn't fit in a Kessler-sized box and God didn't either. Why do you think we try to put God, ourselves, and others in boxes, all neat and tidy and easy to handle?

12. A difficult subject tackled in *Enduring Justice* is the issue of racism. What does it mean to be color blind? Is it possible to live that way? Why or why not?

13. Sean and Michael both live according to worldviews passed down from their fathers. How does Michael break the cycle? How can we keep from passing on prejudices and other beliefs that don't line up with Scripture?

14. Lee tells Michael that you can't "judge a box by its wrapping." In a sense he's reminding us all to look deeper. Into ourselves and into others. Why is this so hard to do? How can we help each other dive below the surface and come up with real relationships?

15. The close-knit community and family bonds the Kesslers, Rollinses, Michael, and Lee share aren't found just in fiction novels. But as these fictional people experienced, relationships are messy. They require time and risk and don't always go the way we plan. Colossians 3:12–17 is an amazing passage on living in community. What can you glean from these verses and apply to your friendships and family relationships?

Therefore, as God's chosen people, holy and dearly loved, clothe yourselves with compassion, kindness, humility, gentleness and patience. Bear with each other and forgive whatever grievances you may have against one another. Forgive as the Lord forgave you. And over all these virtues put on love, which binds them all together in perfect unity. Let the peace of Christ rule in your hearts, since as members of one body you were called to peace. And be thankful. Let the word of Christ dwell in you richly as you teach and admonish one another with all wisdom, and as you sing psalms, hymns and spiritual songs with gratitude in your hearts to God. And whatever you do, whether in word or deed, do it all in the name of the Lord Jesus, giving thanks to God the Father through him. (Colossians 3:12–17, NIV)

Here's to taking risks, getting messy, and choosing healing. May you do all three under the shadow of the cross and in the shelter of His perfect love.

CAN DREAMS BE REDEEMED?

GRACIE LANG lost her family and her faith all in one tragic moment. Now she gets through the days with nothing but the drive for justice propelling her forward.

STEVEN KESSLER is an FBI agent with an important job - rescuing other people's children during the day and caring for his son during the night.

Now a very real threat to a child dangerously intersects Steven and Gracie's worlds—a collision that demands a decision. One thing is certain…neither one of them will ever be the same again.

"*In sickness and in health*"
is about to test Sara to her core.

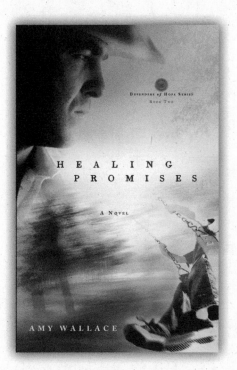

Sara Rollins is an oncologist with a mission—beating cancer when she can, easing her patients' suffering at the very least. Now the life of her tall Texan husband is at stake. As FBI Agent Clint Rollins continues to track down a serial kidnapper despite his illness, former investigations haunt his nightmares, pushing him beyond solving the case into risking his life and career. Everything in their lives is reduced to one all-important question: Can God be trusted?